D0397609
RECEIVED
OCT 13 2022

shades of rust and ruin

shades of rust and ruin

A. G. HOWARD

BLOOMSBURY
NEW YORK LONDON OXFORD NEW DELHI SYDNEY

BLOOMSBURY YA
Bloomsbury Publishing Inc., part of Bloomsbury Publishing Plc
1385 Broadway, New York, NY 10018

First published in the United States of America in September 2022 by Bloomsbury YA

Library of Congress Cataloging-in-Publication Data
Names: Howard, A. G. (Anita G.) author.
Title: Shades of rust and ruin / A. G. Howard.
Description: New York : Bloomsbury Children's Books, 2022.
Summary: Nix and Clarey search for Nix's uncle in the parallel world Mystiquiel, where Nix discovers there is more to her family curse and otherworldly artwork than she ever imagined, and unless she can solve the Goblin King's maze before the clock strikes midnight, the curse will claim more lives.
Identifiers: LCCN 2022004866 (print) | LCCN 2022004867 (e-book)
ISBN 978-1-5476-0808-9 (hardcover) • ISBN 978-1-5476-0810-2 (e-book)
Subjects: CYAC: Blessing and cursing—Fiction. | Goblins—Fiction. | Friendship—Fiction. | Fantasy. | LCGFT: Novels. | Fantasy fiction.
Classification: LCC PZ7.H83222 Sh 2022 (print) | LCC PZ7.H83222 (e-book) | DDC [Fic]—dc23
LC record available at https://lccn.loc.gov/2022004866

Book design by Yelena Safronova
Typeset by Westchester Publishing Services
Printed and bound in the U.S.A.
2 4 6 8 10 9 7 5 3 1

In honor of Christina Rossetti, whose lyrical narrative and evocative descriptions planted wildling seeds in my teen heart, which flourished to a passion for dangerous magic, sisterhood, and devilishly enchanted creatures

shades of rust and ruin

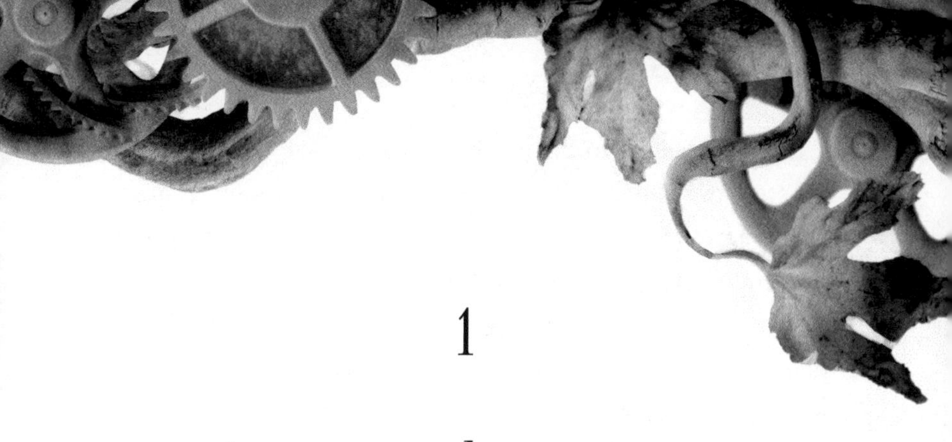

1

sisters and monsters

At the age of fourteen, I found my twin sister dead in the bunk bed beneath mine, and my relationship with goblins began. Not one day since have I regretted their arrival. Without them, I would never have survived the guilt. The very same guilt I battle tonight as I honor a morbid obligation.

I flip over on my mattress and squint at the eyes glaring back at me from my nightstand. Their faint glow smears the darkness. I blink heavily until the lights resolve to my digital clock's display in the same instant the alarm begins to sound. Stifling a yawn, I press the off button. My room falls silent, and I open the calendar on my cell phone to wait for the next fifteen minutes to pass as October twenty-ninth becomes the thirtieth.

Honestly, at this point, I don't need an alarm. I've been waking up at a quarter to midnight the whole month, just like I did the past two years during October. The alarm is a precaution—to ensure the timed awakening will be as spontaneous as blinking by tomorrow night; to ensure Halloween doesn't sneak up on me and steal away my heartbeats and breaths like it did my sister's.

My gaze wanders from my phone to the bookshelves on the wall. It's where I keep my goblins—locked inside sketch pads, handcuffed to paper with chains of colored ink. I used to visit them when I needed escape, when I felt vulnerable and alone. But lately, their power has been fading.

As they are now, they're no match for my sister's looming death-iversary. Nothing can lift that weight. Not even the sweetest dreams.

Maybe because on that fated night, before the badness, I had been dreaming of all the best things: sunshine and salted air, laughter and comfort. When I woke, I could still feel grains of sand between my toes—the subliminal embodiment of a summer vacation Lark and I once took with parents only remembered through photos. On *that* night, what startled me awake wasn't a schedule or an alarm . . . it was a jumble of sawing, dragging, and guttural grunts that were completely out of place alongside warm ocean breezes and laughter.

The commotion made me sit up and strain to listen over my heartbeat. Somehow, the thumpity-thumping had ascended from my chest to my neck and ears, adding to the confusion of wavery silver light that seeped from the window at the head of the bunk beds. Colored-pencil masterpieces I'd sketched earlier that day and sprinkled with glitter—jack-o'-lanterns, ghouls, and a patchwork Frankenstein—had been tacked to the walls and flapped like captive ghosts as the screen rattled behind our open curtains, letting in a chill October gale. With each gust, the seesawing motion of the screen's wires sliced the moon's glow into microscopic squares that moved along the walls.

Weeks later, during an in-depth session with a child psychiatrist, I would describe the shifting light as a strobe effect. I would also remember that the clock said 11:45 p.m., only fifteen minutes before November first arrived, and the window's screen had been slashed at one corner so the edge curled in the gusts like a rough, lapping tongue.

"Lark . . ." I remember mumbling my sister's name in the darkness. "Did you hear something?" It was the lack of her answer that set my spine tingling, causing visions of costumed monsters and bloodied masks from our earlier trick-or-treating venture to rattle through me. At the ladder end of the bed, eerie shadows congregated around Lark's latest project—deconstructed doll and clock parts—piled atop a desk in the far corner. To avoid them, I held tight to the frame and slid down the mattress's edge. Balancing the balls of my feet on Lark's bunk, I nudged her with my big toe. The dim light quavered again, prompting a roiling sensation in a stomach already thick with too much candy.

The phantosmia of ocean air wilted to a wild stink: animal muskiness soured by a damp, mildew scent. Maybe that's when I noticed the screen's flapping tongue . . . or maybe it was later. But my most indelible observation in that moment was this: I couldn't *feel* my sister there.

Yes, my foot pressed into her side against a barrier of static ribs. Yes, her skin was cool beneath her pj's, carbon copies of my own save for the fabric—hers a pattern of pink polka dots, mine a striped yellow. What I *didn't* feel was her presence in the room beside me. It's something Lark and I had always shared, a thread that tied our sensory receptors together, making us aware of each other's physical experiences and emotions via a keen intuition.

Instead, what I felt—what *she* was feeling—could only be described as an earthy uprooting . . . the stench of loam and minerals, the grit of soil, being pulled into a darkness both exhilarating and horrifying.

I dropped to the floor to link my pinkie with hers. With them interlocked, our thoughts could fully connect. We could deliver messages . . . ranging from "Are you okay?" to "I'm mad at you" and everything in between, without even speaking. It all depended on how tightly we held. It was a secret kept between us . . . something we never told anyone. Why try? They wouldn't understand. They'd either laugh or think we were lying.

That night, in that moment, I squeezed as if Lark was my lifeline in a choppy sea. When she didn't squeeze back, I moved closer and my knee shoved aside the opened *Goblin Market* book. Although she had it turned to our favorite verse, my focus strayed back to her—how her spine curled, stiff and arched, and her limbs twisted at unnatural angles, as if she were a felled tree with snapped branches.

"Lark?" Hand trembling, I released her pinkie to shove long strands of black hair from her forehead. Moving past her silvery eyebrows (a by-product of our partial albinism, much like the startling white freckles flecking our noses), I stroked her eyelashes—short, clustered, and dark like my own, though hers remained locked in an empty, unblinking stare.

Repulsed, I yanked my arm back, fingertips grazing her lips. Their bluish tint could've been blamed on the shadows, but not the cold absence that met my hand . . . not the lack of warm breath. Or any breath at all. The strobing moonlight shifted across her face, revealing hollows where I'd never seen them, gutting her eyelids and brows, voiding the space beneath her cheekbones—crevices so deep and yawning it was as though her skin had shrunk to a tight gray sheath and left me caressing a misshapen, monstrous skull. Her arms and legs even appeared to be stubby, withered versions of themselves. Everything about her was disproportioned.

I cried out. By the time Uncle Thatch rushed into the room to soothe my sobbing screams, the moonlight had moved again and Lark appeared natural—her face and body the mirror image of mine, except with ashen complexion, eyes agog, and limbs akimbo. I wriggled out of Uncle's comforting embrace, falling against a wooden floor as harsh and cold as the realization that knifed through my gut: Halloween had stolen away my sister, just like it had taken our parents years before.

Reliving the memory tonight clogs my throat with anguish, compounded by the sensory overload I've been suppressing all month, the inability to go anywhere without being slammed by haunting details. Even school isn't safe right now—with the miniature jack-o'-lanterns on teachers' desks, ghostly shoe-polish window decorations, and paper skulls strung from the ceilings. I drag the covers up to my chin while the autumn chill continues to wrap around my bones, unrelenting.

That favorite picture book found on the floor by my sister's bed—a rare 1933 first edition of *Goblin Market* by Christina Rossetti, filled with beautiful illustrations by an artist named Rackham—holds me riveted from its spot beside the clock on the nightstand. It's another reminder of all I've lost, including the mother who passed the book on to her baby girls before leaving forever. I curl my lonely pinkie around the blanket's edge, then close my eyes and recite that final verse under my breath:

For there is no friend like a sister
In calm or stormy weather;
To cheer one on the tedious way,
To fetch one if one goes astray—

I stop before the last two lines. These words, which once made Lark and me feel invincible together, now sever my heart like a monster's talon. In the *Goblin Market* poem, the stronger sister saves the weaker. Despite that I was born eight minutes before her, I'd always known Lark was the stronger one. The fact that I lived and she didn't was infallible proof, because I'd been too weak to help her.

The coroner cited the cause of her death as an undiagnosed epileptic condition. It explained the seizure-like stasis of her limbs; the guttural and dragging sounds that woke me were due to her inhaling vomit as her fingers snagged the window screen above her head while she thrashed in an asphyxiated state.

Upon learning how she died, I couldn't find my REM . . . couldn't sleep deep enough to dream. Identical twins form when a fertilized egg splits apart; Lark was half of me, and I of her. More than anyone, *I* should've sensed her struggle—rolled her over and opened her airways. At the very least, I should've been wary of the date that claimed our parents' lives; I should've kept us both awake until midnight brought November safely to our bedside.

Uncle Thatch tried to break my insomniac cycle. Finally realizing the sleeping pills prescribed by the child psychiatrist had

no effect, he opted for valerian root. The first night of drinking the tea, I slept long and hard, and my dreams bloomed to life: brilliantly colorful, filled with smog and daggers and snapping metal wings and teeth, each detail so bright with the lux of cyberpunk gloom, my real life in coastal Oregon—gloomy in its own right—paled in comparison.

The next morning, Uncle Thatch couldn't hide the troubled twist to his lips as I sketched a rendition of my industrial-faerie tableau on a stray notepad, using a more skilled hand than I'd ever achieved. The setting mirrored our hometown: similar terrain, shops and streets, an endless ocean; yet it was devoid of humans—with brass-hooved horses, copper-feathered birds, and chain-link-tentacled things in place of trollies, cars, or boats. A parallel world powered by magic, voltage, and metal. I scribbled *Mystiquiel* at the top, having seen it slathered in paint across a dented whitewashed sign along the borders of my dreamscape.

Frowning, Uncle had tried to explain away the phenomena. "Don't worry, Nix. Valerian can jack up the subconscious. I'm guessing that picture book your mom gave you doesn't help, either. We'll put it in the attic. Then once you don't need the herbs to relax, your nightmares will stop."

Within a matter of days, I could sleep without the tea; yet the goblins and faeries calcimining my subconscious—horrific and disturbingly elegant grotesques that were part lore and part mechanism—remained, regardless that Uncle Thatch had boxed up the *Goblin Market* book. He was wrong, and I was glad for it, because those nightmares provided sanctuary. Although Mystiquiel couldn't make me forget the excruciating loss of my other half, it was the one place Lark had never existed, which meant

there was no hole left by her absence. In turn, it was the one place I wasn't a traitor for being the sister who survived.

Now, three years later, I no longer visit a psychiatrist; *Goblin Market* occupies my nightstand again; and those first drafts once scribbled on scrap paper have evolved to a collection of graphic novels, chronicling the adventures of my goblins and faeries as seen through my eyes each night when I sleep.

I've composed over a dozen volumes so far, and there appears to be no end to the dreams. However, I've recently lost the desire to draw them. I haven't finished a single scene in months, but I've concocted a plan to jump-start my muse. Since it hinges on resurrecting the dead, I'll need to be well rested.

My attention returns to the pile of sketch pads cluttering the shelves, and I defer to the one trick that always helps me sleep: counting goblins instead of sheep. Silver paper clip placeholders become spiky metallic spines, scaly copper hides, and tails of electrified coils—each catching glimmers of moonlight as their sharp points and blunt curves frolic within the gently flapping pages. I cast one last drowsy glance at the open window where the breeze sweeps in, then yawning, find my way back to dreams again.

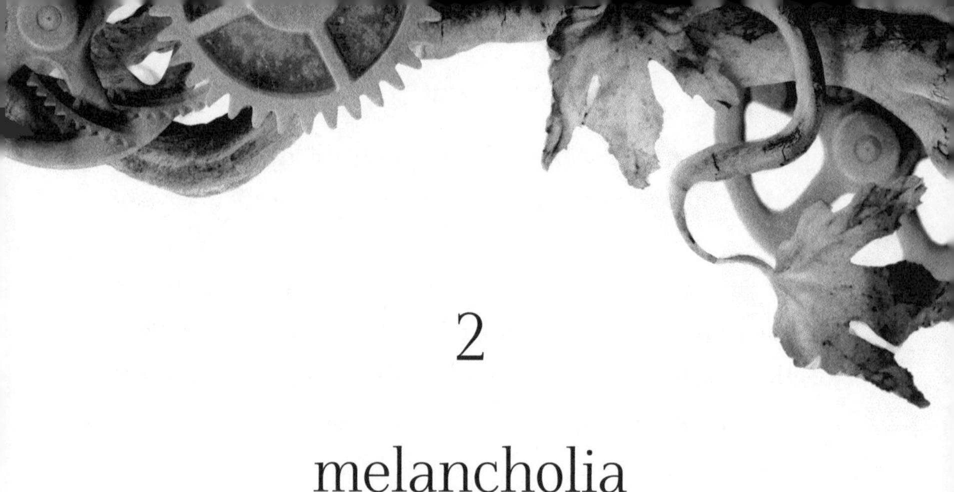

2

melancholia

The trolley door opens, and damp air snakes over my seat in the back row, setting the perfect tone for a portrait of a ghost.

I've spread Lark's velvet hoodie across the wooden bench on the other side of the aisle. Studying the sketch pad in my lap, I shade the lines with my pencil, having already captured the wrinkles in the hoodie's form and the shape of the glittery wings with elasticized straps stretched around the shoulder seams.

A group of commuters step single file off the trolley and onto the rain-drenched street. Goose bumps erupt across my exposed nape and I flip up my leather jacket's collar, inhaling the wet scent. I smile sadly, thinking of the day Lark and I learned the word "petrichor" for the third-grade spelling bee, when our teacher taught us it was easier to say than the mouthful "that fresh sweetness on the air during a long-overdue rain."

Back then, I loved this kind of setting—the promise of newness hidden behind a curtain of fog, the chill of a storm's

fingernails parting my hair and scuffing along my neck, and the squelch of moss, mud, and spongy leaves beneath my boots. Now, it's just another detail that seeps through the sieve of my heart, reminding me how as kids Lark and I waded in water puddles, raced paper boats, and mixed mud pies; we did everything together, until we turned twelve and began to argue over who had to mop the floor or who got to hold the umbrella . . . until we started growing apart.

Up front, a family of five and two older girls wait for the people exiting so they can board. My throat constricts on a stifled demand that everyone stay to the unoccupied middle sections. Given the date, Sam, the official afternoon conductor, would've kept the entire back row taped off as a personal favor to me (perks of having an uncle who owns one of the city's most beloved and lucrative bakeries . . . fellow locals will bend over backward for a free cupcake or macaron). Unfortunately, Sam's visiting his sick brother, and Patty, his temporary replacement, has only lived here a little over a month. I tried to explain the situation to her, but she only frowned and said she was here to man the controls, not play favorites.

I squint, locking my lashes in a thick clutch of mascara while I dig the phone from my jacket pocket and scroll through my earlier text to Clarey.

> Sam's MIA. Open seating. Want to drive over to Maritime Museum and hop on the trolley? You can keep any unwelcome flies out of my web. 🕷

My hold tightens around the phone as I reread the response:

Sorry to flake out. Makeup malfunction. 💄 I'll meet you at 11th with bug repellent prepped and ready. Flannie is always up for noshing flies. 😉

Clarey was with us on Lark's final October thirtieth, when alongside a group of friends, we took a city bus after classes let out. We jumped off at Maritime Memorial Park, strolled the Riverwalk, then hopped the trolley and claimed the two back rows as our own. Our destination was Eleventh Street, where shop owners had set up temporary booths along the sidewalks to hand out goodies—totes full of candies, toys, and bottled water with labels displaying the participating shops' logos. It was the practice run for their updated versions of trunk-or-treat, a means to boost the economy along with the children's pride in their port city. Lark and I had so much fun on the outing, we finally began to bridge the giant rift I'd put between us.

Sighing, I tuck the phone away. My pencil taps the corner of the sketch pad. Using the empty hoodie and wings as a prop, I've drawn Lark exactly how she was that afternoon: the way her arms filled those sleeves; the way she rolled the hems so her shirt's lacy cuffs would stick out, perfectly framing a French manicure that shimmered with carnation-pink polish to match the fairy costume she would wear the following day for Halloween.

My fingers twitch as I prepare to complete the portrait. From the open army duffel at my side, resting atop a few of my latent graphic novels, the blendable markers taunt me. I have to force myself to look at them, because I'm afraid of what I'll see. Or rather, what I won't. Sure enough, no matter how hard I stare,

the colors are lost on me—each pigment as indecipherable as shades of ash. The flavor of frustration sits bitter on my tongue.

I can no longer create the perfect blush for her nails, or the lavender for her hoodie; and simply choosing a marker for its name won't commit her memory to paper accurately. I thought if anything could pump the vividness of color back into my art, into my vision, into my *life*, it would be portraying Lark on this day, when she was at her happiest.

Growling, I erase the sketch, scrubbing until the scent of hot rubber and graphite burns my nose and holes score the paper. I rip off the page as if the action could hide my failure, but the jagged edges along the spine mock me. Crumpling the ruined drawing, I shove it under the markers.

Outside, the Columbia River glimmers along the horizon to the right of the rails. The overhead lights juxtapose against the dreary sky and cause a mirror effect in the window, flashing a face made up pale enough to blend with my white freckles and matching eyebrows; black hair with choppy mini-bangs that barely cover my widow's peak, and shorn sides and nape in contrast with the style's chin-length crown. Sometimes I wear the peak stiffened to a faux hawk, but today it flops over my left ear like a raven's wing.

My former psychiatrist would say it helps me feel tougher on the inside when I look fierce on the outside. Truth is, ever since my sister's face has been glaring back at me from my reflections, this is the only way I *know* myself. I blow a deep breath, fogging the glass before Lark's angry eyes can lock me in.

Across the aisle, the rhinestone-fringed fairy wings blink in a fluctuation of light as people begin to board. The married couple and their boisterous kids enter first. I don't know them by

name, but they're fellow Astorians and regulars at our bakery, so they're familiar enough with our family tragedy to give me wide berth this time of year. It's the two girls getting on next that cause my already tense muscles to cinch tighter.

They appear to be college age, and have matching bags that say "Welcome to the Goondocks"—a touristy catchphrase referencing *The Goonies* movie, shot in Astoria sometime back in the '80s. The comedy-adventure film earned a cult following that in turn earns our town an annual income via souvenir shops and film locale tours.

"Ugh. Almost five o'clock." The first girl glares at her watch.

I frown, unaware it was getting so late. My attention strays to my duffel and the antique pocket watch sewn onto one corner. Even though the hands move counterclockwise, Lark couldn't bear to let it run down. The watch, like the bag, was our father's, and she believed—as long as it was ticking—it somehow kept him with us. Illogical as it is to carry an antique that doesn't keep time, it's a tradition I uphold to honor her.

"The trolley service ends in an hour, and we've barely seen anything in this slog," the girl continues, stalling beside the center row. "Should've went to the hotel hours ago."

"I tried to tell you," her friend answers, dripping behind her. "Hey, that guy on the Riverwalk said some good restaurants are off Eleventh. We can stop for dinner there, then Uber back to the hotel. Want to?"

Nodding in agreement, the first girl tucks away her folded umbrella. After considering the empty spots close to the family and their hyperactive tots, she crinkles her forehead. Her damp curls resemble muddied rose petals, meaning they could be anything from auburn to poppy red.

"It's too noisy up here."

I stifle a groan as she heads toward the back and points at Lark's hoodie. "Do you know who this belongs to?" She directs the query my way.

"Um," I stammer. "Yeah." In an attempt to appear combative, I furrow my eyebrow where a gear-shaped ring spikes the hairs.

The other girl catches up, her swinging ponytail a stale beige under the fluorescent trolley lights. I'd speculate it's golden because it reminds me of the free-range egg yolks Uncle Thatch uses in his cupcakes, but I wouldn't place a bet on it.

The blonde jerks a thumb toward Lark's empty hoodie, jangling her shimmery bangle bracelets with the movement. "So is she on here somewhere?"

Only in spirit. I touch the tip of my tongue to my bottom lip's piercing and maintain silence, hoping they get the hint and move on. If these clowns hijack Lark's seat, I'll lose my shot at drawing her. This is the one place I can capture her essence. Here where she sat, three years ago to this day, when our bond was finally growing strong again.

"Well?" The first girl shakes some droplets off her flip-flop, dimpling the puddles gathered atop the rubber floor. "Is your friend coming or not?"

I suppress the prickly sensation in my gut and shake my head.

"Okay then." The blonde lifts the hoodie—wings strung loosely around the floppy sleeves—and offers the bundle to me. I clutch the tiny motor box affixed to the back of the fake appendages, cradling the on/off switch against the groove of my palm. "Next time you see her, tell her invisible fairy princesses can't hold seats."

Next time . . . Next time . . . Next time. The words pound at my temples, overplaying the conductor's five-minute warning for people to find their seats. The last time I was with Lark was at the funeral. She looked so alive I half expected her to link our pinkies. To ask why I let her die. When she didn't, I leaned over the coffin's edge and pressed my nose to hers, close enough to count the stitches clamping her eyelids shut. That was when it hit me that my sister was truly dead, and we would never mend those busted fences between us.

Both girls slide across the bench, leaving soggy streaks over Lark's empty seat. They may as well be smearing her memory with their wet yoga pants. I watch her smile fade; her eyes—lit up as she demonstrates the flapping fairy wings, her latest robotics innovation—grow dim; the machine oil smudging her fingertips—which juxtaposes with the dried glitter on her palms—peels off and erodes along with her fingerprints. Her very identity wafting away on colorless, tattered tulle appendages. Grief swells in my throat.

No. I won't let these strangers see me break down; won't let them know how hard it's going to be to get out of bed before midnight tonight to face the date that stole my family; won't admit how often I wish the calendar would skip straight through to November first every year so I could abandon staying awake for twenty-four hours—the one means to ensure my survival and the safety of those I love.

Gulping down the knot of emotion, I thread my jacket's arms through the elastic straps of Lark's wings, centering the mechanism at my back. With a flick of a switch, the wire pinions flap behind me.

I reposition my right hand around the pencil and skim

through a dozen storyboard panels—disparate-size boxes waiting to be filled with unnatural creatures formed of metallic slivers that sprout from enchanted flesh. When I first began drawing Mystiquiel, I tried to veer away from the dreams, choosing instead to conform to the traditional fey lore I'd heard all my life.

The eldritch species—dryads, elves, trolls, gnomes, piskies, sprites, wights, sprigs, and more—were flesh and blood, scales and bones, all stitched and sealed with leaves and twigs and sap. They looked like their images in books and movies. But my muse wouldn't let those changes stick. I couldn't move forward with my stories and drawings until I abandoned those attempts and reverted to the blueprints and the denizens I saw in my sleep: an urbanized Astoria, inhabited by cyborg faeries and goblins, and warped by magic, steam, and galvanism.

I turn several unfinished pages, until I arrive at a partly drawn figure of Angorla, a feisty goat-faced hobblegob. Hobblegobs, a dwarfish breed of goblin with mismatched legs that make their gaits floppy and off balance, deceive their attackers by blending into the scenery. This gives a false sense of calm before they reappear, razor-sharp claws morphing into deadly harvesting tools. One sideswipe of a sickle, and they leave their enemies in a pile of shreds.

I cast a cursory glance at the tourists in Lark's seat. With my body blocking my work, I draw myself as Angorla, shading and smoothing the grayscale lines that in my dreams are prismatic: copper ram's horns, patinated green and protruding from my head, red circuit board eyes flashing at the top of my cheeks, my skin the texture and tensility of silvery spider silk.

Patina and brass . . . which markers do I blend together to depict antiquity? Or the luster and depth of new metal? I wriggle

against the plastic box poking my spine. The wings have already run down because I forgot to replace the battery after fishing them from Lark's keepsake box.

I clench my jaw and burrow deeper into the scene appearing on the paper. Under my pencil, the trolley morphs into a rusted serpentine beast—Mystiquiel's living, mobile dungeon. The sides of the cars become metallic ribs, and the floor scaly flesh. I can almost smell machine oil combined with musk, feel heat rising in white vapors, hear the pings of metal and the buzz of voltage and the feral snarls of eldritch prisoners peering from behind the seats.

Next, I sketch the two girls as caricatures in clown masks. Their exaggerated features quickly come into view—triangle-lined eyes wide with shock to find themselves aboard a living trolley alongside a monster wearing my face and clothes. Moving on to my hands, I draw steel weeding forks in place of fingers. The prongs twist in the girls' hair, braiding dual-toned strands into a thick rope that tangles around both their heads until they spin off their bench like a two-headed top, splitting their clown masks in half and revealing their true horrified faces.

I tune out the rustle of last-minute arrivals boarding the trolley, barely noticing when people amble down the aisle toward the middle section. A flush of heat rushes through my ears and cheeks as my pencil dances to an uninhibited rhythm I haven't managed in months. Lark's image appears in the panel, her wings and fairy costume swirling effortlessly from the graphite tip. She perches right where the girls pushed her off, and the two of us high-five while the tourists writhe on the floor beneath a frenzy of rat-pack sprites brutally ripping away all their shiny jewelry. A shadow comes to loom over us all—tall, horned, and

powerful—in the shape of my goblin king ready to claim his newest captives.

For the final touch, I etch puddles across the floor around the girls' supine bodies and busted masks. Then I stretch out my sketch pad for inspection. Did I mean for those puddles to be formed of raindrops or blood? My stomach flips at the question, because I really don't know. And no matter what color I choose, it will all look the same to me.

As daunting as that thought is, an even more disturbing realization surfaces: this is the first time I've drawn Lark alongside characters from my graphic novels, and the first time Halloween masks have made an appearance in my sketch pads. My dreamscape is the one place in my life where Lark hasn't left a footprint, where our family curse hasn't infringed. I must keep Mystiquiel separate and secret, so I'll always have that sanctuary.

I've barely managed to erase Lark's face when a warm, strong hand cups my shoulder and stops my eraser at the tip of her wings, just as the trolley door whooshes closed.

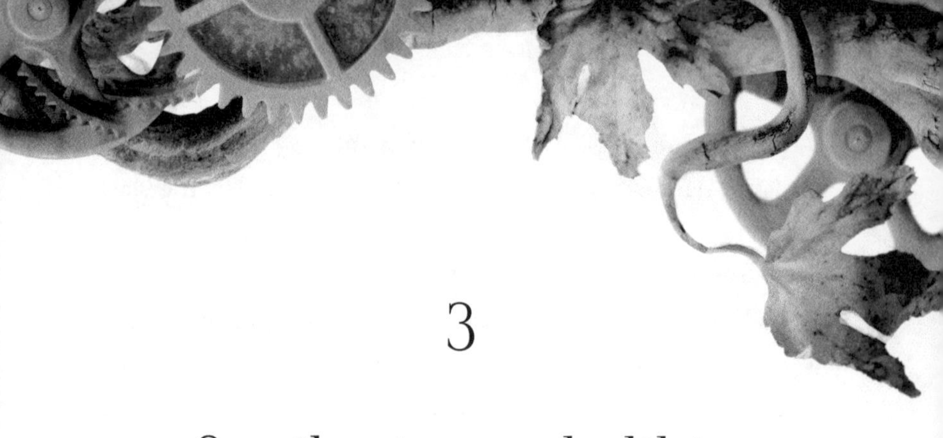

3

family ties and alibis

"It's so great to see you drawing again!" the perky voice greets me.

I glance up at Uncle Thatch's adorably goofy grin. He's slim and a good five inches taller than me, and while I'm seated and he's standing, he looks exactly the way I used to see him when I was a little girl: larger than life . . . a hero . . . my mother's younger brother who became my and Lark's guardian a couple of months after we turned three, when our parents died in a car crash along Highway 101—on Halloween night.

I'm so surprised by his appearance, it takes me a second to realize he's carrying two Styrofoam cups in a cardboard holder and napkins from my favorite bistro.

"Hey," I mumble, hiding the sketch pad against my chest in hopes he didn't see the violence of my freshly drawn scene. I scoot myself and the duffel closer to the window to make room for him before the trolley lurches forward. "How did you know—?"

"Where to find you?" He sits down, offering one cup to me. His large, dark eyes bulge with emotion, magnified by the black glasses resting on the bridge of his nose. "I know how much this date and place mean to you, kiddo."

I take the proffered coffee with my free hand and hold it close to my face. Brown-sugar-and-cinnamon-scented steam curls around my cheeks, lips, and nostrils like a caress. "Mmmm. Cinnamon Dolce. Nectar of the godssss." I practically purr as I take a sip and let the cozy flavor roll over my tongue and down my throat.

"Since it's been a few weeks, figured you might be needing a fix," Uncle teases, spurring a genuine smile out of me.

"You're the best." I take another swig and give his elbow an affectionate nudge.

October is the month I avoid all my favorite haunts, no pun intended. Lark and I were too young when Uncle came into our lives to remember or understand the incident that brought him to us. And over the span of a decade Uncle managed to convince me and my sister that the date was normal, ensuring we took part in traditional fun activities and encouraging us to trick-or-treat even into the beginning of our teen years—so we wouldn't "grow up too fast." All that effort fell to rot once we lost Lark, too. There's no denying that Halloween is out to get you once it's slaughtered almost everyone in your family.

Now, during this season, things once familiar become strange and sinister beneath the black light of Lark's glaring absence. The gory costumes and ghoulish decor—images that are benign to most—rise as nightmarish relics that chase me inside, force me to avoid the streets at all costs every October thirty-first . . . to stay holed up like a mole, burrowed and blind beneath my own safe traditions.

Even in this moment, as the trolley picks up speed, the rail's click-clack-clickety-clack, the falling rain, and my jacket's jingling chains merge together in a harmony that should be nostalgic and relaxing. Instead, it feels off-key—rusty chimes strummed by a ghostly fingertip—melancholic and hollow, just like my sketches.

I lick a dribble of coffee from my lip ring. Uncle Thatch gives me a napkin. I take it, then nod at his bakery T-shirt and gray khakis. "I thought you were at work. Isn't there a shipment today?"

He slurps from his cup. "Not until six thirty. Which gives you plenty of time to get there and do the recycling." He winks at me. "For now, I'm going to keep you company."

"So . . . Clarey texted you." I hike my pierced eyebrow, feeling the hardwire stitch as it pulls tight.

Uncle shrugs. "Let's just say neither of us wanted you doing this alone." His long striking nose wriggles as he pastes on a worried smile I've grown far too accustomed to seeing.

I breathe in more fragrant steam. "I wasn't asking for a babysitting service. Just someone to hold Lark's seat. And . . . well. Infestation." I motion to the girls having their own quiet conversation on the other side of the aisle.

Uncle Thatch glances at them before turning back to me. He gulps some coffee when he notices Lark's wings sprouting from my shoulders. It's obvious he's battling whether or not to fish for details. Instead, he motions to the sketch pad still pressed against my midriff.

"You were drawing like mad when I got on. Should we toast to your writer's block being over?"

Writer's block. I take a long draw from my cup, letting the hot liquid scald me, punishment for the latest lie I've told him to

downplay my lack of interest in drawing. I also haven't been honest about why I dropped art class this year. Better to let him think I want to pursue a mechanics elective in honor of Lark, just like I'm riding on the trolley today as some kind of "tribute" to her—not a last-ditch attempt at rebooting my retinas.

If I come clean, he'll want to send me back to the psychiatrist. But there's no need. I've already googled my condition: retinal sensitivity affected by depression . . . changing the way the world looks—washing out all the vibrancy. I know the root of my despondency, and am pretty sure they don't make meds that can cure guilt. Most importantly, I can't have Uncle worrying more about me than he already does.

"Sure." I tap my cup to his, the deception souring on my tongue. "Just needed some inspiration, I guess."

Uncle grins as the girls on the other side of the aisle giggle over something on their phones. "Good. And I see you even found a couple of new characters to put in the story."

"Oh yeah. Kind of." So he did see the sketch. Since there's no longer any need to hide, I lower the pad to my lap.

Uncle finishes his coffee, then places the empty cup between his feet so he can study the drawing closer. He looks at the wings on my back again, as though making a connection. "Aha. *Inspiration*. And . . . is that you or a hobblegob?"

"Me, becoming one." I force a smile from behind my cup.

He keeps his attention on the drawing, and something passes over his face . . . a disturbance that drains his olive complexion. He rakes fingers through his thick black hair. The silvery strands that developed after we buried Lark make a temporary appearance before blending into the rest again.

“Those are just rain puddles,” I say, feeling my own face grow pale as I try to decipher what caused his discomfort.

He nods, dabbing his mouth with his napkin. “Oh sure. Didn’t really notice those.”

Then I understand. Even though I smeared away most of her face, there’s no missing Lark in the fairy costume. A blatant reminder of her final Halloween night with us. I want to reach out and hug him, but instead I say, “I—I was erasing her because it didn’t feel right . . . putting her alongside monsters and masks.”

Uncle releases a sound, something between a cough and a groan. “Sure. I mean, whatever you think. It’s a great start to a new panel, either way. You should show it to your art teach—um, to Miss Sparks.”

“Nah. It’s only a doodle.” The trolley arrives at Fourteenth Street, and the hissing brakes muffle my quiet response. Still, Uncle heard me. He’s wearing the same determined expression he dons when he’s concentrating on an intricate icing design or nailing down a new macaron flavor.

I drink the rest of my coffee in silence while at the front half of the car, plastic shopping bags rustle and all the other commuters—besides the two tourists, Uncle, and me—stroll down the aisle to take the exit. No one’s waiting to board at the stop, so the door swooshes closed and the trolley dings, announcing its surge toward Eleventh. Patty must be eager to wrap up her conducting shift.

Uncle clears his throat, flicking off some errant eraser dust from my sketch pad. “Don’t you think it’s time you stop treating your art like a hobby? You have a gift, yet you’ve never shown

your teachers or classmates what you can really do. It's like you're ashamed."

Although I'm touched by his faith in my talent, I can't admit why I've only ever allowed him, Clarey, and Clarey's aunt to read my graphic novels. Why I won't let Mystiquiel seep outside that inner circle and into school or friends or the world I once shared with my sister.

The point is moot anyway, since I've stopped drawing my stories altogether.

I stuff the napkins into our stacked empty cups and drop them along with the sketch pad and pencil into my duffel. "I just . . . am busy expanding Lark's horizons, you know?"

Uncle tweaks the fairy wing closest to him, causing the wire to waggle against my shoulder. "I get that. And she'd appreciate what you've done with her inventions. But don't you think what she'd really want is for you to be *you*?"

As per usual, he avoids her name, as if it physically hurts him to speak it aloud. He's always battled the same guilt as me for not knowing she was in danger that night, and I'm just shameless enough to capitalize on that vulnerability.

I roll my left arm to work out a kink, reminded of the tattoo under my T-shirt and jacket—a two-inch lark soaring beneath the outer edge of my collarbone, its twin tail feathers grazing the front of my shoulder. I got it in ninth grade, while going out with a guy named Ebon, a sophomore who worked evenings at the local auto body shop detailing cars and tuning engines. It wasn't his soulful eyes or his muscled arms spotted with oil and grease that attracted me; it was his knowledge of combustion, gear-shifts, drive belts, suspension systems, and transmissions. And

him being an unlicensed tattoo artist was just frosting on the cupcake.

After we broke up, Uncle Thatch found out about the tattoo, but I escaped being grounded by sharing that Lark and I had always planned to get one together. Hers would've been a phoenix. Uncle dropped the subject immediately, like I knew he would.

"Maybe," I say, answering my uncle's question still dangling in the air between us about what Lark would want for me. "But shouldn't her goals take priority? Since she's not here to make them happen? I've got my whole life to achieve mine."

Uncle clamps his mouth shut, validation that I've won this round.

It's a special kind of twisted, to manipulate someone with a heartbreak you share. Yet I can't seem to stop when it comes to Lark's memory; even the tension created between me and my last living family member is just another way to pay penance.

The bell announces our arrival at Eleventh, and I shrug off Lark's wings. After zipping them and her jacket into my duffel, I secure the straps over my left shoulder and stand behind Uncle Thatch. Together, we clutch the cold metal handle on the seat's edge to brace against the stop.

He nods at the tourists, giving them the go-ahead. They gather their things but freeze a few feet from the rear exit.

"Would you look at that," Uncle Thatch says in reference to the lone figure outside, dressed in black and huddled at the empty stop next to the railroad-crossing sign. A hoodie hides its face; gnarled fingernails, brittle and dingy, dip out from the frayed sleeve cuffs. Something scaly and lizard-like stirs at

the level of the silhouette's knees—its two heads bobbing and its four legs dancing.

Normally, I'm not a fan of the monsters that frequent this time of year, but these are something vastly different—something born of my own sketches. Overhead, clouds swirl in a deep gray sky, adding to the aura of gloom and doom. I couldn't have staged a better scene using my own markers.

The blonde points when the hunched silhouette begins to shuffle toward the trolley's opened door with the mutant quadruped loping behind. "Wh-what is that *thing*?" Her voice trembles.

"Bug repellent," I mumble, biting my inner cheek to tamp down a smirk as the gruesome duo gets closer. The humanoid drags its left leg and groans, leaving a dark smear on the wet concrete behind each footstep. I know that trademark streak of blood enough to imagine the crimson standing bright against the asphalt. A mechanical click echoes through the air with the loping movement of the two-headed beast bringing up the rear.

I glance toward the front of the trolley where Patty remains inside the control box with her back turned, playing some game on her phone that emits electronic music louder than the street sounds around us. Satisfied, I scooch from behind Uncle and sidle into the spot in front of him. "Hey-a, Flannie," I holler.

The four-legged monster darts ahead of its biped companion and clears the steps, nearly bowling over the two girls as it boards. They yelp and leap back into their seats. The redhead drops her purse, which Uncle manages to catch, but the blonde's bag falls open when it hits the floor. Lip gloss, a brush, and other personal things roll out under the surrounding benches.

Wedged in the aisle, I crouch as low as I can, the metallic

gears and screws laced through the front of my jacket tinkling as I gather up the spilled contents.

Trotting over to me, the monster reveals herself as a border collie draped in a hide of scales made from painted, repurposed aluminum cans. A life-size prosthetic troll's head bounces next to her muzzle as she noses my hand to explore the girl's fallen items.

"Sorry about that," I apologize to the blonde, stopping short of admitting it was fair dues for them stealing Lark's seat. I know the grudge is illogical, but a little harmless payback felt good.

I gather a tin of mints and a cylinder of lip gloss as Uncle scratches Flannie's head. She looks up and yips a greeting. Her tufted tail wags, causing the aluminum costume to clank and reveal her dancing paws. A mechanical leg, formed of black-oxide-coated steel and carbon fiber rods, is attached to the stump where her left hind never grew. The hinge on the black device bends with a motorized whir, mimicking a dog's real leg and foot joints—albeit a bit jerkier.

The blonde takes the items from my hand and wrinkles her nose. "What kind of costume is that dog wearing?"

"An automaton troll." The raspy answer drifts from the steps as the dog's accomplice boards the trolley, still dragging that left foot for full effect. "A goblin's best friend," the voice continues, vacillating between a hiss and a snarl. Dirty corkscrew fingernails yank down the hood to uncover a glowing, delicate mane of white fiber-optic floss. Underneath the hair, ghastly gray goblin features lurk: beakish nose, pointed ears, and slimy lips. Tiny jagged teeth open on a creepy sneer, and the veins along the cheeks and neck appear to bulge.

The girls' chins drop.

Uncle whistles in admiration. "Best costume you've made yet," he says to Clarey, releasing Flannie so she can greet her owner.

"Thanks." Clarey's gaze flits over to me from beneath the mask, seeking approval.

"Pretty impressive." I stand and cross my arms, smiling big enough that the ring at the edge of my lower lip tugs.

"What, so you're some kind of SFX wannabe?" the blonde tourist asks as she studies the fake blood smudging the floor.

The redhead peers over her friend's shoulder at Flannie. "And how'd you make the robot leg look so real?"

"Well, I can't take credit for that masterpiece," Clarey says with a whispering snarl, staying in character to the bitter end. "This one's responsible." The goblin's gnarled fingers gesture my way.

Before the girls can respond, Patty steps out of the conductor box and glares at the activity in the back of her trolley. "Hey, the rules say no animals on board. And look at that mess!" She points to muddy paw prints alongside the streaks trailing from Clarey's left shoe, her plump cheeks flushed. "Either you pay a fine or I call animal control. You choose." She holds her phone at the ready.

"Wait!" Clarey spits out fake silver pin-teeth, then peels off the latex mask along with the skin cap and attached wig. From beneath leftover splotches of latex, the same sickly gray as the mask, appears his deep brown complexion and wide-set eyes—one iris an almost neon hue, like a blue-raspberry Icee, the other an amber hazel. Although I can't make out their brilliance today, the variance between the gray shades tells me he

didn't wear his cosmetic contact lenses. I'm guessing it was mainly to up the shock factor of his costume, but still, it's my favorite way for him to be: au naturel and embracing who he is.

"She's not just some animal." He attempts to charm Patty with a baritone as smooth and rich as Uncle's maple star-anise frosting. "She's my emotional support troll."

"And he"—I pat Clarey's chest—"is my emotional support geek."

Clarey snorts and rubs adhesive off his forehead, furrowing the tracery of a scar that dips from his hairline to intersect his left eyebrow, while I peel off a stray piece of latex swinging from the cleft in his chin.

The conductor steadies her gaze at Flannie's costume. "I don't see an official vest, unless it's hidden under those scales."

Clarey shakes his head.

"Okay. Then do you have your documentation?"

"I didn't think I'd need it for this short walk." He punctuates the answer with a sheepish grin.

"You thought wrong." Scowling, Patty begins to punch numbers into her phone.

Uncle gives me and Clarey a meaningful look, then nudges past us into Patty's path. "I can vouch for the dog being an ESA."

Patty sneers. "And why should your word matter?"

"I'm a local businessman. Thatch Griffin . . . I own a bakery." From his pocket he pulls out one of the bite-size-sampler bags he always carries. If I didn't see the name Blueberry-Cheesecake Roonie printed on the tiny bag, I couldn't be sure which flavor it is. The vivid turquoise macaron with its deep purplish-cream

center may as well be black mud sandwiched between gray stones. "The place is straight down Eleventh—little ways past the winery. Just before the intersection, there's an alley that leads to a roundabout street called Eveningside."

Reluctantly, Patty puts her phone in her vest pocket and takes the bag. She opens it and places the quarter-size macaron in her mouth and chews. Within seconds, her frown softens to a beatific smile. I would say it's Uncle's effect on people. That his friendly manner and uniquely handsome features make him a top-notch salesman—but it's more than that. It's the ingredients he uses in his pastries. Simply by letting the conductor try one, he's roped in another loyal customer.

All it takes is one taste and you're hooked for life . . .

As Patty swallows, Uncle slips her a coupon for a free sampler platter at Eveningside Enchanted Delights. "Once you hit Eveningside, head left then go four buildings down on the right. The roundabout is easy to miss, so be sure to pay attention to the map on the back."

"Thanks," Patty answers, her bucktoothed grin spreading. "I've heard about this place. Been meaning to try it." She tucks the coupon away and dabs some cream from her lower lip before licking it off her finger. Her eyes dance with an inner glow—almost gleeful. Turning back to the conductor box, she fishes out a canister of wet wipes and hands them off to Clarey. "I'll give you a few extra minutes to deboard. Just make sure the dog doesn't leave any messes behind. And clean up that fake blood."

"No problem," Clarey assures her. "This evaporates to dust when it's dry. Easy-peasy, see?" With his boot's tip, he blots some dark powder from the floor, leaving no residue behind.

Patty returns to the box, humming a happy tune the entire

time. The two tourists wait at the steps, preparing to exit, but seem transfixed by Clarey now that he's demasked.

Their reaction isn't anything new. With his shoulder-length, tousled black curls and two dimples bridging high cheekbones to a squared chin—he's a striking contradiction to the monster that boarded. Yet in his childhood he was treated like a monster by other kids and even some insensitive adults . . . called everything from "skunk-head" to "elf-boy." Partly because of the four-inch-wide white streak through his bangs that also pigments his skin, seeping past his hairline and into his forehead in a triangular shape like dribbles of milk, but mostly due to his large, wide-set eyes. His long, thick eyelashes combined with the dual-color irises add to their striking appearance.

He's beautiful in an unusual, ethereal way, and sometimes people react awkwardly, like he's "a thing" that should be stared at or turned away from, as opposed to a person like anyone else. It made him uncomfortable enough that he escaped inside makeup and masks at the tender age of twelve. But in the five years since, he's had modeling gigs and won awards for his SFX creations, all of which helped boost his confidence. He now recognizes it's the people treating him differently who are awkward, not him or the way he looks.

As though making my point, Clarey laughs off the girls' dumbfounded expressions, yet today his reaction seems a little strained.

He bows his lithe six-foot frame. "Sorry we spooked you, ladies. I'll be sure to keep a better handle on my genius from now on." He pushes the mask, wig, and teeth into his hoodie's front pocket, then opens the canister of wipes with long-nailed gloves to start on the floor.

"A robot troll," the blonde marvels. "What is it with this place? Invisible fairies holding seats and dogs wearing costumes. Is every day Halloween here?"

Halloween, every day. That would be the definition of horror. Blood drains from my face, leaving my skin clammy.

Clarey touches my fingertips with a cool wipe—an effort to ground me, just as Uncle comes up from behind and holds out a couple of coupons to the girls while patting my back.

"Sorry for any trouble." He smiles at them, then tips his chin to me. "See you at the bakery in a few? Remember, I want you done with the recycling before our delivery gets there."

"Got it," I answer, taking the wipe Clarey still holds—my phobia overshadowed by thoughts of our deliveryman. If anything can out-weird this time of year, it's Jaspar. "Be there as soon as we clean this mess."

Uncle wends around the girls and starts down the steps. "You two, be sure to stop by before you leave town," he says over his shoulder where the tourists wait to descend behind him. "You haven't really experienced our little slice of heaven until you've tasted the ambrosia."

"But beware." Clarey revives his hissing creature voice while scrubbing at a muddy paw print. "Once you eat the faerie food, you can never leave." He grins at the girls, flashing straight white teeth.

The tourists smile tentatively and descend the steps, following my uncle into the petrichor-tinged wind.

4

puppy love

Clarey, Flannie, and I wait beside the railroad crossing sign as the trolley pulls out of sight. The bell dings and the wheels clatter, a musical cacophony underscoring autumn gusts and street noise. Clarey absently touches the spot behind his left ear where a magnetic sound processor is connected to a titanium implant in his skull. The BAHA hides beneath all his hair, but I've seen it many times.

When he first got the bone-anchored hearing aid at the age of eight, he had a buzz cut and all the kids at school saw the metal protrusion. Having lived with Waardenburg syndrome his whole life, he accepted the surgery and new hearing strategies without blinking since he had family members who, along with sharing inherent physical traits, were deaf in both ears. But two fifth-grade boys couldn't resist teasing him, so I got into a fistfight with them, winning them both a black eye, me a fat lip, and two days' suspension for the three of us. Lark's solution was subtler

and more effective: she won Clarey instant popularity by claiming he'd changed into a robot overnight.

Clarey pulls up his hood to protect the BAHA from any stray raindrops, then kisses a clawed fingertip and salutes the clouded sky in silent tribute to my sister. He and Lark crushed on each other after the robot incident, and in sixth grade officially became boyfriend and girlfriend. As pure and true as that puppy love was, I'm convinced they'd still be a couple today had she not died at the beginning of eighth grade.

Clarey's jaw twitches, and he drapes an arm over my shoulders. He's only a few inches taller than my five-foot-nine-inch frame, so I fit perfectly in the groove of his lean body. His scent of flowers and special-effects chemicals—an amalgamation of nature and synthetic that brings more comfort than it should—envelops my senses.

A gust rushes at our backs, nudging us to start our regular route along Eleventh. Flannie trots a few steps ahead, her mechanical leg humming and clicking. Streetlights flicker to life up and down the curbs, a soft glow against the backdrop of clouds and the sun perched just above the horizon, ready to dip into the river. Fellow Astorians wave from passing cars and sidewalks bedecked with jack-o'-lanterns, plaid scarecrows, and miniature haystacks. Clarey raises a clawed glove in response and I mimic the gesture with one hand while gripping the duffel strapped over my shoulder with the other.

The snarling pumpkins and skeleton-shaped lights strung across storefronts make me ache to be home where there are no decorations. I look off in the distance, past the commerce and traffic, where Craftsman houses climb hills glistening with wet grass and fall foliage. Normally, the bright patchwork architecture

and the warm oranges, reds, and yellows of the trees cheer me. Instead, I'm greeted with washed-out beiges, browns, grays, and blacks. As if to add insult to injury, a rainbow catches my attention where it peeks out between branches in the early evening haze. With the absence of color, the curved lines look more like talon marks scoring the screen of an old-timey noir film than a promise of clear skies.

Clarey catches the direction of my gaze and draws me closer. "All seven are there. Red, orange, yellow, green, blue, indigo, and violet." He lists the hues in a whisper, his warm breath hovering over my ear, keeping my secret shame between us. "The offer still stands," he adds.

I shake my head in answer. He's said all along he'll fill the role of temporary colorist for my graphic novels, show me what shades to blend, what tints to add for depth or clarity. But my art is the one part of my life I've always had control of. I'm not handing it over to anyone, no matter how much I trust and admire them. It's a matter of pride . . . of power. I'd rather give it up than admit I can't do it alone. Being a tortured artist himself, Clarey understands my resolve on a level few others could.

Several store owners shout out salutations as our trio passes, a few offering appreciative comments on Flannie's bobbing troll head and scaly hide. Having the only dog in town with an automated leg, Clarey gets more attention than he already did. It trickles down to me, since I'm the one who designed the metal prosthesis. Although, truth be known, I had some help from beyond the grave with that. I stiffen my shoulders under Clarey's arm, determined not to let Lark seep into my thoughts again.

"Okay. Assessment time." Clarey takes my tense muscles as cue to initiate distraction tactics. He drops a bone-shaped treat

for Flannie on the sidewalk, then tugs the mask out of his pocket. He holds it up where mist clings like ethereal cobwebs around a streetlight. Empty eye and mouth sockets gape at me—jogging free that unwanted memory of Lark's unmoving corpse when I found her on the lower bunk.

I bite my lip, wishing I could bring the piskies from my novels to life. I'd happily inhale their magical dust so the tiny particles could open my mind to the power of suggestion—allow me to change the memory's details to something more palatable. If I could, I'd carve out that last moment with Lark and replace it with her smiling and blissful . . . however false it would be.

"Earth to Nix." The mask's beakish nose stretches out like an accusatory finger as Clarey shakes it to reclaim my attention. "Thinking of the gilded piskies again?"

I give him a chagrined smirk. "I thought you were a goblin today. Pretty sure telepathy is a Dracula thing."

"What I *am* is the number one fanboy of *The Goblin Chronicles*. And you know I've wished for a sprinkle of piskie dust myself sometimes."

Sadly, even if such magic were to exist, their nirvanic dust only works on freshly made memories. Time has etched every detail of Lark's death in place so it's a permanent part of me. The same holds true of Clarey's final months with his mom, Breonna. Shortly after we lost Lark, Breonna developed pancreatic cancer. Clarey's blond-haired, blue-eyed, Ken-Barbie dad jumped ship at the diagnosis, so Clarey and Breonna packed up and moved to Chicago where his grandparents could take care of their daughter and grandson.

While he was away, I reached my lowest low, and so did

he—as Breonna withered and died within eight months. Not long after, Clarey found Flannie in the alley behind his grandparents' house. She was just a puppy with a two-inch stump for her left hind, and had stayed warm by wrapping herself in an old flannel shirt discarded beside the dumpster. It was love at first sight for them both. He needed her to fill a void, and she needed him to survive—just like me with my goblins.

But despite having survived, neither Clarey nor I can ever forget what it's like to see someone you love changed to a form you no longer recognize.

"Back to the here and now." He ruffles my hair with a clawed glove. "To have a chance at that scholarship next year, I'll need a top-notch portfolio. And who better to coach me than Mystiquiel's most notorious paint slinger?"

The compliment once grounded me, reminded me I ruled over a land of monsters sketched and commanded by my hand. Although lately the mood lifter doesn't pack the same punch, Clarey hasn't dropped it as his default yet.

"So sock it to me." He flips the mask around to face him and starts forward again, whistling at Flannie so she'll follow. "Still working on the copper-wire horns and electric neck coils. But other than that, I nailed Scourge this time, right?"

Stepping in time with them, I lift one eyebrow. "The wig is phenomenal. And the features are perfect. You'll have to help me with the rest . . ."

He squints upon realizing I'm referring to the paint job that's ambiguous to me. "Well, you can almost see oily blood pumping through these veins."

What I can see are the wheels turning in his head as he avoids the subject of color.

He tilts his head in thought. "The only way I could get more realistic would be to actually *become* a goblin."

I smirk. "Don't say that out loud, Clarence Eugene Darden." I use his full name like his aunt does when he's in trouble, in hopes of slowing his backpedaling. "We wouldn't want the Goblin King to hear you and drag you into his realm to grant your wish."

"If he's anything like Perish, I'm already a goner. Unless I can get on the Motherboard's good side." Clarey laughs, the tension easing as we arrive at a subject on which we can both contribute.

I offer a half smile, thinking of the Goblin King in my graphic novels. Perish's barbaric, scrap-metal-meets-flesh form would be considered disturbing at worst, monstrously beautiful at best, when viewed through a conventional human lens. Yet still I've managed to elevate his seductive abilities by refining his character. He's a master of illusions and mind games, and a brilliant strategist with the intellect of any card-carrying Mensa member—qualities that make him almost impossible to resist or outsmart.

The only entity that can match him play for play is the Motherboard . . . a biomechanical being with a hive-mind consciousness, buried in the heart of Perish's kingdom. Though Perish's voice and image are crystal clear in my imagination, I can never quite picture the Motherboard. Her dialogues are always in the "royal we" and poetic, and I've placed her lair in the center of Mystiquiel, with a pinnacle that rises high enough to disappear into the clouds. This way, there's no need for a detailed image.

In my stories, Perish and the Motherboard are locked in an eternal power struggle. When I'm writing their scenes, they

draw me in with a bold fascination—often surprising me by the savagery of their maneuvers, by how each one takes the plot in directions I never expected.

I didn't extend the same depth of characterization to Perish's brother, Scourge. He's a skinny, ruthless lackey—with a sharp tongue and a knack for deceit. Which is why Clarey prefers that likeness for masks. Scourge is one-dimensional, monstrous without complications.

Still, if Clarey's going to get into New York's Make-Up Designory after graduation next year, he has to devote equal attention to all the specs.

We arrive at Eveningside Street. Flannie is closest to me so I grab her collar where it peeks out from her aluminum scales. After looking both ways, I release her and together the three of us drop off the curb to cross.

"You've read all my novels," I say, continuing our conversation. "You know the canon. Does he look the part of Scourge?"

"No. The coloring is still off." Clarey's feet slosh through puddles along the asphalt. "Your goblins are only gray if they're full blooded."

It's a relief to realize the gray of the mask is true, not just a result of busted retinas. I halt as two cyclists roll by, splashing us.

Flannie's ears perk, as if she's considering giving chase, but all it takes is a cluck from Clarey's tongue and she's glued to his heels again. "Since the royal family has frost elf in their lineage," Clarey continues musing aloud, "I've got to find a way to showcase Scourge's lustrous complexion."

Swiping water off my face, I fall into step with them. "When I'm working on my goblin panels, I always use blending stumps and metallic-colored pencils. So you need a medium that's fluid

and flexible . . . that will coalesce like the belly of a seashell. You know, that shimmery shift from pearly white and petal pink to silvery blue." I wince while describing past techniques, knowing I couldn't possibly accomplish the same precision in this moment.

Clarey peels off his gloves and tucks them into his pocket alongside the mask. "Not so easy with 3D latex. I've used all the iridescent paints out there. Nothing captures the fluctuation . . . the luminance. I even tried stirring pearl powder into the paints. The tonalities still blend together. That's where I'm getting stuck."

I cock my head. "You know . . . maybe you could try some of Uncle's squid ink. Make your own paint with flour, salt, and water, then—"

"Use the ink in place of food coloring," we say simultaneously as we step onto the sidewalk a few shops from the bakery.

Clarey looks impressed. "That could totally work. The color variants would be boss!"

I smirk, wondering where the idea came from, and also why I've never considered it in the past with my own art; it's almost as if someone whispered it in my ear.

Uncle Thatch is the only baker I know who uses the rare squid ink in his recipes—partly to replace the salt, but also for its unique multi-tonal effect on the pastries. Drawn from a deep-sea albino cephalopod, the ink looks black until the instant air touches it, then pales to something resembling melted pearls. Uncle places one drop in each batch of batter he mixes, except in our bestselling Berry-Berry macarons. These contain two drops and no other coloring, which makes its effects more visible. The cookies themselves are glossy and opalescent, as if formed of clouds gilded by a sunrise. The subtle, shifting pastels are

magical enough, but the visual takes a back seat to the exceptional flavor. The filling contains butter and heavy cream, sweetened and tinted with mulberries, blackberries, gooseberries, and pomegranate juice. The shimmery cookies, sandwiched around a velvety center as red as clotted blood, are most popular during Valentine's Day and the Christmas season, but remain a steady favorite any time of year.

"But . . . wait. That stuff's expensive." Clarey voices my own unspoken concern while scratching Flannie behind her ear. "Do you really think your uncle would let me try it?"

I shrug. "I'm not sure he'd be up for sharing, and he's the only one with a key to the safe. Maybe I could sneak some when the shipment first arrives, before it's put away. I wouldn't need to take much."

"Only a drop or two will do," Clarey says, reciting my uncle's personal adage for using the ink in moderation when he cooks. "But he'll know, right? When the air hits it . . . it'll lighten in the vial. A dead giveaway."

"Well, it darkens again after a couple of minutes once the stopper's back in place. So . . . as long as I can get it done with time enough for the ink to return to normal before he checks the shipment, I can pull it off."

"There's my naughty kitten." Clarey gifts me with a sexy wink.

I narrow my eyes. "You realize that doesn't work on me, right?"

"So sad." He tweaks the sprocket-shaped piercing at the outer edge of my eyebrow. "All that mechanical know-how and you still can't jump-start your heart."

I scoff and push his hood off playfully, releasing his white

streak along with all the dark locks surrounding it, and relishing that his hair isn't affected by my mood blindness.

"It's got nothing to do with mechanics, Buster, and everything to do with chemistry," I say. If I gave in to the urge to run my fingers through his curls, he'd see right through that lie.

His hands catch mine when I start to pull back, latching us together. "So maybe I should buy you a chemistry set this Christmas." He rests his thumbs against the thin skin of my wrists where my heart drums an undeniable rhythm of excitement. His eyes glitter with something between playfulness and daring.

I try not to think about the pallor of his irises, concentrating instead on the softness of his skin and the heat of his touch against my pulse points. There's no lack of chemistry here. But Clarey liked Lark first . . . used to call her his little gearhead. So I can't help but think any spark he feels is because I remind him of her.

Worse yet, Lark told him she loved him a couple of months before she died. She fell hard, for all the reasons I have: his witty and artistic mind, his eclectic love of music, his eccentric fashion sense, and his appreciation for outdated words such as "ratfink," or dicta like "check out this newfangled gadget" and "I'm in a funk."

Hijacking my sister's robotics is one thing, but stepping into a romance that should've been hers feels like a betrayal. I have enough guilt piled on my plate, and can't afford for my world to get any more anemic than it already is.

So, squelching the flutters in my belly, I deliver Clarey a snide one-liner to get myself off the hook: "Just buy me a microscope so we can look for your mind—'cause I'm pretty sure you've lost it."

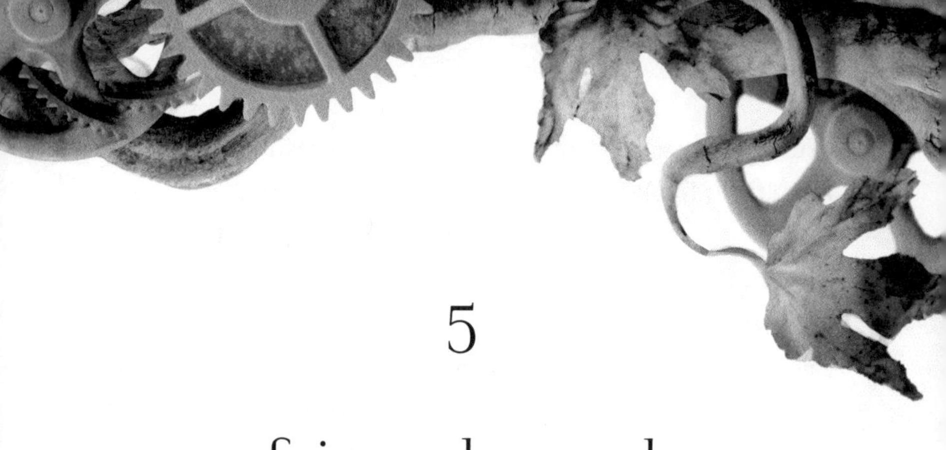

5

fairy-cakes and goblin-roonies

Clarey chuckles as we share an awkward, wobbly grin. We break our hands apart and walk a bit farther, pausing a few feet from the bakery as the bright neon lights wash over us in a prismatic wave.

The longing in my gut to really *see* those lights as I remember them, to decipher the colors fluttering over my face, manifests in nauseous pangs that evolve to a growling stomach at the scent of fresh-from-the-oven macarons.

Uncle Thatch dabbled in cooking throughout our childhood. He makes a mean frittata, and no one can rival his stuffed clams, although his specialties were the featherlight cupcakes and sandwich cookies baked up for me and Lark—no special occasion necessary. At the time, his official job as a portrait photographer made just enough to rent us a two-bedroom-one-bath Craftsman home, but six months after we lost Lark, he quit, found a business space to lease, and opened a bakery armed with nothing more than his meager savings and those homespun

desserts. The one change he made was substituting organic ingredients in place of the less healthy counterparts.

When I asked him why he wanted to take that kind of chance, he said, "Life's too short not to live your dreams." I inferred the unspoken reference to Lark. He went one step further and dedicated the bakery to our family by hanging the quote from my mom's *Goblin Market* book on the front door as a greeting to customers:

Morning and evening
You'll hear the goblins cry:
"Come buy our fruits,
Come buy, come buy."

Two other signs frame either side of the bakery's large display window—yellow silhouettes on a background of dark green. One is a flying faerie, and the other a crooked-nosed goblin. To reflect the rainbow hues of his macarons, Uncle Thatch had the shop front painted in oranges, yellows, purples, turquoises, and greens. For the final touch, he installed neon lights in the same colors, so his bakery draws the eye—day or night. It's all part of the magical theme, meant to lure people in and make sure they return, but he never really needed it; his baking skills and fresh ingredients did that on their own.

Within a few months of our grand opening, Uncle had already raked in enough money to buy our rental home, pay off the café space, and invest in a healthy 529 plan for my collegiate future.

"I'm heading over." Clarey nods toward the twinkling white lights draped like icicles around a potted wisteria tree on the sidewalk two shops down. His aunt Juniper opened the

boutique around the same time Uncle Thatch opened his shop. Since her last name is Wisteria, it seemed only logical she should sell creeping vines and climbing flowers and name it Wisteria Rising.

Another fringe of white lights outlines the French-style glass doors. Flannie sniffs at their base, waiting to be let inside where everything flickers with the same inviting, angelic glow that emanates from the woman who owns the place. Shortly before Clarey's grandparents ended up in a retirement facility—worn down from caring for their daughter—Clarey got into some trouble in Chicago. He needed a new start, and without hesitation, Juniper welcomed him into her heart and home at the beginning of our freshman year. Her not actually being Clarey's blood relation (she was his mom's best friend when they originally lived in Astoria) made the gesture all the sweeter.

"Still plan to come by?" Clarey asks, his body leaning away from the line at the bakery's entrance; it doesn't matter that aluminum isn't magnetic, it's as if he's being pulled toward Flannie's shimmery costume.

I don't blame him for that anxious spasm in his jaw or the tremble in his voice . . . for not wanting to venture inside Uncle's packed bakery.

"Yeah, I'll be by," I answer. "I've got to shade the letters and tweak that mechanical arm." I don't say the rest since we both already know: I *have* to get the carnival mural done tonight. Once my twenty-four-hour vigil against Halloween begins, I won't leave my house for anything.

"Cool. Tootles, poodle." He touches two fingertips to his temple—the Clarey version of a wave—then buries himself in his hood and carves a wide beeline around the crowd. He

developed enochlophobia after the incident in Chicago—the details of which he's never shared, other than that it has to do with the scar on his forehead. He manages going to school with Flannie by his side; but congregated events that aren't regimented or scheduled can take unpredictable turns and trigger a deep-seated fear of having a panic attack in public.

Though Fridays after school are among the bakery's busiest times, second only to Saturdays, today is worse than usual because of the rain. We have a waiting area with benches on the patio, but with everything dripping wet, customers choose to cluster at the storefront under their umbrellas—listening for their numbers over the intercom so they can claim a spot inside.

Their eager expressions remind me of the warning Clarey gave the tourists earlier . . . of people not being able to leave after sampling my uncle's desserts. In truth, it's not that they *can't* leave; it's that they don't want to.

Uncle Thatch bakes the best macarons and minicupcakes this side of the Columbia River. The fact that he uses only organic ingredients—with flavorings such as basil, lavender, citrus, and anise in combination with natural colorings like beets, paprika, saffron, matcha, red cabbage, and coffee—only makes his success all the more mystifying.

He decorates his Fairy-Cakes with lacy spun-sugar wings so realistic it appears tiny flying creatures crash-landed into the all-natural frosting. And his macarons, aka Goblin-Roonies—named in fond tribute for the goonies of our city's fame and for the goblins I draw—are every color of the rainbow beneath their luminous squid-ink glow. Some customers say he bakes with magic. There may be something to that, considering he receives

weekly shipments of exotic fruit for his creations that are so flawless, plump, and juicy they could've been grown in an enchanted orchard.

Thereby the name of his shop, Eveningside Enchanted Delights, is the perfect fit.

As I make my way to the door, several regulars smile and clear a path. I pause long enough for small talk, acutely aware of the sympathetic frowns on their faces as unspoken thoughts of Lark swirl around us like phantoms. Relaying my goodbyes, I step over the threshold before anything can be voiced aloud.

The aroma of baked goods—paired with the glow of candle jars centered on each wooden table—greets me with a familiar warmth that doesn't quite reach my eyes. Four years ago, in seventh-grade chemistry class under our teacher's careful supervision and instruction, we learned to make white flame using Epsom salt fueled by methanol. Today, that's the only color of fire I see. No oranges or yellows, no reds or bluish tones.

It's even more of a kick in the teeth here, where our special candles emit rainbow-hued flames. Uncle doesn't even play background music, so as not to interfere with the ambiance. Instead, the sound of customers talking and laughing provides its own soundtrack.

Resituating the duffel on my shoulder, I wind through a faded kaleidoscope that teeters between sepia and grayscale on my way to the front counter. Our two servers, Stephen and Tori, and Pete the busser are all busy working the tables so I skip any hellos.

"Hey, Nix!" Three of my classmates, seated at a tall, four-top table in the corner, wave me down. They don't have a candle or plates yet, so they're still waiting for their order.

Jin's salt-and-pepper braids shimmer beneath the soft overhead lights. "Do the candle trick!"

Brooke, a cheerleader who volunteered to pose for a "portraits on canvas" unit back in August, then decided she herself wanted to learn to paint and switched over to art, adds, "Yeah, Émile hasn't ever seen it."

Émile enrolled in mid-September as a French foreign exchange student. "I don't believe what they're telling." He beams his wide, inviting smile.

I furrow my brow teasingly. "I don't blame you, it's pretty unbelievable." In the past, I would have happily hung the duffel on a chair and joined them for a game of Name That Dessert.

Unfortunately, I'm no longer the same girl. I glance at the digital clock on the wall. I still have plenty of time before the deliveryman comes, but my classmates don't know that. I'm the only one Uncle trusts to do the recycling, and since he has a strict rule that I'm never to have direct contact with the deliveryman, I have to have the box ready so Uncle can hand it off himself.

"I know you're here to work, but hang for just a few. Please? I never see you anymore." Jin's dark eyes sparkle with supplication before I can offer my excuse. She and I were in art class together from seventh through ninth grade, so she took it personally when I dropped it this year without warning.

Resigned, I scoot into the empty spot between Émile and Brooke with my duffel in my lap. Since there's nothing sadder than a broken trick pony, I'm not about to make it obvious I need help. That leaves me with only one option.

"Okay," I say, "but let's kick things up a notch. Blindfold me with that napkin."

"Ooooh, I like where this is going," Jin squeals. Standing

behind me, she secures one of Uncle's tie-dyed cloth napkins across the top half of my face, shutting out all the lights and sights.

I check the knot, then nod. "Okay, Jin. You're my eyes."

"You got it, girl." Her clothes rustle as she returns to her chair. "There's a two-seater table. Diners have their backs to us, blocking their plates. A pink flame burns on the candle between them."

I tap my lip ring. "Okay, they both ordered the Avocado-Guava Roonies."

There's a scribbling sound as someone jots my answer on paper.

"Another," I say, rearranging the blindfold so it won't pinch the bridge of my nose.

"Four-topper with three people, too far across the room to make out what they're eating. The flame is flickering between green and blue."

I smirk. "Hibiscus Fairy-Cakes and Berry-Berry Roonies."

"I tried those hibiscus ones once," Brooke inserts. "Didn't like them. They made me feel too sad."

"Shhh," Jin shushes.

Brooke makes a huffing sound.

"Sorry, boo," Jin says, followed by the sound of a noisy peck. "You're going to break our girl's concentration."

"Last one," I say, itching to pull off the blindfold and look at the clock as my concern for the recycling becomes genuine.

"Okay, a six-top in the middle . . . a business meeting."

"How do you know?" Brooke interrupts again.

"Why else would they have a flow diagram propped on an easel, huh?" Jin scolds. "I can see everyone's plates, but they've all

finished eating so there's just crumbs. One candle, the flame goes from red to blue, then turquoise to orange."

"Is the cycle repeating?" I ask.

"Yeah."

I chew on my lip hoop. "Hmmm . . . they had the Poesy Sampler: Strawberry Mead Fairy-Cakes, Lavender-Blue-Dilly Roonies, Nectarine-Cardamom Cakes, and Peach-Curd and Maple Roonies."

As I take off the blindfold, Brooke finishes jotting my answers. Jin takes the list, gets up, and makes a sweep of the room, pretending to look at the colorful artwork on the wall. What she's really doing is surreptitiously glancing at everyone's food, or in the case of the six-top, the itemized check on their table. When she gets back to us, she confirms all my guesses were right.

Émile's eyes widen, and Brooke busts out giggling. "See? She never misses one."

"She has a gift," Jin adds.

"Or a touch of *sorcellerie*. How's it done, eh?" Émile asks, leaning in so his beaded paisley neck scarf grazes the tabletop with a soft clack.

I hesitate, thinking that sorcery would be the perfect explanation. Uncle Thatch buys the candles from the same distributor who provides our fruit, and the wicks are rumored to absorb emotions then showcase them through the flames. When we first opened, I asked my uncle how that was even possible. He said, "You know, kind of like a mood ring." Uncle then made me promise never to talk about the emotion-emitting wicks, or we'd risk losing everything. I've always assumed he meant the distinctiveness of our bakery—what sets us apart. So we just let

everyone believe the candle flames are simply colorful, with no rhyme or reason.

Over time, I learned to read the fire. I could predict what each person was having because I knew that each dessert inspired a distinctive emotion, having sampled them all and noted how they affected me.

If the glow at the table was pink, someone ordered the Avocado-Guava macarons, and the odd combination of flavors had them feeling indecisive or uncertain. If a flame sparked green, someone chose the Hibiscus Fairy-Cakes, which make people wallow in sorrow—maybe over a recent heartbreak or a bittersweet memory of a lost loved one—since the sugar-glass wings glisten with a pink Himalayan salt and sugar mixture that tastes like candied tears. Blue came through when someone felt bold or ambitious, brought about by a boost of antioxidants in the Berry-Berry macarons. Turquoise was happy, red was angry . . . and deep orange energized.

There is an entire palette of emotive colors, each triggered by the herbal and fruity combinations Uncle Thatch bakes into his wares, and I hope to one day see them again.

For tonight, I plaster on a fake smile and give Émile the only answer I can: "A magician never reveals their secrets."

6

waxing poetic

The table's order arrives, complete with a candle waiting to be lit.

I ease from my chair and say goodbye as the waitress ignites the wick. The clock on the wall reads 6:10. Uncle Thatch and I have to be home before midnight—no exceptions—which means I need to hustle to finish the recycling so I'll have enough time to work on my mural next door.

As I pass the counter, I wave at Dahlia, our evening cashier.

She waves back a little too enthusiastically—an obvious effort to downplay her concerned expression. "You okay, sweetie?"

"Yeah." I force the reply against a tweak behind my sternum. Bad enough that she and her husband, Carl, have volunteered to man our booth tomorrow at the carnival so Uncle and I can hole up at home like every year on Lark's death-iversary, but seeing how tired she looks makes me feel even worse. My bleak traditions should be secondary to toting around a whole other person day and night.

"Isn't your shift about over?" I ask, already knowing the

answer; I'm in charge of schedules and payroll while Uncle manages the baking and supply side of things—and I lined up Tori and Pete to shut down. "It's okay if you duck out early. Pete can do cash till Uncle's done with the delivery."

"That's all right. I had a break thirty minutes ago when we changed out the bank drawer." Dahlia grins, and her face beams with the perfect example of pregnancy glow. She lifts a water bottle and takes a sip. "I'll be fine until your uncle gets the produce put away."

My shoulders tense because I still have to get Clarey's squid ink before Uncle locks it up. "Is Jaspar already here?"

Dahlia glances toward the kitchen, smoothing her tie-dyed apron over a bulging abdomen. "I don't think so."

Although Uncle's never clearly explained why I should avoid the deliveryman, I'm okay keeping my distance; Jaspar's in his early twenties and disturbingly pretty with pale ivory skin, sculpted muscles, sharp cheekbones, heart-shaped lips, and a thick shock of burgundy-red hair, but it's not so much the way he *looks* as it is the way he looks *at me*. Or rather, into me. He has the creepiest black irises I've ever seen, like beetles digging beneath my skin with their oil-slick carapaces . . .

"You should still have time to get the melts ready," Dahlia assures me. "I had Pete put today's jars under the sink."

"Thanks."

I enter the kitchen, a pristine white slate that shines with marble-topped cutting board islands, stainless steel cooling racks and commercial floor mixers, and spotless, scrubbed convection ovens and sinks. Other bakery and pastry supplies line the shelves along the walls, pots and pans sharing space with stoneware plates and beverage glassware. Two copper

refrigerator-freezer combos take up most of the back wall, framing the storeroom's door between them.

I avoid looking directly at the glossy surfaces then place my duffel and jacket in the bottom left divider of the plastic storage cabinet. The unwelcome sight of Dahlia's bag of Halloween candy greets me from the shelf above. Cringing, I slam the cabinet shut.

Taking an apron off a hook, I tie it over the red-lipstick mouth and the Silently Screaming lettering on my black T-shirt. At the industrial-size double sink, I fill one side with a shallow layer of hot water and partly submerge the twelve candle jars so liquid rises to engulf their outer bottom quarters. I brace the jar in the middle to keep them all from tipping over.

Our product supplier is big on recycling and conservation. So much so that other than his teensy sampler bags, Uncle adheres to a strict dine-in-only policy as part of his contract. No carryout boxes are provided. This earns us a hefty discount, and since customers order exactly what they can eat—never more than one treat per person—they leave nothing on their plates. Maybe that's the most magical thing of all about Uncle's bakery: there are never leftovers, and everyone always goes home satisfied. Also, per the contract, the supplier insists we recycle each and every candle, and the melts have to retain their shape when we send them back, as though they're precious gems or something. We get charged extra for our next shipment if any wax gets crumbled or broken, which makes for a very slow and tedious process to remove each stump from the jars.

My muscles twitch while I wait for the steaming water to soften the wax inside; even with my duffel tucked away, I can't help but sense the ticking as minutes pass by. A rising cloud of

heat caresses my face, and I lift my chin to escape it. It puts me eye level with a stand-up mixer seated on the shelf above the sink's steel backsplash. In the silver bowl's reflective surface, I catch a glimpse of my nose, eyebrow, and lip hoops all shaped like miniature cogs and sprockets—tributes to Lark's mechanical talents. I stare a moment too long, and before I can stop myself, I've locked eyes with my image.

A loamy scent, bleak with mildew and rot, seeps into my nostrils . . . so close it's as if the sink is gurgling up mud. A sensation like a skitter of dirt and pebbles rolls beneath my skin. The gaze looking back at mine turns accusatory. My nerves tug against their roots. I bare my teeth so I can see their tight, straight lines. The absence of the gap my sister had between her central incisors grounds me: it's not Lark . . . it's my face . . . it's my face . . . it's me . . . Phoenix Loring.

The jar I'm holding clinks its neighbor, and a slosh of hot water stings my wrist, delivering me from the brink. I rip my attention from the bowl, feeling the separation like a physical snap inside my chest.

It's been this way since we lost Lark. Each time I look in a reflective surface there's a sensory rush—that same tugging on my nerves and loamy tinge on the air I sensed on the night she died—that triggers a misstep of reasoning, where I think I see her glaring back from somewhere I can never reach.

I don't need to be psychoanalyzed to deduce it's my imagination, warped by how much was left unfinished between Lark and me. It's manageable as long as I use a handheld mirror to do my makeup and hair so I can flip it around before I'm captured.

The only part of my life it's really affected is that I opted out of driver's ed last year—not trusting myself to keep a clear head

while glancing in a rearview mirror—making me one of the few seventeen-year-olds at my school without a license or a car.

I shake off the residual tremble in my hands, then return to the recycling, easing a butter knife into the first jar's mouth. After levering the softened wax free, I wrap the used-up stump in brown paper before placing it in a cardboard box already half-filled with others I prepped earlier in the week. Following the same technique, I pop out the melts one by one, then set each empty jar aside to be washed and fitted with the new candles arriving in our shipment.

As I pry out the next-to-last melt, Carl, our assistant baker, exits the storeroom with an unopened pack of pastry bags. He tugs a hairnet into place over his balding head and smiles my way. The familiar sight calms my nerves. He and Dahlia met here when we first opened, so Uncle and I had front-row seats to their love story, making them more like family than employees.

"Hey there, Doodle-bean." Carl enjoys razzing me with assorted nicknames I made Uncle stop using in the ninth grade.

I point my butter knife at him. "If you weren't going to be a daddy in a few weeks, I'd shiv you for that."

He laughs.

"Thought you were done for the day. You need to go home . . . and take your wife since you're both working the booth tomorrow." I use the back of my glove to blot sweat from my forehead as another cloud of steam rises.

"I will." Carl opens the package, takes out a pastry bag, and fills it with batter before snipping off the tip. "Just wanted to make an extra batch of Pumpkin-Pie Roonies for the carnival. The evening rush left us short a dozen."

"Ah." I lift the last jar from the water. "You know, if you used the cookie carousel, you'd save some time," I tease.

Carl grimaces at the stainless-steel machine in question. "Making macarons is an art form, not a carnival ride."

The carousel is my latest invention, designed for extra credit in my mechanics class. Springboarding off the concept of a conveyer belt, it has a giant bowl at the top to hold macaron batter and a spout at the bottom that rotates as it presses out uniformly shaped circles; when used at full speed, it can spit them out on the silicone-lined belt at a rate of two dozen per minute. Our part-time baker, Lydia, uses it every time she works; Carl and my uncle, however, have too much pride to let a machine interfere with their creations.

I look over my shoulder toward the storeroom. "Is Uncle Thatch waiting for the truck?"

Carl settles at a long marble cutting board where he's lined up stenciled baking sheets. "Actually, Jaspar arrived early. About fifteen minutes ago."

"Crap." Leaving the final candle jar unfinished, I pick up my box and aim for the storeroom.

"Not sure you should interrupt." Carl's observation stops me at the threshold. Concentrating on piping macaron batter into perfect circles atop each sheet, he glances my way from the corner of his eye. "Jaspar's in a snit, something about seeing supplies in the storeroom that your uncle bought elsewhere. They're both in the alley, hashing it out." Having filled one sheet, Carl lifts and drops it several times to release any air bubbles from the raw circles. "You ask me, that guy needs to learn some respect. Customer's always right, you know?" His cheeks darken with annoyance.

I thank Carl for the heads-up, then step inside the storeroom. I'll have to go against Uncle's rules and hand the recycling off myself. I know from past experience how upset Jaspar becomes when the melts aren't ready for him to load. Uncle doesn't need our deliveryman getting more worked up than he already is.

But first, Clarey's ink . . .

I wind around shelves and tables loaded with crates of fresh fruits—as bright and polychromatic as their scent is mouth-watering, at least for those with working color receptors. Many times, I've been tempted to stop and sample them, but I don't dare. Uncle forbids anyone to eat the fruit raw. He says it has to do with the organic fertilizers used to grow them. It affects their seeds somehow. They have to be cleaned very carefully and prepped in a special way. He always filters their deseeded pulp three to four times through a strainer before he'll even put them in our recipes.

On the other side of a box of pomegranates sit three squatty bottles of black, brackish liquid. I'll take just a small amount from each and Uncle will never miss it. If he does, I'll forfeit my next paycheck to pay him back.

I push aside a carton of fresh candles and other new supplies to make room. The carton's corner hits a container of silver dragées, making the tiny decorative balls rattle against their plastic walls. I fit my box of melts in the opened space on the table.

Several empty vials wait on the shelves behind me, ready to be filled with natural extracts and colorings. I take one and pour a tiny drizzle of ink from each of the bottles, watching the liquid pale to an iridescent white as I fill the vial almost halfway. Plugging it up with the stopper, I push the vial into my right front pocket, then shut the original bottles tight once more.

Tapping my fingers on the table's edge, I look toward the alley door. It's slightly ajar, allowing a sliver of moonlight inside. I bide my time, waiting for the ink to coalesce to black in its bottles. Goose bumps erupt along my arms, partly from the chilly gust filtering in, but more from Uncle's indecipherable conversation outside. He already sounds upset.

"C'mon, c'mon. Hurry," I whisper to the ink, then shudder a sigh as it finally darkens. The relief is short lived, though, because I catch Jaspar's words seeping through the door, as clear as crystal.

"You think we're blind to what goes on up here?" The young deliveryman's voice is slick yet scratchy, like dead leaves scraping underfoot on wet pavement. Recyclables in hand, I move to the crack to peer outside. "Only a fool would be so careless with our generous bargain. If you breach it, there will be payment due. And you know what *he* will take."

"To hell he will," Uncle snarls, clutching the lapel of Jaspar's rain jacket. "We've kept to the bargain . . . both here and there."

Jaspar huffs, shaking free of Uncle's hold.

Uncle leans in until they're almost nose to nose. "At this point, a little shortage of smoke isn't going to make any difference. This is the consequence of *his* choice, so you'll all just have to suck it up. You can relay that to your boss for me."

Both here and there? Smoke shortages? Consequences of his *choice?* What's any of that mean? And what does it have to do with our fruit deliveries?

My goose bumps evolve to a foreboding shiver along my spine. Uncle is the most chill person I know. I've never heard him sound so defensive and tense—never seen him get physical with anyone.

Determined to intervene, I shove through the storeroom exit with the box of melts. Just as I'm about to step out, I notice the truck's cargo door remains open. A streetlight pours a soft white spray inside to reveal a maw of crates and folded-down shelves. A burlap blanket hangs across the back half of the interior, curtaining off the rest of the view.

Uncle and Jaspar stand in the alley next to the passenger side, whisper-arguing, as unaware of my presence as they are that the mist has turned to drizzle. As if triggered by the soft plops hitting the truck's aluminum roof, the burlap curtain sways and the darkness behind it seems to shift. Four lights—two amber and two green—blink on.

Wait.

Amber and green. My throat clenches, cutting off a gasp. I *see* the colors . . . brilliant and vivid. The only pigmentation anywhere in my world right now—like I've stepped into one of my pencil sketches right at that moment when I'm starting to add color.

I'm still trying to wrap my mind around the realization as the lights illuminate the shadows, revealing serpentine silhouettes. The lights bob back and forth, and a grinding hum of gears keeps time with the movements.

It takes a minute to understand what I'm seeing, and I have to bite my tongue to keep from screaming because it's *impossible* . . .

I squeeze my eyes shut, then look again. Wind blows the curtain, opening it farther. The two colorful sets of lights grow brighter while seeming to narrow. A black slit elongates in their centers like cat pupils.

Before I can react, the drizzle becomes a downpour, pounding

the truck with rhythmic pings. Two distinctive yet strangely synchronized voices invade my ears and drown out the rainfall, as if having a direct line to me:

"There be no friend like a sister, Slinx . . . ," voice one hisses.

"Aye, e'en in stormy weather, Binx . . . ," voice two answers with a mewling, purring sort of sound.

A frantic pulse hammers at my temples in recognition. "No, no, no," I whisper to myself. Slinx and Binx are two characters from my graphic novels. Actually, one character with two heads . . . part feline and fur, part metal and whir. A grimalkin, to be exact.

I'm always pretending to see my characters, inserting them into my real life—maybe I even use them as a crutch sometimes. Still, it's just imaginary. I never actually see them. And I never, ever *hear* them. It's like this one stepped out of my dreams into real life.

But that's not possible . . .

"Aye, a sister will cheer along the tedious way," the first voice says, taking the lead again. "To fetch her should she go astray."

"Unlesss," voice two says, taking its cue, "one sister should turn away."

My fingers go limp. The box I'm holding drops to my feet and I slap a shaky palm over my mouth. The shapes behind the curtain are disturbing enough on their own—seeing the vibrancy of green and yellow in the feline eyes is both unsettling and exciting—but those voices reciting the one verse in *Goblin Market* I can no longer bear, pulls me over the edge.

As I wrestle the confused agony in my chest, the dual voices synchronize to a crooning yowl. Their blinking gazes begin to spin—the light and dark swirl of a hypnotic binary spiral. The

eyes flip back and forth, as if bouncing from one face to the other, but I know better. They have necks made of springs, longer than swans', that in the darkness behind a burlap blanket could be interpreted as snakes, and they like to entwine them, then loosen them, and entwine them again in a slithery, silky dance, as a means to mesmerize their prey.

I know, because I gave them those characteristics.

My face feels feverish. Nausea flips my stomach. Maybe the spiral is hypnotizing me. Maybe that's why this moment feels like I'm dreaming. No, hallucinating. Their dizzying gazes slip back behind the curtain, growing dim. Then the burlap's edges billow shut, and darkness fills the truck again.

I need to get inside that vehicle—whether to prove I was having a Halloween-induced panic attack or to get another look at those prismatic eyes, I can't be sure.

Suppressing a moan, I nudge the box aside. The cardboard shoves the door wider, causing the hinges to squeal. The sound captures Jaspar's and Uncle Thatch's attention, and they turn my way, simultaneously.

Cold rain pelts my face as a slash of lightning spotlights the deliveryman's burgundy-red hair—another unexpected spatter of color in my bleached-out world. With a second lightning flash, his glistening wet face is revealed, but it's no longer pretty. Chasms appear around his eyes and brows, empty valleys beneath his cheekbones—a bleakness so deep it's as if his features have sunk away, leaving his skin to shrink-wrap a hollowed skull. Everything about him seems disproportioned.

Disproportioned. Just like my sister.

Lark's image, dead in the bed beneath mine, blinks through my brain.

An agonized wail scours my lungs and throat, and I stumble backward in an effort to escape. Uncle rushes toward me through sheets of rain, shouting my name.

I trip over the box of melts and the back of my head thuds to the floor. A hot jolt races from my nape to my jaw, then everything fades to black. The darkness folds over me and unrolls like a carpet, spitting me out into my moonlit bedroom where I jerk to a sitting position on my top bunk. I know this night . . . and I don't want to be here again.

I hear the sounds that startled me awake the first time, see the colored pencil sketches flapping in the wind; then, I see something else entirely . . . a dark silhouette, hunched and clawed, blinking a set of eyes that spark bright with electricity. Or is it two sets of eyes? It's impossible to know.

As my gaze adjusts, it's clear only Lark and I are in the room—her face and body appearing warped and distorted. Whatever monster I imagined creeping along the floor was actually her all along, lying in the bed, motionless.

Horrified screams claw their way out of my mouth. I barely notice Uncle Thatch rushing into the bedroom, barely see him lean across Lark and howl in shock. Even when his arms surround me for comfort, all I feel is the absence of my sister.

"Nix," Uncle soothes. "Talk to me . . . Nix."

He rocks me gently, but I can't speak. I struggle to even breathe as the darkness gathers around me again.

7

creepers peepers

"Nix . . . Nix!"

I snap awake to Uncle Thatch's hand cupping my cheek. I'm seated on the floor in the storeroom with a throbbing headache, my back and shoulders propped against the wall.

Squinting at the overhead light, I shake off the dregs of my memory. It was too real this time . . . too harrowing. I still feel that earthy uprooting I experienced through Lark's senses—the one part of her that lingers in every reflection. Not a calm, happy relief, but a dark, critical weight.

Uncle Thatch kneels beside me and holds a cup of water while Dahlia and Carl crouch on the floor. Although with Dahlia, it's more of an awkward slouch because of the baby bump.

"Where'd you two come from?" The words seem senseless even as I'm saying them, so I focus on the boxes and fruits surrounding me to collect my wits. I rub the knot at the base of my skull while struggling to remember why I'm on the floor.

"We've been trying to help your uncle wake you." Dahlia hands me a foil-wrapped eyeball. "Here."

Seeing the themed candy gives me goose bumps. I shake my head, refusing it.

She tilts her chin and an ebony coil slips out of her bun. "Hey, I don't share my creepy-peeper stash with just anyone. I know you don't like reminders of the holiday, but this is full of peanut butter."

"I told her how you fainted," my uncle explains, his thick dark eyebrows drawn together behind his glasses. I make the silent observation that his chef's hat is the only part of his uniform that's dry.

"That's why you need this." Dahlia takes over the conversation. Her mom's a doctor, so she's our go-to for anything health related. "You're either lacking protein or your blood sugar's low. This will fix both. Now eat."

"C'mon, Nix. They're no Goblin-Roonies, but they're still tasty," Carl presses.

"Okay," I say, surrendering at last. "But I'm pretty sure child services would frown on strong-arming a kid into eating candy."

The three of them offer relieved smiles as I peel off the painted foil, crumpling it so the veined eye is no longer visible. I pop the chocolate ball into my mouth and chew. The rich taste of peanut butter coats my tongue, and I do start to feel better. Until the truth of why I'm on the floor comes rushing back.

I didn't faint. I tripped, running from what I saw through sheets of rain: colors . . . real and vivid, such a stunning deviation from my dreary reality, tainted by what they were attached to—a grimalkin and a hollow-faced Jaspar.

How could it be? My characters coming alive and taunting me seems as impossible as Jaspar's face warping like Lark's on the night she died.

I gasp, inhaling the remnants of the candy. A cough rattles my throat.

Dahlia slaps my back. Uncle offers the cup he's holding. Still coughing, I observe him through watery eyes. That's why his chef's hat is dry. He didn't have it on outside when he was talking to Jaspar.

Why did he lie about my fall? He knew the box toppled me. He saw me. Didn't he? Or did I imagine everything? Has the Halloween curse finally cracked me wide open?

My stomach flips as I glance toward the closed alley door. I meet my uncle's gaze. "Where's Jaspar? There was something . . . off with him."

Uncle's lips slant upward, a smile that looks forced. "There's always something off with him. Why do you think I want you to avoid him?"

My heart pounds in fitful beats. "No . . . you remember that night . . . the way Lark looked? What I told you I saw—"

"Maybe," Uncle interrupts, molding my fingers around the cup, "we should take you to the emergency room. Check you for a concussion?" He glances from me to Dahlia.

She cradles my chin and studies my eyes. "I don't think so. Her pupils look good. She's going to be all right once that knot on her head shrinks."

"But we can agree that she needs to stay hydrated, right?" Uncle asks pointedly while staring me down.

I sip the water from the cup and frown at him. I shouldn't be surprised he's changing the subject. He's always been sure the

psychiatrist was right: that the shifting distortion I witnessed in my sister's appearance that night was a result of my horror to find her deader than the walking corpses we'd seen while trick-or-treating. And now, for some reason he doesn't want to discuss the events of *this* night, either. At least not with our friends here.

I take a few more swallows; the aftertaste of peanut butter and sugar lingers on my tongue along with a faint mineral-metallic flavor. We need to change the filter on our faucet.

"Shouldn't you two be headed home?" I say as Carl helps Dahlia stand so she can stretch her lower back. "Carl, you already earned overtime baking those extra roonies for tomorrow."

They look at each other and smile.

"We just wanted to be sure you were okay," Carl answers. "But it sounds like you're back to yourself, Boss."

Uncle Thatch manages a chortle that's tight and grinding, not nearly as musical as his authentic laugh. I aim a suspicious glare at him and he lifts his eyebrows in a pleading gesture.

Downing the rest of the odd-tasting water, I hand the empty cup to Carl. "I'm okay. You two go. We'll finish the roonies for the festival. You need to take your wife home and give her a warm bath and a foot rub."

Uncle Thatch stands and squeezes Carl's shoulder. "Nix is right. And don't worry, I'll make sure she gets home soon and relaxes, too."

Carl snorts. "I'm starting to wonder if these two were in cahoots. Did you gals plan this whole thing so you could get pampered?"

Dahlia laughs. "Busted." Then she pats my bruised head with sympathy. "Bad choice of words. Sorry, honey." She drops a few

more creepy peepers onto my palm. "Seriously, take it easy the rest of the evening."

"You too," I say, careful to tuck the candies into the back pocket of my leather pants to avoid my front pocket where the squid ink vial pokes my lower abdomen—snug and hidden.

Dahlia and Carl exit the storeroom hand in hand. In the kitchen, I hear the door to the plastic cabinet open and shut, a few whispers and shuffling steps, then finally silence.

Uncle Thatch turns and looks down at me, rearranging his tie-dyed apron over his T-shirt and pants—a nervous gesture. With his chef's hat drooping to the left, it's like a cloud dropped onto his head. He may as well be up in the sky because he feels as if he's miles away.

"Ready to stand?" he asks, straightening his hat.

I nod.

He offers his palm and pulls me up. My head swims as I struggle to stay balanced; the wooziness falls in line with a fainting episode, although I'm sure it didn't happen like that.

"Take it slow, Nixie-girl." Circling one arm around my shoulders, he helps me out of the storeroom. The aroma of his damp clothes blends with that of the kitchen around us: spicy, soapy, and nectarous. It's the routine scents of daily life, yet this night feels anything but routine.

"I'm fine," I mumble, the flash of dizziness fading to mental fog. "*Physically.*"

"But not so much emotionally, huh?"

I nod, unable to put names to all the things pushing down on my chest and making it hard to breathe. We both slip into disposable gloves. Grabbing a parchment-lined basket, I pause at the cooling racks where Carl left the roonies. I glance at the clock

on the wall. It's seven fifteen now, and I remember it being just after six when I came into the kitchen. Maybe it took twenty minutes or so to do the recycling, but still . . . there's a big chunk of time missing.

"How long was I unconscious?" I ask, rubbing my nape again.

"Oh, I don't know. Maybe a few minutes."

I shake my head. That can't be right. Even if the clock didn't confirm my suspicion, an hour had to have gone by since Carl's macarons have had time to dry, bake, and cool. I try to form a follow-up question, but can't put my finger on what exactly I want answered.

Uncle stops at the batter-and-icing fridge and takes out the spiced mascarpone filling so we can construct the macaron sandwiches before boxing them. "You know, I expect you to be out of sorts this time of year, kiddo. Everyone understands."

"It's more than the date." *I think?* Annoyed with my sudden absentmindedness, I test if the macaron shells are ready to come off the racks by nudging a few. They move freely without their feet sticking, so I place all twenty-four in the basket.

Uncle watches me as he puts the bowl of filling beside the box of pastry bags waiting on the counter. "You overheard me arguing with Jaspar, didn't you?"

Dragging a barstool up to the counter, I sit down and slide the cookie basket next to the bowl. "I did hear . . . something."

Then, my mind goes completely blank. Wasn't it more than an argument? Any images of what happened in the alley seem slippery and ephemeral. All I remember is lots of rain and strange voices. And lights . . . something to do with lights. Can hitting your head knock so many details loose?

After placing twelve shells upside down, Uncle squeezes

filling onto them, releasing a medley of cinnamon, ginger, and cloves into the air. That longing for vibrancy nips at the back of my eyes. Normally, the bright orange cookies, topped with the maple-tinted cream, represent fall's warm, cozy mood. But without any depth, their pale, sepia tones look cold and empty as winter.

"Nix?" Uncle prompts.

It's my job to top the filled macarons with their remaining halves, but I can't seem to move. I need to remember . . . I'm forgetting something important.

Uncle sighs. "Okay, I shouldn't have lied about you fainting."

"You . . . lied?" Honestly, that's the least of what's bothering me right now.

"I didn't want to discuss Jaspar in front of Dahlia and Carl," he says, oblivious to my mental turmoil. "You're right. He was throwing a tantrum. When we were carrying in some crates, he saw the macaron sleeves and cupcake boxes I bought for the festival tomorrow. Then he saw the booth panels in the corner. He says I'm going against our contract by selling our items outside of the restaurant and contributing to the world's landfill issues. Like one night of to-go boxes makes that much difference."

Placing the tops on the macaron sandwiches, I grind my jaw. "So . . . I fell instead of fainting. I backed into a box. I was upset because this is my fault, because it was me who talked you into helping with the carnival."

At first, when it was announced there'd be a PTA-sponsored fundraiser contest at the carnival, I didn't give it much attention. Then I learned the contest would be between our school's five main electives—art, shop, journalism/photography, mechanics/design, and theater/music. The mechanics department voted to

charge people to play a mechanized carnival game, but our teacher wanted one more lure—something sure to bring in the money. That's when my classmates suggested selling the bakery's goods.

"No, Nix. You didn't *talk* me into anything. This is an arrangement. Quid pro quo . . . I help raise money for your class, and next year you apply to some art colleges along with the robotics institutes you had in mind." He shakes some acorn-shaped seeds from a jar and drops them into a handheld grinder. As he cranks the handle, fragrant nutmeg floats down over each macaron like a dusting of sand.

I trace my glove-tipped finger through some nutmeg that has drifted onto the counter.

"I want you to see what art programs can offer over engineering classes. You were born to be creative, not technical. You could be doing storyboarding, animation, gaming illustrations. There are so many possibilities out there. See what you can make of yourself by honing *your* talents instead of . . ." His voice trails off, leaving that empty space in the shape of Lark's name. "Jaspar will get over it. The supplier needs us more than we need them."

"Really?" I ask.

He pauses, as if he didn't mean to say that last part aloud. "Well, I don't see anyone else lining up to use them."

I nod, though I can't help but think that's by design. They don't advertise anywhere. They don't have a title or logo painted on their truck. Uncle makes all our payments in cash, so I've never seen check stubs. It's been two and a half years, and still the only company employee I know of is Jaspar, without even a last name attached.

Uncle claims an acquaintance recommended them when he first opened shop; otherwise, he'd never have found them at all.

"Anyway"—Uncle resumes the conversation—"ours is a done deal."

"Actually . . ." I tap the counter. "My end is only valid if my class wins the contest."

He scoffs. "Right. We both know it's as good as in the bag."

He punctuates the statement by drizzling some icing onto the counter and giving me his goofy smile. I can't help but return it as I peel off my gloves and dab my pinkie into the drips. The spicy-sweet flavor makes my tongue tingle with delight. I should never have given him this much leverage over our ongoing argument—especially since any chance I have of excelling in an illustrative field hinges on the ability to assign lifelike colors to my creations.

Uncle wipes off some filling on his apron, raking a washed-out brownish streak across a tie-dyed rainbow that's lost on me. "Life is a gift, Nix. Live it. Stop hiding in someone else's shadow. Otherwise, it was all for nothing."

I crinkle my nose so hard the piercing cinches my right nostril. "*What* was all for nothing?"

He squeezes the leftover cream from the bag into its bowl, then presses a lid over the top. "Crossing Jaspar and our supplier for this fundraiser. What else?"

There's something omitted from that answer. Something he's not willing to specify. It's obvious by the way he keeps his eyes hidden under his lashes, avoiding my frown.

As he slides the roonies into the cardboard macaron sleeve, I clean off the counter, still feeling unsettled. "Is it okay if I go to Juniper's? I've got to finish that mural." Everyone in art class is

required to work a shift at the carnival as seventy percent of their grade for the project, but my teacher took pity on me; he said if I made a mechanized mural to hang on the bakery booth, it would suffice in place of my attendance.

I worked on the majority of the piece at home in our garage the past couple of weeks, but brought it to the bakery a few days ago so Clarey could help me match its color scheme to the other booth panels in our storeroom. I'm using latex paint since it's weatherproof and cheaper than acrylics for larger blocks of color. The chemical scent doesn't pair well with fresh baked goods, so Juniper's been letting me use her courtyard in the evenings.

"Can I duck out early?" I ask.

Uncle hesitates. "If you're absolutely sure you're feeling all right?"

"My head's good now." I flick my gaze to the clock, seeing the digital "7:30" blare like a floodlight. "Just don't forget that I need to be home before—"

"I'll pick you up in an hour," Uncle assures me. "We'll have you home early enough to catch a catnap before your alarm goes off at midnight for your vigil."

I smile gratefully and carry the pastry bags to the sinks for Pete to wash later, then stop at the cabinet to get my things. After secretly tucking the vial of squid ink in the smallest interior compartment of my duffel, I notice something lumpy in the back pocket of my pants. I dig out Dahlia's three creepy peepers. They've melted. One still has a lopsided eyeball staring back, but the other two foil illustrations disappear where the chocolate caves in, making them look like sunken eye sockets.

My jaw drops as several images rush back into my head: Jaspar in the rain with brilliant red hair, his eyes dark, empty pits,

his mouth yawning and cavernous . . . the grimalkin blinking emerald and amber eyes behind the canvas sheet and taunting me with that painful *Goblin Market* verse.

I yelp and drop the candies on the floor.

I turn to tell Uncle Thatch everything, but he's already there. He tugs me into the storeroom and closes the door. Before I can ask what he's doing, he pops off his hat and digs something that looks like a large cricket from his damp, rumpled hair.

Only it's not a cricket—it has two arms, two legs, and a body made of emaciated, intertwining wire.

"*Ting*?" I whisper on a shaky breath.

The spindly creature blinks large, beady eyes and wiggles its pointed brass ears as if acknowledging its name.

Brass ears . . . reddish gold. *Colorful.*

Uncle holds out his hand, urging me closer. I gulp the knot of disbelief from my throat and lift a finger to touch the teensy piskie—risen to life from the pages of Mystiquiel and seated on his palm. Two filigreed wings of patinaed copper flap lazily on its back. It tilts its head, the upper metallic half of its face frozen in an inquisitive arch of the brow.

A tidal wave of joy from seeing every pigment that blooms alive in the creature washes over me, only to be dammed up by logic and skepticism. *Ting can't be here.*

The piskie studies me, then my uncle. Pink skin covers its nose, mouth, and chin. Fleshy lips form a word: "Extirpate?" Its voice trills with a fragility that matches its body—the sound of tin chimes clinking against a glass pane.

Uncle nods.

I'm so shocked I can't move. Lifting itself off my uncle's hand with buzzing greenish wings, the gilded piskie begins to

spin. Shiny gears and sprockets spring out from hair made of downy white feathers and coiled black wires. The wires glow red and sizzle. An instant later, the piskie vanishes and reddish powder puffs into the air in its absence—like a miniature explosion of rust.

In a rush of insight, the rules that bind my imaginary faerie realm shake me out of my trance. As impossible as the piskie's appearance is, I know what it came to do . . . and I can't allow it. I hold my breath, trying not to inhale the brainwashing particles.

"Phoenix Francesca Loring!"

Uncle's shout startles a gasp out of me, and I strangle against the metallic-mineral tang seeping into my lungs, recognizing the taste from my glass of water.

"I'm sorry, Nix. Mixing it with water only diluted the details. You need a concentrated dose. I want to tell you every—" His voice breaks on a slobbery, gagging sound, like his tongue is suddenly too big for his mouth.

He grips his neck, his eyes bulging even larger than usual. Something in his pained expression—a mix between despair, remorse, and determination—reminds me of the look he wears every time Lark's name comes up.

After several guttural coughs, he manages to speak again. "I'll make you a safer memory . . ." His pronunciation clears with each word, as if his tongue is gradually shrinking back to normal. "I owe it to your mom to protect at least you. And I will. No matter what."

I have so much to ask, but my voice box locks closed. Then piskie dust leaks into my brain, swallowing every question whole.

8

death-iversary

I awaken to a bright light and drag my blankets over my face. Silence swells around me, as if the house holds its breath. Chiseling through my brain fog uncovers a few hazy memories—me slipping in the storeroom and hitting my head; Uncle driving me home sometime after 8:00 p.m., helping me into bed, and plying me with Tylenol before tucking my blankets up to my chin. He told me to take a nap, then kissed my brow and tiptoed from the room.

I dozed, deep enough to dream: feline ears and noses upon metallic masks shaped like human faces . . . rusted-wire whiskers swaying in time with swanlike necks and hypnotic, swirling eyes. The grimalkins, in pairs of six or more, chanted something in synchrony, though I can't remember what exactly. Those images and words, so vivid in my sleep, fade as the sun warms my blankets.

The sun?

A terrifying realization creeps over me: it's morning and I

overslept. I slap the covers down, and harsh daylight meets my gaze. The sled-style bed frame curves higher and tighter than usual. Shadows creep around the edges . . . shadows that only appear around noon. I chance a look at my digital clock and it reads 12:45 p.m. I should've woken up over twelve hours ago.

Heart racing, I bolt upright. October thirty-first has arrived, and I'm lying around like a corpse-in-waiting, vulnerable and unprepared.

The hush over the house becomes a dangerous pulse . . . static in my ears . . . a sticky raze of electricity along my nerves—lifting the hairs on my arms as if lightning pumps through my veins. When Uncle's cell phone rings in the kitchen and his muffled voice answers, my nerves scatter in a confusion of relief and anger.

Why didn't he wake me? Did he turn off my alarm last night? Why would he take that chance? He knows how dangerous this day is for us; how we have to keep our guard up.

I tamp my fear and frustration, determined to let him explain before I bust his chops. Dangling my feet over the mattress's edge, I muster the courage to step into the remaining hours before midnight's reprieve.

The clang of dishes sloshing in the sink eclipses Uncle's conversation. I strain to hear bits and pieces as I drag a hoodie over my tank and sweatpants and ease into the hallway.

"—under control. No problem."

More sloshing followed by his laugh—and not the fake one. Genuine and hearty.

"Uh-huh . . . uh-huh. Such an exciting time!"

It feels wrong for him to be so upbeat on this dark day. What could have made him forsake the traditions and precautions I've set in place?

I stop at the shrine of photos hanging in the hallway, determined at least one of us will uphold the rituals for today in hopes of getting us back on track. I start by mentally honoring the lost members of our family standing beside me in the images, tracing their outlines with a fingertip: Lark, Mom, and Dad—in candid, unprofessional shots.

One of us at the beach, Mom bowing low, dark hair blocking her face, hands side by side with mine and Lark's as we smooth out sandcastles; another of Dad next to the tide, his white-blond hair shining as he bends down with his back turned to help us fill our buckets; a picture of four pairs of feet—two adult size and two babies'—sinking in the wet sand, then a follow-up shot after the tide came in and we all stepped aside, leaving toe-and-heel-shaped hollows filled with frothy water.

Even in our sole photo album in the attic it's that way . . . faces covered by hair; profiles muddied by shade; dark silhouettes against a backdrop of bright light. It used to bother me and Lark that we never saw our parents' faces front-on in pictures, considering we were too small to remember them in person. Uncle insisted it was because Imogen and Owen, aka Mom and Dad, loved doing things with us . . . making us the center of their world. All that mattered to them was being together—never posed, never staged. Until our time together came to an abrupt halt because of a freak accident on Halloween night when, according to an anonymous witness, my parents' car swerved to miss a deer and crashed into a tree. The final page of that album doesn't contain a picture, but instead an old newspaper clipping of their obituary.

At the end of the hallway shrine hangs the last three framed memories: the first is of me, Lark, and Uncle together—in a

professional sitting the year before she died. The last two are of me and Lark standing side by side on auditorium stages—one taken in fourth grade at a spelling bee where Lark took first place and I took second. The other was taken in seventh grade at a Young Edison's Challenge where Lark wrangled the third-best spot. Uncle had us pose together with her holding up her green ribbon. She would've been holding the first-place blue had the tiny rotary electrical motor that doubled as the robot's heart not developed a glitch and stalled midpump before it could animate all the robot's extremities.

I tense against the impending flood of guilt and loneliness. The emotions echo inside where a family tree once grew—a tree now reduced to phantom limbs and a hollow trunk. It makes sense that I see Lark in my own reflections after the role I played in her Young Edison's failure, something she knew but kept between us. But it's always surprising how much guilt I feel toward parents I don't even remember having.

I catch a whiff of Uncle's Florentine and bacon quiche, and a vacant, hungry growl rolls through my stomach, as if echoing the void in my chest. Turning away from the pictures and their half-told secrets, I step into the kitchen in time to see Uncle saying goodbye to his caller. He stands at the sink, his back to me. Although his conversation seemed happy, his body language belies the act. His shoulders sag, and the towel draped along his left side begins to slide. He catches it midfall as a sob shudders his whole body.

"Uncle Thatch?" My voice comes out ragged and hoarse.

He stiffens, dragging a hand across his cheeks before resituating his glasses. His grand efforts to hide the grief we share softens my irritation, but it doesn't curb the uneasy tangle in my

chest . . . the sense that we've started this day all wrong and there will be consequences to pay.

"Oh hey, kiddo!" He faces me—false vibrato in place. "Don't be mad, all right? I just . . . I didn't want to wake you. You had such a rough night. So I stayed up instead, and see? We're both doing fine."

The bags under his eyes attest to a lack of sleep, and I kick myself for being skeptical of his loyalty. On Lark's first death-iversary, I insisted Uncle and I hold vigil at home to keep us both safe, and he's honored that request ever since—no questions asked. Even though it's hard for him, staying shut in. Even though he'd rather find solace by working at the bakery, to show me by example that it's a harmless holiday. Still, he respects my need for us to lie low, never making me feel weak or irrational. In fact, since Lark's been gone, he treats me more like an equal than his dependent—always asking for my input in every decision, always being straight with me.

Uncle's proven he deserves my complete trust, and I won't doubt him again.

"Sit down," he says, motioning to the table with his towel. "I made brunch." From the fridge, he removes a wooden tray half-filled with homemade buttery croissants and orange marmalade. Then, opening the oven, he levers out a fresh slice of hot quiche with a spatula and plops it onto a plate. He sets the spread on a place mat in front of me along with a freshly made protein smoothie. I struggle to guess the flavor without resorting to taste . . . it's always either green, orange, or purple, depending on his ingredients of choice.

Faced with nothing but washed-out beiges and grays, I inhale the quiche's fragrant steam instead. The warmth billows inside

me, temporarily thawing the shivery ache that clings to my innards ever since my world's begun to fade.

Uncle claims the seat opposite me and reaches for one of the croissants, spreading preserves before taking a crispy bite. "How's the noggin today?"

I devour a forkful of quiche, letting the cheese, bacon, and spinach flavors melt on my tongue. "Okay, I think. A little fuzzy about last night. Who was on the phone?"

Uncle frowns. "First, you tell me what's fuzzy. I can fill in anything that isn't clear."

I shrug, indulging in citrusy marmalade on flaky, buttery layers of pastry. Licking a fingertip, I answer, "There was . . . a plum." Even as details start seeping into my brain, the experience feels detached—distant. "I slipped on it after I told off Jaspar for arguing with you in the alley."

Uncle nods. "Yep, good so far." He takes another bite. "Do you remember why we were fighting?" He's trying to hide it behind his chewing, but his jaw muscles appear tense.

"The carnival . . . the to-go packages. I can't remember what was said exactly. But I ran into the alley, dropped the box of melts at Jaspar's feet, and told him to back off. Then he apologized, saying he wouldn't step out of line again." I almost choke on those words, they're so out of character for the guy.

The knot in Uncle's Adam's apple makes me wonder if he's having as hard a time swallowing his croissant as I am believing what I'm remembering. Did Jaspar really say that?

Uncle finally gulps down his bite and his mouth flips to a smile. "I was so proud of you, materializing out of thin air to take down the enemy. Angorla should make you an honorary hobblegob."

"Huh, right."

"What happened next?" Uncle presses.

"I went back in the storeroom and wasn't paying attention. There was a plum that had fallen and busted. I didn't see the pulp and skidded off balance." That doesn't feel right, either. Uncle is meticulous with his shipments. He wouldn't let a single cherry drop to the floor and be wasted, much less the bigger and more expensive produce.

Didn't something trip me? Something hard that caught my heel?

Unsettled, I glance around the room. Beige light seeps through the lacy curtains on the window over the sink, and something about the way the sun pierces the holes in the fabric, imprinting them on the tile floor in pairs like eyes, makes me think of the grimalkins from my dreams. Curtains and glowing eyes. Why do they feel like they go together somehow?

"Excellent," Uncle says, polishing off the last of his croissant and disrupting my bizarre musings. "Glad you're feeling better today. I need you in tip-top shape." He swipes a paper napkin across his mouth, smothering a sigh behind it. "I have to attend the carnival tonight . . . to run the booth."

"What?" I shove the tray to the middle of the table, nearly toppling the smoothie I've yet to sample. "No! I can't watch your back if you're not here! I can't be sure—"

"Nix." Uncle catches my hand on the table between us. "I'll be fine. I promise. And there's really no choice. That's what the phone call was. Dahlia went into labor."

Suddenly I'm on a roller coaster, dipping between terror for Uncle and concern for our friends. "Isn't it too early?"

"Nah. She was only three weeks away, which Carl says the

doc calls 'near-term.' Close enough to be safe. It's just . . . things kicked into overdrive and their baby's already here. A little girl. Carl says they're still trying to decide on her name, but they're at the hospital and everyone's doing great. Anyway, obviously they're out for the carnival and since all our other employees are scheduled for the Saturday rush—"

"What about Aaron or Ryann?" I stop myself short of asking why Lydia can't do it, because of course we need at least one baker working the shop.

"Aaron's out of town, and Ryann's down with a cold," Uncle answers—details I already know but have conveniently buried beneath my hysteria. "Just, don't worry. I won't be alone. Juniper's closing her boutique early so she can help me. And Clarey will be here with you, so we're covered."

My argument that the only way we can be "covered" is to adhere to the guidelines that have kept us safe for the past two years doesn't even make it past my lips. Uncle's already spouting off his itinerary: carrying the booth panels to Cannon Beach ASAP so he can find a good spot before everything's taken; then returning to Astoria around four o'clock to pick up the roonies and fairy-cakes from the bakery along with Juniper before heading back to be in place at least a half hour before the six-thirty carnival opening.

When I ask about my mural, Uncle trips me up with another unexpected wrinkle.

"Well, in all the confusion last night, I forgot to grab it and bring it home." Uncle removes his glasses and polishes the lenses with a clean paper napkin. The glass isn't even smudged, so I can't help but think it's a ploy to avoid my panicked gaze. "I'm sure Clarey won't mind bringing it to you a little early since he'll

be coming over anyway. Just be sure it's dry in time for me to pick up on my way to the bakery."

Since I can't offer any argument that doesn't feel weak or selfish, I coax a promise out of him that he'll text me every hour so I know he's okay. Then, after a hug he's forced to break because I can't, he leaves.

For the next half hour, I'm on autopilot: putting away leftover food, doing the dishes, and shooting Clarey a text about my mural that sounds way more composed than I actually feel.

My pulse pounds inside my head . . . a disorienting rhythm. I turn the stereo in the living room full blast to drown out the silence, then step into our one and only bathroom for a soak, staying as close to my Halloween routine as possible.

Inside, I flip on the tub's faucet and plop a lavender-scented bath bomb into the cascading water. Glimmers of sunshine stream from the skylight, painting the resulting foam in sepia prisms as I shed my clothes.

I overslept by more than half a day . . . Uncle is out in the world . . . and Dahlia's innocent little baby was just born on the most malicious date of the year. My thoughts settle there, and I hope with all my heart that their little girl will never have to see the true face of Halloween unmasked.

Naked and waiting for the tub to fill, I avert my gaze from the steamed-up mirror toward the dirty towels piled behind the door. Laundry, vacuuming, and dusting are next on my to-do list. They're great distractions, and have always served as justifications for Uncle staying home, giving us something productive to do together while being locked in.

Upon lifting the top towel, I notice a protrusion sticking out from the terry cloth mountain—patchy tufts of dark hair. A rush

of goose bumps curdles my skin, contrary to the balmy heat enveloping the room. I fling the second towel aside and a doll's blinking eyes glare up at me from the head attached to the legless torso of Lark's final creation. She sliced the face in half horizontally, separating the bottom and top lips before rehinging the jaws shut with a pair of dentures between them, and another shock races along my flesh as the false teeth begin to chatter while the doll's arms jerk up and down.

It's as if the thing has been lying in wait to demonstrate Lark's robotic skills as a macabre reminder of her genius. My chest gives an anguished squeeze at the thought—a mix of misery and horror.

No. I disassembled this project two years ago when I needed the legs to help me design Flannie's artificial limb. The remains recently developed a short circuit, activating at random times. Since I couldn't get it figured out, Uncle took it to his room, saying he'd look at it. Maybe it ended up in here as a diversion, in place of his usual crossword puzzles.

I tap the doll's brow, and the teeth, eyes, and arms go still. Relieved, I fling towels over its face again, only to uncover the *Goblin Market* book under a curled corner of terry cloth on the opposite side.

"What the . . ." I kneel. Last night it stood open on my nightstand. I vaguely remember studying it while I was changing into my tank and sweats.

So how did *it* get from my bedroom to here?

I scoop my hands under the spine. It's turned to the final page—those excruciating words that Lark had it opened to when she died. Reading the verse gives me clarity: *this* is the song the grimalkins were singing in my dreams.

A ray of sunlight catches the book and reveals strange pockmarks marring the text. I rub my thumb across them. An unsettling awareness follows the gesture; something gnawed on these pages—something with multiple pointy teeth. Maybe even a short-circuiting doll head fitted with a set of dentures . . .

Beneath the towels, the teeth begin to chatter again.

Yelping, I drop the book and scramble backward. My calves hit the edge of the tub. I snatch a breath as I flip butt-first into warm water. Foamy waves slosh out and flood the floor, ruining the pages of Mom's *Goblin Market*, and fully sealing my and Uncle's fate.

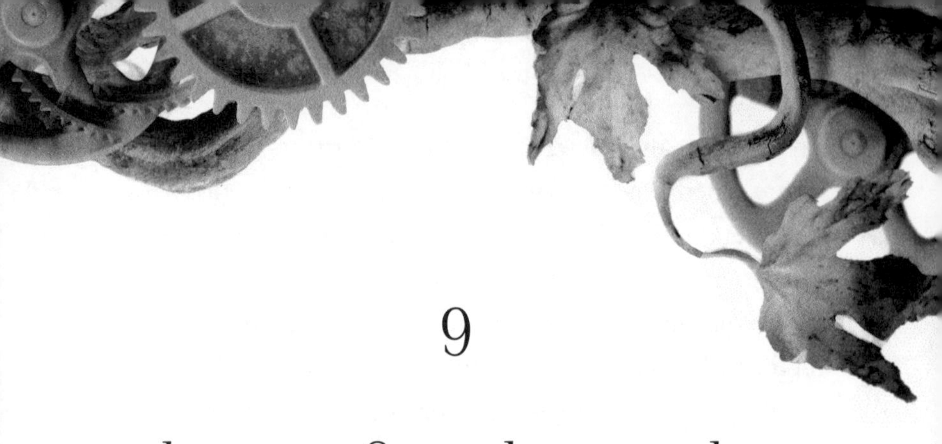

9

lemons from lemonade

I steer my bike across the trolley intersection onto Eleventh Street, averting my gaze to avoid people dressed in holiday shirts and costumes. After forcing myself to finish all the housework and laundry in hopes of staying distracted, I rushed out of the house at 4:00 p.m. I left despite my rules—not even stopping to fix my hair or put on my fiercest face. I was worried that even an encounter with my handheld mirror would be risky. Yet it was *leaving* that was truly dangerous.

My wheels wobble on the loose asphalt as I ride along the once familiar street where fresh crops of giant cotton cobwebs, Styrofoam tombstones, and human-size ghosts formed of chicken wire and cheesecloth sprouted up overnight. My lungs contract with each scene I pass.

A group of ghosts grabs for me. I swerve. Flung outward, the duffel bag strapped to the back of my seat knocks two of the cheesecloth ghouls down. The bike frame slams sideways, and

my knee hits the sidewalk. A jolt of pain rushes along the bone where concrete meets skin through the rip in my jeans.

Several pedestrians stop but I wave them off, my ears growing hot. After assuring my dad's pocket watch didn't get cracked, I leave the ghosts in knots of wire and gauze, reposition my feet on the pedals, and push onward with my throbbing knee.

Not receiving a single text from Uncle Thatch—besides the one he sent upon arrival at Cannon Beach—may not warrant imaginary ghost attacks; but bungling all our rituals, finding bite marks on Mom's picture book, and having the reality of the date—signs on street corners advertising parties, trunk-or-treat locales, and professional haunted houses—heaped on top make hysteria unavoidable.

My knit beanie, snug under my helmet, warms my ears while my face and eyes sting from the crisp air. No matter that the sun came out today, the northern gusts promise we'll be facing cloudbursts again tonight. It doesn't bode well for the carnival.

I have to make sure that Uncle won't be there to weather any storms, and the atmospheric variety is the least of our worries.

I arrive on Eveningside and coast in front of the bakery. The absence of Uncle's Chevy Bolt triggers a nervous clutch in my throat. It's a twenty-minute jaunt on bike from our house to here. I expected he'd be picking up the macarons and cupcakes by now.

So deep in thought, I accidentally cruise past Wisteria Rising. I force a U-turn against my knee's objections. The boutique is already closed, but Juniper's sedan remains parked out front. I'm hopeful she's heard from Uncle Thatch. I'm also hoping she'll be willing to run our booth by herself with the help of someone other than Uncle. There are always extra volunteers at PTA events.

Clarey's Subaru takes up the space in front of the sedan. Once I finish my project, we can load up my bike and drive to my house, shutting ourselves in before this evening's trick-or-treat infestation gets under way. It's the bitterest irony about Clarey's phobia, that despite creating the most magnificent costumes in town, he can't bring himself to attend any crowded festivities. Yet that very neurosis makes him my ideal companion.

Just like last year, he's getting paid to do Halloween makeup at his aunt's boutique for a few hours today. Afterward, he'll come to my place with his portable record player and we'll listen to his mom's vinyl collection until midnight—with one intermission to watch his DVD of *Oceans 11,* the 1960s version starring Clarey's two idols, Sammy Davis Jr. and Dean Martin.

Ever since Clarey's been joining us on All Hallows' Eve, Uncle has taken a liking to jazz and blues himself; I'm banking on that shared interest to convince him to return home with us where he belongs.

I squeeze the hand brake. Alighting on the sidewalk, I pop off my helmet and limp-walk my bike to the french doors. Juniper believes plants are ornamental enough on their own, so, short of a few Mexican flame vines and orange black-eyed Susans in the display windows, her shop is blissfully free of themed decorations.

My gloves muffle my knock, but the lacy curtains on the interior tremble—proof someone heard me. Glancing at the potted wisteria display on my right, I tap one of the flowers so it releases a vanilla scent. The plant will have to be shut inside tonight, to protect its blooms against foot traffic and oncoming weather.

Then it hits me: I'm no better than wisteria. I've become as fragile as a flower petal.

Teeth clenched, I shove my emotions down . . . a last-ditch

attempt to resemble the tough-as-iron and rough-as-grit girl I once was.

The right door swings inward, and Clarey fills the opening.

A sharkskin vest covers his gray long-sleeved Henley, rolled to the elbows to showcase lithe forearms. Pencil-thin dark pinstriped pants taper down his slim legs. A pair of calfskin loafers completes the look. Although my retinal perception can't fill in the particulars, my memory still can: the main body of the shoes is printed with indigo and green platelets that resemble the hide of a dragon, and gold metal toe tips complement the claw-shaped buckle.

The Rat Pack ensemble isn't a costume. It's trademark Clarey. He buys most of his clothes through online thrift stores, but shoes are his one extravagance. He has at least seven pairs, each with their own color scheme and theme, all of them embellished with various metal toe tips.

"What are you doing out?" he asks, unable to hide his shock while shooting a glance at the decor lining the streets. In honor of the date and Lark's love of all things that sparkle, SFX scales shimmer along his temples and under his eyes—as if he's some sort of ephemeral aquatic creature with oddly placed gills. He told me he was going to match them to his eyes: bright turquoise and gold.

I prop my bike against the brick wall, too distracted to even ask if he managed to coordinate the tones. "I sent you a text earlier, then called. Needed you to bring the mural by my house. My grade hinges on it, you know . . ." It's a good cover. Keeps me from admitting that when he didn't answer, an overwhelming sense of panic forced me to hit the streets.

"Oh shizzle!" He drags his phone from his pocket and fumbles with the buttons. The sun hangs low in the west, and a stray

beam pierces through the wisteria branches to highlight the white pigmentation at his hairline where it fades into his darker forehead. “Sorry about that. I forgot I muted my phone during a makeup session.”

“Makeup, or make-*out*?” I fake a smirk, desperate to maintain the cool facade. “Oh, wait . . . forgot about your dry spell.”

In the two years since Clarey’s been back, we’ve both gone out with a handful of people, but neither of us can seem to muster enthusiasm for the process. It’s so much more fun to bust on each other about our lack of prospects than to actually search for anyone ourselves.

“*My* dry spell? That’s the Sahara calling the Mojave a sand trap,” Clarey responds to my barb, grinning. He slips his phone back in his pocket. “Pretty weird, though. How we’re both so content in our droughts,” he adds, meeting my gaze pointedly.

I’m mortified to feel heat flush through my ears, cheeks, and forehead.

“Wait, am I about to witness a Phoenix catching fire?” His smile widens. “Or is Nix Loring actually blushing?”

I roll my eyes, in no state to navigate the complexities of our circuitous relationship today. “As if. Don’t you recognize frostbite when you see it?”

“Okay. Park your stick, little Popsicle.” He gestures to the bike. “Aunt Juni brewed some lemonade-cider for the carnival. We’ll get you a cup and a gingerbread scone.”

Juniper has an open courtyard in back with a greenhouse roof. Three evenings a week, she serves her own unique hot brews and treats for high tea, a tradition she shared with her British father and Indian mother as a child growing up in London. Customers sit by the fountains in the outdoor lighting, sample her

latest recipes, and admire the lush flowers and ivy hanging overhead from old Victorian streetlamps, repurposed gazebo panels, and patinaed chandeliers.

Gelid air seeps through my ripped jeans and sears my raw knee as I dig in my duffel's outer pocket for my bike lock. Shivering, I wrap my yellow-plaid scarf tighter around my jacket's collar. "Any chance your aunt heard from Uncle Thatch in the past hour or so?"

A burst of wind lifts Clarey's curls, making them dance. "Not sure. He texted her last night when you fell, then this morning about the carnival."

I kneel to snap the U-lock into place around my front spokes and a rain pipe that runs from the roof to the sidewalk—wincing as my injured skin stretches.

"I thought you hit your head. What's with the leg?" A concerned frown tugs at his lips.

I fasten my helmet around the handlebars, then dust off my knees. "Head last night. Knee today. I crashed my bike on the way over."

Clarey frowns. "Wait. You're telling me that Nix Loring, dirt-bike virtuoso, king of the hill, and tree-climbing wunderkind, fell twice in two days? Clumsy isn't in your wheelhouse."

His pronunciation of "wunderkind" the correct way, with a *v* sound—when most kids our age don't even know the word—would typically make me smile. Yet all I can think of is that I've got to see Uncle. Not just to be sure he's okay, but so he can explain why Mom's picture book and Lark's doll contraption were in the bathroom earlier.

"What can I say," I mumble. "I'm off my game." *Understatement of the year.*

"O-kay. So . . . you want a Band-Aid?"

I scoff. "Yeah, because I'm five. Just get me off this sidewalk, would you?" The request comes out sounding more desperate than I like.

Clarey moves aside. Once I'm in, he secures the door's lock and pulls something from the inner pocket of his vest, anchoring his hand behind his back before I can see what he holds.

I feel one degree better as the scent of flowers and greenery seeps into my nostrils. Even though the main showroom is indoors, a row of skylights gives it an airy feel, like a French bistro. The whitewashed brick walls and weathered benches also serve as props for assorted potted vinery. Flower arrangements—jelly jars half-filled with water and fresh blossoming bouquets—hang from twine on vintage hat racks or hunker inside antique suitcases with lids yawning wide like clamshells.

There's an eager *ruff* followed by claws clicking speedily across the stained cement in time with a metallic whir.

"Hey-a, Flannie." I bend down to hug her furry neck. She drags her wet nose along the edge of my beanie, pushing it loose. I shove staticky hair off my face and check her mechanical leg and harness for signs of wear, although it makes me oddly queasy to look at it today.

She breaks free, snuffling her way around an old wooden wheelbarrow filled with flowering sweet pea where she dropped a rubber mouse. As she gnaws on the toy, the squeaks feel louder than they are . . . disproportioned alongside the quietly trickling garden fountains that break up the winding paths throughout the showroom.

I bend closer, studying the bite marks in the plastic, thinking of the damp, swollen pages in my *Goblin Market* picture book

now stashed inside the main compartment of my duffel bag with my paintbrushes. A sour taste fills my mouth.

"So, want to tell me what happened last night?" Clarey jerks me out of my dark musings. His lean body reclines against a trellis wrapped in ivy. "Your uncle said you were out for a sec after hitting your head."

I lower the duffel from my shoulder and lift a bouquet from its display. It's Clarey's responsibility to prep the fresh merchandise each day. I bury my nose in the blossoms, inhaling the floral scent that always clings to his skin and clothes—seeking the comfort it provides. "Can't remember much. The details feel hazy to me, like it was someone else's experience."

He cocks his chin. "Cranial swell-age?" he teases.

"Something like that," I answer, any effort to appear calm shattering all around me. "Could you get your aunt for me? I need to talk to her." I polish the glass jar with my gloves, then set the flowers back in their suitcase.

Clarey puts his other arm behind him; his shoulders twitch, like he's passing the hidden item back and forth from hand to hand. "I don't know," he baits. "I think we should test you for head injuries first. Riddle me this . . ."

And in that moment, I know what he's hiding. Clarey likes to dip into his arsenal of music-related trivia questions when I'm being too serious or morose, and he keeps his harmonica on deck in case I need to hear a riff as a hint. It's how his mom used to quiz him when she introduced him to her favorite genre of music. And the way he brightens up when playing songs that remind him of Breonna—the way he becomes that animated boy again, the one I knew from elementary to middle school

before we both lost loved ones—always manages to put me in better spirits.

"First hint: He was the original star of folk blues in the 1920s. And hint number two . . ." Clarey draws his left palm from behind his back and surprises me by brandishing not his harmonica, but a small lemon wearing a pair of permanent-marker sunglasses. I'm actually disappointed; I could've used a song.

He laughs, mistaking my frown for confusion. His irises reflect the skylights in facets—as do the scales that glimmer on his skin. "C'mon. I'm practically handing the answer to you. This lemon should be on a silver platter."

I nibble my lip ring and peel free of my gloves, dropping them next to my duffel bag. "Who is Lemon Brite?" I ask in the required *Jeopardy!* format, substituting Uncle's preferred brand of dish soap in place of the musician's name that I can't remember.

"Sorry. The answer should've been: Who is Blind Lemon Jefferson?" A smug smile underscores his usual expression of pity for my ignorance. "To think this lemon gave up the spotlight in my aunt's cider for such a sad display."

Losing all patience, I cup my mouth and shout, "Juniper! Are you here?"

Clarey snorts, juggling the lemon. "Chillax, okay? She's in the courtyard." He points to the keys hanging below the door's handle. "Hand me those, would you?"

I work them loose, and he drops the lemon to catch them midair. "I'll tell her you're here. Then we'll set up the tarp and get out your paint cans."

I'm confused for an instant before remembering my

trumped-up reason for venturing out, and that I do still have a class project to complete. "Thanks."

Scooping up the lemon in her mouth as if it's a tennis ball, Flannie trots after her owner, but pauses to look between the two of us.

"Stay." Clarey jangles the keys over his shoulder and disappears through the french doors leading to the courtyard.

Flannie plops down at my feet. I'm mesmerized, torn between fascination and fear as her teeth indent the lemon's rind.

"All this time, and I'm still gobsmacked by it." Juniper's British accent shatters my trance.

"Huh?" I dig my fingers into my hair, massaging my scalp.

"What you did for our little cyborg pup." Juniper smiles at me, looking like spring in a crocheted dress and headband of fresh flowers. She offers one of the steaming cups of lemonade-cider in her hands.

"I don't deserve credit. The technology wasn't mine." To quell the chill around my heart, I take a sip and the sweet-tart flavor warms me from head to toe.

"Tosh. It's not like you nicked your sister's invention."

In theory, I know Juniper's right. But in practice, I can't forget that I would never have thought of the prosthesis on my own. It was Lark's animated arachnid-doll invention, the way its eight glittery metal legs moved—crablike and hinged like real knee joints when activated by an intricate gear system connected to the movement of the vinyl cranium—that inspired me. I simply took it apart and let her vision guide me. Now, after my scare in the bathroom with the doll, I can't imagine ever touching it again.

"You honored your sister's design by expanding on it." Juniper tilts her head, causing the salt-and-pepper layers over her

ears to splay out like soft horns from the edge of her headband. The white in her hair is the only betrayal of her forty-five years, given that her dewy skin has barely a wrinkle. "You made it something useful. That's teamwork at its finest."

It's a lovely sentiment, yet the word "teamwork" reminds me of the grimalkins' taunting song from my dreams: *A sister will cheer along the tedious way . . . and fetch the one who went astray.*

I fight the urge to tear up. "That's what Lark always wanted . . . to build things that mattered," I say absently.

What I don't say is that she also wanted to win notoriety, and I put a crimp in that. Which makes me taking home the local Young Inventors' postgrad engineering internship last year—by reworking her innovations into a dog's mechanical leg—an undeserved honor.

Juniper pulls her glasses down from their perch atop her headband and settles them over her nose, narrowing her doe-eyed gaze. "And you helped her accomplish it, Nix. Now, frame that Young Inventors' award. Then patent the design, sell it, and use the payoff for a fabulous art school."

I groan. "Really? This is what you and Uncle talk about when you hang out?"

I know better than to say *on your dates*, because they'd both deny it. Even though they plan their lunch breaks so they can eat together every day, they text constantly, and she's dubbed him "an unusual kind of handsome" while he calls her "a most alarming sort of pretty."

"Can't you two think of anything more interesting? Politics maybe . . . global warming. I can make a list of grown-up topics for you."

She laughs—an adorable wobbly sound that's always reminded me of a goat's bleat—sputtering her sip of cider back into her mug. Steam fogs her lenses, and she lowers the drink to give them time to clear. "*You* are his favorite topic, little bird. He's absolutely chuffed anytime you come up."

Her response is the perfect opening. "Have you heard from him since this morning?"

"No. He hasn't answered my texts. I assume he's a trifle busy. Last one I sent, I told him I'm over to the beach myself with the fare in a half hour. No need for him to make the trip back this late. I'll carry your art piece, too."

I gulp down the rest of the warm cider, unsure how to answer.

"Won't it be dry by then?" she asks in response to my silent hesitance.

"Yeah. The paint only takes thirty minutes. But . . ."

"Something else gutting you?"

"He hasn't checked in with me like he said he would. And . . . now he's not showing up *when* he said he would. It's not like him. Not on this day."

Her forehead folds to empathetic creases. "Sure, sure. I was assuming he was just lagging about. But I'll call the bakery, see if they've heard anything. Sound good?"

"Yeah." I hand off my cup; it's a testament to how scattered I've been that I didn't think of that myself before hitting the streets on my bike. "Awesome new recipe, by the way."

She smiles gently.

We both turn when Clarey shuffles loudly through the double doors in back, lugging my mural. "I thought this scene was of you and your uncle."

"Well, yeah." I originally penciled it out on graph paper, and

was pleased how the idea transferred to fit a two-by-three-foot particleboard. Clarey went with me to buy the paints, choosing bright purples, reds, greens, oranges, and blacks per my request. As much as I hated asking for help, I couldn't let pride get in the way of a good grade.

In the finished product, Uncle and I stand side by side with exaggerated features . . . malformed eyes, giant toothy smiles. His hair hides under a chef's hat while mine sweeps up in a chaotic Mohawk to spotlight my widow's peak. Gears and sprockets spring out from my skin in tribute to my piercings. Hunkered beside us, as if luring us into the forested background, are two goblins—not the kind from my books that are as tall as humans, but dwarfish green creatures like from the movies, with long hairy chins and pointed heads. They're both holding baskets of fruits that glisten, dewy in the moonlight. Their expressions are comically sinister—with gazes as black as coal. Once I complete the mechanism hinging the smallest goblin's wooden elbow, his forearm will move in a beckoning motion.

"So . . . when did you make these changes?" Clarey appears both puzzled and disturbed as I wind my way around flower-and-leaf-filled benches, trunks, and wheelbarrows to see where he's pointing.

At first, I don't catch his reference. It's the image of me I painted—overblown Mohawk and cheesy smile. Then a chill raises the hairs along my arms as I home in on the subtle details: a gap in the girl's front teeth, the absence of a widow's peak at the tip of her forehead, and not a single piercing in sight.

The residue of cider on my tongue curdles to an acidity more bitter than raw lemons—because standing next to Uncle Thatch, in my place, is my dead sister Lark.

10

goblin market

Like a bad omen, storm clouds roll over us the minute I see the changes in my mural. It's five fifteen, so dusk is settling in, yet it's as dark as if it were midnight. Fuzzy gray fog weighs so heavy on the greenhouse roof that Juniper has to turn on all the courtyard lights to help me see while I try to fix everything on my piece.

I appreciate her attempt to assure me that I'm not losing it—that it makes sense I'd include my sister in my painting subconsciously, since Lark is on my mind so much this time of year. I appreciate, too, that Clarey says he probably just didn't notice the minutiae of the scene when I first brought it over. But as soon as his aunt leaves the courtyard to call the bakery, he grills me about my entire day. I spare no details, then hand him *Goblin Market* from my duffel and pull out my paints and brushes.

"Could be a mouse," Clarey offers as we sit, legs criss-crossed, opposite each other on the tarp. He angles the book in a strand of light that streams down from one of Juniper's upcycled streetlamps—studying the pages that are half-dried, bloated,

and scented with lavender. He has it open to the masticated text and his thumb trails the bite marks.

My mural is centered between us, facing me. Lark's eyes glare back with a hint of disdain. I concentrate on unscrewing the lids from the miniature aluminum containers I use for touch-ups. The sharp scent of latex paint overpowers the fresh greenery and blossoms surrounding us.

"A mouse," I answer as Clarey leans over to help me choose the palette I'll need to change Lark's likeness back to mine.

"This one . . . coppery gold for the piercings," he says.

I nod, coating a round brush and dabbing the excess on a towel. "So, a rodent opened my book to a verse I was dreaming about?"

"Well, it's either that or grimalkins popped out of one of your sketches and opened it," Clarey says, a hint of teasing returned to his voice.

"Or my sister's haunting me through a pair of dentures," I pretend to joke back. I'm actually starting to believe it . . . that somehow, she's reaching out from beyond the grave, that it really is her face I keep seeing in the mirror instead of my own.

Clarey frowns, knowing me well enough to call me out on my half-hearted attempt at sarcasm. "Why would Lark haunt you?"

I bite my inner cheek to silence my answer: *Because I didn't save her, and now I'm stealing pieces of her life*. I begin to add a lip ring on the girl in the mural. The sooner I get Lark out of my sight, the sooner she'll be out of my mind—at least for a little while.

"I'm sorry, Lark." I allow the confession to slip, hoping at least my mural-sister might forgive me. "I let you down again."

Clarey's jaw muscles twitch, causing the shimmering scales along his temples to catch the overhead lights. He turns pages, taking care not to tear the damp paper. "Why do you always blame yourself?"

"Because sisters are supposed to look out for each other." I jab my brush toward the bloated book. "Our mom gave us this, to teach us that. If our places had been switched, Lark would've saved me that night. *And* she wouldn't have ruined the one thing our mom left behind."

Clarey's expression hardens. "I think it's time you give me the Cliff Notes."

Over the past couple of years, he's had plenty of chances to read Christina Rossetti's nineteenth-century masterpiece, but other than admiring the watercolor illustrations—showcasing scenes with stumpy, beak-nosed goblins and anthropomorphized animals alongside two Alice-in-Wonderland-esque girls—he's barely skimmed the verses, claiming they're too "poetic and flowery." You'd think a guy who thrives on the fashion and diction of the sixties' era could make allowances for antiquated writing.

I lean across the mural to complete the jagged edges of my eyebrow ring, and let the book's details unwind as prosaically as possible. "Night after night, two sisters would walk through a forest outside their cottage. One time, while peering through the trees, they noticed an enchanted market run by goblin men on the other side. The goblins noticed the girls, too, and called out from behind their baskets: 'Come buy our fruits . . . blah-blah-blah.' "

Clarey riffles through the pages. "Ummm . . . I don't see that blah-blah verse in here."

"Ha." I coat my brush with more paint. "I'm paraphrasing

the Victorian lingo, to hold your feeble twenty-first-century attention."

He grins, his dimples deepening. "It's working . . . but the original reads pretty saucy for a kids' story. Check this out: 'We must not look at goblin men, we must not buy their fruits: who knows upon what soil they fed their hungry, thirsty roots?' "

" 'Come buy,' call the goblins hobbling down the glen," I recite the next lines from memory. " 'Oh,' cried Lizzie, 'Laura, Laura, you should not peep at goblin men.' "

Clarey meets my gaze. "Innuendo much?"

"Yeah, it's pretty sensual. Even the fruit descriptions. I don't think the author wrote it for kids. It's about the conflict between sisterly love and dangerous passions." I point to the illustration opposite the title page where one sister, having no money for fruit, clips off a lock of her hair to trade. "See, this is Laura. She gives away a piece of herself because she can't resist the goblin's call, even though they had a friend who'd already been lost to them." I find the relevant verse and nod for Clarey to read it aloud:

Do you not remember Jeanie,
How she met them in the moonlight,
Took their gifts both choice and many,
Ate their fruits and wore their flowers
Plucked from bowers
Where summer ripens at all hours?
But ever in the noonlight
She pined and pined away;
Sought them by night and day,
Found them no more, but dwindled and grew grey;
Then fell with the first snow,

While to this day no grass will grow
Where she lies low:
I planted daisies there a year ago
That never blow.

Clarey leans back with his forehead crimped thoughtfully. It's my favorite expression to sketch, and although I always show him the finished products, I've never admitted how many hours it takes to capture that tiny indention where his scar slices through his eyebrow.

"Okay," he says. "Some friend of theirs ate the magic fruits and then fell prey to goblin enchantments."

I nod.

"And this one sister . . . Laura . . . she still sneaks out to visit the market."

"Right. Despite Lizzie's warning that the goblin men will come between them."

"So this poem is the foundation for the 'sisters before misters' movement." Flashing a mischievous smirk, Clarey flips to the front of the book.

"Something like that." I nibble on the brush's handle to hide my discomfort at another secret reason why Lark would haunt me . . . because I'm losing the battle against my feelings for her first and only love.

As if drawn by the clicking of my teeth against the wood, Clarey focuses on my mouth. My cheeks threaten to overheat again, and I point at another illustration, steering his attention back to the book.

"Here, Lizzie goes in search of the market because her sister's addiction to the fruit is killing her. Laura tried to find the market

again herself, but the goblins are hiding from her now that they got what they wanted."

"Typical misogynistic pigs." Clarey shakes his head. Having watched his father abandon his mother, he harbors strong opinions on "misogynistic pig" syndrome.

"Right?" I resume painting my piercings on the mural. "So Laura lies around in bed, her cheeks growing gaunt and her eyes hollowing out." The image of Lark in the moonlight on her final night flashes through my mind; I clear my throat to steady my voice. "Somehow, the fruit drained her instead of filling her up."

"Huh." Clarey concentrates on the illustration of Lizzie standing by a tree while spindly goblins offer fruits and climb on and around her like monkeys. "You sure this poem wasn't written about Halloween? A piece of fruit sucking the life out of someone. That's like a Twix bar growing arms and cracking a person in half . . . the ultimate trick-or-treat prank."

I inhale slowly, uneasy with the turn of conversation. I've considered that before. The author mentions cooling weather and that it's harvest time. It could definitely be set in the fall.

I swirl my brush in turpentine to rinse it, choosing to skate past Clarey's comment. "Anyway, the goblins appear to Lizzie and tempt her with their baskets of fruit. She wants to be strong for her sister, so she refuses to taste anything. They try to force her—shoving food in her face. She closes her mouth so nothing can get by, and lets the juices cover her lips and chin. Then she runs home and cures Laura with a sticky, dripping kiss. Years later, they share the memory with their kids around the fireplace . . . to warn them about goblin men, and to remind them of the power of sisterly love."

Clarey turns to the back flap where the author and artist bios

are. "Man. That's some twisted hokum. What would make her write a story like that?"

Blotting the brush bristles dry on a rag, I shrug. "I read somewhere that she had a nervous breakdown when she was a teen. She pasted strips of paper over passages in other poetry books to censor them. I've always wondered if whatever caused her trauma inspired this poem. She dedicated it to her own sister, after all."

"Ah," he responds quietly, and it's obvious his mind is going to his own breakdown in Chicago. I've asked about the experience only once. When he said he wasn't ready to talk about it yet, I told him I'd trust him to tell me when he is, because that's what friends do. They wait as long as it takes.

Clarey lets out a breath and returns the book to my bag, pausing to rub the pocket watch at the corner. "As Aunt Juni would say: That was a *ripping* good yarn."

However adorable his flawless British imitation is, I still can't muster a smile.

"But," he resumes in his natural northwestern vernacular, "your family's tragedies aren't lifted from a fictional poem. Goblins and magic played no part. Your parents had an accident. Lark had a medical condition. And *you* couldn't have stopped either of those things."

Despair knots in my windpipe. My brain gets it, but not my heart. Dipping the brush in a pigment so dark it can only be black, I begin the process of adding in my widow's peak.

Clarey cups a hand over the toe of my boot, stalling me. "You know what *I* think? Your uncle saw the book on your nightstand and found that chewed-up page. He took it from your room so you wouldn't see it and be upset until he could get some mousetraps."

I drum my knee with the brush's wooden end. "We already have traps in a box in the garage. And it still doesn't explain the doll's head. And if something's not wrong, why hasn't he called?"

"His phone battery died, and there's nowhere to recharge it at the beach?"

I clench the brush, struggling to keep my hand from shaking. "Sure, we can make pieces fit the puzzle. But we have to cut them into shapes to *make* them fit. It feels forced . . . it's not organic, you know?"

"Organic, like the bakery next door . . . that my aunt is calling now."

"What if they haven't heard from him either?" I whisper. "I can't lose my uncle, too. He's all I have left."

Clarey leans in and squeezes my shoulder. "Not so. It sucks you've been alone today, that you had to get out and ride over by yourself. But that took some platinum guts. Especially with the way this date shakes you up. You proved you could do it, and now you're not alone anymore. I'm not going anywhere. Okay?"

I meet his thick-lashed gaze, feeling even more off balance under its gentle scrutiny. The warmth of his fingers around my shoulder blade seeps along my neck and into my ears. It's overwhelming—this bond. After losing Lark, I never expected to find someone else who could see inside me. Someone who knows exactly what I need to hear at any given moment.

The only drawback is that *this* someone's empathy and kindness make me want things from him that I shouldn't even contemplate.

"Thanks." I force my attention back to my work in an effort to slow my stomach's somersaults.

Clarey pauses, as if waiting for more. He's still way too close,

and his warm breath—scented with sugar and citrus from the cider—tufts my hair where it hangs across one ear. I keep my jaw hinged tight, forcing myself not to look up. I'm not strong enough right now. If I see those beautiful eyes, those soft lips, inches from mine . . . it'll be my undoing.

Finally, he stands, and the tension snaps free. "I'm going to find out if Aunt Juni's heard anything yet."

I nod in relief, telling myself the hoarse quality to his voice isn't disappointment; that being around the latex paint and turpentine affected his allergies, even though it never has before.

After he leaves, I use white paint to fill in Lark's teeth so there's no longer a gap, resisting the urge to apologize to her as I'm doing it. With the last of her attributes gone, I trade the round brush for an angled one. Dipping it in swirls of dark purple and gray that Clarey blended for me, I shade the edges of the glittery lettering at the top left of the mural:

On All Hallows' Eve,
You can hear the goblins cry:
"Visit Eveningside Delights,
Come buy, come buy!"

I finish the goblin's mechanical elbow, then turn it on and lean back to examine the scene. The forearm makes rotary-whirring sounds as it slants to the side of the mural, as though pointing toward my painted forest. I hunch close, noticing something between the branches: swirling eyes in the shadow of the trees . . . two pairs. Barely discernible at first, but the longer I stare the more brilliantly they glow—until they're suddenly crystal clear, in *full color.*

I inhale a sharp breath. A grimalkin's eyes, appearing more vivid than the world around me. But I didn't put them there, any more than I added Lark.

Flannie trounces into the room, wearing her emotional-support vest. My effort to keep her from toppling the paints or stepping on my touch-ups distracts me from the mural for an instant. When I look at the scene again, those brilliant eyes have disappeared and I'm faced with sepia and grayscale once more.

Clarey comes in carrying his SFX organizer—a large, repurposed metal tackle box. His eyebrows furrow.

The worry in his expression capsizes the fear and disbelief fluttering in my chest. "What?" I ask, hugging Flannie's neck, both to hold her still and for solace.

He puts his box down with a thud, calls Flannie over, then holds the store's key ring under her muzzle. "Go find my car keys, okay Sherlock?"

She sniffs the keys, shakes her floppy ears until her collar jingles, then trots into the boutique—her bionic limb clacking in time with her nails.

Clarey opens the box's lid. He takes out the top two inserts with dividers loaded down by makeup, then sorts through the sculpted prosthetics stored in cloth sacks in the spacious bottom compartment.

"Your uncle called the bakery earlier, on his way over to the beach. To fill them in on Dahlia and Carl." Clarey pulls out an emaciated mask he designed last year—a twisted mix between a skull and a jack-o'-lantern. I imprint the color orange from my memory. "He told them he'd be back around four to pick up the macarons and cupcakes, since he'd be getting your mural. That's the last anyone at the bakery heard from him."

My stomach plummets into my feet. “Then he must still be at Cannon Beach, right?”

Clarey’s frown deepens. “Aunt Juni called the PTA president for an update. She says his car is still there, but she hasn’t seen him since he set up the bakery booth. She figures someone must’ve convinced him to help set up stalls or game booths in one of the other tents.”

An icy rush chills my body. “I have to go with your aunt.” I start to stand.

“Hang on,” Clarey says, coaxing me to stay seated. “Aunt Juni’s got to get stuff together here and stop at the bakery. You and I can leave now. We’ll load your mural in my Subaru; it can dry on the way. We’ll take Flannie to help us search, in case your uncle’s not where he should be once we get there.”

“I—I don’t get it. You’re going *in* with me?” The ivy-coated heirloom grandfather clock in the center of the courtyard shows it’s a quarter to six. Depending on traffic and weather conditions, it can take over an hour to drive to Cannon Beach; by the time we get there, the festivities will be well under way. It’s a dizzying seesaw, teetering between concern for Uncle and shock at Clarey’s willingness to brave a sea of carnival-goers, many of whom we won’t know.

“Just let me do one thing first . . .” Clarey kneels. Utilizing the mirror welded on the inner lid of the tackle box, he peels off the scales from around his eyes. He then covers his eyelids and skin with thick black makeup until his irises stand out like achromatic gemstones embedded in an onyx setting. Next, he dabs spots on his face with spirit gum adhesive, waits for it to get tacky, then pulls the mask into place—taking care not to

dislodge his BAHA—until his forehead, high cheekbones, and chin disappear beneath the cadaverous pumpkin's ridges.

Clarey once told me that ever since Chicago, he often wishes he could wear a mask all the time; that the shaped features and their unchanging expressions feel like armor. An impenetrable wall to hide any panic he might feel. So of course, to face the crowds tonight, he needs some refuge for control.

Thinking of the shiny surfaces that will be in abundance at the event—aluminum food trucks, reflective carousels, and fun house mirrors to name a few—I wouldn't mind having some protection myself. I want to look as different from Lark as humanly possible . . . *inhumanly* would be even better.

I dig out some white makeup to go with the black tube already on the floor, and find a piece of white zipper tape and a tube of lipstick marked Ruby Red. "When you're done, I want some metal."

His eyes glitter bright within the mask's triangular eyeholes. "One zombie rag doll, coming up."

The pumpkin's ridges cave in on one side of his head, as if dented. There's a stem and circular top that attach with Velcro to the skullcap that covers his hair. The prosthetic topper is shaped and painted to resemble a gash around the stem that gapes open, revealing stringy guts and goopy seeds. Paired with the face mask, it forms the illusion of a smashed pumpkin.

Two long nostril holes and fat lips carved into the face's surface complete the effect. The result is so realistic, all Clary needs is to don the brown withered-leaf cloak and the gloves with gnarled-vine fingers, and he'll be every inch a demented jack-o'-lantern goblin.

Dread prickles around the edges of my heart—not because of his costume, but because of Uncle's absence, Mom's picture book, the mural, and the unshakable sense that something bad is in the works.

Clarey's earlier observation rattles through my head like a deadly toss of dice: *the ultimate trick-or-treat prank . . .*

I was right all along. Halloween hasn't finished with my family yet.

11

all hallows' eve

Flannie brings Clarey his harmonica instead of his car keys. An understandable mistake since it hangs on the same hook and is affixed to a chain so he can wear it. He places it around his neck and sends Flannie off again; with one more try she drops the keys at his feet and wins a liver-flavored treat.

On the way to Cannon Beach, traffic moves reasonably fast as the fog clears, and the storm clouds—though growing darker and more ominous as twilight moves in—seem reluctant to dump out their contents. By the time the silhouetted forests spread off to one side of the highway and the beachfront homes and shops appear like whitewashed shadows on the other, it's ten till seven, much earlier than we expected to arrive.

Recognizing the cars of several students and teachers in a small lot on Hemlock Street, Clarey pulls in and parks next to a glass studio. I see Uncle's Chevy, but can't find much encouragement, considering the driver himself is still missing.

Clarey and I open the back of the Subaru and drag out my

mural to wrap it in a plastic tarp now that it's dry. I'm reminded of the spontaneous appearance of the grimalkins and Lark in my scene, and I can't fight the niggling sense that I'm missing chunks of last night . . . that something happened I can't quite put my finger on. And that's why, ever since, I've been off balance—making mistakes. I won't be able to relax until I see Uncle with my own eyes and we're all back home, waiting out the night in safety.

Clarey tucks the harmonica on its chain inside his shirt, then hands off his leafy cloak and twiggy gloves for me to carry in the duffel. Rearranging them alongside Juniper's leftover scones makes me glad I left my paints, pens, and sketchbooks at the boutique to save space.

Clarey lifts the back end of the mural. I lead with the front, my gloved hands angled behind me to hold the panel parallel to the ground, as if it's a piece of scaffolding between us. Flannie's collar jingles and her mechanical leg whirs as she trots alongside us. I toss a look over my shoulder and catch Clarey's troubled gaze within the eyeholes.

"You sure you're up for this?" I ask.

"I was wondering the same about you," comes his answer, muffled by the mask.

"Well, it beats being alone." Recalling what he said back at the boutique—how I'm no longer alone—warms me head to toe like Juniper's cider, and I'm overcome with gratitude again. I still have that squid ink stashed in the bag on my shoulders. Helping him perfect a new Scourge mask will be the token of my appreciation—once the danger of October thirty-first is behind us.

Chilly, damp gusts finger through my hair, carrying the

appetizing scents of local cuisine and brine. I ate one of the gingerbread scones Juniper sent with us but am still hungry enough my stomach would be growling if it wasn't sunken like a rock.

I glance at the asphalt streets—glistening and black but mostly empty due to dinnertime and the activities drawing people to the beach. I've always been captivated by the creative atmosphere here and have taken many a day trip with my uncle and Clarey to visit the eclectic shops and art galleries. At night after a rain shower, the sidewalks and thoroughfares are even prettier—splashes of glitter reflecting the streetlights.

As we navigate a crosswalk to the closest beachside inn then swing around to the back where the pavement stops, the town's charm fades to the sight of Haystack Rock rising offshore in the distance—a monolithic imprint against the inky sky. The sea stack, over two hundred feet tall, hunches like a beast lying in wait between swirling charcoal clouds and the ocean's frothy white waves.

In agreeable weather, the volcanic rock is a popular tourist attraction, mainly for its cameo in the opening scene of *The Goonies*, when the Fratellis race across the beach to outrun the police. Yet to locals and a few discerning visitors, there's so much more magic happening at the base and on the rock itself.

Even from this distance, the cries of seabirds colonizing the surface vibrate in my ears: the puffins' growling wails that sound like garbled chain saws; and the shrill *kee-ar*s of the terns. There's a thin strip of rock and sand that connects the beach to the sea stack at low tides where starfish, crabs, sea slugs, and other intertidal life populate the resultant pools of water.

Lark and I used to come here with Uncle Thatch for afternoon picnics and kite flying. On our twelfth birthday, he brought

us late in the day because—although the cave inside Haystack Rock is usually unreachable—the sand levels had risen high enough that people could slip in for some spelunking. By the time we arrived, sunset filtered through the back entrance and flooded the tunnel's corridor with a pink glow—Lark's favorite color. Lark and I spent the next half hour squatted on outcroppings in the cave's jagged interior, counting crabs and starfish. The experience inspired my earliest attempt of a comic about a girl who sprouted gills and fins, and her adventures in an underwater kingdom where glowing starfish lit up the ocean like a night sky. As for Lark, watching the crabs' hinged claws sparked the idea for the robotic appendages that would later inspire Flannie's bionic limb.

Desperate to escape the nostalgia, I return my attention to Flannie. She bounds from my ankles to Clarey's as we take the gradual slope to the beach. Tail wagging, she yips in excitement the instant we hit sand, and I envy her unfettered enthusiasm.

Beach lanterns on tall poles light the way to the carnival in the distance. Flannie trots along the shoreline several feet ahead of us, sand spraying up around her paws as she attempts to herd a couple of terns fighting over some smelly fish the tide uncovered. Before we came, we put on her waterproof snowshoe attachment; it's the same thickness and shape of her real paws, to allow her mechanical leg to skim across sand—or snow—instead of sinking. However, the circuitry inside the leg joints won't survive a dousing of salt water any more than Clarey's calfskin loafers and their metallic toes would.

Before she can get too close to the ocean, Clarey shouts, "Flannie, come!"

She aims a final scolding bark at the birds, then scampers

back to us. Our trio veers toward the warm beigy glow coming from the black-and-white circus-style tents clustered along the beach a few yards behind a local resort. In an announcement at school, students were told that the three big tops would have a central height of thirty-three feet and a forty-foot circumference, so they could house a large selection of rides and fundraising attractions.

It's overwhelming to see the spread in person, knowing we may have to comb each spacious tent, one by one, to find Uncle.

Lightning streaks overhead, and the sky fractures as if we're inside a black Fabergé egg embellished with electrical netting. Clarey and I break into a wobbly sprint with the mural swaying between us. My biceps and shoulders stretch at their awkward positioning, but I push on. Rain pours down the minute we plunge through the closest tent's entrance. I glance at Clarey, shaking my head at how close we cut it. The mural would've been protected beneath the tarp, but our makeup wouldn't have fared so well—and we both need our hiding places.

The sugary essence of fresh-spun cotton candy and the greasy balm of crab puffs and funnel cakes overtake the scent of the rain—even before the sounds and sights hit. Flannie lifts her nostrils to sniff the carnival fare.

"Don't get distracted, poochie," Clarey says quietly from beneath his mask. "You've got a job to do before you can earn yourself some junk food."

I smirk when Flannie wags her tail in answer and finds her place at her master's side.

The sweet moment shatters like the sky outside as I take in our surroundings: the lights on the rented games and rides—which should be every color of the rainbow—blink in sepias and

grays, as though I've stepped into an old-timey carnival documentary. The droning buzz of motors, the grinding swirl of wooden Skee-Ball machines competing with the pop of air guns, and the *clack-clack-clack* of a thirty-foot drop tower taking passengers up to the central dome of the tent's roof so they can plummet down at breakneck speed all make me grateful my other senses remain sharp.

Everything presents a gruesome theme, from a Clowns-Go-Round carousel with circus animals—elephants, seals, tigers, and ponies, their heads masked in white with eyes and muzzles blotted black and bulbous noses that I'm guessing are red to mimic evil bestial clowns—to a Bloody-Bits-in-Jars sensory game, where participants blindly stick their hands behind a screen and attempt to deduce what they're touching . . . "slimy eyeballs," "amputated appendages," or "broken teeth."

For the first time since losing Lark, I've stepped out of hiding and directly into the world of fabricated monsters and synthetic gore. I swore I'd never celebrate this holiday again, yet here I am in the thick of it.

I nibble my lip ring, counting on the familiar metallic tang to calm my nerves, but it's futile. My heartbeat slams in my wrists and neck—a thrumming that picks up tempo when, to better see all the sights in the tent, we're forced into the midway, swarmed by a throng of costumes.

There are the traditional Frankensteins, Freddy Kruegers, Draculas, and Jasons; then there are the homegrown tributes: Sloth, Mama Fratelli . . . the Datas, the Chunks, the Mikeys. Some are wearing Hey You Guys T-shirts, others have donned jackets with the logo Goonies Never Say Die.

In spite of hidden faces, it's easy to identify strangers by those

who gawk at Flannie's leg as we pass. Our fellow Astorians glance and wave but walk on undeterred.

However, almost everyone—stranger or not—makes a point to compliment the realism of Clarey's pumpkin prosthetic. He offers the occasional "Thanks, man," but keeps his head down.

I pause in the midway when two ski-masked revelers—one a ninja and the other a cat burglar with fuzzy black ears and tail—relay excitement at seeing us. I recognize the voices as Jin's and Brooke's and set down my end of the mural while Clarey props his on the sand, leaning its weight against him . . . effectively walling off one side of himself from the crowd. He turns his face into the board, his shoulders raising on shallow breaths.

"I can't believe you're here!" Jin shouts over the drop tower's whooshing air brakes, the carousel's distorted circus music, and bursts of laughter and chatter. She absently wraps Brooke's tail around her plastic ninja staff. "And such amazing costumes!" In deference to Clarey's obvious discomfort, Jin shifts her attention to me. "Dang, those look so real."

Using the end of Brooke's tail, she gestures toward the zippers razing my chalky made-up face—one severs my forehead, another my cheek, and the final my chin. Clarey made them by cutting the zipper tape to fit, dotting the white fabric backing with spirit gum, then pressing them into place using tweezers and dabbing on latex texturing before blending the edges into the white makeup. Plumping up my lips with the Ruby Red matte, then adding harlequin-style black triangles around my eyes and a few oozing drops of fake blood along the interlocked zipper teeth, created a ghastly rag doll effect. Nothing too terrifying, but macabre enough to be a creature completely separate from myself . . . and more importantly, from Lark.

"So what made you come out tonight?" Jin's familiar enough with my Halloween routine to understand I'm out of my element.

"Had to bring my mural," I shout back, trying to keep my footing as people accidentally jostle the board. A hand-holding couple with a funnel cake get close enough I can almost taste the sweat, sugar, and greasy smoke emanating off them. I worry for Clarey. He's stiff as a scarecrow in an ice storm, though Flannie's doing a great job preserving his personal space by dancing around him. Still, it's obvious—by the pinched, painted skin surrounding his eyes under the mask—he won't last much longer.

"Do you know where my uncle set up?" I ask.

"The middle tent," Brooke answers from beneath her fuzzy-eared ski mask as she wrestles her tail away from Jin. "Right next to the art class's face-painting stall, just on the other side of the flap."

I ask one last question while dreading the answer: "And he's already there, right?"

"No. Mrs. Ruiz is watching the booth, but she doesn't have anything to sell," Jin says. "We thought maybe that's why you came. We haven't seen your uncle since we got here, and people have been asking. There was a line for a while, but not sure if anyone's still waiting. Maybe he's there now."

"Thanks," I manage. My thoughts flicker faster than the grayscale lights on the carousel, and my fears escalate until I feel like I'm in a gut-twisting free fall—as if *I'm* the one descending from the top of the Grim Reaper's Drop Tower, my spine pressed against a tombstone seat back as we race toward a speedy plunge.

Without a word, Clarey uses the mural between us to nudge me forward.

We resume our two-person hold on the panel and use it to

push a path out of the midway and back to the edges of the canvas where the crowd thins, providing a faster route to the middle tent.

"He's got to be manning a game or something," Clarey says from behind as my feet shuffle on autopilot. I clench my jaw, because it sounds like he's trying to convince himself as much as me.

We scutter by a "Haunted Hovel," basically a temporary shed painted to look like a Victorian manor that houses some prefabricated scares. Eerie music, groaning zombies, moaning ghosts, and hysterical yelps can be heard as the door opens to let in new victims. The seasonal sounds burrow inside my belly, heightening my nausea.

Next, we pass a couple of fundraising booths. The photography class painted a board to look like a giant black widow, with a hole for the spider's head where people can pose their faces for keepsake pictures—five dollars a sitting. There's also a line at my mechanic class's three-dollar-per-try game—a hand-built striker that tests a contestant's level of scariness by how high they can send the puck up the nine-foot tower with a mallet. There's Barely Hairy, Fairly Thrilling, Goose Bump Raising, and Spine Chilling.

A customer swings the mallet as we pass. He reaches *Spine-Chilling* status, and the bell's celebratory *ching-ching-ching* reverberates deep in my chest.

Ching: No one's heard from Uncle since this morning. *Ching:* He would never have allowed a line of eager customers to go unattended. *Ching:* He's not here but his car is.

An icy sensation prickles my skin. *What's happened to you, Uncle Thatch?*

12

ringmaster

I pick up the pace, my sights set solely on the opening to the next tent. I duck through with Clarey and Flannie close behind, and the bakery's booth appears a few feet away—unmistakable once Clarey points out that there are multicolored Christmas lights wound about matching red, purple, green, and gold panels.

The PTA president, Mrs. Ruiz, sits inside wearing a school-spirit shirt and jeans. She assures a few customers that someone is on their way with the bakery's popular treats, and says to please come back in fifteen minutes or so.

My hope she's been in contact with Uncle bursts as soon as she spots us.

"*Gracias a Dios!*" She claps in relief. "Miss Wisteria said she'd be coming, but I guess she sent you instead?"

A discouraged breath shunts out of me, and I lose my grip on the mural. Clarey manages to keep it from slamming to the ground. I crinkle my forehead apologetically, a movement that tugs the fake zipper above my eyebrow ring. He grasps my

forearm in a comforting gesture, even as his gaze darts at some passersby.

"I'll hang it. You two talk." His voice sounds tremulous, and his fingers shake as they glide to my glove and squeeze gently. Our eyes meet before he releases me to drag a few dog treats from his pocket and coax Flannie out of the main path. The two of them then press up against the side panel. It's a good spot to unwrap the tarp and even better for seclusion.

In front, I lift the wooden serving counter, allowing Mrs. Ruiz to exit.

She carries a set of wire cutters that used to belong to Lark. I don't have to be able to make out the pink of the handles to recognize them. There's no mistaking those spatters of dried glitter glue along the blades. "Found these in the booth. I'm guessing your uncle used them to cut the wire that hangs the lights." She offers the tool to Clarey as he comes from around the side. "Thought you might need them for the mural."

Clarey takes the wire cutters, and I see the pained recognition when he drops them into his pocket. On my end, I'm confused. Uncle never delves into Lark's toolbox. He has his own stuff. He would've had to climb into the attic to get to hers. The weirdness just keeps piling up.

Together, Mrs. Ruiz and I step out of Clarey's way so he can hang the sign. Focused on his work, he rises on metal toe tips and loops the mural's rope hanger over the hook already screwed into place along the center of the top panel.

While he's activating the goblin's arm, I turn back to Mrs. Ruiz—shutting out every other sight and sound. "When did you see my uncle?"

She twines her hands at her waist. "A few hours ago while he

was setting up. I stopped to ask him if he needed anything because he seemed distracted . . . kept looking at that mirror maze." She points to a fun house on the other side of the face-painting stall.

Some of the art students—dabbing bat wings and skeletons into place on customers' smiling cheeks—catch me looking their direction and shout a greeting. I offer a cursory wave, though my attention strays to the fun house's huge, hand-painted facade. The scene looks like the inner workings of a clock: gears, suspension springs, dials, and pendulums—in black, white, and every shade of gray—interlocked together in a maze. In the maze's center, a key-shaped tree sprouts, jagged branches ripe with fruits bejeweled in dewdrops.

Across the top, painted letters entice visitors while adding a splash of glitter: Ringmaster Mystique's Mystical Maze: Tame the Pendulum, Breach the Plinth, Face-Off Time in the Labyrinth.

Underneath poses the eight-foot depiction of a top-hat-clad-and-caped man, one hand holding a plum to his lips, the other splayed to present the doorway that leads inside—a door that from here looks tightly shut.

White circular bulbs outline the entire frontispiece, casting shadows in strange places, making it difficult to see the magician's illustrated features. Yet one thing stands out beneath the hat's brim—sharp eyes that shimmer like black diamonds. It rocks me with an unsettling and familiar sensation, as if that faceted gaze could peel back the layers of my skin and poison my blood.

Thunder rolls above the tent's roof, loud enough to be heard over the carnival sounds . . . distracting enough to break my study of the facade.

Mrs. Ruiz tugs Uncle's cell phone from her jacket pocket.

"Your uncle asked me to watch the booth while he spoke to the guy who brought the maze. I saw them go into the fun house together. I must've missed them when they came out. I don't think he realized he left his phone behind. I found it under the shelf."

I curl my glove around the cold vinyl casing, wishing it were his warm hand instead. At least there's a logical reason he hasn't been answering.

"Nix, I can see you're worried," the PTA president continues. "But I'm sure he'll be back soon. He said something about a delivery. I assumed that red-haired young man had placed an order and your uncle planned to pick it up at the bakery when he left to get the booth's food. Maybe he stopped for a quick bite first. Everyone's been working so hard to get things—"

"Red hair?" I interrupt, my sights returning to the maze. I gulp a gritty stickiness from my throat. "A delivery?"

My feet start moving before my tongue can sever the threads of conversation. I ignore Mrs. Ruiz's and Clarey's calls from behind. I'm laser focused. A few kids from school block me, saying the fun house isn't open for the public . . . that there's no one to unlock it or take tickets.

As if I want *to go in; as if any part of me thinks facing warped mirrors and winding pathways on Halloween would be fun.* I bite back my response, and instead push silently through the crowd. Stopping a few inches from the facade, I look up-up-up until my eerie suspicion is validated: despite that I can't make out the color of hair, the painted magician looks exactly like Jaspar.

My shoulders stiffen.

Why would our deliveryman have an attraction here after the hard time he gave Uncle? Is it to keep an eye on us? Is this some kind of passive-aggressive powerplay?

I've always known something's off with the guy . . . but this is beyond creepy.

Punctuating that thought, thunder rumbles again, this time accompanied by a flash of lightning that spreads across the tent's top.

In contrast to the chill skittering along my spine, a breathy warmth rushes my ankle. I look down to find Flannie sniffing around my boots. With a short yip, she darts to the back side of the mirror maze, her tail high and erect as she disappears from view. Clarey hustles up to me, avoiding the crowds milling through the midway. Our classmates hang a few yards back, waiting for the fun house to open.

Clarey clutches Uncle's tie-dyed apron; the whiteness of his knuckles indicates he's using it as a lifeline. "I gave Flannie a sniff so she could—" His explanation stalls as his attention catches on the painting overhead. "Whoa. Bizarre-o."

"The hair color?" I ask, studying the dark tufts poking out from the hat's rim.

"Burgundy red," Clarey says softly. The circular bulbs shadow the dented ridges of his pumpkin mask as he stares upward. "It's totally your deliveryman."

Before I can respond, Flannie woofs.

"She's found a trail," Clarey announces.

The two of us rush to join her behind the fun house. Clarey visibly relaxes once we leave the crowd and step into the abandoned area; there's an employee entrance to the maze, but a padlock secures the latch. Thick cables and cords tangle on the sandy ground, powering the structure's chugging electric generator. Flannie sniffs alongside them, and I fall in line with her.

A snap of lightning flashes high outside the tent, followed by

sparks and a loud pop. All at once, the lights snuff out around us—every ride, attraction, and booth losing electricity. Gasps, awkward footsteps, and startled shouts fill the sudden silence on the other side of the fun house.

Clarey's hand captures mine, and I squeeze back, grateful he's still with me. I take a step toward him but something scrapes my boot. I kneel and blindly rake the ground. My glove glides along smooth lines and slick surfaces.

I turn on Uncle's phone. The screen's glow reveals an all-too-familiar pair of spectacles, but with a cracked black frame and one shattered lens. A tight ball forms in my gut. "Just like his car," I murmur. "His glasses are here, but he's nowhere near them."

Clarey puts my uncle's apron on the ground and holds Flannie's vest handle so he can kneel beside me. He draws me into a hug. I press my head against his shoulder, clinging to his warmth and flowery-chemical scent as fear lacerates my heart.

"This is bad, Clarey." I wince at the crack in my voice, at how tight I'm clenching his shirt—like I'll sink if I let go. "It's a *part* of him—busted up and left behind."

Clarey releases Flannie and cups both my shoulders. He leans his pumpkin skull against my forehead zipper. "We could try these to get into the locked door." He drags the wire cutters from his pants pocket.

"But they're not strong enough for cutting a padlock. Are they?"

Clarey considers my question, then drops them back into his pocket. "I saw some cops around the carousel. We'll get them to help. It'll be okay," he promises.

I want to crawl inside the mask with him . . . I want to watch his expression match his voice's confidence. But the phone's dim

glow hints at the worry in his eyes and I know, if exposed to bright light, his assurance would be revealed for the lie it is.

I shine Uncle's cell phone on the glasses again. This time, the shimmer catches a subtler detail: bite marks, just like the ones on my picture book's pages . . . all along the earpieces.

I hold them up. "Look!" A burning sob builds in my throat. "Unless the mouse hitched a ride with Uncle—"

Clarey interrupts me with a finger on my lip. "Listen."

I strain my ears, trying to pick out the panic-filled rush of voices and feet sloughing through sand on the other side of the fun house. There's nothing but the pounding thrum of rain overhead.

"Why's everything so quiet all of a sudden?" I whisper.

"Exactly," answers Clarey, his voice thick and shivery.

Uncle's phone blinks off, abandoning us to darkness again. I jab at the button, but it won't reactivate. Clarey and I huddle closer.

"Maybe we should try one of our phones?" I offer.

A clunk of metal at the back of the fun house disrupts the suggestion, followed by a scratching, scraping sound. For a moment I'm trapped again on that horrible night—the sawing, dragging, and grunts that woke me . . . Lark's fingernails against the screen when she was struggling for breath.

A high-pitched whine shatters the memory.

"Flannie?" Clarey jumps up, his spine stiffening beneath my hand. I latch onto his belt loop to keep us together in the darkness while tucking Uncle's phone and broken glasses into my duffel. The straps eat into my shoulders through my jacket as I'm tugged sightlessly forward.

"Flannie, here girl!" Clarey calls out.

She yips excitedly from a few feet away. The employee entrance opens on moaning hinges. Even though the generator sits silent, light radiates from within. And not just any light . . . bright, retina-piercing neon red.

"Clarey, what color is that light?" I ask, needing the validation to believe what I'm seeing.

"Red," comes his answer as the glow illuminates the fallen padlock and Flannie bouncing on her hind legs.

I don't even have the chance to tell Clarey that I can see it for myself, because Flannie digs at the door's edge and vanishes inside before we can reach the threshold.

"Flannie!" Clarey shouts.

A warm waxy-scented mist—reminiscent of candle smoke—sweeps out along with the light, both spreading toward us in an eerie luminous path. Clarey curses and peels off his mask and cap. I know what it took for him to shed them . . . but it's the only way he can see clearly in this smoky haze. I hand him my bag, and he zips the costume inside, then hangs the straps over his shoulder.

Worry for Flannie and Uncle merge with my desire to follow the colorized glow. I inch closer to look around Clarey, my chest pressed against the bumps of his spine beneath his sharkskin vest. The smoke clears in patches, revealing a floor awash in that same red light. Though it's not just any floor; it's an intricate system of gears—brassy and stainless steel metallic teeth turning and interlocking to form moving bridges and pathways that lead to upper and lower levels.

My stomach flips over, both from the recognition of gold and

silver metals and from the fact that the maze appears to be four or five stories high; much bigger inside than out, impossibly so.

"Are you seeing—?" I ask.

"Yeah."

"How can it—?"

"Don't know."

I cringe then, making note of the glimmering mirrors that form the walls and ceilings, so many of them, stretching into oblivion. On and on and on . . . a thousand reflections waiting to be born . . . waiting to accuse me. To ambush me.

For an instant, I see two pairs of eyes, swirling and bright—amber and green, like the ones on my mural—peering out from a mirror on the upper level. They blink twice, then vanish. Tiny hairs along my arms bristle as the grimalkins' song from my dream last night scores my psyche like steel claws: *Fetch the one who goes astray . . .*

It was a warning all along, except it's Uncle who's gone astray. Were they leading me here so I could find him?

No. Grimalkins are a figment of my imagination . . . my own creation. They live only in my mind.

It's that logic that stops me from spilling everything to Clarey—how I can see the colors inside the building, how I see the eyes of my characters blinking in the reflections. Because how can those perceptions be real when everything else around me still looks anemic and drab?

As if in response to my strained silence, he grabs my free hand where it hangs at my side and holds my palm against his sternum.

"I have to get Flannie." His heartbeat rattles his ribs behind his lapel, a thudding rhythm that penetrates my glove, and his

breaths burst—short and ragged. He's as afraid and confused as I am, but for a whole other set of reasons.

"Right." I lace my fingers through his. The only way to find our loved ones is through this maze. "We go together."

He nods, then hand in hand, we cross the threshold.

13

grunge and grudges

We pick our way across gears that are constantly in flux . . . horizontal copper teeth clutching and spinning to form paths both serpentine and shuddering. Smoke twines around our ankles, broken up by the shifting metal. The muscles in my legs and feet strain to hold ground, and my scraped knee resumes throbbing. A thick, goopy sludge spurts up sporadically from the interlocking seams—some hydraulic lubricant that keeps the wheels turning and smells of exhaust fumes.

I struggle to focus, my attention divided between the brilliant colors I haven't seen for months while keeping my footholds and listening for any signs of Uncle. I breathe deeply, a concentrated effort to stay on the path beneath us and avoid the cogs.

I'm torn. One half of me wants to avert my gaze from the numerous reflections on either side and overhead, to keep from seeing terrifying things—Mystiquiel's denizens warping my reality, or images of Lark, angry and accusatory—while the other, the artist's half, aches to stare without blinking, to memorize

each prismatic flash of hair and cloth, of shadow and light, as beautiful to my hungry eyes as rainbows bouncing along a geode's crystallized facets.

Yet my spirits don't feel any lighter; it's as if my guilt-induced depression has peeled back like a scab, bleeding color into the raw wounds left behind.

"There she is." Clarey points at the fourth level where multiple likenesses of Flannie appear in the mirrors. The reddish glow tinges her gray and white patches of fur to soft pinks and reds. Clarey resituates the duffel bag's straps alongside his collarbone. Although he's not wearing the mask now, his face is hidden by alternating plumes of smoke, so I can't make out his eyes. "I'm betting she's got your uncle's scent."

When I open my mouth to respond, I inhale a throat-burning gulp of waxy smoke and motor grease. Suppressing a cough, I nod instead.

In sync, Clarey and I step sideways and grab a metal rail, hitching a ride on a pinion joined to a rack. The swiftly climbing motion reminds me of a cherry picker lifting its long neck. I sway at the upward swing, tightening my grip. The gears below grow smaller as we pass levels—exactly like being inside a giant clock.

The thought triggers an unexpectedly euphoric rush. Although Lark would've loved to have seen this, she couldn't have handled the journey. I've never minded heights . . . my sister was the one afraid of them. Other than drawing, it's the only thing I ever did better than she did.

"Flannie!" Clarey calls out as we step off the framework of steel bars onto a new moving path.

The collie barks, altering her route in answer to her master's voice. Together, their greetings echo, the sound amplifying to an

uncomfortable pitch above the clanging of metal and grinding of gears. I clench my teeth, worried we might draw unwanted attention. Who knows who's hiding along the turns of the shifting corridors, or worse, what might be lurking inside the mirrors?

After everything that's happened today, and now stepping from a sepia-gray world into this polychromatic maze, this is starting to feel strangely like a trap.

The image of Uncle's busted glasses resurfaces on that thought. He can barely see without his prescription lenses and would never have managed these dimly lit automated walkways and lifts on his own. He was obviously forced inside, and it must've been Jaspar behind it, but why?

My stomach churns, a spastic counterrhythm to the oiled and metrical movements beneath my feet. A trio of Flannie reflections appears a few feet away, resolving to one as she steps out from a corridor alongside us. It's a miracle the gears haven't snagged her delicate foot pads. Even her snowshoe attachment remains intact as she picks her way gracefully, never faltering. The grinding and humming of the motorized walkways don't seem to faze her, maybe because she's one part mechanized herself.

Letting the duffel drop to his elbow, Clarey opens his arms and Flannie bounds to him. "Good to see you, pooch!" He hugs her as his voice ricochets around us.

I pat her flank, and we all keep our feet moving to stay in place. Knowing she came into this maze led by my uncle's scent confirms he's here somewhere.

I don't get the chance to relay my hope before the flat, whirring gears beneath each of us grow larger . . . from the size of dinner plates to manhole covers. The teeth release, and our metal

platforms break apart, carrying Clarey and Flannie away on one conveyer belt as I hurtle in the opposite direction. A steel frame drops down from overhead and seals me in for the ride, reminiscent of the domed jungle gyms I used to climb as a child, but not nearly as fun or familiar.

Multiple reflections of Clarey and me whiz by in the mirror walls. We both reach for the wrong likenesses in passing, and always a moment too late.

"Clarey!" I call. He shouts my name simultaneously, moments before he and Flannie disappear around a corner. A mirror folds down to close the opening.

"No!" I shout. Looking back from my reflection, a set of swirling grimalkin eyes emerges as if laughing at my misfortune. They blink twice, then shut and vanish.

I look away before the mirror can cast any more unsettling images, or capture me within my own. I stand trapped in my dome. The gear stops spinning and chugs along on a belt, headed toward the far side of the maze. Farther and farther away from Clarey. Panic scrabbles through me and my muscles twitch, eager to leap. I grip the bars surrounding me, silently willing the mechanism to perch somewhere and open the frame.

I could be lost here forever, considering how huge it is. My fraying ability to reason says maybe the dimensions are an optical illusion caused by the mirrors. If that's the case, I'll be found when they deconstruct the carnival. Until then, I could be imprisoned for hours; afloat in isolation, without Uncle or Clarey or Flannie or even my sketchbooks and pencils. Left with nothing but regrets and distorted reflections.

I don't want to be alone with myself on this night . . . I don't think I can handle it.

I slam my eyes closed at the alarming possibility, unable to watch. A part of me is relieved that at least wherever this crazy maze has taken Clarey, he has Flannie to help him stay calm. Another part of me envies them both.

My stomach flutters on a sudden downward drift, forcing my eyes to open on the chance I'm landing. The soft red light of earlier has disappeared, leaving me in total darkness. I whimper and clench the bars, trying to find something to focus on—a silhouette, a glimmer of glass—all the while keeping my guard up for more surprises.

Looking over my shoulder toward where we first arrived reveals a red pinhole growing smaller and smaller, as if I'm shuttling through a tunnel. The sound of clanging metal fades to a whir and a click. A robotic hum, reminiscent of Flannie's leg.

"Clarey?" I shout. No answer, only my voice boomeranging in the black void.

The motorized hum grows louder and more clicks join in, as if there are multiple legs scuttering about outside my moving platform. Reminded of Lark's doll, I shiver in my blindness and shove my spine against the farthest bars of the cage—trying to put distance between me and the disturbing sound.

A flicker appears up ahead, orange and purple, like a misty October sunset.

The closer I get, the more details come to light. It's a giant mirror, yet the scene on the surface isn't reflecting anything around it. It's my and Lark's bedroom, with the props set perfectly in place for that Halloween evening three years ago: a life-size diorama behind glass.

The metal plate beneath my feet skims faster and faster toward the display. I hold so tight to the bars my palms sweat

inside my gloves. I'm thrust toward the glass, the bars slipping through my grip and disappearing from around me. I cry out and wince, anticipating the impact of the shattering mirror, of razor edges dicing me in a thousand places. Instead, I shimmy through with a pop, as if penetrating the skin of a bubble. My gloves vanish and I land soundly in my chair at the desk with a colored pencil in hand, the orange tip at rest on a pile of monster sketches.

Behind me, the sunset filters through gauzy curtains on the bedroom window, warming my back. The familiar scent of machine oil and pencil shavings fills me up, puts me at ease; reminds me that I belong here, and makes me forget Lark ever left.

We're both fourteen again. She sits on the floor, right where she should be, in the shade of our bunk beds and surrounded by butter tubs filled with clock parts—sorted according to size and style. In her lap, she holds the pieces of three disassembled dolls. Arms and legs stick up from the pile like gruesome pieces of kindling. One dark-haired decapitated head rolls around. Earlier, Lark lacerated its bottom and top lips, then inserted a pair of dentures before hinging them back together. The false teeth chatter and the doll blinks its eyes sleepily as Lark tinkers with some wires jutting from its neck.

"Eureka!" she says, more to herself than me, pleased at her accomplishment. I'd know her mood without seeing her upturned lips or hearing her voice. I feel it in our symbiotic bond—in the fuzzy contentment that fills her chest. She leans into the fading sunlight to thread a needle with ultrafine wire. We both yelp in shock when she accidentally pricks her thumb, then we share knowing smiles as I stick my own throbbing finger in my mouth.

I can even taste the vanilla-orange hand cleaner she uses to keep the grunge and grease at bay while working.

Blissful serenity surges through me, just to be here. Us, together. Inseparable.

"I almost have it." Lark's white eyebrows crimp as she concentrates, pulling the looped wire through an opening Uncle Thatch helped her cut in one doll's cavernous torso. Earlier, Lark assembled an intricate rib cage system to hold and power the main mechanism using spindles and various gears. At the end of her threaded wire hangs a small pendulum from a miniature grandfather clock Lark found at an antique store. "You have to tell me, Nix. Is this heart going to be a good one?"

The question is pointed, accusatory, and exactly what I deserve.

We both know: The heart controls the mechanism's actions. If it's a good one, it will synchronize every movement. If it's bad, it will rot the doll from within and she'll never work again. Lark had a good heart for her Young Edison's Challenge a year ago in seventh grade . . . but I interfered. I tried to replace it with one I built, in hopes of proving I was as good at making things come alive as she was—so she wouldn't be the one with all the power.

My tweaking cost her the first-place ribbon and a summer internship.

No one knew my part in her failure, except her. She sensed my guilt and linked my pinkie with hers, and there was no hiding what I'd done.

"I haven't touched this one," I promise from across the room. I've been trying to get back in Lark's good graces for months now, and if her cyber doll is a success, she can enter it this year

and win like she deserved to last time. Then she'll finally forgive me.

I try to focus on my incomplete sketches, although I'm much more captivated by what she's doing. Earlier, I borrowed some glitter—her signature design element—to highlight the lines of my monsters . . . to give them layers and texture, yet still I can't help feeling like they're lacking something.

Lark cuts and crimps the wire with some pink-handled tools moments before Uncle Thatch knocks on the doorframe leading from the hallway. He peers around the corner. My pulse leaps happily at the sight of his goofy smile. For some reason I was worried about him, but can't remember why.

"You girls still don't have your costumes on? Aren't you going trick-or-treating with your friends?"

In that moment, Lark inserts her doll's head onto the body, clicks a tab, and the tiny motor kicks on, making a thump-thump-thumping whir—a mechanical heartbeat. The doll's eyes blink in time with the rhythm, pulses of white light flashing behind them, and its head turns back and forth while the dentures snap at the air. The vinyl torso and arms twist and lift, and the long robotic legs, made from a garage-sale Erector kit that's coated in glitter glue—much like Lark's palms and fingers—move the toy across the floor with the stride of an off-balanced crab. I saw Lark install the pulleys and sprockets that are activating everything, but that doesn't make it any less miraculous as the doll scuttles left to right, sparkling in the late daylight.

"Whoa!" Uncle steps into the room, and a pink sun ray reflects off the lenses of his glasses and illuminates Lark's beaming face. She's never looked more angelic, and I can see why it's

her favorite color. I can also see why Clarence Darden likes her so much, but that doesn't change my liking him first . . . all the way since kindergarten.

"You got this one to work, Songbird?" Uncle grins at her. "Great job! You'll nail this year's challenge. I'm sure of it!"

"Thanks, Unca-thunk. Just glad the heart's a good one." Her words are meant for me, as both an acknowledgment and a warning. As she lifts the doll and demonstrates how she did the wiring, her tongue tip peeks through the gap between her two front teeth.

Turning back to my colored-pencil sketches—stagnant lines and stilted shapes—I let my tongue trace the absence of a matching gap in my teeth.

Lark's eyes flit up to mine, and her smile droops. "Nix has been drawing," she offers. It makes me feel even smaller, to know she sensed my jealousy and felt the need to throw me a scrap, to know how transparent my insecurities are to her now.

She's intimately aware of how I envy that she can bring her multidimensional pieces to life while mine lie flat and motionless—tiny corpses on paper, mummified in pencil lead and eraser dust. How can I possibly insert a thumping heart into a drawing?

That's why she's so much stronger than me. So much surer of herself. That's why she already knows she wants to be a robotics engineer one day, to invent mechanisms to help people or make them smile.

Maybe, if my drawings could breathe and move, I wouldn't worry that she'll eventually leave me behind like an unused cog or discarded wire. I'd have my own clout, my own "someone important" to be. It was that desire that caused me to ransack her robot last year. A selfish move that almost cost us our bond.

Uncle steps over the butter tubs to consider my work. My cheeks grow hot with shame, and I start to cover the papers.

He stops me, shaking a head of thick, dark hair that matches mine and Lark's, as well as my mom's in every picture I've seen. "Never hide your talent, Doodle-bean. Behind every good inventor is an artist who can map out their visions. What's a clock without the diagram? A house without a blueprint? Okay?" His big brown eyes, bulbous like a frog's yet somehow all the more appealing for it, are intent on me, searching out my response.

I slide my hands down so he can see, and then I smile—half-heartedly—hoping Lark doesn't sense the direction of my thoughts.

"Nix, show me your sketches, huh?" Lark asks, but I can't respond because my drawings are shifting before my eyes, changing shapes, curves unfurling into lines, and lines forming letters: *Tame the Pendulum, Breach the Plinth, Face-Off Time in the Labyrinth.*

Where have I seen that verse before? I rack my brain to remember . . . Lark and I once had to spell "plinth" in our spelling bee. It means a pedestal, a podium, or a stage. I remember the definition, because with that word, she won first place and I dropped to second.

Uncle cries out from behind. I glance over my shoulder just as the floor opens up and swallows him whole. Too late, I twist in my chair to grab him, jostling my knee. A sharp ache awakens behind the scraped skin. My hands feel swollen and hot, and I realize I'm wearing woolen gloves.

Everything comes back to me then: my encounter with Lark's doll at home and ruining Mom's book; my fall on the way to Juniper's boutique; the mural's discrepancies; Uncle's

disappearance at the carnival; the fun house and Jaspar's painted image on front; the verse on the facade; Clarey's and Flannie's separation from me in a maze filled with colors and sounds.

Most importantly, the unavoidable reality that tonight is Halloween, and Lark has been dead and gone for three years.

An agonized scream fists in my throat, unable to release. I've been reliving a memory—locked inside my last evening with my sister. Did I fall and hit my head again? Am I dreaming? Or is this some kind of trick . . . a fabricated reality meant to torture me?

I don't know what's up or down here, but one thing I do know: I hate this moment in time, ever since the child psychiatrist made me talk it out, made me face how jealous I had been of Lark. The doc said it was why I harbored so much survivor guilt—why I couldn't let my sister go. That until I could forgive myself for those negative feelings and the wedge they caused between us, I wouldn't be able to move on.

Instead, I cultivated my guilt and lost the ability to see color, and with it the passion for my art. And to stay afloat in life, to keep moving forward even a little, I commandeered the one part of my sister I both loved and envied most—her mechanical aptitude.

I slump in the chair, my back to the room . . . afraid to see the synthetic narrative again; to playact when Lark's not possibly here.

Deep inside, I want to beg her forgiveness, but this version of her can't be real. Which means she's something else entirely. Something *unreal.*

Icy prickles climb my spine. I turn back to Lark, gripping the chair arms to stay balanced.

The sun becomes a ball and rolls into the room, pulsing like a strobe overhead. Lark faces me, the intense flashes shifting

across grayish skin too tight for her bones, as if the fake daylight has dried her to a desiccated shell. Her jaw stretches inhumanly wide in a silent scream, her bone structure caving in; blackness oozes out of her eye sockets, an inky overflow of criticism and rage. Her arms and legs wither, crinkling and coiling until they vanish inside billowy pant legs and sleeves.

An animal's primal cry pierces my eardrums, and the strain in my vocal cords tells me it's coming from me.

"This isn't happening," I shout. "I don't believe it. None of this is real!"

My hoarse refusal booms like thunder. The sun rolls back outside the window, settling on the horizon in the distance, pink and luminous. In the midst of the dissipating sparkles, my sister's warped image transforms to a young man with wild red hair snarling out from the edges of a ringmaster's top hat; high cheekbones sharp enough to cut glass; and a heart-shaped mouth twisted in a grim sneer.

At last, the deliveryman is here.

14

the plinth and the pendulum

Jaspar stands across from me, overdressed for a school carnival, but on point as a player in a steampunk creep show. The rose-gold pinstripes in his emerald green suit and cape of copper-colored silk match the impervious lenses in his round-framed goggles. His fitted paisley pant legs are tucked into knee-high utilitarian boots with grommet buckles that jingle as he taps his left toe, as if impatient. The cape unfurls at his waist with the movement, baring a dagger with a spiraled handle that blinks through a glowing rainbow of colors. Steam puffs out from three miniature black tubes threaded through the back of his shirt and stretching to the tip of his top hat. They remind me of the smokestacks I've seen on factories in Astoria.

Somewhere underneath my awe of the kaleidoscopic view, there's a niggle—an inkling of déjà vu—where I sense I should fear the shift from a hollow-skulled creature to an unsettlingly pretty guy. Yet I don't. It feels . . . expected. Like I knew all along

he wears more than one face. Yet how could I know something I've never witnessed?

"The famed Phoenix." His whispery husk of a voice breaks the silence between us. "Such lengths, getting you here. Getting you to come out at all. Never seen anyone so afraid of a holiday. Especially one with traditions so quaint and charming as All Hallows' Eve. Corpses walking on their own . . . pumpkins casting flames from empty sockets. To think, of all the monsters we could've chosen to smoke you out, it was a baby doll that forced you from your hidey-hole."

His taunts drizzle over me like a sleet storm, chilling and intrusive. I have to fight the urge to shiver. "You . . . you were in my house?"

"Oh, not exactly me. I had help—a concerted effort, really. We've been making arrangements for this visit for some time."

That's all it takes to slam me back into the moment and why I'm in this maze to begin with.

"We, who?" I ask. "You and our supplier? The owner of the orchard?"

Jaspar chuckles. "Technically, yes. Exclusively, no."

I clench my teeth, annoyed with his evasive-speak. "What's this all about?" I aim my most intense glare at him. "What have you done with my uncle?" I try to stand, but my legs seem to be rooted to the chair. I hold my ground—figuratively—determined to at least appear brave. "*Just tell me where he is*," I hiss.

"Where, indeed?" Jaspar shoves his hat so it hangs off the back of his head, propped up by the smokestack tubing. He rakes long fingernails—silver and coiled like springs—through his hair, getting several stuck before wrestling them free, illustrating

why he always looks so disheveled. "That's yet to be seen, isn't it? It all depends on you."

"What are you talking about?"

He removes his goggles so they dangle from a leather band around his neck, then locks me in that beetle-sheen gaze. "Well, you're the artist. The builder of worlds. Why not simply draw your uncle where you'd like him to be?"

I look down at the sketches on the desk. Is he serious? "How could you know that about me? And how did you reenact this memory?" I glance at the diorama setting still in place around me. This has to be some sort of virtual simulation, but where did our deliveryman get his details? It's impossible that Uncle ever shared anything about me with this creep, considering how protective he is when Jaspar's around.

"Ah, memories." The deliveryman taps a spiraled fingernail against his forehead. "They're the building blocks of your kind. Thus, the stage is set each time you look in a mirror. And, as an artist, your creations are extensions of those past experiences, as well."

Your kind?

He steps closer and his grim sneer widens to show his teeth. In that moment, I'm seeing all his features come into focus for the first time. His teeth are metallic at their pointed tips; and as for his roach-black irises, there's a flicker there I've never noticed. It's as if a curtain drops, revealing two tiny red pupils in each eye, as small as pinholes. When he blinks, white sparks fountain up between the twin dots, like a short circuit passing between electrical wires.

An uneasy twinge unfurls in my belly as I remember a profile for a character in Mystiquiel that I started a while back but

haven't finished yet. It's a changeling-like fey called a dopplegan-glia, with the same dual-pupil peculiarity. The doppleganglia can mimic other characters by adjusting its own inner circuitry, forming a glamour of sorts. Actually, more like a hologram. I planned to incorporate it into my novels, but each time I started adding it in, other than the eyes, I couldn't make out the face clearly. So I scrapped the idea. Now that character sits languish-ing in a spiral at home. Or does it?

Is my doppleganglia imitating our deliveryman?

My throat catches at the absurdity of the thought. No. The *right* question is: How can I be buying into any of this? My draw-ings, my world . . . they're all imaginary.

They can't be here.

My earlier attempt at bravery drains away, leaving my blood cold. I clench my hands around the chair's arms, feeling the weight of makeup, piercings, and zippers across my face as I struggle not to show the horror and incredulity in my expres-sion. "Are—are you saying I somehow brought my memory to life in the mirror? That my imagination created this whole maze without me even knowing it? How can that be?"

"Ah. That's the rub of being an artist, isn't it?" He pauses, clacking his metallic teeth together so they underline his ques-tion with a high, musical ping. "Imagination is like a garden. You must water only the plants you want, and rip out the sneaky weeds winding their way in. If you're not mindful of the gaps between the good seedlings, that's where the wicked off-shoots will crop up. It's your job as the creator to lop off their heads. Otherwise, they could lop off yours—or those of the ones you love."

My heart sinks. If such nonsense were true, it would be more

guilt heaved on top of what I already carry. "So you're saying I caused my uncle's disappearance? This is *my* doing?"

Wearing an annoyed scowl, Jaspar polishes his hat's copper-wire band with a thumb, triggering a few more hazy puffs from the tubes on his back. "Oh, stop being so dramatic. You're not all-powerful. Nor are you power*less*. You have the means to get in and bend things to your will. Your uncle's already there, waiting for you to find him. Simply watch for clues that will lead you to him. Just don't be afraid to take off those mitts and get your hands dirty. Understand?"

Speechless, I look down at my gloves, more confused than ever.

Jaspar slides the goggles into place over his electrified eyes. "I suppose you'll figure it out once you get inside." He prods his hat back onto his head. "But I suggest you don't tarry too long here. The clock has just begun to tick, and time passes on a knife's blade in this maze. When you find the key, don't hesitate to use it."

I flinch as Jaspar drags his prismatic dagger from its sheath and jabs the razor-edge into the skin beneath his jawbones. He begins to saw, cutting his face away as easily as slicing a ham. Bile rises in my throat and I gulp as the flayed edges curl and gape. Even while dreading the blood and gore, I can't stop looking. I've seen enough of Clarey's SFX creations that I've developed a stomach for the more gruesome aspects, and I try to convince myself that's what this is. A costume . . . a performance.

However, instead of a mix of corn syrup, nondairy creamer, and red food coloring drizzling out from a severed prosthetic, there's a white glittery shimmer, like light hitting a thousand facets in crackling increments.

In a blink, the effect spreads to his skin and clothes, as well

as the bunk beds, floor, and wall—transforming the diorama to diamonds.

Yet it's not diamonds . . . it's an infinite number of tiny mirrors.

Within moments the sunbeams from the window burnish to dazzling hues and catch fire to Jaspar and the room. There's no heat radiating from the reflections. Instead, they give off a frosty chill.

My mind spins in disbelief and confusion; Jaspar or someone working with him was in my house this morning after Uncle left, putting everything in place to chase me out. How did they get in without me seeing them? How did they know what buttons to push?

Maybe the same way they knew intimate details of my private memory . . .

I don't have time to speculate on any optical illusions or the things Jaspar said. The mirrored chair I'm seated in begins to crack—the snap of a lake freezing over. I leap off just before it shatters into pieces along with the diamond desk and its pencils and papers, each one casting off blinding chinks of light. If my drawings were the key to anything, they're gone now. I wince, and using my gloves for shade, back away.

A masculine wail sounds in the distance. A dog's frightened bark joins in. It's Clarey, shouting for help. Either he found Uncle and he's hurt, or Clarey himself is in trouble.

Determined to find them, I wield my arm across my eyes to ward off the brightness and start forward. The ground quakes beneath me. Stumbling, I grab blindly and catch a railing. A loud clang rattles my bones as the metal frame of earlier drops back into place, caging me again.

The whoosh of pistons and motors muffles Clarey's screams, but I still can't see over the mirrored prisms of sunshine. Only the harbor of my arm salvages my sight.

I'm at the mercy of the platform, the motor thrumming beneath my feet. It carries me away, leaving the spectacular inferno behind, and shadows rise around me again. Soon a grouping of lights appears in the air just inches away—flickering bluish Edison bulbs, a soothing balm after the blinding light I just left. The bulbs float freely in a cluster, as if they were glassy balloons with copper ribbon tails. I shove a hand outside the bars, catch the ribbons, then wind them around the framework to keep the gentle glow close so I won't be left in the dark again. There's not a mirror in sight now, only other metal walkways as far as I can see within the circle of light.

I yelp when the gear shuttling me slams into something solid. The cage lifts, breaking the bulb-bouquet's tails. The lights hover out of reach, yet oddly, still follow close behind, like they're tied to me with invisible strings. There's a crunch of steel on steel beneath my feet, interlocking gears that propel me forward. The progression is swift, and with no railings on either side, I have to keep up the pace or I'll tip off the edge and into the snarling, pounding machinery below.

My entire body lurches when the conveyer-style walkway comes to a jolting stop, as if someone put the brakes on; I manage to stay balanced by lunging and landing on my good knee.

An excited woof makes me look up. Flannie leaps down from a sinking ride that could double as a Ferris-wheel's bucket seat. The soft light tints her fur to cornflower and powder blue. I call her name, my throat swelling with relief. She licks my chin and I

nuzzle her fuzzy head. Clarey drops down, just a few steps behind.

My happiness to see him shrinks to worry when I realize he's lost the duffel bag, and is wearing his mask again. Something bad had to have happened for him to seek his hiding place. Did Jaspar or something from my imagination attack him?

The irrational thought would make me laugh aloud if I hadn't seen for myself that my characters . . . my world . . . appear to be making live appearances somehow.

I shoot to my feet and rush over. Clarey wraps his arms around me—holding on so tight I feel every tensed muscle.

For one elated minute, I bury my nose against him, inhaling flowers, chemicals, and his own delicate brand of sweat. Then I notice his erratically beating heart and how the brittle tension stretches from his muscles to his trembling bones. I've never seen him have a panic attack, but I'm guessing this could be the start of one. Or the end . . .

I stretch him to arm's length to study his eyes inside the triangular holes. I can't even appreciate the ability to see their color again; they're watery and racked with fear or dread. Maybe both.

"You saw Uncle, didn't you? He's hurt. Is that how you lost my duffel, trying to help him?"

Clarey shakes his head and clears his throat behind the mask's bulging lips, as if searching for the strength to answer. "I—I didn't see him. My BAHA . . . it broke." He says this as if in a trance. So he's not in shock over something he saw? He's just worried about the expense Juniper will have to shoulder for replacing his BAHA?

But I don't get the chance to clarify. A loud clank shakes our

platform, and a rusted chain-link fence, at least ten feet tall, rises from the edges and snaps into place, penning us from all sides in a space no bigger than a walk-in closet. Though I'm relieved our trio managed to stay together this time, Uncle Thatch is still alone somewhere, possibly at the end of one of the walkways now out of our reach.

As if to compound my unspoken fear, the gears and cogs making up the maze—all the winding bridges and paths—start to shift, taking vertical, parallel positions. Clarey and I watch helplessly as, with a loud grinding creak, they whir outward, locking into notches on the walls like tiles, leaving our domed space suspended alone in the dark void. The gears spin in aimless loops on the distant walls, jagged wheels going nowhere, and leaving me no pathway to Uncle Thatch.

Biting back a sob, I look down. There's nothing below—only deep unseeable depths where the blue glow won't reach.

"How high are we?" I shout over the chugging gears surrounding us. "Are we just drifting here, or is this a pedestal?"

No sooner have I said this than I think of the odd quote on the front of the fun house, the same one that I saw transform from my sketches in the memory trap.

"A pedestal . . . is a plinth," I mumble.

Clarey's eyes brighten with something akin to understanding, but a shuddering gong, like the voice of a giant clock, sounds off three times and interrupts his response. Before my skeleton has even stopped vibrating, Clarey grips my biceps and drags me into a crouch as a huge shadow swings across us from the emptiness above. A rush of wind follows in its wake. Flannie yelps and cowers between us. The giant form swoops back in the opposite direction, and the bluish light flashes across a gargantuan silver

blade—shaped like a hatchet—strung by thick ropes from the upmost center of the endless, obscured ceiling.

"A—A clock's pendulum," I stammer. This must be what Jaspar meant, about time passing on a blade.

A scraping, metallic screech prefaces a shower of sparks, the blade eating through the top of our fence like a knife cutting butter while leaving behind the stench of burnt sulfur. The deadly pendulum drops closer and closer to our heads with each sway, slicing through the chain links—inch by inch. Clarey and I drop to hands and knees.

My pulse ratchets up, and I curl wool-tipped fingers against the metal floor. What was it the verse said? I try to concentrate in spite of Clarey's ragged breaths inside his mask, still wondering in the back of my mind what happened to him while we were apart.

"Look," Clarey says, surprising me with the steadiness of his hand as he points down where another pendulum appears from out of nowhere, moving perpendicular to the first. This one must be suspended from the ceiling off-center, because the ropes glide by without touching our fence, and the sequence of its swaying is timed perfectly with the pendulum above, so they pass like deadly cradles swinging from tree branches in the night.

On each undulation, the lower pendulum's top surface skims by a few inches below our pedestal; it's flat and looks as wide and long as the storeroom's floor at the bakery. Unlike the first one, this pendulum continues without descending in elevation, back and forth, holding its bearings. It's close . . . close enough we could touch it if we could somehow get out of our chain-link prison.

And then it hits me: "'Tame the pendulum. Breach the plinth.' The quote on the fun house's facade?"

Clarey's eyes widen to the size of the mask's holes. "Right . . . tame the pendulum. You tame a horse by—"

"Riding it," we say simultaneously.

Clarey and I initiate army-crawling, scooting with our elbows and dragging our torsos and legs, trying to stay as low as possible to avoid getting caught by the blade, which has already eaten through half of the fence's height. We choose opposing sides and search for some weakness in the metal links, or a gate that's camouflaged somehow.

No luck. The fence is solid.

Another squealing, jolting swoop slices by, ripping through metal and missing us by a mere two feet or so. "Lay, Flannie!" Clarey yells, and drags her close as he and I sprawl on our bellies. Our gazes meet and I feel the terror reflected in his eyes burrowing inside my own gut. Just a few more strokes and we'll all be left in shreds.

As if triggered by the press of his clothes against the platform, Clarey digs in his front pocket and draws out Lark's wire cutters. Somehow, we both forgot about them.

"Do it!" I shout.

Clarey springs into action, using the tool to bite through the steel wires. The diagonal jaws cut at an angle, leaving flat tips behind. Clarey's propped on his elbows, cutting the last link to open a big enough hole to squeeze through, when I shove him flat to the floor just as the pendulum gores into the tip of the pumpkin stem on his headpiece. The latex topper sticks to the blade and lifts away, taking his Velcro skullcap with it. His black curls spring free, then his white streak follows suit. Only his mask remains, leaving him oddly half-formed . . . part jack-o'-lantern, part Clarey, but at least he still has his head intact.

Although my tackle caused him to lose the wire cutters, he nods in gratitude. As the pendulum sways away, dropping the stem and cap into the darkness below, Clarey shoves the outline he carved in the chain links free. It falls without a sound, causing me to question if there's a bottom to this place at all.

Since my hands are gloved, I bend as many sharp edges outward as possible so we can ease through without catching clothes or fur, or gouging skin.

Once we've belly crawled enough to clear the fence, we pause at the edge. Clarey grips Flannie's vest harness to keep her close as the lower pendulum moves toward us, slowly aligning beneath our pedestal.

The moment it's centered, I take a breath, and holding Clarey's free hand, I nudge the three of us to leap. We land, grunting and rolling along the moving expanse. I snatch the rope rooted at the axis. Clarey grips my hand tight while he helps Flannie climb closer to the middle. As soon as we're balanced, we wrap the rope around our arms with Flannie sandwiched between us and sit up to catch our breaths, grateful to be out of the hatchet blade's range.

We swing, gusts of hot, fumy air raking over us with each fluctuation. A wailing screech sounds above as the blade finishes off the remaining chain links and grinds them to dust. The gears that formed our pedestal split apart, allowing the dangerous pendulum to continue its downward course while altering trajectory just enough to slant toward our pendulum's rope.

"It's going to cut us loose!" I scream.

Clarey and I both look downward into the darkness. Just then, my flickering Edison bulb bouquet drops lower, its light illuminating a stage some two stories below. The same key-shaped

tree that I saw on the fun house's facade, heavy with fruits, is painted in its middle, although this time I can make out all the colors.

The key . . .

Jaspar said not to hesitate to use it.

I nudge Clarey and nod toward it. "That's our way out."

"How do you figure?" he asks. "All I see is a painting."

"There's got to be some way to go through the stage; maybe a trapdoor. Why else would it be a key?"

He looks above us at the oncoming hatchet, then mimes concern about how we'll get close enough to jump safely onto a platform so far down.

It's then I notice Flannie digging at a small metal box that protrudes from the surface where we sit, right next to the suspension's core. One hand anchored to the rope, I prod her muzzle aside and lift the lid. A red tab rests in the middle, with a space above and below, suggesting it's a switch that controls our rope's length by either taking up slack or loosening it. That's only a guess . . . because there are no instructions.

"Should I try it?" I ask Clarey.

"Worst case," he mumbles behind his mask, "it'll blow us to kingdom come. Pretty sure that beats being sliced in half by a giant ax aimed at your back."

It would lift my spirits to hear the sarcasm beneath the huskiness of his voice—if there wasn't the possibility he's right.

I'm still debating when Flannie shoves my hand aside and nudges the button with her nose. It flicks upward, and Clarey and I tense, waiting.

A sudden jerk of our rope stops us midswing. We're dangling in place like toys on a clothesline—a rag doll and a pumpkin

puppet hung out to dry—when a loud creak, followed by a pounding snap, erupts overhead. We have little time to react as the pendulum above us releases from its rope and plummets our direction.

Not even thinking, I slap the switch downward, and at the last second, our pendulum reactivates and we swing out of the way, barely missing the giant hatchet rushing by at breakneck speed. With a gut-clenching crack of splintering boards, it severs the wooden stage below wide open.

The sound of an ocean and the scent of brine burst upward at the breach. Our pendulum sways, lifting us high to the right, and then dipping toward the center. We're no lower than before, but there's an opening now that we can jump through, should we dare.

Clarey cups where his left ear hides in his mask, obviously worried about water damage. I don't have a chance to convince him or myself before a giant crest of white swells up from the darkness and snatches the three of us off our perch.

The last thing I can think to do is catch my breath and hold, as the wave curls its fist around us and plunges us into the roaring ocean below.

motherboard

Through the crystal ball—our eye in the sky—we observe her fall into the sea. We can't react. We won't remit. Even as the crown and throne begin to crumble, our heart persists on its assigned algorithm. Though the beats skip and groan to the demands of synthesis and assimilation, though we strain for the actuality of individuality—to taste, to touch, an eager and angry lust—our work is yet unfinished. She will not deter us. She'll not lose us what we crave. We have earned this destruction. Yes. We have earned the end to everything.

15

skin to bone, steel to rust, ash to ash, and dust to dust

I bob up from the depths, gasping for breath, and drag myself onto a sandbar where the water shallows out, unconcerned that my gloves stayed dry while the rest of me shivers wet and cold. It's not the strangest thing to happen today. Not by a long shot.

My eyes burn from the brine, making everything blurred. A shadowy sanctuary loops around me, spacious and scented of fish and a pungent sort of mustiness . . . maybe rust combined with algae? Every sound bounces off the walls, rounded and swollen. The trickle of water underneath and beside me brings clarity: I'm in a sea cave.

"Clar-ey," I call out, sputtering salt water between syllables.

"Here," he responds at my right, his echo playing tag with mine.

"Your BAHA?" I ask.

"It's working now. Maybe the impact of the water? I guess my mask protected it like an aqua sleeve. There's some static in the background, but I can make out vibrations super clearly.

Flannie's panting feels like a whirlwind in my skull." Rustling movements follow as Clarey inches toward the collie over the rocky terrain.

Strange that I hadn't even heard her. "So, she's okay then?" I ask, propped up on my elbows while I blot my eyes with woolen fingertips.

Flannie shakes her fur from somewhere between us, slapping us both with droplets of water.

"Yeah." There's relief in Clarey's voice. "Good girl. Let's check your harness. Wait, stop licking." He half snorts. "If you let me get the mask off, I can kiss you properly."

His comment is simultaneously adorable and surprising. I thought he already had the mask off; his voice isn't as muffled as it was in the maze—possibly an effect of the cave's acoustics.

Flannie whines, and Clarey makes a pained grunt. "Quiet, girl."

She whimpers again, though softer this time—a confused, disoriented sound. I can't blame her after what we just went through.

Clarey coos to soothe her. The sweet interaction bolsters my gratitude that the three of us made it out of the fun house alive. There's still so much to figure out, but I'm thrilled they're here with me.

Still, that leaves Uncle out there somewhere. Our delivery-man said he was *inside*, which I can only hope is this beach where we landed; he also said that I'll have to "bend things to my will" to help him—whatever that means.

A worried frown stretches my lips and my eyebrows, tugging my piercings in familiar places, assurance that the rings in my skin remain intact. This, I expected, but I also notice a pull through my costume zippers. They didn't wash off, which is almost as

weird as the cloth around my hands being so warm and stiff it could have dried in the sun.

I sit up and lean my back against a large rock, blinking hard to clear my vision. The far end of the cave yawns wide, revealing a beach outside. Luminous moonlight glitters silver on the sands, a few strands reaching inside to glaze the cave's dark, jagged walls. I'm instantly reminded of my spelunking excursion with Lark at Haystack Rock. In fact, this place looks so similar—minus the pink sunset—that I could be tripping down memory lane again.

As if triggered by the thought, I feel a flutter at the outer edge of my left collarbone where my lark tattoo sits; I must've strained the muscles while escaping the pendulum, causing them to spasm.

I press my hand across my T-shirt, willing the sensation to stop. The sounds of Clarey and Flannie provide proof that I'm not reliving a memory again. Neither one of them accompanied us on that day in the cave. It's a relief. Not only do I *not* want to endure any more painful, shaming moments like the one in the maze, but I can't have Clarey be an audience to them. I can't have him know that I was the cause of Lark losing that first-place ribbon in seventh grade. I don't want him to glimpse that flaw, to see me for the jealous and insecure girl I once was.

Then my logic kicks in: whatever happened to Clarey while we were apart threatened him personally. Jaspar mentioned mirrors setting the stage for our memories. Most likely, like me, Clarey faced something from his past. The loss of Breonna, or that incident in Chicago he won't talk about.

I'm a jerk to be relieved by that. But he can never know how much I envied Lark—for her relationship to him, but even more, for her talents; otherwise, he might question, like I do, if I

somehow subconsciously wanted to be the only sister. If that's why I slept through Lark's final, thrashing grasp at life.

My heart withers at the appalling possibility. It's something I've struggled with for so long; something I didn't even share with the psychiatrist or Uncle.

Uncle.

I've got to get my bearings so we can find him. My stomach clenches with a hollow growl, and chill bumps raze my skin. I'm such a mess, I don't even know where to begin.

"Seriously, stop licking," Clarey grumbles to Flannie in the darkness. "If you let me get off your wet vest, we'll go exploring. Okay, Sherlock?"

Exploring. He's right. We begin by going outside. I start crawling my way across slimy rocks toward them, wheezing when my bad knee rakes a pointed surface.

"You okay?" Clarey asks.

"Yeah." I rub the sore spot, my focus shifting to the cave floor where the rocks break up to form small basins.

I inch closer, captivated by glimmers of ghostly white inside the inky puddles. It takes a minute to make sense of them, but I soon recognize the blurred shapes of starfish. There are other tiny sea creatures, too—spiky slugs, seahorses, shrimp, and even frogfish walking on their front fins in the shallows—all varying in size from cigars to fingernails to pinheads. The one thing each one has in common is a bleached-out bioluminescence: soft, hazy outlines of white beneath ripples of dark water.

Has my renewed guilt over Lark stolen my ability to see color again? Or is something even weirder going on?

Ignoring the sounds of Clarey and Flannie across the cave, I fixate on a starfish the size of my hand—leaning across a puddle

to refine the details. Its spiny translucent skin encases a framework of wires and circuitry that lights it up from inside. As I'm watching, a slug, with luminous spikes that sway in the water like fiber-optic strands, gets too close. The starfish extends its stomach out of a metallic, beakish mouth to cover the digestible parts of its prey, regurgitating the spikes now coated in rust. While digesting, the starfish curls its five legs outward and inward in an inflating and deflating motion, similar to how pneumatic car suspension systems pump air in and out of rubber bellows. It's like the SYFY and Animal Planet Channel came together for an under-the-sea special.

I exhale slowly, afraid to stir the water with my breath. The starfish looks almost engineered, yet it's a living organism, needing nourishment to survive. At the same time, parts of it seem to be severely damaged, as it spews out rust after catching its prey. The colony of starfish surrounding it share the strange attributes. Even the tiniest creatures, the shrimp, appear to be galvanized, stimulated to move by the sparks inside their bodies that cast starry imprints along the cave's ceiling and walls, while also leaving currents of rusty red to trail their movements in the water. Come to think of it, the rust is the only color I see in here.

The whole scene is bizarre, beautiful, and unsettling—all at once. This kind of marine life doesn't belong in any conventional ocean, yet fits perfectly in the world I've been drawing for almost three years.

Mystiquiel.

My empty stomach flips at the name. I recall Jaspar's implication that I should just draw my uncle where I want him. It was an obvious nod to my artistic ability . . . to my creations. He even mentioned me being a builder of worlds. So has Uncle slipped

into my dreamscape somehow? Did the gear-and-mirror maze form some kind of bridge to my novels?

No. It makes more sense that I'm not really seeing or experiencing any of these things; that I hit my head harder than I thought last night and have an injury causing episodes of delirium.

I rub my nape, craving someone else's eyes, someone else's logic. "Hey, Clarey, can you come check this out?"

He groans. "Give me a sec. Flannie's acting cuckoo. I thought she was just uncomfortable in her vest but— Hey!"

I glance up at his shout. Clarey's silhouette shifts back and forth, he and Flannie engaged in a tug-of-war. He yelps in pain and moves into a pale beam of light refracted off one of the puddles.

"Flannie, *release*." He wrestles against her teeth clamped over his latex nose. "Ouch! That . . . hurts. RELEASE!" She lets go then, her tail drooping. With an annoyed *ruff*, she spins around and shoots out of the cave onto the beach.

"Flannie!" Clarey grunts under his hands where they cradle his fake nose.

The moonlit sands illuminate her trek. It strikes me that I've never seen her run so smoothly. It's a wonder her leg's harness and snowshoe managed to stay in place, and that the salt water didn't damage the inner workings. Another oddity I can't reconcile.

"She's found something," Clarey says, about three beats before I hear the collie's eager woof outside. His BAHA's ability to pick up sounds has definitely risen to a new level.

I carefully pick my way over the slippery rocks to where Clarey's still cradling his prosthetic.

"Did she ruin it?" I ask as I squat in front of him. He shrugs.

I peel free of my gloves and drop them atop Flannie's discarded vest, so I'll have a better grip to help loosen his costume. I tug at the pumpkin's ridges where they curve around his chin, but can't find the edges. "It's hard to see over here. Maybe we should get you into the moonlight."

"No, wait." He strains against my next attempt at pulling. "Something's wrong. It feels stuck. Like, *really* stuck." As if just noticing my own costume, he cups my face. "Your makeup didn't even come off." He taps a finger first across the black triangles around my eyes, then across my zippers. He studies me, thoughtful and intense. My stomach flutters with each line he traces, the warmth of his touch along the metal teeth almost painful somehow. "Whoa. Maybe the salt water strengthened the spirit gum . . . but that's not supposed to happen. It's not normal."

"Huh. Seems to be a lot of 'not normal' going around tonight," I say.

"Yeah, can't argue that." His palm still cradles my chin. I'd like to lean closer for comfort, to sit down next to him, face-to-face, and sort this all out. I've got to tell him about the grimalkins in the mirrors, my ability to see color, about Jaspar. About the marine life and the weird theory taking shape in my mind—but no time right now. We have to get outside and find Flannie before she wanders too far.

As if spurred by my thoughts, the border collie returns to the mouth of the cave and yips at us scoldingly, then trots off again, prompting an unusual jingly sound across the sand.

Clarey's intense focus drops from me. He rubs his masked nose again absently. "Maybe she's found your uncle's scent again. We'll take care of our costumes later. I've got adhesive solvent in your duffel."

He and I both catch our breaths, coming to the realization simultaneously: in all the chaos of escaping the pendulum, we forgot that we lost the bag and everything in it. A pang of regret trails along my sternum. Not only have I lost Dad's pocket watch, I've lost my mom's book, too.

"Oh shiz. I'm so sorry, Nix." Clarey tilts his head, and a strand of moonlight captures the apologetic gaze embedded in the eyeholes. His irises burn bright blue and gold against the black makeup.

I'm shocked that I can make out his eye color. In fact, his mask looks orange now, as it should've all along. *Weird.* And weirder yet, his makeup hasn't smeared any more than mine.

"It's all right," I finally answer, because I'm pretty sure there was nothing in the duffel that could help us figure out what's going on around us.

Together, we clamber toward the cave mouth. We step out onto an abandoned coast that looks so much like Cannon Beach it makes me do a double take. Even in the distance, through sweeps of moonlit fog, I can see the tops of circus tents, strips of black and white appearing intermittently. Their entrances are hidden on the other side. But judging by the moving silhouettes within, the carnival appears to still be going. We must've only been in the maze for a little bit, although it felt like an eternity. Which begs the question: How did it spit us out all the way over here?

Flannie prances in circles around us, stirring up that unfamiliar jingling sound, but I barely notice. I'm fully focused behind me, staring at the cave we just left. Somehow, the ocean's waves have carried it off, impossibly far. Far enough that its full shape rises to the sky, monolithic and imposing, confirming my suspicions.

"That's Haystack Rock, right?" I ask Clarey, unable to look anywhere but at our surroundings.

"Uh . . . yeah? It's like we stepped back out where we first went in. Our walk to the carnival," he says. "We're on Cannon Beach."

"Or a reasonable facsimile," I amend.

"Yeah, a black-and-white facsimile. Those tents were red and orange striped earlier . . ."

"You mean, you don't see any colors either?"

"Everything looks grayscale—silver sands, ashen mist, black water, and slate rocks. No color except for the three of us."

"Clarey, I'm seeing exactly the same thing. It's like I took a set of markers to you and Flannie and me, but haven't filled in the setting yet."

"What?" He turns to me. "So . . . your retinas?"

"I guess they're fixed somehow? It happened when we stepped into the maze."

"No way." His stunned reaction is proof I don't have a head injury. He's seeing all the same deviations I am; I'm not sure whether to be comforted or terrified by that fact.

Flannie yips at us, bringing our full attention to how each paw jingles as it stirs up the terrain. Frowning, I burrow my boot's tip into the filaments and kick up a spray. It flutters down in a tintinnabulation similar to coins drizzling into an aluminum bin—yet smaller, brighter, softer. Musical and stirring. We're not standing on grains of sand; instead, it's remnants of steel or iron, or maybe even silver, judging by the absence of warm color tones.

Clarey drops to his knees and scoops some in his palms, letting them slip through his fingers to release another tinny song. "Wait. Is this—?"

"Metal shavings," I answer, sharing his awe as I take in the scope of the beach . . . how many millions there must be. It's hard to be sure, with the swirling mist blocking our view in places.

"Yeah . . . I've seen this stuff. In sixth grade, Lark went through that phase where she crafted sculptures out of it."

I nod on a private memory of my own. She once wove a bird's nest from copper fibers, to cradle an egg I found under the porch swing. I wanted it to belong to a phoenix . . . she insisted it would be a lark. It never hatched, so we finally broke it open. Inside, there was nothing but pale gray powder. I said it was a phoenix turned to ash; Lark claimed it was dust from a lark's bones. Both guesses were illogical. Uncle—ever the voice of reason—said it had been a rotten yolk that dried out due to a microscopic crack we hadn't noticed in the shell. Lark shrugged it off, but I regretted being so irrational. What were the odds a mythological creature would've set up camp in our front yard, after all?

I glare at the circus tents in the distance. *What were the odds, indeed.* My throat burns on each inhalation as I'm bombarded with thoughts of grimalkins and doppleganglias.

I stare up at the moon, desperate for orientation. It's a mistake. The orb appears glossy and iridescent—a glass ball hovering in the sky with light refracting through the center. Kind of like a giant, magical eye.

I shudder as the thought awakens the sense of someone watching us. I shake it off; it's just my imagination filling in the blanks because of the thick gray fog that diffuses the moon's light and blurs its outline. The scent of melting wax fills my nostrils, suggesting that instead of fog, it's smoke or smog.

Closer to the ground where we stand, the haze clears in

intervals, as if on a breeze, though the air is motionless and claustrophobic.

"Clarey . . . there's no wind."

"Um, yeah. I noticed that, too," he answers upon standing, then clicks his tongue at Flannie when she appears a few feet away between clearings of smoke.

She bounds toward us through the gray murkiness, then races back to dig at something slumped in the shavings. Dread grips my heart tight.

"Uncle?" The word stumbles out on less than a whisper.

Clarey takes my hand, and we freeze in place, waiting for the smoke to thin so we can see the contours more clearly. As the object comes into view in intervals, a wrinkled army-green lump with straps is exposed.

"Is that your duffel?" Clarey says skeptically. We release hands and shuffle forward, stirring a symphony through the metal shavings. "It's like someone dropped it here, knowing we'd end up on the beach. How's that even possible?"

"How's *any* of this possible?" I reply, and catch his arm so he'll stop for a minute. "Okay." I steel myself. "I've got to tell you what I'm thinking, but you won't believe it. About . . . this place. Where we are . . ." I squeeze his elbow and turn him toward me so he'll meet my gaze. "I saw Jaspar in the maze, and he told me—" My explanation breaks as I see his face fully illuminated.

Clarey crimps his brow. "Told you what?"

I gulp, studying the wrinkles as they move along his mask's orange forehead . . . staring at the thick eyebrows matching his hair. His mask didn't have eyebrows before, did it? The furrows in his forehead deepen, highlighting his scar—which

shouldn't even be a part of the orange latex. It's like the indentation rose to the surface somehow.

"Nix, c'mon. What about Jaspar?" He shuffles his hand through his white curls, weaving them into the surrounding darker strands. His orange slitted nostrils pulse, drawing my attention to bite marks and dried red drizzles, as if Flannie's tug-of-war from earlier drew blood. From a prosthetic . . . ?

A dizzying nausea swarms my belly.

The movements on his mask . . . they respond like real muscles. The way his high cheekbones jut out above the pumpkin's ridges and move when he talks and blows out a frustrated breath. Those weren't there before. And how the bulges in the orange-colored rind taper and fade into the smooth brown skin of his chin. The only things still the same are the triangular eye openings with his thick lashes and beautiful eyes set deep inside, surrounded by bruise-tinged makeup. Otherwise, there are no seams . . . no gaps. No open edges.

"Nix, what's with you?" His swollen latex lips turn down, and I notice minuscule lines in the fleshy rolls, the same as a real mouth.

"You're . . . frowning," I manage.

"Well, this is a lot to take in. I think a frown is warranted about now." He pauses then. "Wait, how do you know I'm frowning?" He feels around the lower half of his face. "Did the bottom of my mask come off?"

Eddies of smoke snake around him. Upon each momentary clearing, I'm slammed with the inconceivable theory: *No, it didn't come off. It's becoming part of your skin and bones.* My stomach drops, skidding all the way into the ends of my toes. *That's* why Flannie attacked his face. She *was* confused. Just like me.

No. I refuse to believe it. We just need to peel it off.

I jump into action, striding toward the duffel where Flannie has resumed digging her nose inside a half-opened pocket. "We have to get that adhesive solvent. *Now.*" I kick up metal shavings with my determined pace.

"Wait . . . I hear something, up there." Clarey grabs my elbow to stop me and looks toward the sky, but I can't see anything.

In a matter of seconds, a shadow appears, high overhead, silent and stealthy, emerging in intervals where the smoke clears, then disappearing again where it thickens. The BAHA really is working overtime for Clarey to notice it before Flannie. A second later, she starts barking in frenzied circles.

Clarey tugs me backward. My butt lands in his lap and he wraps his arms around me. Any other time, any other place, my nerves would have come alive at the intimacy of the action. Instead, every part of me shuts down with dread at the thing descending from the sky toward us.

"Don't move." Clarey's command stirs the fine hairs behind my ear.

The silhouette slices through the fray—wings spread wide and reflecting the moonlight in shiny flashes. Now I hear it: the whir of gears, gusts of wind stirring through our hair.

With a triumphant hooting call, an owl swoops in and seizes the bag's straps with metallic talons, lifting it away. Flannie leaps forward and snaps her teeth, missing its rusted tail feathers by only a breath.

16

filigree, feathers, and fetlocks

Clarey and I sit with mouths agape, watching the mechanical thief lift into the sky, lugging my duffel like a prized fish it snatched from the sea.

"Whoa. Wowee-wow-wow," Clarey mutters under his breath, his arms tightening around my waist for anchor. "That looked like . . ."

"Filigree," I finish when he seems unable to close the thought.

His thighs stiffen underneath mine. "Nah. Can't be."

"It looked exactly like her," I insist. Still captivated by the silhouette overhead, I battle an odd twinge . . . something between pride and panic. "Wings and body of both synthetic and real feathers. What other bird has silver aluminum and white fleecy down over a gut of gears and cogs?"

Clarey doesn't answer, so I roll off his lap onto my knees, and use one naked fingertip to sketch the owl's shape into the metal shavings. Her snowy-owl's head that could've come off a taxidermist's shelf; her steel black talons. My fingertip moves on muscle

memory alone, buried in the filaments, as I stare up where the winged silhouette hoots and circles in the hazy moonlight, as though waiting for something. Or *someone*. My pulse spikes at that thought and my finger stalls. "I didn't get a good look at her eyes. Did you?"

Instead of responding, Clarey touches my wrist and nods toward the drawings I've blindly made in the shavings. Only then do I see *and* feel the changes: the wiry filaments have shifted to a saltlike grittiness everywhere I touched. In the pale light, a warm, golden hue chases the outlines. I frown, then splay my bare palms on the ground. The metal responds in kind, first leaving imprints of my hands, then spreading across the entire beach—a transformation from silvery shavings to luminous golden granules.

I meet Clarey's bewildered gaze, once again shaken to the core by the way his mask seems to be reshaping into something lifelike.

"Sand," he whispers. "You turned it into glowing sand."

I'm sorting through my jumbled thoughts when Clarey belatedly answers my question about the owl: "Yeah, the eyes. You're right. One looked real . . . the other sparked electric. That bird is the spitting image of your Goblin King's pet."

The spike in my pulse climbs. What if Perish is also real? What if he somehow already knows we're here? And where *is* here, exactly?

It can't be what I'm thinking. It just can't.

"An endless ocean without any color." Clarey looks all around us. "No other humans in sight. If we were to walk farther, I'm guessing we'd find a town like Astoria. With goblins and faeries and more of your creatures . . . things of metal and magic. Nix,

it's like that fun house was a pathway that opened to your graphic novels."

Just that easily, he blurts what I haven't had the guts to admit to myself. Clarey is like my uncle; he's the voice of reason. For him to think stepping into Mystiquiel is reasonable enough to conjecture out loud . . . well, that makes it a lot harder for me to deny.

"Maybe it's too wild a guess, but this place just had a major reaction to your touch." He gestures to the lambent sands, punctuating his point. "Seeing is believing." Then, voice deep and strained, he asks: "But how could we be here? How could any of this be—here?"

I chew on my lip ring, struggling not to focus on his face. Trying not to compare the altered state of his mask with what just happened to the beach. Jaspar told me to take my gloves off and get my hands dirty . . . he said I could bend things to my will. But I *can't* be responsible for the changes in Clarey, can I? He's not my creation.

"Please, oh please." My voice cracks on the plea. "Just let us be asleep."

Clarey shakes his head. "What are the odds we'd both be dreaming the same thing?"

I moan and search for my gloves in my pockets, terrified to touch anything else without them on, but they're gone.

"Wait . . ." I pat down my jacket and jeans. "Where are my gloves? Did I leave them in the cave? I need my gloves!"

Clarey lifts himself to his knees and cups my leather sleeves to stop my searching. He raises me so we're face-to-face. "Calm down, Nix."

I fake a laugh to keep from screaming. "Calm down? If what

you said is right, you've no idea what kind of havoc these hands can wreak."

"Would you stop that? I mean, look. Just like everything else you've ever drawn or painted, it's beautiful."

Sweet, supportive Clarey. It hurts to watch him scan the glimmering beach in awe, as if that's the only thing I've touched, the only thing I've altered.

Flannie yips excitedly, demanding our attention, moving efficiently despite the wavering terrain. Her leg is still hairless, formed of black-steel and carbon rods, but there's no ignoring how smooth her gait is now. How the snowshoe attachment appears to have melded to the metal, and how quietly the mechanical limb runs. The harness straps no longer make parts through her hair; they've disappeared into her skin—become part of her. I haven't touched her leg since we've been here, but it *is* my design, my creation.

I steal another glance at Clarey, who's studying Flannie's leg, too. He rubs his chin, deep in thought, then his hand moves across his latex lips. The golden sands reflect off his eyes, and the perception forming there fills me with dread.

I've had longer to digest all of this, so he's a few steps behind; but he's gaining ground fast. I can't let him connect the dots and be slammed with the blow of what's going on with his face. Whatever happened to him in Chicago was enough to make him feel the need to hide behind masks again, but that's a far cry from *becoming* a mask.

I'll tell him, but only after I discover how to fix it. How to fix everything.

"Did you find something, Flannie?" I blurt for a distraction. Relief sags my shoulders when Clarey drops to hands and knees

to help the collie explore the dent left in the sand where the duffel lay earlier.

"What is it, Sherlock?" he asks.

Bits of white poke out of the shallow pit. She clamps one with her teeth, tugging a cloth free—the same object she pulled from the bag before the owl took to the sky. It must've been buried when the shavings became sand.

As she yanks it loose, a band of silver-wired beings, the size of monarch butterflies, comes with it, clinging to the opposite edge. They chirp and chatter angrily while trying to drag the cloth back underground.

Pack rat faeries.

I gasp and scramble to stand. Making the connection the same instant I do, Clarey jumps to his feet and releases a hysterical sound, somewhere between a cough and a snort.

In my stories, they're the collectors for the Goblin King, bringing him anything that washes up on the beach and doesn't belong in his world, so he can destroy it or send it back where it came from.

The faeries glare at us, baring teeth the color and size of pencil leads. They're similar to the bird's nest Lark made years ago: bodies, arms, legs, heads, and wings woven from pieces of wire. Several have corrosion dusting their limbs; some are even missing a hand or a foot where they've rusted off. The gray wiry manes on their heads bristle with circuitry from end to end, causing a globular effect that illuminates velvety ratlike faces—the only part of them that's natural and not synthetic.

Cursing and spitting, they surrender the folded cloth to Flannie, then flutter into the air. The band forms a cloud around us—electric dandelions gone to seed and caught on the wind. Flannie

barks, attempting to herd them like she did the birds when we first arrived at the carnival earlier . . . what seems a lifetime ago.

The faeries hiss, making coordinated revolutions that stir her fur and our hair. Upon reaching her leg, they move away in reaction to the motor whirring within.

They pass over Clarey next, first puttering around his mask, spending an inordinate amount of time around his left ear, as if sensing the BAHA under the latex. Then they spiral down to his shoes to admire their reflections in the gold-metal toes.

They murmur, teensy susurrations that remind me of a breeze sweeping across meadow grass. Interlaced with their "oohs" and "aahs" are words that sound suspiciously like "belong" and "tinker."

Then it's my turn; they twirl around me, some jangling the chains on my jacket, others tangling and pulling my hair before tugging at the fake zippers stuck to my face.

"Ouch!" I screech, surprised by the jolt of pain that follows when the metal runners don't peel free. In a knee-jerk reaction, I slap at my attackers, my fingers accidentally grazing one. The faerie contorts in midair, buzzing and whizzing. Then, amid a poof of silver glitter, it reappears, its body woven of brown twigs and bright pink flowers in place of wire. Its wings transform to golden gossamer webs, and its mane, no longer aglow, becomes feathery and soft like real dandelion tufts. A rodent's smile curls along its whiskered muzzle, showcasing pearly white teeth.

It's a fully organic being, with no remaining bits of metal. Which means it no longer fits in with its counterparts.

I yelp and shove my hands in my pockets as the other faeries snarl and attack their mutant companion. It screams with the voice of a baby bird. Flannie barks again while Clarey tries to

intervene, but the flock rises too high in the sky. Showing no mercy, the metallics spin around their organic counterpart, wrapping it in a net made of circuitry from their hair. In their wind-wispy voices, they chant: "Spoils for the king, spoils for the king," while dragging their captive up and away into the smoky haze until the charged currents disappear from view.

Clarey and I stare at each other in shock.

"Told you." I bury my hands deeper in my pockets. "Havoc."

He raises an eyebrow, stirring crinkles along his pumpkin forehead.

Flannie trots over, dropping the cloth she saved from the faeries.

"Is that blood?" Clarey holds it up to showcase dried dribbles of brownish red around one edge of the white fabric.

Recognizing the pleats, I slip my hands from my jacket and take the cloth. When I shake it out, the folds unfurl into a chef's hat. My chest muscles seize tight. I hold the brim to my nose, breathing in the unmistakable scent of Uncle Thatch. The threat of tears burns my lower lashes.

Clarey cradles my elbow. "You okay?"

I shove aside all the doubts and inconceivable theories crowding my mind, homing in on the need to save my uncle. "I didn't put this in my bag. He must've had it on when he went into the fun house. Which means someone else stuck it in with my things, just like they left his glasses for us to find. And . . . Clarey, he's *bleeding.*"

Clarey's jaw clenches—an action that bundles the orange ridges under his cheekbones. "I shouldn't have lambasted you with that." He runs his thumb along the stains on the hat. "It

could be raspberry-beet icing for all we know. Even pomegranate syrup. There's other explanations."

I swallow the lump from my throat. "His glasses were smashed. It wasn't that far of a leap." I glance up, shocked to find that Filigree is still overhead, whirring and grinding in circles. All I can see from this distance is her one electric-bright eye looking down on us. "This is a clue. We're being led to him." Hands shaking, I refold Uncle's hat and shove it into my jacket and zip up.

As if prompted by my words, Filigree stops her rotations and slants through shirrs of smoke, making her way toward the carnival. She adjusts her wings' trajectory, soaring lower and lower, then in a blink, glides around to the other side of the closest tent. Her silhouette skims the interior, confirmation that she slipped through the opening.

"Follow her!" I shout.

Riding the shock wave of our discoveries, we give chase with Flannie in the lead. Golden-lit sand puffs up beneath us like swirls of fireflies. The closer we get, the thinner the haze of smoke grows. It seems to be channeling out of a striped protrusion in the middle tent's roof, and spreads thicker in the sky the farther it drifts from the "chimney."

As we get closer, a carousel comes into view in front of the first tent's opening. It's similar to the one we spotted at the carnival in the real world, although this one sits outside, all alone. It's impossible to make out clearly, hidden by smoke and the remains of some leviathan sea creature slumped on the shore.

The skeleton's ribs spear the sky and curl down into the beach. Golden sands, magnified by silver moonbeams,

illuminate the elephant-size form like a macabre halo as we weave around it. The putridity of organic decay and metal oxidation burns the back of my throat. I cover my lips and nose to keep from gagging and notice in my peripheral vision that Clarey's doing the same.

From the corpse's hind, eight tentacles spill out, formed of roller chains—giant versions of the ones on my bike at home—completely mismatched with the two front legs similar to a zebra's: black-and-white scaly hide and rusted hooves. An aluminum dorsal fin fans out from the withers. Matching gills stretch across the bend of its neck, and the striped head is equine in the way of a seahorse: pectoral fins, cheek and eye spines, and jaws gaping open at the tip of a too-long snout. Vapid, lifeless eyes reflect the ethereal lighting as we pass—silent and horrified by the eerie juxtaposition. Even Flannie knows better than to bark; she sticks to Clarey's heel, tail down and ears pricked.

We give the snout wide berth, staring at back-to-back rows of sharklike teeth on top and bottom jaws strung together with corroded muscles and tendons. A slimy brownish-red substance oozes from the lagging tongue—resembling a mix of rust and saliva. The similarity to the stain on Uncle's hat strikes me, but I'm reluctant to speak until we're farther away from the beastly funk.

As we step over dregs of seaweed wrapped around the corpse's dorsal fin, Clarey braves uncovering his mouth to mime the word: *kelpine*. I nod, having already recognized my creation.

Kelpines are inspired by kelpies—mythological fey shapeshifters that live in water and hunt on land. In traditional lore, they shift from a beautiful human to a horse to lure prey into the depths where they feast on them. In Mystiquiel's version, a kelpine's inner circuitry can reroute itself, enabling the creatures to break in half

yet continue to function as two separate beings. One takes the shape of a mammalian seahorse and the other a kraken. They live and hunt as a pair, both on land and in water, using their size and split abilities not to seduce but to trap and shred violently with constricting tentacles, razor-sharp hooves, and snarling teeth.

Nothing is safe on the water or shore—not even a ship or a boat. It appears this one was in the process of splitting apart when it died.

An almost maternal pang of remorse washes over me, similar to the time I colored an entire story panel and spilled a water bottle, smearing it all. But that momentary anguish fades upon remembering the most disturbing detail about kelpines: they're virtually impossible to kill. So whatever caused this one's tragic end is something we don't want to meet.

"We have to get off this beach," I tell Clarey the moment we're safely past the rancid corpse. He makes a shushing sign with his forefinger. I go silent. Standing still, I wait and wonder. Whatever he hears is lost on me. But then, suddenly, I can *feel* it . . . a rolling hum along the air. Then I see it, the carousel beginning to spin in the distance to our left.

After two revolutions, it emits the soft, haunting notes of a song I vaguely recognize from my childhood. First, it's only the tune, a slower discordant version of the original—like an old windup music box dragging its prongs against a steel comb. Next a robotic voice, genderless, off-key, and eerie, takes up singing the chorus:

"Que sera, sera, whatever will be, will be. The future's not ours to see, que sera, sera."

It's from an antique record Lark and I used to listen to back in fifth grade. Uncle found a vintage turntable at an estate sale

and brought it home for Lark to refurbish and repair. She and I especially loved the lyrics of this particular song—about a little girl who wonders what she'll be when she grows up: pretty or rich, a painter or a singer. Our favorite verse was always when the mother would answer that the fates would decide, because it felt like something our own mother might have said had we known her.

The tattooed lark along my left shoulder and collarbone twitches again, as if the inky bird is trying to fly. It's the song; the melody tugs at a place deep inside me, makes me ache for so many things I no longer have.

Why is it playing here? First the mirror memory, then the metal fibers, now this. It's like my most private and intimate moments with Lark are being preyed upon . . . manipulated.

With the carousel's spinning movements, the smoky haze thins, stretching into vaporous ribbons and showcasing the ride more clearly. This isn't the same Clowns-Go-Round carousel of earlier. The platform and poles are monotoned, and instead of circus menagerie animals masked in clownish paint, they're something entirely different, yet startlingly familiar.

"The royal mounts," Clarey whispers.

It doesn't matter that he's saying something I already know; I barely hear him. The haunting song has seeped inside and holds me spellbound.

The tinkly music grows louder, the computerized voice more malevolent, as the merry-go-round spins faster, displaying thirteen unicorns. The white silken hides on their flanks, hindquarters, and heads wear thin in places, leaving gaping holes that display the inner workings of clocks—spinning gears and cogs. They flick lionlike tails tufted with fleecy balls of steel wool and

shake angelic manes of real glistening feathers. They'd be majestic if not for their bodies reflecting the same decay I've seen so far: corrosive mechanisms and electrical cord innards tucked in a skeleton of rusting, metal bones. The glassy horn spiraling from the center of each forelock burbles with liquid light, like a lava lamp—although the illumination is colorless here—unlike my finished sketches at home that pulsate rainbows. In a moment of clarity, I recall Jaspar's dagger handle. It was obviously carved from such a horn, yet somehow it retained the color these are lacking.

Everything on this beach is a grayscale panel, a basic draft before I've added tincture with markers. It's exactly the way the real world has been looking to me over the past few months, other than places dusted with reddish rust.

When the music reaches a fever pitch, I snap out of my musings and turn to Clarey. He slams a hand behind his left ear, as if to muffle the vibrations in his BAHA.

The unicorns choose that moment to leap off their platform, high enough to blot out the moon before landing some ten feet away. Their fetlocks—steel and spiny—spin around their cloven hooves like propellers, spraying sand. Clarey and I cough in the fray, struggling not to inhale. Flannie barks, placing herself between us and the silhouetted riders that materialize before our eyes—Perish's biomechanical regiment seated on the backs of their mythological mounts.

The pack rat faeries of earlier appear in midair. Their interwoven manes blink with light, and each time the trapped faerie I altered hits a thread, electrical currents shock it like a bug zapper—throwing its twig, flower, and furred form back to the center.

"Let it go!" I blurt after its third try to escape, unable to handle any more screeches of pain.

Clarey grips my wrist to shush me as one of the mounted riders pushes through the others, taking the lead. I know him immediately; I've studied those lines and angles so many times I could draw him in my sleep. His muscular build, his hair—thick and wavy—gathered in a braid that reaches midback. The strands are ombre, dark roots that match the inhuman burgundy of his irises, fading to lightened ends, as pale as frost. His voltaic-white pupils and spiky antlers . . . I don't need to see them—or his iridescent shell-sleek skin and feral features—clearly to know it's Perish. His crown says it all, emitting lightning-bright zigzags, electrical pulses from prong to prong.

"Are you responsible for this creature's state, Phoenix of the Somatic Realm?" His voice, grinding and deep, rumbles loud, then soft, then loud again, like a motor revving up. Everything around us grows still and silent in response to his authority; even the hazy atmosphere itself seems suspended in time.

Somatic realm?

Reeling over the fact that he called me by name, I gulp. "I—I am."

"Then let your fate be one and the same." With a sneering glint of razor-edged fangs, the king lifts a silver metallic arm and snaps his fingers. The faerie net short-circuits and the lights withdraw into the heads of the pack rat band, sending them in a tumbling, buzzing whorl mid-sky, like bees blown through a windmill. Upon realizing it's free, the altered faerie dashes toward me, seeking refuge.

"Catch it!" I direct Clarey, afraid another touch from me could cause more harm.

Clarey opens his palm. The faerie lights on his skin and hugs

his fingers in gratitude before Clarey tucks it safely into his vest's pocket.

Perish blows into a trumpet, bringing the unicorns and their riders to full attention.

"Ravage the human souls!" Scourge, Perish's henchman brother, shouts from the back of the regiment in a voice that's rattled my dreams. He's the commander of the boggle knighthood—my own warped version of the bogeys and bogeymen of lore. The squadron raises ogre-like arms in tribute.

That's all I need to see to know what "fate" the king was referring to.

"*The Wild Hunt*," I whisper to Clarey. "We're the prey."

Heading the hunt are the pack rat faeries, fully recovered from their spinning spill and eager to reclaim their prisoner. Clarey's eyes widen with terror. I share the sentiment, but two other emotions—astonishment and pride—hold me rooted in place.

I've done it; my creations live, just like Lark's once did. They're more than paper and pencil marks; they're flesh and metal, magic and mayhem, and most importantly . . . mine.

"Nix, snap out of it!" Clarey grabs Flannie's collar with one hand and my elbow with the other to jerk us into motion. We resume running, now driven by self-preservation. My legs pump and my knee throbs with each slam of my bones along the beach, but the stampede on our tails drives me onward. Mere seconds before the clouds of sand, roaring soldiers, whirring faeries, and pounding hooves can overtake, the three of us duck through the tent's opening, not daring to look back.

17

mystiquiel

The pack rat faeries, Perish, and his mounted infantry turn sharply behind us the moment our feet land within the tent. In their place remains only wind, a blast of sand and grit that shoves us several feet forward.

I allow myself one cautious glance over my shoulder, only to find that the tent flaps have folded closed, leaving the cloth wall solid and seamless as if the opening itself had been a mirage. We're stuck inside with no way out.

Flannie whimpers, and the altered faerie in Clarey's pocket peers out, screeches, then ducks back into its hidey-hole.

"You're right, Toto One and Toto Two," Clarey says. "We're not in Kansas anymore."

In keeping with all the weirdness we've encountered so far, there's no tent roof up above, just a low-hanging firmament—cloaked in spumes that rise from each building and house to smudge the sky. The surroundings are lit to a grayish, dreary

"daylight" by the glassy globe slipping in and out of sight overhead.

Flocks of finch-size sprites soar on tin-feathered wings through the smoky clouds. Their computerized tweeps and chirps take the place of birdsong. I inhale the waxy scent weighing down on us, oddly reminiscent of the candles always burning at Uncle's bakery.

We're in Astoria, but not really; our hometown on a grayscale cybernetic mind trip: hills, shops, and streets identical to those at home, though devoid of trees, grass, or foliage of any kind. The atmosphere, arid and dry, almost crackling with static . . . doesn't seem capable of bringing rain. And the denizens are a far cry from the humans we know.

Shimmery-gilded fey creatures with iron hooves, aluminum-wire horns, or electric neck coils, with chain-link tails and circuit-sparked eyes, fill the streets and skies; their chatter, bleats, growls, and hisses fill our ears. It's the same magic, metal, and galvanized dreamscape I've been visiting in my sleep since Uncle cured my insomnia. Except the only vivid colors I see are red slashes of powdery rust and patina streaks of corrosion.

Clarey hasn't budged from ogling all the biomechanically engineered creatures soaring above and sauntering around us. He lists every eldritch species under his breath, knowing them as intimately as I do from my novels: dryads, elves, trolls, gnomes, piskies, sprites, hobblegobs, wights, sprigs, and more. There are no goblins, boggles, or grimalkins in sight, but that could change just by turning a corner. Like in my stories, the anthropomorphized classes wear clothes, whereas the more feral castes are naked. Yet *unlike* my stories, they're wandering

aimlessly en masse, as though they're lost, or have been brainwashed.

My mind immediately goes to Clarey's enochlophobia. "You okay? I mean . . ." I gesture to the crowded streets and skies.

"Yeah. Maybe because they're not exactly people? And they're not strangers, either. Thanks to your novels." He meets my gaze and flashes his white-toothed smile almost shyly. It doesn't even matter that his face is tangled up with a grisly mask; he's still Clarey, through and through, and the adorable gesture makes my heart flutter, like a feather trapped beneath my sternum.

I smile back, thrilled he's okay, although I can't shake the sense that so much about this feels different from my drawings. Mystiquiel is an ethereal realm of sneaky creatures and eerie mystique—yet the denizens here seem to be keeping their distance instead of attacking us or pulling pranks.

"They seem so aimless," I say absently.

"Right?" Clarey responds. "It's like they're so preoccupied with wandering, they don't even care that we're here."

Exactly my point. Some move to our left and others to our right on a whir of gears or a grind of motors, parting like the Red Sea along the sidewalks and streets. Each time a weathered metallic tail or tattered scaly wing wends a bit too close for comfort, Flannie growls, yet stays by her master's side.

I lock gazes with every one of them in passing—some with one eye, some with two, others with multiple sets. Whether towering over us, matching our height, or even smaller, they return my stare, yet move on. Don't they realize I'm their creator? If so, shouldn't they be as astonished by our meeting as I am? Yet even more baffling than their odd behavior is how this can even be happening.

"The fun house." The term tumbles out of me. "It led to the beach. The tent . . . led here. And now both passages are inaccessible. It's like we just dropped in, out of nowhere. But how?"

"I have a theory," Clarey answers. "Perish mentioned the somatic realm."

I crinkle my nose. "Yeah, pretty sure I missed that word on our last vocab test."

"It's a synonym for reality."

"Okay . . . go on."

"The old-school version of Halloween . . . didn't you once tell me that people used to think a portal appeared or something, just for a few hours?"

"On All Hallows' Eve." My throat dries as I recall the Google searches I did over the past couple of years to help me stay one step ahead of my family curse. I could never have predicted I'd be using the knowledge to piece together a moment like this. "It's why people started wearing costumes. They were convinced the veil between the spirit world and ours thinned, so they hid from the spirits by looking like them. It's the entire basis of the pagan holiday."

"So could it work the other way around? Letting things into their world, like a doorway?"

"You think these"—I gesture everywhere—"are spirits?"

He shakes his head. "No. I think we somehow stepped through a loophole leading from our everyday life to—"

"My imagination," I interrupt.

"Or imagination in general," he corrects. "What if it wasn't spirits the olden-day folks saw, but figments of their imaginations coming to life? What if *that* was the veil wearing thin—the one between fantasy and reality?"

"So," I reason aloud, "we walked through the veil and entered their side."

"Exactly. And we'll have to find some way back out there"—Clarey motions toward the tent wall we came through—"to find the portal again. Haystack Rock."

"*After* we rescue Uncle," I add, tamping down the image of the bloody stain on his chef's hat before panic can get the better of me.

I recall what fun house–Jaspar said: *You'll figure it out once you get inside.* Inside. He was referring to this place . . . a world of fantasy. The doppleganglia must've stepped into reality when the veil first thinned this morning, in search of me—then stole our deliveryman's persona. But why?

Needing Clarey's input, I admit to seeing "Jaspar" in the maze and everything about our interaction—all but the details of my virtual memory.

"So you're saying one of your off-scene characters glamoured themselves to look like you guys' deliveryman?"

"Yeah, and after hearing Perish say my name, I think doppleganglia-Jaspar is helping the Goblin King lead us around."

"That's heavy." Clarey shakes his head.

"Agreed. Why bring me here at all?" I ask. "And using my uncle as bait? There were lots of other ways to lure me in."

"Not sure. But I'm guessing Jaspar knows. Probably even knows how to get us out again." Clarey rakes his free hand through his hair, blending the white and black curls for an instant before they spring apart in coils across his orange forehead.

I frown. His portal-to-imagination-in-general theory isn't completely watertight. Still, even with a few dribbly holes, I'm eager to accept it because that would mean I'm not responsible

for his mask. *Clarey* created the prosthetic. It's part of *his* imagination.

I nudge the zippers he earlier dabbed across my face, inciting a sting just like when he tapped them in the cave and when the pack rat faeries tried to tug them. As if they're connected to nerves and tissue. I glance at Flannie's leg, and that feathery twitch around my tattoo starts up again.

Maybe the wings and tail feathers are actually moving under my T-shirt, and the lark is trapped inside my skin. I'm not the one who guided the ink-filled needle, but I did sketch the stencil that Ebon used as the outline.

The only explanation I can think of is anything Clarey or I made has become real upon our entry through the sea—as long as it was attached to us somehow, physically.

My entire body tingles with reverence; what artist doesn't long for a chance to walk among their fantasies, to breathe the same air as their creations? But then logic overtakes and slams me with a disturbing thought.

"Clarey," I mumble.

"Yeah?"

"If we did slip through the All Hallows' Eve veil, it only stays passable for a while. According to all the lore I've read, it closes at midnight, when Halloween ends. I'm not sure how long we have left. And even if we had our phones, there'd be no way to get a signal here to keep tabs on the time."

"Time," Clarey says, thoughtful, his finger touching the mask above where the BAHA hides. "I've been feeling ticking vibes ever since we stepped into the tent. It's like a clock. Somewhere. Do you hear anything?"

I shake my head. The only sounds I'm getting are mechanical

hums, shuffling hooves, and fluttering wings. It's impressive that what helps Clarey hear better in the real world has now become his superpower.

Grabbing Flannie's collar, he looks around; his jack-o'-lantern mask creases as he strains to pinpoint the direction. I'm curious if it's starting to dawn on him yet . . . the irrational rationale to why his prosthetic feels so snug.

"There's one more reason to hurry," I continue, reluctant for him to open that particular can of pumpkin guts. "We both know my characters and creatures. What they're capable of when they decide to misbehave. Just because they're too distracted to notice us doesn't mean they reacted the same to Uncle."

"On it," Clarey says, and points toward a gaggle of trolls and some sky-high dryads. "There. On the other side of that crowd. The ticking."

We both hear a familiar ding then, the sound of a trolley crossing a stop, and push between the trolls to get through. Though they only come to our knees, they're intimidating with crinkly aluminum faces and vicious glassy teeth that glint like shards of mirror in their mouths. Luckily, like all the others, they don't seem interested in us at all.

Clarey and I arrive a few yards from the stop, both of us cautiously eager as we wait to see Perish's half-serpentine, half-train mobile dungeon I've been drawing for years.

The heat hits us first: lines of flame—reds, oranges, yellows, and blues, dominated by fingers of blackened soot and steam—racing along the electrified rails. Before we can react, the ambling eldritch crowd around us barks, cries, squawks, and screeches, diving out of the way.

Through the resultant opening, the trolley slithers off its

rails. A giant, scaly serpentine head whips left to right, intent on capturing two gnomes wearing prison garb. Two metallic fanged jaws open wide, then clamp down on the unlucky escapees—mere inches from where we stand.

The faerie hiding in Clarey's pocket screams as oil- and copper-scented gusts rip through our hair. I suppress a gag, watching the gnomes' bodies erode, the snake's deadly acidic venom disintegrating them from the inside out within seconds, leaving nothing organic or metal behind, just a powdery pile of ruin.

I grab Clarey, who's still holding tight to Flannie, and we leap out of the way as the trolley shifts course and returns to its flaming rails, charging past us as if nothing out of the ordinary took place.

Clarey and I gawk, speechless, at the progression of the long and winding black-scaled body. Gaping holes reveal sinew and cartilage strung around a rusted metal skeleton, with all the king's prisoners peering out from between the ribs. I study each passenger to ensure Uncle isn't onboard, feeling almost frantic until there's no one resembling him. Close to the end, the two tourists from yesterday appear—their lemon and rose petal hair suddenly clear and vivid to my awakened sight. Both girls grip a curved bone on either side of their faces and watch us while they pass. Only a flicker of light in their eyes, an electric blink, saves me from a cold sweat. They're no more from the "real" world than anything else. It must be that the moment I drew them on the trolley, their likenesses became part of Mystiquiel. I'm more grateful than ever that I erased Lark from that scene. Seeing another false representation of her like the one in the maze would've destroyed me.

As the trolley's tail slithers away, the flames on the rails snuff

out, opening the rest of the cityscape to our view. We're already on Eleventh Street, without even having walked that far. Exchanging a confused glance, we pass over the tracks and instead of a railroad crossing warning, come face-to-face with the metal sign that I've seen in my sleep so many times.

Rows of tiny Edison bulbs line the edges, flickering and popping to spotlight the word "Mystiquiel" in neat script. Black glitter makes the letters sparkle and draws the eye. And then I see it: there—close to the *l*—hangs my duffel, its straps slung loosely around the upper right corner.

Clarey reaches up to flick the pocket watch dangling at the side. "Of course this was the ticking. Our one link to the outside is a busted timepiece. So much for keeping up with how long we've been here."

Maybe he's disappointed, but I don't share the feeling. Releasing a jubilant yelp, I grab the bag. It's impossible not to hug it, to bury my nose in the canvas like I used to do as a little girl . . . to pretend that residual scent of brine and fish is somehow tied to oceanside excursions Lark and I took with our mom and dad. I turn the pocket watch around and the ticking hands read 8:15 p.m.

I suck in a stunned breath.

"What is it?" Clarey nudges me.

Unable to believe what I'm seeing, that for the first time in my entire life, the hands are moving clockwise, I flip its face to show him.

"No way." He leans closer.

He knows the story, how Lark's obsession with tinkering started with trying to repair this watch when no one else could; but no matter how many times she took it apart and put it back

together, it couldn't be fixed. Those failures led her to practice tirelessly until she had a knack for rebuilding almost any machine, and for designing her own from scratch.

"Do you think it's accurate?" Clarey asks. "We arrived at the carnival close to seven. It feels like we've been at this longer than an hour. But things happened so fast inside the maze, you know?"

"The maze." I nibble on my lip piercing. "Jaspar. He mentioned something in there, about the clock 'beginning to tick.' And that time passes differently here. Maybe my dad's watch activated the second the duffel came through the portal. It could've come alive because it's technically Lark's design."

It surprises me that I actually want this to be true, considering how hard I've always worked to keep my sister separate from this world.

"Why wouldn't all those painstaking hours she took it apart and reassembled it finally pay off in a land of imagination?" I finish the unexpected thought.

"That's an incredible sentiment, Nix," Clarey says, bumping me with his shoulder. "But like you said, Jaspar mentioned *time*. It's more likely this is Perish, laying out the precepts of a game through his henchman. You wrote your king to be manipulative and wily, but he also sticks by his rules and offers clues so he can 'appear' to help along the way."

"Volume ten," I interject. "When his first knight, Automata, betrayed him and begged for a second chance to prove himself."

"Perfect example. Instead of killing the boggle outright, Perish gave him that candle where he'd trapped his last breath, then invoked a hurricane and laughed as the boggle tried to keep the flame from snuffing out. That's his idea of fair . . . the fae's idea."

"Like fixing a watch my sister and I always wished would

work, just to taunt me that there's only a little over three hours left to escape being trapped in our make-believe world." Anxiety knots my stomach. Anxiety and disappointment as any possibility for a postmortem connection to Lark shatters. I groan and shove my fingers through my hair. "Why did I have to make him so cunning and ruthless?"

"Name one goblin who isn't. So we both agree, Perish was herding us here, to land us in this exact spot."

I nod. Clarey's hypothesis makes perfect sense; otherwise we'd still be in the chase. The Goblin King doesn't give up on a Wild Hunt unless he's caught his quarry.

Clarey holds Flannie back with his leg as a lizard-size wight skitters by her paws before creeping up the sign's pole and disappearing within a hole at the top. "And the duffel was dropped strategically by Filigree, right where we'd find it—"

"Because he's leaving us crumbs." I slide the chef's hat from inside my jacket. "Leading us to the bakery."

Clarey drags some dog biscuits from his pocket and scatters them on the ground for Flannie. "Well, at least we're going somewhere where they serve food. I'm starving."

"You know better. There are rules about faerie food."

"So, what then? You want to share some of Flannie's biscuits?"

Flannie looks up at us and wags her tail, merrily crunching away.

I sigh, realizing how hollow my own stomach is. "We'll just have to ration."

Unzipping the duffel, I dig out the baggie containing Juniper's three remaining gingerbread scones and take a bite of one while handing another off to Clarey. Someone has definitely

rifled through the bag's contents, because the vial of squid ink is now in the main compartment along with everything else. I search for more "clues," but find only the things we packed ourselves—our phones that won't turn on, Clarey's cloak, Mom's picture book. Another surge of relief swells through me upon seeing those pages intact.

I shove the chef's hat inside next to Uncle's broken glasses then fish out the pair of twiggy gloves Clarey brought to complete his costume. Holding one corner of the scone in my mouth, I slide them on. Once the bag is arranged over my shoulder, I resume eating.

"What do you say?" I pause to loosen a doughy bit from the grooves of a molar with my tongue. "Are you ready to follow some crumbs?"

"I'm *game* if you are."

I force a laugh in hopes of tamping down my reservations. My maternal-artist instinct kicks in, and I pat Clarey's vest pocket, coaxing our tiny refugee to shove its rat muzzle out. It blinks large, pink eyes hungrily at my scone. I offer it a pea-size crumb. With the twigs, flowers, and vines that make up its arms and fingers, it takes the treat and nibbles at the edges, then gobbles it down.

Chewing his scone, Clarey snaps his fingers for Flannie, then tugs me forward like we're starting our usual stroll along Eleventh. As if there's anything usual about this night.

I cast a glance inside each shop window on our route: a haircutting place, a coffee shop, a bike store, a winery, and a bookstore. From inside, humanoid facsimiles of the store owners in Astoria—part metal, part motor, and part flesh—look back at me. Although I've never sketched them onto the page, they're here. It's

as if just seeing them on a daily basis imprinted them upon my mind's eye, which in turn conjured them to life in Mystiquiel. However, some of the owners, newer ones who I don't really know, have been replaced by eldritch creatures, as if their faces haven't been in my mind long enough to make an impression.

Like everything else, each of them is rusting; some have lost noses, ears, or fingers. Their shops are also falling into disrepair: missing shingles, unhinged doors, crumbling bricks, and masticated siding that makes me think of the chewed-up page in my *Goblin Market* book.

I'm so focused on the decay, I nearly trip where the sidewalk buckles steeply, revealing more corrosion underneath the cement. In place of dirt clods, tufts of grass, or sprouting weeds, there's black mold and brownish-red flakes, moistened to a wet, burbling paste. I've no idea how it could form without rain, but it's like a compost heap gone to mud. Maybe water has seeped in from the ocean somehow.

There's an underlying stench of loam and minerals that I recognize with sobering intensity. As I inhale, a familiar prickle of nostalgia pierces me through; if I were staring at my reflection, I'd be seized by Lark's accusatory glare. Yet the predominant odor, the salt-sour tinge of rust, is just different enough to keep me grounded.

It appears the sludge has been absorbed by the sidewalk, obvious only by the veins inside the jagged surface of the open crack, and barely noticeable when looking at the top. However, now that I know what to search for, I can see it: faint reddish threads running through the cement in every direction, winding toward the shops and making contact with everything that walks across it. The rust appears to be contagious, spreading with only

a touch, a pandemic in the heart of this land, sucking the color and luster out of every creature and character I've ever drawn or conjured.

It's almost like they're being eradicated . . .

Maybe this is why some of the denizens are no longer playing the roles I wrote for them, why they seem so absentminded.

Studying the muddy offshoots in the walkways, I'm reminded of the creeping vines sold at Juniper's boutique—innocuous plants like wisteria and honeysuckle—that come with a warning to sow them in an isolated patch of ground due to their tendency to overtake a garden.

Jaspar said imagination was like a garden. Is this rust and corrosion the weeds he was referring to?

"Maybe they're in on it, too." Clarey gestures to all the wandering fey that step out of our path, as if trying to shake me out of my quiet reticence. "I mean, why else are they clearing the way?"

I frown. "Perish wouldn't petition the common populace for help. Maybe they think we're from here."

As we walk on, a couple of human-size fey with metallic torsos connected to organic legs and arms—long and hinged like those of a cricket—move aside.

"We have metal bits." In demonstration, I tip my chin at the creatures, and they tip theirs in passing. "Flannie's leg, my zippered and pierced face, your BAHA. Even your shoes. The pack rats saw the toe tips and called you 'tinker.' "

Clarey nods. "Oh yeah, I didn't make the connection. The blacksmith gnomes, they're called tinkers in your stories."

"Exactly. So everyone here thinks we belong. But this little critter"—I gesture to the pack-rat-faerie-size lump moving around under the cover of his pocket—"no longer does."

Clarey snaps his fingers. "Right. Because it's bona fide."

"Bonbon?" The eensy fae's voice slips out from the other side of the fabric. The tip of its wings appear, trembling. "Me, Bonbon!"

Clarey and I exchange tentative smiles. "So it has a name now," he says.

I drop my final piece of scone into his pocket, and the faerie jabbers contentedly. "I couldn't have thought of a better one myself."

"As for us looking like them," Clarey continues while polishing off the rest of his scone, "I'm guessing my mask helps, too. Makes me appear piecemeal like they are. But once your zipper glue wears off or I use the solvent on my prosthetic, the jig is up. So do we have to keep our costumes on the whole time we're here?" He raises his dark eyebrows, furrowing the latex skin around them.

My stomach crimps. Enough is enough. I have to tell him—though the shock might make him completely unravel.

Our quartet arrives at Eveningside Street. There are only two shops along the sidewalk, unlike in the real Astoria. Both Enchanted Delights and Wisteria Rising stand three times wider and taller than our hometown stores, and both are depreciating at the hand of dribbles that ooze out from the wood panels and bricks like reddish-brown sap. The same sludge that's beneath the sidewalk and streets.

Clarey starts toward the bakery door.

"Wait." I drag him into the shadows of the dead-end alley at the side of the building and push him against the brick wall so we're face-to-face. Placing my gloves on his shoulders, I lean in

to look him in the eye. "There's something I have to do now, because I don't know when I'll get another chance."

One side of his prosthetic lip quirks upward in surprise, and his eyes fill with the daring mischief that always makes my pulse pound. "Seriously? *Now?*" He shrugs. "I guess we don't have time to waste, huh?" He grips my elbows and pulls me so close I smell the ginger from his scone on his breath. "Like I told Flannie. Let me take my mask off first so we can do this properly."

"Oh, Clarey." I groan, putting space between us so I can fish the glue solvent from the duffel. "That's exactly what I'm hoping this will do." I squeeze the tube, aligning the nozzle with what were once the mask's edges along his chin and jawline.

Nothing changes. Just by looking I know. It's still a part of him. Defeated, I step back, leaving Clarey to tug at the mask.

"Ow!" he screeches when it won't release. "What's going on with this thing?" His hands pause, then in an awful light bulb moment, he trails his fingertips along his features—a blind person feeling their way to illumination. "No. Oh god, no!"

motherboard

We watch. We wait. And we wonder. We turn our ears to listen, lapping up the boy's cries, gorging on her pain. We gobble their emotions, fill our bellies to brimming . . . supping on the flavor of life. Uncertainty reigns the closer they gain: no rust rots his toe tips, no sparks light his eyes. He seems familiar, like one of our own, yet we do not know this face. It is a deception, and he belongs because *of it. To us, and to her. He has a role to play. Test his mettle; force her hand. She bathed our world in soft summer sands, now let her baptize us in autumn storms. Let the skies cry, and seal the fates of the soulless. For should the clock strike midnight and the world still stand, our battle will be lost.*

18

feels like rain

Flannie whines and Bonbon slips from Clarey's vest pocket to hover beside me, frowning at the rising pitch of his screams.

"Clarey." I stop his hands where they've started yanking at the mask again. "You're not alone, okay? Just . . . watch." I swallow hard, then catch the zipper's tab on my forehead. It's something I've been afraid to try, but if what I suspect is true, it may help soften the blow for him. My twiggy gloves pinch tight, tips curling like a tree's offshoots as I tug the metal teeth open. I wince, feeling the air sear my raw, wet flesh.

Clarey's astonished expression confirms my fear: underneath the hardware is an open wound, oozing with blood. Which means the same is true for the other two zippers on my face. I seal it closed again and shiver against a wave of nausea.

Emotions blink across Clarey's carved features, ones I've already faced myself: disbelief, revulsion, then finally, horror.

"We'll fix this. I swear. Once we find Uncle, we'll get back through the portal before it's gone, and everything will be real

again . . . we will be *normal* again. I'm sure of it." I hope I sound more convincing than I feel; my dad's watch keeps ticking away, as though to mock me.

"Right-o. Right." Clarey takes a few gulps, then leans forward and braces his hands on his thighs to calm himself. "Until then, you're a walking piece of luggage, and my head is a jack-o'-lantern."

The moment he quips the sarcastic words, the orange latex pales and he presses his spine against the wall. Then he's sliding to the ground and holding his knees to his chest as he shudders with laughter. At first, I'm shocked by how well he's taking the news. So much better than I expected.

Then it hits me he's not laughing. He claws at the buttons on his vest, opening and closing his thick latex lips like a fish gasping for water. He's having trouble breathing.

Sweat beads on his forehead. "My . . . heart . . ." He rolls from the wall, flat on his back, still gripping his chest.

I drop to my knees and peel off the gloves. I've never witnessed a panic attack; he's held himself together remarkably well since he's been back. Now I understand why he feels so vulnerable while having one.

I've done research to try to be prepared. I know the symptoms: it can feel like his heart is stopping; there's sweating, shortness of breath, chills, and so many more. What I don't know is how to help, because everyone's different. Why haven't I ever asked him?

Am I supposed to touch him? Will that make it worse?

"Clarey, tell me what to do," I say, plucking at the frayed holes in my jeans to keep from reaching out, from doing the wrong thing. "What do I do?"

Bonbon flutters around us, its tiny whiskers quivering in concern. Flannie's the only one who's proactive. She pads up to him and lays her body over his, front paws rested atop his hands where they clutch his sternum, bellies aligned. Next, she tucks her cold, wet nose in the groove of his collarbone and whimpers a soothing tone.

I wait, tense and nervous. We need to be finding Uncle, getting out of here before we're locked inside. Each missed minute stretches out too long, like taffy folding over us and expanding—a sticky discomfort that makes my jaws clench and my teeth ache.

At last, Clarey comes back to himself, nuzzling Flannie's ears and praising her. What she's trained to do . . . what she remembered without hesitation . . . it was amazing and beautiful. And most importantly, effective.

I sigh with relief. "I'm so sorry I couldn't help."

Clarey shakes his head. "You . . . didn't know how to."

"So, is that what you need? To be hugged?" I'm determined to learn, in case it ever happens when Flannie's not with us.

He sits up, shuffling Flannie's ears affectionately as she wags her tail.

"I don't always want to be touched. She has a way of knowing when I do; animals' intuition or whatever. But her nose, the coldness . . . it always helps. My therapist used to have me hold an ice pack against my chest. Keeps me from falling into bad memories. Keeps me in the here and now, you know?"

"Okay. Something cold." I pause, trying to cover my awkward ineptitude. "So all those times I used to pound you with snowballs, I was actually doing you a favor?"

He laughs. It triggers a wonderful moment of acceptance

between us—and a calm that's unfortunately too short lived. Because it's then I notice Clarey tense up while looking over my shoulder at the eldritch creatures that were ignoring us earlier.

I turn to face them. Drawn by either our emotional outbursts or Bonbon's agitated hovering, they've stopped on the street and sidewalks. They stare our way, grumbling among themselves. The flocks in the sky drift down like falling ash, settling on the gnarled wooden shoulders and metallic antlers of the tallest faeries, the dryads. There they perch—vultures gathering among stark winter trees in anticipation of a feeding. A collective sound begins to emanate from the masses, a chittering hum that evolves to something loud and unwieldy, eerily similar to the giggles of hyenas—yet synthesized and robotic.

Lowering my fingers, I curl them in invitation to Clarey. "Can you get up?"

He fits one hand to mine and holds Flannie's thick scruff with the other. Trembling, he stands. "This is bad," he says, his voice steady, considering what just transpired. "You know what happens to pumpkins when the pranksters come out." He cringes at the maniacal laughter. "They get smashed."

"Go!" I shout.

Before we can dart around the corner and duck into the bakery, two trolls rush into our path, chomping broken-glass teeth and penning us in the alley. Behind them, more creatures advance from every direction. There's nowhere left to run.

Then I remember: they're not just creatures. They're *my* creatures. I tamp down the knots in my stomach, reminding myself that I dreamed up everything here; sketched these things to life

with pencils, ink, and markers. Gave them breath. Surely there's some way for me to control them.

I hold up one bared hand, relying on the power it can wield. "Stay back!" When they keep moving, I squat and flatten my palm where cement meets asphalt, to light the world up beneath their feet and throw them off our scent.

"What are you do-ing?" Clarey sing-songs the question nervously as nothing happens. The fey keep inching toward us, heads cocked and teeth gnashing.

"I was trying for a magical distraction." I peel my hand off the concrete. All that's left is a rainbow handprint, like a slap of neon graffiti. The effect isn't widespread as it was with the sands of the beach. All I've managed to do is apply a bit of color.

I just can't figure out the rules here.

The eerie cackles grow louder as the creatures overtake the far side of the street. My pulse skyrockets. In just a few more steps, the first line will be crossing the sidewalk to our alley.

"I hate to rain on your parade, Gandalf"—Clarey grips my elbow and forces me to stand—"but your wizardry isn't working."

"I can see that, genius." I crinkle my nose; even the familiar tug of my piercing doesn't comfort me now.

Behind us, Flannie growls. The trolls latch onto her fur, holding her in place as she twists and turns, trying to snap at them.

"Scram, you ghouls!" Clarey shouts.

I use my bare hands to jerk one loose. Knocked off balance, it rolls onto the ground in front of me and screeches as if in torment. Within moments it's transformed by my touch like Bonbon: crinkly aluminum hide reshaping to colorful bony

platelets. The scales shimmer red, orange, and blue, as bright as a school of rainbow fish leaping from the water and catching sunlight along their fins. The flesh-and-blood troll scrambles to stand just as its biomechanical counterpart totters toward it. There's something unsettling and sad in the way they look at each other, perfect reflections, yet not. It's too much like how I feel when I look in a mirror and see Lark.

The rusted, metallic version beats its chest—a gorilla challenging an interloper. The altered one displays white, sharp teeth. Bonbon drops down, attempting to mediate, only to get waved off like a bothersome bee before the cyborg troll catches its transformed comrade around the neck. The duo tumbles to the ground and wrestles, blocking any chance for us to make a break for the bakery door.

In the same instant, the hyena cackles surrounding us shift to something much more terrifying: utter silence. A feral glint blinks through each oncoming creature's eyes—fragmented electrical sparks that home in on the altered troll and Bonbon. I can't decide if they want to capture them, *eat* them, or punish me for changing them. Whatever the case, Clarey and I are stuck in the middle and it can't bode well to be in their path as they march forward in sync—like a gruesome parade.

I glance at the sky, catching the orb through sheets of smoke. It feels for a moment as if it's looking right back at me; and then, an idea lights up my brain.

"A *parade* . . . so all we need is rain," I say, drawing inspiration from Clarey's earlier mockery. I cast a sidelong glance in his direction as we tighten our flanks with Flannie secured between us. "Time to use your magic, Merlin."

"What are you talking about?" Clarey backs another step

toward the dead end behind us, and I follow—toe to heel, toe to heel.

"I'm not the only one who has power here." I point at my zippers, reminding him how his creations have become as real as my own. It must mean his imagination works like mine. "You don't just create masks and costumes. You create music. Use your harmonica."

He frowns. "These aren't field mice. They won't fall for the Pied Piper bit."

"You're right. That's why you're going to make it rain. Metal and water don't mix. Now, get your harmonica."

Dragging the small instrument out from under his shirt, he holds it up by its string. He looks beyond rattled as mere feet away, our fey assailants start across the sidewalk. Shimmery metal tusks, teeth, and fangs snap in rhythm to the click and whir of gears alongside clomping hooves and clacking claws. The winged creatures flap their appendages, still perched on the dryads, but threatening to take flight any minute. The tattoo along my shoulder thrashes wildly, as though the inky lark is desperate to escape my skin's chains and join them.

Flannie growls low at the approaching masses, and Clarey stands there, watching the harmonica swing in midair, bewildered. "Any requests?"

"Play the song by that Bud guy. That blues guitarist. Play his song about rain."

Clarey has the audacity to look exasperated. Like *I'm* the most vexing thing he's seen tonight. "You mean by *Buddy Guy*."

"Really? We're about to be faerie fodder, and you're going to quiz me on a stupid name I can't remember?"

"It's Guy."

"Yeah, *that guy*."

Clarey groans. "Whatever. You want me to play 'Feels Like Rain.' "

"Yes, that's the one!" I growl.

"Okay, okay. I'll try."

I'm not sure what he means by *try*. He's quizzed me with his accompaniment to that song uncountable times over the past couple of years. He never misses a note. He's a master of the mouth organ.

Then I see him work his lips back and forth, and I understand. It's something I hadn't even considered, his needing to adjust to their meatier latex shape—like me trying to draw with gloves or swollen fingers.

"Play it for your mom, Clarey," I whisper. We're at the end of the alley, backs against the brick wall, with creatures stepping off the sidewalk in our direction.

Pressing the harmonica into place, he blows. The first effort is shrill and off-key; too airy to carry a tune, but it makes our attackers pause.

Taking advantage, Clarey readjusts his mouth along the harmonica's holes and begins to learn how the metal fits his new lips. Within moments, his hands and fingers shimmy along the grooves, and he inhales and exhales to push the familiar strain through the brassy reeds—pitch perfect this time.

He taps a metal-toed shoe, becoming engrossed in the melody, just like he always does, just like I hoped he would. He stands at the end of the alley, eyes shut, head tilted to one side, cupping the harmonica in his hands lovingly. He releases his song into the sky, as if sending it up to his mother. The notes bend beneath his mastery, rhythmic and throbbing; they plunge

and rise, mimicking the pattern of droplets pinging off rooftops, pelting velvety leaves, and skidding down umbrellas.

And that's when it happens: each arpeggio and ambling octave becomes a tiny, fluttering thing, like transparent butterflies that disappear into the smoky haze overhead. There, the notes liquidize then fall back down, at first clear like water until they hit the ground and leave glowing, colorful smears behind.

The droplets hiss when they bombard Mystiquiel's denizens, the polychromatic streams fizzing along their metal parts. The fey crowd backs away, wailing and frightened. Some shield their heads with paws, others spread wings or fan out feathery tails to form makeshift canopies, but it doesn't stop them from getting wet. Several fall to the ground, left crippled by appendages and limbs that have rusted solid, and though I'm grateful they're no longer a threat, I can't help but feel sad for their sickly state.

Others, those that can still move, retreat, abandoning the chase to find cover in houses or shops around the corner on Eleventh Street, out of sight. At last, we're alone, nothing in the air but smoke and drizzling rainbows; nothing on the street, sidewalks, or alley but the incapacitated fey, their eyes shut as if in some sort of enchanted slumber.

I let out a whoop and inhale the welcome splendor of petrichor, then tilt my head back so Clarey's raindrops can skate along my lips and cheeks, soothing the zipper teeth where they sting my skin. Giddy with relief, I laugh. Clarey stops his serenade and joins me, catching my hands and spinning us around under the gentle downpour. Bonbon and its new troll friend splatter through the vibrant puddles building at the edges of the curbs, doing their own dance.

Flannie rears up, placing her front paws against my lower

back and then Clarey's as she bops alongside us. The wetness tastes sweet, like real rain, but tinged with the salty redolence of tears. *Loss.* That's why Clarey always looks so happy when he plays; this music, born in the depths of his soul, carries his blues away, purges him of sadness—for a little while.

He and I slow our twirling, grinning at each other. The lines and curves of his mask curl endearingly. Breaking myself from his gaze, I crouch and cup some water in my hand to sip it. Clarey follows suit, smacking his lips as he notices the flavor.

"All we need now are some paper boats," he says, observing the deeper pools filling the street edges and sidewalk cracks, referring to how we used to race them back when we were kids.

"Those times were the best." The patter of rain lulls me into a momentary state of nostalgia.

"Remember that one summer, when we finally beat Griffin, Spence, and Tanner?" he asks. They were a trio of brothers who lived on our block. Me, Lark, and Clarey were always competing with them, be it computer games, mountain-biking contests, or school fundraisers. "You painted those wolf faces on our sailboat flags—with fangs that looked real enough to devour their scrubby little lunch-bag canoes."

It surprises me that he remembers that detail. I chew my inner cheek in thought. "Yeah, but we won because of that rubber-band paddle Lark attached to their boughs." After she wound and released them, our boats moved so fast they were like lupine water bugs skimming along the gutters.

The rain slows to mist, and Clarey blots some wetness gliding down my cheek with the back of his hand. My skin responds with a tingle of pleasure. "Is that why you started dabbling in mechanics? A way to keep her with you? I've wanted to ask you

so many times since I've been back. But you seemed touchy about it with your uncle. I mean, when I saw your graphic novels—*amazeville*. I couldn't understand why you'd do anything but that. Making stories come alive in other people's minds, it's the closest thing to magic I've ever seen. Well, until now."

Though he refers to our surroundings, I can't stop admiring the colorful droplets clinging to his white curls, glistening like the fiber-optic wig he made back home.

"For most my life, I never felt like my stories were alive *enough*, if that makes sense?" I answer. "Then I lost the drive to sketch altogether when I lost myself."

"I get it. That's why you took over Lark's inventions. Hoping to find yourself through her?"

"Yeah," I mumble, feeling far too exposed. "But then, tonight . . . standing in this grayscale world and stamping rainbows with my fingertips, I finally realize *that's* how I give my art life. Color."

Clarey rubs some raindrops between his fingers while dropping his gaze to the harmonica strung from his neck. "You know, I never thought my music could do anything half as amazing as this, either."

I glance at Flannie, who's lapping up the water puddling at our feet. "Really? I never doubted it. There's magic every time you play. And now I understand the *why*."

"The why?" He furrows his eyebrows, then catches himself and touches them, as though just noticing how the hairs now poke through the latex. The orange mask begins to pale again.

I snag his hands and hold them in mine. "Why you like the blues, why you play the harmonica." My smile reaches higher when I see him visibly relax.

"How many times do I have to tell you? It's called a mouth organ. And if I wasn't trapped inside this pumpkin-nightmare, I'd show you my mouth can do more than just play music."

My pulse flutters at my jawline. I'm about to tell him I don't care about what's happening to his face. That he's still Clarence Eugene Darden, and I've wanted to kiss him since the day I punched two guys in the mouth to defend him. Mask or no mask, I'd leap at the chance. But before I can feel guilty for betraying Lark, his gaze falls from mine and I sense an awkward chasm spanning between us. I waited too long, and he thinks I'm shutting him down again.

"So"—he buries his fingers in Flannie's fur—"how did you know that rain would stop them? That's not official Mystiquiel canon."

"No." I glance at my boots, feeling flushed at the way his eyes follow my lips when I talk now, like he's holding on to every word. "I noticed on our walk over that there's this weird corrosion on everything." An unexpected pang jolts through me, too close to sympathy for my comfort, so I focus my attention on Clarey and avoid looking at the fallen faeries behind him. "Rust killed the kelpine on the beach, and is making the sea animals sick. Logically, it made sense. The ocean is rotting them faster than the ones living here."

I pause and look at the orb overhead, almost an afterthought. "My gut told me if we made it rain, they'd have no recourse but to take cover. I'm an artist; my touch affects what already exists in different ways, but it doesn't create something from nothing—not without paints, pens, or markers. So I figured we'd test *your* theory—about this place being as much your imagination as

mine. Because you can make music out of thin air. Amazing music, that pulls others into the experience with you."

His gaze drifts up to mine again, and this time, those beautiful blue and amber eyes don't waver. "No one gets me like you do, Nix. I don't think anyone ever has."

Not even Lark? I stanch the unwelcome question, and opt to keep things light, to veer my mind off her. "Well, that's just 'cause everyone else is stupid."

He snorts, then grows somber. "When this is all over, we need to talk. Really talk. I'm tired of running away from what's right in front of us. Aren't you?"

His assertiveness makes my toes curl both in anticipation and apprehension. I've suspected all along that his patience would reach a breaking point, but am I ready to admit everything to him? The penance I owe Lark and why.

What about him? Is he finally willing to tell me what happened in Chicago? Because if I have to lay bare my most sacred fears and shame in order for us to move forward, it's only fair he do the same.

"When this is all over," I parrot back, then shift my gaze from his to the watch ticking on the duffel. It's 8:40. Time is definitely passing slower here, but it's still passing. Until we find Uncle and cross back to Astoria, we have to choose our moments wisely.

That in mind, I take the duffel and lead Clarey and Flannie around the corner, leaving our newly organic fey companions to their antics in the puddles.

"Is that your—?" Clarey asks, pointing toward the bakery.

I crane my neck to get a better view as a man steps inside the glass-paneled door. Although I can only see him from the back,

he has the same dark hair, that same tall form and lanky gait. He's wearing a white apron tied around his waist and neck, but is missing the most important component of his uniform, because I have it in my bag.

"Uncle Thatch!" Without waiting for Clarey and Flannie to catch up, I sprint toward the entrance despite my aching knee, digging the chef's hat from my duffel bag. Now that we've finally found him, we've beat Perish *and* the Halloween curse. We can all make it safely home with hours to spare.

19

truth like flame and lies like honey

"Nix, wait!" Clarey calls from behind. "We forgot the gloves in the alley . . ."

His words nail my feet in place. The door has already shut behind Uncle, so I pause under the awning and squeeze the chef's hat to keep from touching anything. My entire body tenses, wanting to go inside; still, I force myself to wait.

I squint at the overhead lights that should be neon but instead blink black and white, then peer through smudges on the glassy panels to keep tabs on my uncle. Smoke seeps through the seams in the doorframe, filling the air beside me. The waxy scent is even more noticeable in the absence of any fresh baked goods or burning wicks. It's strange—I should be able to see candles lit up; yet there are no flickers of fire anywhere. So what is causing the smoke to fill the bakery? To fill the skies above every shop and house in this pseudo town?

"Uncle Thatch!" I call again, my fingers clutching the white, bloody fabric like a lifeline as he stops to talk to someone at a

table next to the door. I pay no mind to the fey customers. I don't even let it register that all the rainbow tables and walls are nothing but colorless forgeries of the originals—just like they looked at home when my retinas failed me.

I'm too busy anticipating his reaction, how grateful he'll be that we're here; that we found him. He'll step outside and wrap me in a hug. I anticipate the smell of home and safety he carries with him—the cooked fruit and lemon detergent always on his hands and clothes—and a happy effervescence rises in my chest when he begins to turn.

Then all my muscles clamp down. Like every other shopkeeper on the way here, this isn't the real Uncle Thatch. His arms hang too long at his sides, fleshy fingers and hands paler than snow. His face shimmers unnaturally, those familiar features now metallic and silver. He's missing his nose and right ear. Bloody red rust cakes the indentions left behind. I lift the chef's hat and contemplate the stains on the brim, how they look like the kelpine's rusty saliva; how they match the patches on the creatures we passed on our trek here.

When I look up again, Uncle Thatch's facsimile stares back—a malformed mental image of what I see every day, warped by my subconscious to fit this cybernetic alternate world. Without any hint of recognition, he whirls around and strides to the counter.

My cheeks grow hot, feverish. Where's the *real* Uncle Thatch?

Perish wasn't dropping crumbs at all; this was a misdirection. To piddle away more of our limited time. I'm back where the whole thing started: Uncle lost and in danger, and me with no idea how to find him. Yet now, I'm feeling minutes and hours slip through my fingers.

Growling, I throw the soiled chef's hat to the sidewalk and

spin on my heel to escape my mixed emotions. I'm stopped short by red snarls of hair peering out from a ringmaster's top hat and that grim, tinny-toothed sneer looking down on me.

Filigree perches on Jaspar's right shoulder, shaking her dual-feathers—metal brushing plumage in a harsh rustle—proof that the "deliveryman" is indeed working with the king. Emitting an eerie hoot, the owl lays her tiny ear tufts back, like an angry cat. She blinks her one real eye while the other turns on a whir, telescoping out to get a better view of me.

Jaspar stands there like an oil painting, his bright rose-gold and emerald suit and copper cape almost searing against the grayscale bird and the background behind him. Interesting how he's retained his color here when nothing else has . . .

"You know what Perish wants from me, don't you?" I bait, lowering my gaze so the reflections in his shimmery goggles won't catch me.

"That would be *His Royal Highness* to you," Jaspar scolds in his swishing, dead-leaf voice. With him standing this close, his breath reminds me of dead leaves, too. Cold, earthy, and over-ripe. I cringe. Despite his attractive and youthful appearance, there's something decaying beneath the surface. Which means he's not as strong as he seems.

The observation lights a fire in my belly. "It's *Perish*. I created him; I named him. I can call him whatever I want."

Jaspar peels off his goggles and dangles them from his thumb. Then without warning, he snatches my chin's zipper. The harsh tug on the metal tab forces me to stare up at the sparks leaping like lightning across his four pupils. Plumes of white swell up from the smokestacks in his hat. "If you truly are the creator, where is your love for these creatures, this place? Where's your

respect? And most of all, your compassion. Don't they deserve at least that?" His gaze flashes from me to the bodies lying in the streets.

I clench my jaw against the tug behind my sternum, telling myself it's simply a phantom pain—backlash from the zipper stretched taut at my chin. Yet I know it's more; that protective, custodial tenderness I've wrestled since I've been here—honestly, since I first started drawing Mystiquiel—has grown more intense upon seeing how my creation seems to be disintegrating . . . suffering. I wince, suddenly ashamed for exploiting their affliction when I insisted Clarey make it rain. My tattoo flutters beneath my shirt, as though to remind me it was for our own protection.

I set my jaw and harden my resolve, determined not to let Jaspar see how deeply connected I really am. "Tell the king I've seen enough. I'm ready to bargain so we can leave."

"Oh, but there's no bargaining to be had. You simply must play his game to the end, and deal the winning hand." Jaspar releases the zipper tab and pulls his goggles back in place over his eyes.

I shift my gaze to his straight, long nose. "So tell him to face me and lay out the rules. Let's begin."

"You've not yet proven yourself worthy to look upon his royal face. And you've already begun playing. The moment you took those wire cutters at the carnival and stepped into the house of mirrors. You're very close to the end now, in fact."

I gawp at him, struck by the mention of Lark's wire cutters. "Wait, so not only did you—or your accomplice—creep into my house and animate my sister's doll, but you also snuck into the attic and dug through her toolbox?" I scowl hard enough to

make all three zippers pucker my skin as he holds up a hand to silence me.

"Time is ticking. Better to not go off the rails trying to parcel out irrelevant details. How you got here is no matter. What does matter is how you end the game. And I'm going to give you a little tip: There's another who's been playing longer than you. Years even. In order to understand how to win, you need to know how spectacularly that player has failed, so perhaps then you'll not make the same mistakes." He bounces his shoulder two times, sending Filigree into the air. "Round up the boy and the dog," he instructs the bird. Before I can screech a warning to Clarey, he comes around the corner and drops the gloves at the sight of the hooting owl.

The deliveryman grips my elbow and forces me to look back through the bakery's display window. He presses long coiled fingernails between my shoulder blades, digging them in just enough to warn me if I twist around at Clarey's shout, I risk getting skewered. "Did you think it mere coincidence that you showed up just when the faeries were about to feed?"

Clarey and Flannie arrive, herded over by Filigree. Jaspar sends the bird away again, with instructions to capture our altered fey wards and take them to the king's palace. A worried pang echoes through me for Bonbon and the troll, but I can't help them. I may as well be part of the sidewalk, cement on cement, for how firmly the scene in the bakery holds me in its thrall.

The smoke, which earlier appeared gray, now rises from each table in prismatic hues. The biomechanical eldritch customers come into view between swirls. In place of fruity pastries, each table has a bowl containing a smoking wax melt—not lit by

flame, *but by magic*. A niggle of unease skitters along my spine as I recognize the used candles so painstakingly boxed up and recycled at my hands. The faeries lean across their dishes, inhaling the colored smoke. Afterward, some laugh, some cry, some argue, and some hug and kiss, as if triggered by the wax.

"Nix, you all right?" Clarey asks from behind.

"Silence. She's being enlightened." Jaspar steps back, giving my companions room to hedge in beside me and share the display window.

I can't even acknowledge their arrival. My tongue is plastered to the roof of my mouth.

Just like at our restaurant, I can read the colors and predict each faerie's reaction. If the smoke at the table is pink, the creatures appear uncertain, confused. If the hazy cloud is green, tears dribble from their eyes. Where blue puffs rise around a bowl, the faerie pumps a fist, feeling invincible. Turquoise leaves them smiling, red leads to shouts and snarls . . . and deep orange makes them jump up from the table and skip around the room, as animated as windup dolls with keys screwed tight into their backs.

After the smoke clears, there's one final result, common to them all—be they winged, horned, clawed, or hooved. They each appear livelier, eyes flashing brighter, movements smoother and less jerky and mechanical, as though the smoldering wax were an outlet and they've been recharged by plugging themselves in.

A few of the faeries look our way and flash electric eyes, trailing lines of light up and down us. It's what my characters do to determine if someone's a threat. Their laser-beam gazes stall on my zippers and on Clarey's mask, then, deeming us harmless, the customers step up to the counter where cyborg Uncle Thatch awaits payment. They snap off the corroding metallic pieces of

themselves: a nose here, a thumb there, an ear, or even a tooth. In return, he gives them a replacement for it, silver, shiny, and new.

It's an odd and confusing exchange, and I can't help but wonder where the pristine substitutes came from, considering there seems to be a shortage of unspoiled metal here.

I turn away before I can witness any more.

Lowering my duffel to my elbow, I finally give all my attention to Clarey. "Those are from our restaurant in Astoria. They're the wax melts from the mood candles that Uncle uses."

"*Mood* candles?"

"He told me the flames emit colors with people's moods." I scold myself for breaking my promise to keep the secret, but these are special circumstances. "That sounds crazy, right?"

Clarey raises his eyebrows. "Um, really? Do you see where we're standing right now? Those puddles back there? This phony over here who can change his face, pretending to be your deliveryman?"

Jaspar snorts. "Who says I'm pretending? And at least I don't get stuck inside my masks, *Jack*."

An anguished expression crosses Clarey's eyes as he's reminded of his state. I glare again at Jaspar's chin, avoiding the mirrored sheen of his lenses. "That's enough. I've seen what you wanted me to see. Per our recycling clause with you, we've been supplying this place with wax."

"But why would anyone here want it?" Clarey asks, bringing my focus back to him.

"It must work differently than Uncle thought. People's moods—their emotions—are *absorbed* through the wicks and stored in the wax. And the faeries . . . my creations . . . they feed off the essence somehow. They've been feeding off it ever since

the bakery opened." It sounds outrageous to say it out loud, but then again, as Clarey pointed out, look where we're standing.

Clarey frowns. "But that would mean your uncle—"

"Knows about the portal? That he's been in contact with my dreamscape for two and a half years? Impossible. He wouldn't keep something like that from me."

"So he doesn't realize he's been dealing with your characters at all, and doesn't know what the candles are for."

"Or what he's been feeding the people in our town. The produce we've been supplied isn't from our world, is it?" I turn to the deliveryman with an accusatory stare. In my self-righteous anger, I forget to avoid the goggles this time. I try to lower my lashes before the lenses' reflections lock me in, but it's too late.

The underlying stench of loam and minerals buried somewhere beneath the sidewalk seeps into my nostrils. That familiar prickle pierces me through, followed by a momentary flicker as the zippers on my face and the piercings disappear to showcase Lark's flawless skin in the mirrored lenses. Her dual images snarl the words: *We must not look at goblin men, we must not buy their fruits!*

The tattoo at my shoulder flaps its wings wildly at the warning so clear on her lips. My stomach curdles, the scone from earlier sitting like a rock. I avert my gaze, shaking off the illusion.

"Hey." Clarey grips my arm, coaxing me to look at him. "You're trembling. Where'd you just go?"

"I can't stop seeing her. Even here."

"Who?" Clarey asks.

"Lark." With my brain still fuzzy, I forget not to think out loud. "I'd guess it was the carousel song . . . or it being Halloween. Or her doll invention, even the pocket watch. If it were just today. If it weren't *every single* day."

"What do you mean by that?" Clarey asks.

His question goes unanswered, because Jaspar's devilish laugh intrudes.

"You put her in my head," I snarl in his direction. "Just like in the maze. Have you been doing it all these years? Is this part of the game?"

He responds with a sigh. "No. You've been getting off track all on your own, guilty conscience and all that. But let's get back to the game. The man you trust so implicitly . . . who you're looking for so diligently while putting yourselves at great risk. Aren't you curious what part *he* might play? Why in fact he's been dealing all this time with a weasel like me? It presents a delicious dilemma. One that, much as you try to avoid it, has burrowed beneath your skin, and is itching. You want to scratch, but fear what's beneath the surface. Am I fooling your uncle, or is he fooling you?" Jaspar rakes a springy fingernail along my jacket, catching one of the chains and jingling it tauntingly. "Just so you know, in all your conjectures about candles and contracts, you got it half right. But which half?"

I square my shoulders. One of Perish's favorite tricks is to pit players against one another in a game; Jaspar is obviously well versed in the king's playbook. "There's no way Uncle would participate knowingly. He'd never sell goblin fruit in our world. It's addictive to humans, it sucks the life from—" I cut myself short, suddenly drawing the parallel between the *Goblin Market* poem and how dangerous Uncle has always believed our produce to be in its raw state. He said it had to do with the fruit being organic . . . the special fertilizers that were used.

Jaspar smiles. "Ah, it's becoming clearer now, is it? Some loose threads lacing up. Let me help you tie a few more."

He takes a fingernail and unzips the duffel bag at my elbow so he can dig inside. Clarey and I watch, too intrigued to stop him.

He draws out the squid ink vial and pinches it between thumb and forefinger.

Clarey's eyes bulge. "Whoa, you swiped some for my—?"

"Masks," I answer softly before he can finish his question. That seems so long ago, and our problems so petty compared to the troubles we're facing now.

Jaspar's eyebrows lift above his goggle frames in interest. "The only thing this *masks* is the addictive powers of goblin fruit. You know as well as I, there's a cure for fey food. If a human imbibes that cure, they can eat without being trapped in the enchantment."

"The king's royal blood." Bile seeps into my throat. If this is true, Uncle's secret ingredient was never squid ink at all. And wouldn't that explain why the liquid has such unusual, almost magical, properties? How it shifts from dark to bright, then back again?

Jaspar opens the vial and sniffs the inky oil as it pales to that familiar pearlescence, as if to punctuate my unspoken point. Then he corks it up once more and places it back in the duffel. "Looks to me like you have just enough to last while you're here. Only a drop or two will do."

I lock eyes with Clarey, fighting a burn along the edges of my lashes, because we've both heard that exact phrase so many times.

My voice comes back in a rush and I lunge for Jaspar. "This proves nothing! They were your directions. Your instructions. You probably even gave him the recipes, told him exactly how to prepare things. He had no idea why!"

Clarey clasps my elbows, preventing me from grabbing Jaspar's prismatic dagger and slamming it into the doppleganglia's beautiful, fake face.

"Ah, such faith. Such blind, pitiful, human faith. I suppose we'll have to do this the hard way." Jaspar unbuttons the flap on his jacket pocket, and a cricket-size creature buzzes upward on shimmery, latticed wings.

"*Ting?*" Clarey chokes out the piskie's name.

A coil of uneasy recognition unwinds within me. I can't shake the sense that I've been here, experienced this moment already, before I even arrived in Mystiquiel. Yet that can't be right. I must be thinking of a scene I've imagined but haven't yet written.

Hovering midair, Ting cocks its chin first in Clarey's direction, then mine. The tin-can top half of its face is locked in a childish, adoring expression. The fleshy lower half smiles sweetly to showcase teeth as thin and sharp as silver straight pins. "Extirpate?" it asks with a voice that chimes like silver dragées raining across an aluminum baking sheet.

"No. There's enough eradication taking place here in our kingdom, don't you think?" Jaspar answers the teensy creature cryptically. It responds with an eager jingling nod. "Good. So let's try something different. Reconstruct something once lost."

The gilded piskie begins to spin, then stops midair and singsongs: "Replevy!" before reversing its rotations. Gears and sprockets spring out from its white-feather and black-wire hair, the gears turning counterclockwise along the wires until they sizzle hot and red. The piskie vanishes in a poof of black smoke and flickering embers.

Jaspar jerks me forward, forcing Clarey to let go. Startled, I catch a breath and suck in the floating cinders. They blaze through

my lungs. I lean over, hacking, unable to inhale. Clarey pounds my back, but he can't stop the flame rising in my chest, burning a trail from my throat to my head. There, in my mind, memories from last night catch fire in spaces reduced to dry kindling, waiting to be relit: *Jaspar and Uncle arguing in the alley; the grimalkin in the delivery truck behind the curtain; Uncle feeding me tainted water, deflecting everything I asked, then unleashing Ting on me in the storeroom; and amid all this, me seeing colors again for the first time in months.*

A barrage of questions follows: How many times has Uncle crossed the veil to this world? How many times has he seen my characters, interacted with them? What other memories of mine is he covering up? How can I ever trust him again?

I finally manage to gulp some air, refilling my charred lungs. "*He lied.*" The hoarse revelation drifts out on a ribbon of smoke that leaves my tongue parched. "I didn't slip on a plum. I saw too much, and he made me forget. He's been lying all along."

"Who?" Clarey asks.

I stiffen against a growling sob. "Uncle Thatch."

"No way," Clarey says. "This rat fink filled your head with some kind of hallucination. He's the liar."

But the fey can't tell lies . . . I'm unable to counter with that tidbit of lore, which Clarey already knows anyway; my mind is spinning too fast. It barely even registers that Flannie has found her way to my side, as if sensing my mental state. Whimpering, she licks my wrist where the duffel dangles, unzipped and gaping.

Jaspar "tsks" as the piskie seats itself atop his hat. "See, here we have the paradox. Humans can tell untruths. In fact, they've made an art of it, much like your uncle's exquisite baked treats.

Your lies are honey, sweet enough to lure, sticky enough to trap. My kind, on the other hand, are held to a standard of candor few of you could ever comprehend. So how is it we have the reputation of being tricksters, when it's you that are liars?"

"Oh, please!" Clarey steps between me and the deliveryman. "You spin trip wires that misdirect and lead us astray. That's *your* bag, and it's way worse than lying outright because there are too many strands . . . too many paths. And guaranteed, you're leading us down one right now. A *wrong* one."

Jaspar laughs. "Good to see you have a spine after all, boy. A shame you didn't have it with you in Chicago."

Clarey hunches as a strange sound—both a snarl and a groan—bursts from his mouth. "How would you . . . ?" But he can't finish the question.

Jaspar chuckles. The attack was perfectly executed, cutting Clarey off at the knees with something so intimate even I don't know the details. Just like the faerie weaseled into my thoughts and memories. Somehow, he's turned us both inside out to view all our secrets.

Wispy clouds stream from the miniature smokestacks behind Jaspar's hat, causing the piskie to cough and take flight on buzzing wings. "I guess you'll know 'who's leading you where' soon enough," Jaspar says, tapping his hat, "should you find the next clue, and make it to the final leg of the game *alive*."

While I'm still trying to make sense of Uncle's deceit, of everything I've learned, Jaspar ducks around Clarey and jerks my duffel's straps off my hand. Flannie growls, but the piskie flutters around her ears as a distraction. Jaspar shoves me hard, causing me to catch myself against the display window—palms splayed wide along the pane on either side of my cheek.

Before I can move, glass fractures everywhere my skin presses, slowly reshaping like a puzzle. There's a shuffle as the fey customers climb over one another, knocking down tables and chairs in their race to the storefront. I back up and we all watch with bated fascination—me standing outside and them within—as a vivid, stained-glass imprint of my profile and hands melts into place. I barely have time to look it over before the faeries' shock-bright gazes drift to me.

"Uh-oh," I mumble, my pulse roaring in my ears.

Clarey charges toward Jaspar for the bag. The deliveryman dumps out its contents and flings the duffel down. Chuckling at the mess he's left for us—both emotional and physical—Jaspar vanishes, along with the piskie, in a poof of metallic beads smaller than BB pellets that plink to the sidewalk and roll around our feet.

The bakery door shakes and rattles between me and those grimacing faeries desperate to come out. Something's holding the latch closed. Maybe Jaspar ensorcelled it . . . but why would he help us at all?

"We gotta scram, now!" Clarey shouts as he shoves items inside the duffel. "Get those things," he says, pointing toward the door. The squid ink vial rests at the base, and Mom's *Goblin Market* lies open a few inches farther. I manage to grab the book but leap away before I can get to the vial as a ripple stirs along the wood and glass panels—a silhouette that steps forward yet retains the appearance of the entrance, as if a part of the door itself has come alive.

I squint, astounded, knowing what's arriving even before she materializes. Her camouflage wears thin, and the hobblegob's true form comes to light. Circuit-board eyes blink up at me

curiously, and her goat-bearded sneer reveals razor teeth oozing with brownish-red drool. One claw, clamped around the bakery door's latch, has shape-shifted to a padlock. The other hangs at her side in the form of a sickle.

"Angorla," I whisper, unsure if she's here to save us or shred us to ribbons.

20

goblin fruit

"The history . . . be forbidden, yes?" Angorla says while holding the bakery door against the raging fey customers inside. She speaks with the exact white-noise-crackly voice I've always dreamed she had. By the shift of her gaze, I assume she's referring to the picture book in my hand.

"History?" I ask, noting the illustration on display before slamming the pages closed.

"They isn't look nothing like us, do they? There a reason for that. Writers. Words be the worst enemy of me and mine. But dreams, what a playground make. Aye? So we shut them silent. Take the tongue and swell it tight. Seal the lips and stitch 'em right. Once we own the parasite, then we sculpt their dreams at night."

Clarey and I exchange uneasy frowns.

"I'm not following," I say to the hobblegob.

"Oh, you followed just fine, you did. All Hallows and Eves we go, dancing and prancing, in leaves that blow. Now here you be, with he and me. But where the hairy one go?"

Hairy?

"You mean, my uncle? He's not so hairy . . ."

She snickers. "I got the door, but they gots the dog. Poof and gone. Look-see, all around."

I whirl to look behind me where Clarey's already caught on and is desperately whistling and calling out, but no Flannie comes running.

My stomach plummets when he finds her collar lying empty on the sidewalk next to the glinting beads. "Oh, Clarey."

He kneels to pick up the leather strand, cradling it tenderly. Then he kicks the silvery balls and shouts Jaspar's name like a curse. "That's why he dumped our stuff." His molded lips warp into a furious snarl as he places her collar inside the duffel bag and zips it. "I had my back turned for one second . . . and he vanished with her."

Thinking of how inconsolable I was when I first found Uncle's busted glasses, I struggle not to reach for him, to calm him; he's better off outraged than worried. He'll keep his head this way. He'll be sharper, well equipped for the fight.

"It's the next leg of the game," I conjecture aloud, suppressing my own anger so I can think clearly. "Jaspar had Filigree take Bonbon and the troll to the palace. I'm betting that's where Perish is holding Uncle, and now Flannie. What did the idiot deliveryman leave for a clue?"

"Just these . . ." Clarey punts the tiny beads once more, sending them on another scattering tirade. "It's those decoration dragées like your uncle uses. But we're already at the bakery, so it's a dead end."

I steal a look at Angorla, who's humming some nonsensical rhyme while barricading the bakery's entrance. She doesn't

appear too willing to offer any other help. I hand off the book to Clarey, then scoop a bunch of silver dragées into my palm. With one coasting revolution around my skin, they become hard, grainy, and straw colored.

Angorla watches me with rapt attention then murmurs, "*The true Architect*."

"Saint Shiznet. Are those . . . seeds?" Clarey asks, touching the grains in my hand.

I furrow my brow, distracted by Angorla's "architect" outburst, but pressing on for the question we need answered most. "Well, are they seeds or not?"

Her electric eyes flash dim to bright. "Yay and nay; some good seeds, some bad," she answers. "Dark hearts yield dark deeds . . . rusty fruits have metal seeds."

"Fruits," Clarey says. "Goblin fruits."

I only partly hear; I'm wallowing in my own tortured thoughts . . . the memory of that Halloween Eve when Lark gave life to her robotic doll—her putting me on the spot about the bad heart I placed inside her Young Edison project, how it rotted all the mechanisms from within. It's so strangely in tune with Angorla's riddle now.

With anguished clarity, I finally understand why everything here contains pieces of my sister: this world was built entirely upon my guilt over living when she died, which means that its foundation, its very heart, is bad . . . wrong . . . ugly.

That ugliness is not only killing Mystiquiel but has leaked into my real life somehow; has lured in my uncle and trapped him here. And now Clarey and Flannie are in danger, too.

My gut clenches, because only I can stop this. And to do that,

I have to move the final game piece, and land us where Perish waits.

"Is there an orchard around here?" I scoot the seeds around my palm, then start to dump them back on the ground.

"The seeds, they priceless be. Best to keep a few, in case you needs a plant or two."

I shake my head at Angorla's meaningless taunt, but tuck them away in my jeans pocket just in case.

Satisfied, the hobblegob leans her body away from the door, pulling opposite of the fey crowd locked inside. She bleats a goatish laugh, teasing them as though they were animals in a zoo.

"Well, where's the orchard?" When Clarey reiterates my question, Angorla's pointy, furred ears twist in our direction.

"Hills of cement, and walls of stone. Smoking clouds, and the eye that roam. No garden do these make." She lifts her gaze toward the celestial orb, unspoken confirmation that it's how the king is watching our progress. "Only one place seeds sprout, where the rot and rust won't push 'em out. One place where things grow; a pottage of harvests, of sun and snow." She nods her ram's horns toward Wisteria Rising. "Being as your kind be magic-blind, you can't find a way in, lest you eat from the vine."

"What vine?" Clarey asks, looking toward the boutique around the corner.

"Guardian of the orchard. Hers not be a easy door to turn. She be fragile and vengeful. Wound her feelings—your skins itch, your eyes bleed, your ears catch flame, and your belly churn. Choose your bite wise so you don't get burned."

"How do we do that?" I ask.

"The guardian want what anyone want. Acceptance. Not for her charms; love her warts and leave her disarmed."

Clarey passes me a dubious glance.

"O-kay?" I say. "But we're not eating anything without that." I point to the vial of goblin blood at her mismatched feet, skeptical she'll let us have it.

"Want your cure, eh?" Angorla's free hand morphs from its normal shape—if thin, metallic fingers curled like a tiller could be considered normal—into a shovel. She scoops up the vial. "It be yours for a wink and a favor."

Warning bells go off inside my mind: *Never make deals with faerie-kind.* They're cryptic, wily, and tricksters. It's one of the rules not just of Mystiquiel lore . . . but of any fey mythos. Just like never eat their food. But we don't have a choice on either front if we're going to win this game and rescue our loved ones before the portal closes.

As though reading my thoughts, Clarey ogles the watch ticking away on the duffel.

"Well?" I ask him.

"Ten till nine."

He holds my gaze. I know we're sharing the same misgivings. What if the hobblegob is another distraction, put in our path to slow us down?

I set my jaw. "If we make this trade, will you stay out of our way?"

Angorla's goat-bleating laugh erupts again, sounding a bit too much like Juniper's giggles for comfort. *Weird.*

"Once trade made," she answers, "I blend into the background, tall as a tree, quiet as a wall. Not stand between you and any door, evermore."

"Except that one," I say, motioning to the bakery's entrance, the only barrier between me and the shouting fey. I'm not about to let her weasel her way into letting them out to attack us by agreeing to ambiguous terms. "You'll hold them off until we're gone."

She smiles then, baring those rust-slicked teeth. "Ah, an earthen bird who knows the power of every word. Impressed I be. I'll siege this door till you can flee."

"It's a deal," I answer, despite Clarey's garbled attempt to stop me. "What do you want in return?"

Angorla shifts her shovel-hand to a tin box that captures the vial inside. She straightens out her arm so the box is only inches from me. "All I ask is you lift the lid. The only favor I'll ever bid."

I start to stretch my fingers toward her.

"Nix, your gloves are gone," Clarey reminds me, although I've already thought of that, and I've also reasoned out it's the means to her end. She saw me change the seeds, saw the stained glass overtake the window. It's possible she even watched me alter the troll. She said I'm an earthen bird, so she obviously knows I'm not from here. Even if she doesn't realize I'm her creator, she's aware of what my touch can do, and craves it.

Angorla wants to be real like me; like Clarey. Question is, would she be more or *less* dangerous to us as flesh and blood?

Hearing my dad's watch click away each second, I go for broke and touch my fingers to the box's edge. In a blink of metal, fur, and bone, Angorla changes. Her metallic horns and teeth become jagged, grayish white, and calcified, free of rust. A thumping heart replaces her internal mechanical whirring. From her head to her ankles, everything metal thins and vanishes—replaced by brown fur and pink skin like a baby mouse's. Her eyes

permutate from blinking lights to doe-eyed irises with slitted-white pupils like crescent moons. She's no longer a cybernetic caricature, but a true organic being.

Throughout the unsettling conversion, she grunts and growls, never releasing the door's latch. The claw that earlier formed the padlock shifts to a cloven hoof with a skeletal finger and thumb curving at the ends, holding tight to keep the faeries—who, upon seeing her transformation, snarl and howl even louder—at bay.

"Praises to you, and cures be yours." Angorla opens the fist of her free hoof to toss the vial my way.

I catch it midair.

"Once you take a sip," she says, "best to swallow no seeds. Lest you wish the moss to grow roundabout, marking you as one of ours, like the orchard's finest trees."

Her warning is reminiscent of Uncle's insistence all this time, never to eat the fruit until he'd cleaned and prepared it. Is that why? Is she being literal? That a seed, when mixed with the squid ink . . . *king's blood* . . . could somehow call the plants here, cause them to bind themselves to that human? I can't afford to be distracted by his betrayal or the danger he seemingly put our customers in. I *know* him, and there has to be a reason for what he did. He'll tell me once I find him.

"So we're even?" I ask the hobblegob, overtly aware of the danger of loose ends in this place.

Her slobbery bearded mouth lifts to a smile of pure chicanery as she tightens the hoof holding the bakery door. "Aye, we be aligned in plot now, you and you." She aims a wink at me, then one at Clarey. "And for my troth, I follow through." The door has stopped rattling behind her. "Best to go then. Afore your face be breaked."

Angorla gestures where my stained-glass likeness shines, glossy and prismatic, then camouflages herself once more with the storefront's pattern, so I can see through her to the happenings within. Several of the trapped faeries take up flinging chairs at the window, causing the image of me to fissure and crack.

Clarey shoves Flannie's collar and Mom's book in the duffel, zips it, and nods at me, looking as wary as I feel.

"Hope that doesn't come back to bite us," he sputters on our sprint for the greenhouse boutique.

"Well, at least now she can't give us tetanus."

He frowns.

I chomp. "Metal teeth?"

We arrive at the boutique before he can unleash the annoyance narrowing his eyes. Thankfully, no reflections look back at us from the shop's glass front; but it's a catch-22, because, be it ice—Angorla mentioned something about snow—or an enchantment that coats the inside, it makes any preparation for what awaits us impossible.

I don't see the vine guardian anywhere. Nothing but a metallic white handle shaped like an S. I start to grab it, but Clarey pulls me aside.

"That thing is breathing." He gestures to the handle, then absently touches the place behind his covered left ear where his BAHA sits beneath latex conforming to flesh.

He waits a beat or two, then steps between me and the door. A soft glow seeps out through the glass's frosty surface—a nod to Juniper's calming lights in Astoria. He grips the handle but recoils when the metal shifts, forming a white, serpentine vine. Only now do I hear the intake and outpour of breath. I also see

it in the plant's stem, a rise and fall of what appear to be ribs beneath the thin fleshy coating.

Next, the plant unfurls wide, opaque leaves, and a fruit the size and shape of an egg droops at the end. It's ugly: fuzzy and brown with protruding carbuncles that look like albino raisins. Were I sketching it as a character in a panel, I'd draw a kiwi with a severe case of acne.

"Blech," I mutter.

"My sentiments exactly," Clarey answers. "Also, how are we supposed to make a wise choice if there's only one fruit?"

I press my lips together in thought. This is nothing I've ever drawn or imagined. "Tap it or something," I offer. "Maybe it will multiply."

Clarey does as I suggest, but there remains only one. However, two notable things do happen: first, the carbuncles burst with a nauseating, gurling hiss. A fog puffs out from the ruptured blisters, releasing a stench like skunkweed and stagnant bogs.

Gagging simultaneously, Clarey and I step back and shield our noses. Two moments later, the leaking, furry-brown husk sheds, revealing a shiny, smooth, and glowing rind underneath, shifting from red to purple to orange.

It dawns on me, the vividness of these colors, as opposed to the grayscale we've seen everywhere else. The vine and fruit are organic, no metal or rust in sight. I uncover my face to share the observation with Clarey, but I'm distracted by a new scent. With each color's fluctuation, the aroma also changes: whereas the brown shade was pungent and off-putting, the red is refreshing, like a splash of sparkling wine; following that comes purple, triggering a waft of earthy sweetness that brings to mind baked

plums sprinkled with brown sugar; and lastly, orange, carrying a delicious note of caramel and citrus.

After the cycle runs through the three bright colors, it starts over again with the brown. The fuzzy husk returns, bearing new blisters that pop and emit a worse vaporous stench than the prior time, before repeating the shedding process. The jewel-toned rinds and their appealing fragrances follow in pulsing sequence. Then back to the zit-faced kiwi. Over and over and over, with no apparent end.

"It's a trick, made to play on our natural instincts," Clarey says.

I pinch my nose tight in preparation for the oncoming brown cycle. "So if we use common sense and eat it in any of its ripe and delectable stages, we're going to suffer the vine's wrath."

"Although bleeding eyes and itchy skin actually don't sound so bad compared to putting that in our mouths." Clarey flattens his entire hand across his lips and nose just as the newest furred and blemished rind releases putrid, wet streams.

When red overtakes, I bare my nose to the scent of sweet wine. "That's the whole point, then. We have to eat when it's at the right stage—or rather, the *wrong* stage. The blighted one; the unsightly one; the most repellent to all our senses."

"Love the vine, warts and all. Does everything have to be literal here?" Clarey complains as he draws his hand away from his mask during our temporary reprieve. No doubt having to cover his face is a constant reminder of his own ever-changing features and flesh. Come to think of it, this whole process is an unusually cruel pantomime of what's happening to him. Almost as if it was planned for that very purpose: to torment and annoy.

And I'm betting that's exactly what Perish had in mind.

If only we had time, I'd convince Clarey he's nowhere close to being abhorrent like this noxious fruit. He's the same irresistible guy, even with a pumpkin for his face.

The brown cycle shoots vapors into the air again. I cringe; the idea of eating something that smells like marshlands and skunk glands makes my stomach flip. Not to mention the thought of the pustules bursting on our tongues. But when glass shatters around the corner at the bakery, indicating the fey have broken out, it prompts me to man up.

"Pluck it off," I tell Clarey, afraid to chance touching it myself without gloves. "The second it goes brown and fuzzy."

Clarey wrinkles his bulbous nose as the deep purple lightens around the stem to a pinkish hue; then an orange, warm as sunrise, spreads across the shiny rind. The moment it begins to grow fur and fades to brown, Clarey snaps it free and holds it by the stem. He glances over my shoulder where the sounds of snarls and growls grow louder and closer.

"Remember not to swallow any seeds, okay?" I clasp the vial of ink I've just uncorked. Clarey rolls his shoulder under the duffel straps—like a soldier preparing for his march to war—his fleshy mask almost gray with dreaded anticipation as carbuncles appear on the fruit.

Pinching my nose to suppress the surge of bile in my throat, I tap the vial, releasing a dot onto my tongue, then do the same for Clarey. I watch the black fade to white, then quickly put the stopper in to contain the rest. Clarey returns the favor with the fruit, holding it for me as I take a bite, avoiding the center where a fat seed appears. I chew while struggling not to notice the seeping bumps and spindly fibers gumming up my teeth. Not even

waiting for my reaction, Clarey shoves the remainder—all but the seed—into his mouth.

The carbuncles dissolve on my tongue, but the horrible stench and flavor I assumed would slam into me never come. Instead, my palate lights up—though not in reaction to a flavor. It's like bands of color smear across every sensory receptor. I'm overwhelmed by a variegation of emotions—free-falling in a thrilling rush: bouncing in a pink bubble of happiness that bursts to black rage then unrolls like a sponge to catch me in a yellow cushion of sorrow. The soft sadness swells to crimson excitement, then becomes a tidal wave, propelling me along blue currents of calm, ending in a silvery waterfall . . . a purge of loneliness.

It's then I realize the king's blood has spread over my tongue with perpetual warmth and raced along my taste buds and throat to form an oily, salty sleeve that repels any conventional flavors. Not only that, it binds all those emotions into one pristine color and feeling: the blank white of longing. Such a wide, yawning canvas, that if it weren't for the dispelling qualities of the royal blood, I'd *have* to have the experience again—regardless of the gruesome conveyer: sizzling warts, wooly fuzz, and foul odors notwithstanding—just to glut the endless expanse, just to survive.

Now I get the allure of goblin fruits, and the danger they present: They magnify human emotions, to an intensity so powerful, it's the closest thing to magic most people will ever know. The emotional overflow rises high enough to sweep one into the drowning depths of oneself, unless it's forced to spill over by the king's cure. The enchanted candles act as a funnel, collecting that overflow.

It makes sense, even in the context of Christina Rossetti's fictional poem . . . Laura craved the goblin fruit to the point of

dying because humans get addicted to that enhanced version of what *makes* them human. But the distillation of goblin blood in each of Uncle's pastries protects our customers from the full potency. So they return to the bakery again and again because they're drawn to that singular reminder of their humanness, instead of being driven to craven madness by an unrelenting hunger that only the rush of every emotion at once can satiate.

They return to *feel* alive, not to stay alive.

Coming back to my senses, I savor the smoky spiciness left on my tongue, something like cloves mixed with cinnamon and black cardamom—the residue of the king's blood. I glance at Clarey, who's already looking back at me.

"Trippy," he says.

"Right?" I answer, breathless.

Before we can expand our one-syllable exchange to concern that the door still hasn't opened, the vine grows to the size of an anaconda and wraps us in a swirl of stems and leaves, lifting us off the ground just as the faeries rush around the corner. The pressure around my chest and waist isn't constrictive or threatening. It's gentle and protective. And when Clarey's eyes widen with awe instead of fear or pain, I know it's the same for him.

The plant continues to grow and raises us so high our would-be attackers below begin to look like metal ants.

"If you're planning to write a story about this, I've got a great title," Clarey comments, his hands clasped around the white stem surrounding his torso.

"Yeah?"

"Jack-o'-lantern and the Beanstalk." He waggles the ridges of his brow.

I snort. "That's bad, Clarey. And I thought the fruit stank."

I'd be questioning how calmly he's dealing with this if I weren't also adrift on the euphoric aftereffects of our sample. Seeing him start to joke about things gives me hope he might make it through this without any more attacks. He knows, once we get everyone home, all will be right again.

At least for us.

My mood plummets at that thought, on an opposing trajectory to the vine swooshing so high it could give the thirty-foot Grim Reaper's Drop Tower a run for its money. I inhale deeply. Being here in the smoky clouds, I can't escape the view below: the city so like the one we know, yet so different. Peering through hazy ribbons from this elevation, I find that the only splotches of color—red patches and dripping smears—look even more like seeping wounds than rust.

Mystiquiel is bleeding . . . dying.

With another breath, I draw in the burnt candle scent swishing around our heads, a reminder of Uncle and all he's hiding. Does he know the root of this plague? Was he trying to help treat it somehow with the emotion-filled wax melts?

All conjecturing takes a back seat once the vine swings off to the right. My stomach bobs when we begin a sweeping descent toward the roof of the greenhouse boutique. I'm still too high up to know if the solid whitish surface is bricks or aluminum siding.

We pick up speed. My anxious screech joins Clarey's and I struggle to keep my eyes open against the smoke and wind sucking them dry. If we don't slow down, we're going to splatter against that surface like bugs on a windshield. Clarey must have

the same thought, because he's wriggling against our binds as desperately as I am.

Almost as if offended by our efforts, the vine releases us and we free-fall—on a collision course for the roof.

motherboard

Our eye strains—foiled, furious. Don't let her out of our sight! But she will be, as will the boy, once the orchard swallows them whole. Only a temporary parting. For though we have no feet and hands to walk or grab, we have greedy minds that bend to our whims. They do our bidding, they worship our commands. It was too easy to lure them, to trick them. Soon, victory will be ours. We will infest all that stands, and bring Mystiquiel to its knees. Ashes to ashes, dust to dust. Let the clock tick its last . . . and the king fade to rust.

21

magic

My scream folds in on itself as Clarey and I plummet faster than a massive drop on a roller coaster. Our clothes and hair whip around us. Gravity fails to compress my organs and hold them steady, leaving them to float inside me like balloons waiting to burst.

Inches away from the roof, the slats begin to move, manifesting as something alive and circuitous. The waxen smoke clears, and giant white vines—carbon copies of the door handle—open like a curtain. They must belong to the same plant . . . or creature . . . that guarded the entrance.

Just before we slam through the opening, one long, winding tendril forms a chute beneath us. We plop down; Clarey first, then me on his tail. Our butts bump over scales and leaves on a progression toward the depths of the orchard.

I catch glimpses of trees, both frost and blossoms somehow simultaneously weighing the branches. Familiar fruits I recognize from bakery shipments burst through in mouthwatering

increments. An opening appears in the thick canopy, and our chute spins us downward like a curly slide. The view of the trees vanishes, obscured by swirls of white stalks and pearlescent leaves.

We're hurled off toward grass and dirt. Clarey hits ground, drops the duffel, and scrambles to his knees to try to catch me. Unable to slow my momentum, I slam into his chest. Gripping my wrists, he thuds onto his back and drags me with him.

Tiny lights hover around us. For an instant, I worry we're being attacked by microscopic sprites. Instead, it's floating seeds not much bigger than dust motes—incandescent and flickering in soft blues and oranges. In the dimness, the effect is both magical and disorienting, as if we're locked within a fiber-optic snow globe and someone has shaken us up.

Dizziness swarms my head, as though I'm still spiraling down the slide. Then Clarey wriggles and reminds me that he's pinned *beneath* me. All my senses grind to a halt, focused only on us: my body pressed against his, chest to chest, belly to belly, leg to leg, just like Flannie earlier; but I'm not having the calming effect she did.

The tension I've always stretched between us to hold us apart now constricts and tethers us together, tighter than the vines that dropped us here. Our faces almost touch, my nose inches from the carved tip of a mask that's mostly converted to flesh now.

My bangs undulate each time he inhales and exhales, and his salt-and-pepper curls do the same beneath my own frazzled wheezing.

"Anything hurt?" He breathes the question, sending several floating seeds on a trajectory toward my face.

"No. You?" My response, just as husky and winded, volleys the teensy lights back to him.

"I'm good."

"Good." Propped on my elbows, I debate rolling off, but every muscle in my body locks in refusal. Clarey's clutching my ribs, and I don't dare move and break this spell. The expectant silence expands, disrupted only by the leaves confining us in a tentlike stasis—shuffling to the same breeze that carries scents reminiscent of Uncle slicing fruit and preparing recipes. Yet there, somewhere behind it, lingers something so cold it burns.

I've no desire to find the root of it all . . . even to see the orchard on the other side. I'm too grateful to be shielded from everything, to finally be cloaked from the orb overhead, to have quiet, with no one or nothing watching us, because this pocket of enchanted seclusion *should* belong to just Clarey and me.

No one else needs to know how his body reacts to mine, the attraction I'm always avoiding undeniable by the changes in us both, the strain of his muscles and the heat radiating everywhere we touch.

Clarey's gaze holds me transfixed, even more dazzling than the magical drifting seeds, aglow with an intensity I've seen in the past but never dared to decipher. His fingers find their way over my T-shirt, grating along the bumps of my ribs, then easing over my leather jacket and bared neck, stopping to push my hair from my face.

A gasp slips from my mouth. I wince at the ineptness of the sound, and my cheeks flush.

What's wrong with me? I'm not some chaste little prom queen at my first after-party. I've had my stints with surface

thrills and lust. Ebon taught me a lot more than just how to assemble mechanical components and diagnose a check-engine light. But I didn't know him inside and out. I've never felt this with any other guy: desire tempered by respect—a *belonging* so bright and real, so pure and lovely—an affection so comforting yet at times so frenetic, that I'm terrified to do anything that could taint or alter it.

Maybe Clarey's afraid, too, by the way his heart pounds against my own.

"We were going to wait to talk, right?" I finally manage.

"Not sure," he answers, jaw twitching and rippling to orange jowl lines. "'*When all this is over*' feels really far away. Maybe we wait on the talking part and skip to—" He stops cold and tenses up. "A mask seems like a weird precedence for a first kiss."

I have to smile then, because leave it to Clarey to use the word "precedence" in a moment like this.

"Shut up. We've only got a minute to spare, so either you do this thing or I'm giving you a fatter lip."

He snorts. "Gourd abuse; pretty sure there's a law against that somewhere."

"Ugh." I start to roll off, but Clarey grips my biceps gently, an invitation for me to wait.

"No more jokes. I promise." He grows somber. His hands settle at my jaw, cradling either side.

The pads of his fingers scrape my skin, rougher than usual, as if some leaves and grass still cling to them from our fall. But it doesn't matter, because I'm too caught up in other sensations—other points of contact—to care. Every curve and hollow tucked beneath my clothes smolders and softens, conforming to the

lean, angular planes of him. I may as well be made of wax and he of flame, melting my barriers to expose everything I keep hidden under the surface.

I skim my hands along the sides of his head, my thumb stroking where his left ear has started to fuse with the prosthesis, wishing more than anything I could touch those soft curls just behind his BAHA instead of carved latex.

I resent the inability to look at his true face—that soft skin, those familiar features. This mask is standing between me and all the endearing parts and parcels of the boy I've been falling for since kindergarten. Still, this creation is also a part of him, the incredible talent I've watched him hone and master over the years, so I don't even hesitate when he coaxes my mouth toward his.

His eyes flutter down, thick lashes framing the barest glimpse of ice blue and warm amber. I let him guide me, tilting my head, willing to take this chance . . . shoving all thoughts—of Lark, Jaspar, masks, Goblin Kings, and time itself—aside. Just for one second. Just for one kiss.

My eyes close. A momentary burst of cinnamon-spiced breath precedes soft, plump lips brushing mine. I moan, ready to take control and seek his tongue, that part of his mouth his costume can't conceal, when suddenly, I'm shoved aside as he yelps and rolls out from under me.

My back throbs where I hit the ground, and grass pokes my nape—as uncomfortable and itchy as the questions plaguing me. Does my breath stink? Do *I* stink? I mean . . . a dunk in the ocean is the closest thing I've had to a bath since this morning.

Then the cruelest question trumps them all: Did Clarey come to his senses and realize I'm only a substitute for Lark?

Dazed, with the spice of his breath clinging to my lips, I stare up at him. He kneels with arms lifted and hands opened wide, turning his fingers from front to back and chanting under his breath: "No, no, no. This can't be happening. It can't."

The glowing seeds drift around him, their serene suspension at odds with his agitated tone.

I shake off my fugue, shutting down the tiny fires inside my body and snuffing out my insecurities so I can focus. His hands look like he's wearing the gloves from his costume: brown and withered, with gnarled-vine fingers that twist and twine. At the ends, where there should be fingernails, leaves begin to sprout.

I bite back a shocked screech. It can't be. He dropped the gloves on the sidewalk outside the bakery . . . at the corner of the alley, when Filigree herded him and Flannie my way at Jaspar's command.

Those are *his* fingers. *His* hands.

I scramble up to crouch beside him. He's struggling to keep it together, but I know that look in his eyes now . . . the way he clutches his chest and struggles to breathe. I also know how to help. Cold is what he needs; cold will keep him grounded.

Snow. The white frost I saw coating the branches on our way down—Angorla mentioned sun and snow. I turn my attention to the surroundings and slap several pearlized leaves aside to open the view. The luminous seeds drift out on a back draft of wind, sailing away through a canopy of autumn colors and mud-brown branches overhead. The covering is thick enough that I can't see sky or sun. Yet strands of bright yellow warmth slip through, printing a dappled pattern on the ground that leads to a path covered with snow, mere inches away.

I turn to Clarey, who's propped his back against a trunk. "I'm not leaving; I just need to grab something to help."

He tucks his chin to his chest, draws up his knees, and gasps. Hoping he heard me, I duck my head through the opening where several tree branches spread apart, inviting soft flakes to drift down like confectioners' sugar. The whiteness coats limbs, fruits, and leaves already gilded with shimmery ice, and speckles red, seedy berries sprouting from green bushes thick with thorns.

As I consider the oddity, it begins to make a strange sort of sense.

Keeping my sights on Clarey, I vow to work it out in my head later. I only have to crawl forward a few inches to scoop a handful of snow, and am relieved when it doesn't change beneath my touch. I retreat back to Clarey. My palm grows numb with the chill as I take his hands and, turning them upward, press the icy clumps into place. He makes fists around them.

His knuckles tighten; the snow begins to melt between the seams of his fronded fingers, seeping onto the lap of his pinstriped tapered pants. His breathing returns, slow and even. Unspeaking, he stares at the leaves along his fingertips, how they're dotted with clumps of frost, then turns his eyes to me and mimes the word "Thanks."

Then he drags the duffel over, stopping to look at the watch that now reads 9:20 p.m. Less than three hours left to get out of here.

Tick-tick-tick.

22

the burden of masks

Clarey growls. "I'm sorry I lost us time . . . and our moment. Gah. I just . . . I'm not broken, I swear."

"Of course you're not!" I kneel beside him. "Who wouldn't freak out at this?" I grasp his cold hands in mine. The vines and leaves tipping his fingers stretch down to tap the back of my wrists.

He shakes his head. "Yeah, right. You barely flinched at the zippers on your face. You're a badass. Hero material."

"Not always a badass. And I'm the furthest thing from a hero."

"You're more of one than me." He sighs then—a colossal intake and exhale so deep, it carries the weight of this weird, wild otherworld we're trapped in. "That thing Jaspar said . . . about me not having a backbone in Chicago. I don't know how he knew, unless he somehow saw my memory in the maze when it played out in a mirror. It was like I was *literally* back there again, reliving it."

My pulse kicks up. So Clarey did share my experience;

having one of his most painful memories ripped out of his head and reenacted as entertainment for a vindictive faerie.

"I've wanted to tell you for so long," he continues, voice trembling. "But—I was worried you'd think I'm a big ole pantywaist."

"First off," I scold, "you hate the word 'panty' as much as I do. So let's go with underwear-band, okay?"

He snorts, then stretches his legs out in preparation to stand. "We can't do this now. We're short on time already."

He's right. This isn't the best place or time, but I wouldn't dream of stopping him. He has to leave this behind to move forward, and he needs all his wits about him for what's coming next in the game.

I press a hand on his chest to hold him in place. "I told you that's what friends do. They wait till you're ready, then they're there to listen. We'll make time." I plop down, my back against the trunk beside his, and nudge his shoulder.

He puffs out his cheeks until he looks like a blowfish, then nods. "All right, I'll make it quick. There was a girl at my school in Chicago. Kendra. She was obsessed with me, but totally oblivious to it, if that makes sense? She always wanted to touch my hair and my eyelashes. We weren't even going out or anything, and she'd come up to me at pep rallies or lunch and rake a hand through my white streak, run a fingertip down my forehead. She had a boyfriend, Jackson—a big shot on the varsity basketball team—and she couldn't even see how ticked it made him when she hung all over me. She sent me texts. Weird ones. Said my forehead felt soft like a puppy's belly. Asked if there were other puppy patches hidden under my clothes."

My hands fist instinctively. "Holy crap. That wretch was

fetishizing you." I gnaw on my lip ring, biting back the million curse words I want to spout.

"Yeah. And I'm the freak, right?" Clarey half laughs, but I see the gesture for the coping mechanism it is.

My gut lurches, a surge of sickness for the intrusiveness . . . the insensitivity. I try to imagine how it would feel to have someone not even care who you are inside. Who treats you like a pet or a windup toy. Like something they could own. And I can't for the life of me understand how any person could treat *another* person like that. I wouldn't even treat a faerie that way.

"So, anyhow, fast-forward to a couple of weeks after the school year ended. Summer break. It was June, when my mom was at her worst. Hospice, you know?" He sniffs, then continues. "She'd always wanted to take me to the annual Blues Festival in Millennium Park there. Since she couldn't go, I promised I'd bring her back a program, and get it signed by the artists. I was just hoping for enough time, maybe even a chance to frame it, hang it in her room. So I went opening night. Had a couple of friends who were going to meet me at the outdoor amphitheater."

His shoulders rise on another sigh, then his fingernail frond traces the divot in his eyebrow. It dawns on me that there's still the detail of that scar, and my nausea surges because this already ugly tale is about to turn violent, and I'm not sure I can suppress all the vigilante justice I'm going to need to expend.

"On the last day of school, I blocked Kendra from my phone. It was so great not to be around her every day after that I almost forgot about her twisted infatuation. Unfortunately, she hadn't, and neither had Jackson. Since she couldn't call or anything, I was totally oblivious that they'd broken up over me and he was out for blood. Kendra had stalked me enough to know I liked the

blues, but I didn't know she'd mentioned it to Jackson. So I wasn't watching for anyone to be following when I stepped onto a quiet path in the trees on the way to find my friends at the festival."

I hear a leafy rattle as Clarey's palm quakes. I grip his hand in mine again, anchoring him.

"I felt someone tug me from behind. He dragged me into an abandoned thicket and shoved me down, pounded me, kicked me. Called me a freak show, and a lot worse . . ." He swallows. "My BAHA busted, my ribs ached, my jaw throbbed, I felt like I needed to puke. I wanted to fight back but didn't have any idea how. You know my dad hated that about me. I was too skinny, too mild mannered. The only makeup he would've condoned for me to wear was the eye-black of football players." Another half laugh.

I squeeze Clarey's hand in encouragement. I remember when he first lived in Astoria. How his dad never approved of his hobbies. Mr. Darden couldn't understand what we as kids already did: that clothes, cosmetics, piercings, tattoos, all those things on the outside . . . they don't define a person. They're just one small fraction of who they are.

"Anyway, I was getting creamed pretty bad. Just laid there like a lump, hoping it would be over soon, that Jackson would wear himself out. I could tell he was drunk, because every word was slurred. Then he pulled a knife and told me he was going to send my skunk patch to Kendra as a present." Clarey's entire body convulses.

I lace an arm around him in solidarity.

"I shouted for help, but the music had already started, and no one could hear. He made one cut." Clarey touches his scar. "That's when the adrenaline kicked in. I grabbed a fallen

branch off the ground and thwacked his leg. I heard his kneecap pop, and he went down. Voices were coming our way, and I knew someone would find him. So I left him there in the dirt . . . left to get that program for my mom. Pretty sure I was in shock. I was bleeding, it hurt to breathe, my hearing aid buzzed like radio fuzz, and my clothes were ripped, but all I could think was I'd made Mom a promise and intended to make good, because it was probably the last one I'd ever get to keep. I didn't tell anyone what happened. When my grandparents freaked out about my broken BAHA and the cut that needed stitches, I said I got drunk and tried to climb the stage and fell. Getting punished for underage drinking was better than admitting the truth. It's not like Jackson ganged up on me. It was mano a mano. I should've been able to fight him off. Maybe my dad was right. It would've helped to know how to defend myself."

"But you *did* defend yourself."

"Yeah, but maybe if I had learned to throw a punch or two, I wouldn't have ruined Jackson's leg. He was never able to go back to basketball after that. Lost any chance for a scholarship. Of course, he didn't tell anyone, either. We had an unspoken pact. But Kendra figured it out. That's the one good thing that came of it. She totally avoided me afterward because she felt so ashamed."

"Nice to know she could act halfway human."

Clarey huffs. "After that, if anyone stared at me for too long, or seemed overly interested, it would take me right back to Kendra's fixation, and to that beating in the park. Especially in crowds; that's when the panic attacks started. My grandparents sent me to a psychiatrist. I used the excuse of falling in front of hundreds of people. That it was why I only felt safe when I wore

masks. Because others weren't scrutinizing the *real* me. Maybe I shouldn't have lied, but . . ." His voice trails off.

"I get it." I lift his wrist and press my cheek to the back of his gnarled hand. Like him, I was never completely honest with my doctor, either. Clarey averts his eyes, sure indication I need to take this in a new direction. Turn it back around to something positive. "So did your mom get her signed program?"

He meets my gaze with an expression that can only be described as pride. "Yeah. With five autographs all personalized to her. Even Toni Price signed it."

Clarey doesn't have to test me on that name. Toni was one of Breonna's favorite singers. I know her well because one of her albums has a very Halloween-ish look to it that always makes me uneasy when Clarey pulls it out for a listen: a model wearing an orange dress that blends with the pumpkin in her hands, while little black cats traipse around her feet.

"Inspiring lady. Sixty years old and still doing what she loves." Clarey grins. "Mom gave me the prettiest smile for that one. Said she wanted the program buried with her. So we did."

It gets unbearably quiet for a minute, then a sob escapes him. His vulnerability tugs all my heartstrings, plays them like a violin. It's got to be the musician in him.

I pull him close so he won't see my own eyes leaking. "Clarey, you were always there for her, making her smile. Spending time together. Sharing your love of music. That means you *were* a hero, to her. Not just that day, but every day."

He hugs me, his mouth pressed to my temple. A sniffle or two later, and I feel his lips curve in a grin. "Thanks, Nix." He kisses my hairline, then eases us apart, but keeps one arm around my waist. "Dang. I can't tell you how good that feels, to finally admit

the truth. Maybe that's where I've been tripping myself up. I haven't been able to work through my panic attacks because I haven't been honest with the doctors. I've got to stop being embarrassed and open up for them to really help me. It sucks, though. To be ready to quit hiding . . . to get this thing off and face my monsters head on. But"—he tugs at his chin and his shoulders droop—"now *I'm* the monster."

His frustration fans the flame already burning in my belly. Not just because he was forced to live such an awful experience at the hand of a birdbrained girl and her vindictive ex, but because he was forced by Jaspar to *relive* it before he was ready; because that's what chased Clarey behind the latex now adhered to his skin. And in this moment of triumph when he's itching to cast off the past, to shed the mask in a symbolic show of courage, he can't.

"I'm going to strangle Jaspar," I mumble before I can stop myself.

"No doubt. Just like you pounded those two guys back when we were in elementary school to defend my honor. Just like you were going to shiv Jaspar earlier for your uncle. And I figure you're planning to assault the king for all of us. Unless I can talk you out of it."

"You're the only one who could." I smirk. "You know, it's good we're geared different. I'm aces with my fists, and you rock the makeup. You're logical and level headed where I'm not. When I can't fix something with my own two hands, I get stalled. I could never have made it this far without you. I would've broken down the second I found Uncle's glasses, convinced myself our Halloween curse had won, and he was gone forever. You talked sense into me, gave me back my will to fight."

"Yeah, we're a pretty formidable team." He pulls the duffel straps over his shoulder. "When we get home, we should come up with a logo, print some T-shirts. Make this partnership official." He offers a sly grin, but there's no hiding the sincere hope behind it. He's ready for us to be an *us*.

I force myself not to stare too long at those lips, because it makes me want to discuss our abandoned kiss, even more, to confess my own secret guilt and shame—so we can do this thing right, with all our cards laid out . . . no masks between us of any kind.

Later. Always later.

I clear my throat. "Speaking of teamwork," I say, tapping my dad's pocket watch absently, "let's put our heads together. I can't pin down how our 'magic' works here. If you were to logic it out, what do you think is happening to your hands? It can't have anything to do with the seeds that were floating around, because I'm unaffected."

Clarey shrugs, the duffel shifting with the gesture. "Maybe, since this was part of my completed costume when I imagined it, it's continuing to change me to fit that mold?"

"As good a guess as any."

"Which would mean I'm going to keep changing until we get out of here."

I suppress a groan. "We can't let that happen. You can't become a goblin for real." My mind snags on that thought—reaching for something tucked away. "*Déjà vu.*"

"What are you talking about?" he asks.

"We discussed this last night . . . on our way to Enchanted Delights. When we were debating how to improve your costume, how to make it more true to life. You said—"

"The only way I'd look more real was to actually *become* a goblin." He gulps, a knot appearing under the edge of his mask, then working its way down his throat to vanish before it hit the top button of his shirt collar. "You warned me not to say it aloud. That the Goblin King would drag us into his realm and grant my wish. But we were just goofing. Right?"

My tongue grates the roof of my mouth, dry as sandpaper. "Unless he heard us. Unless Perish took our joke as a challenge, and that's what started this whole thing."

Clarey narrows his eyes, not fully buying my epiphany. "But the portal wasn't open yet when we talked last night. So how could Perish have heard?"

I growl, frustrated. "I'm done playing twenty questions. And sick of entertaining Jaspar with our bumbling around. It's time we get answers from the king himself." I tug Clarey out from under the vines and onto the margin that separates fall from winter.

He stands up next to me, his gaze roving all around. "No way." He releases my hand and gathers a fresh scoop of snow. Straddling both winter and fall, he sprinkles the caked powder by his right shoe, where dead, faded grass transforms to greenish-yellow blades interspersed with autumn leaves. The snow melts the instant it hits warmer ground. "This place is amazing."

"Yeah." I point to our right. "Perish's castle is that way, where summer bisects spring."

"You saw it? Through all of this?" He gestures to the canopy overhead.

"No. I know because that's how I drew it—years ago."

Prompted by Clarey's bewildered expression, I explain everything I remember about why this orchard's layout seems so familiar: that in my earliest sketches, I had four medieval faerie

courts—spring, summer, fall, and winter—that were inhabited by a purely organic Goblin King and his subjects. Back when I tried to restructure the map of my imaginary world to fit a more conservative model than what I saw in dreams, there was no metal, no smoky haze, no electronics.

Inside this orchard, the trees are divided in tribute to those four seasonal courts, to my abandoned all-natural/nonsynthetic concept. Somehow, we landed on the border of autumn—colorful leaves and apples, cranberries, and figs blooming on bushes and limbs—and winter, where persimmons, pomegranates, cherries, and raspberries burst through sleeves of ice and caps of frost.

It makes sense that the king's palace would be sequestered away here, under vines and canopies, protected from uninvited visitors, be they flying sprites or the giant destructive footsteps of dryads.

"Those are panels you never saw"—I finish my account—"because I ditched the idea. But I guess imagining it was enough, like other things here. The good thing is, Perish doesn't have his eye on us now . . . he doesn't know exactly where we are. That gives us the upper hand. Are you with me?"

"Nowhere else I'd be. Just wish I knew how much longer I'll be me." Clarey snaps his wet fingers, making a frog-slapping-cement sound. Frowning worriedly, he swipes his palms down his pants to dry them. "A jack-o'-lantern taking on a Goblin King. Sounds like a great plot for a Claymation Halloween special, yeah?"

I smirk, impressed by the spot-on sarcasm covering up the quiver in his voice. Not only that, but I'm encouraged, too, because for the first time since I lost Lark, the mention of Halloween didn't make me shudder or regress to awful places in my

mind. This gives me new confidence that I'll be ready to tell Clarey everything once we make it through this crazy night. Once life returns to normal again.

Clarey shifts the bag on his shoulder and gestures for me to lead the way. "Okay. Let's go beat this fink together. Leave his whole kingdom in a pile of rust."

23

seasons and treasons

I can't admit to Clarey that my heart doesn't fully share his sentiment for destroying this world. From what I've seen outside the orchard, everything is already headed for rot because I built it wrong; gave it a bad heart. Not to mention, the sickly fey I left behind in the streets and on the sidewalks, surrounded by rainbow puddles that are rusting them through.

Could there be a way to get Uncle and Flannie, then escape this place before the portal closes, yet somehow still heal Mystiquiel?

Everything we've seen so far—the deteriorating sea creatures in the cave, the dead kelpine on the beach—confirms that the plague affects the metal pieces of the denizens of this world. Since those pieces are part of their very essence, it can potentially kill them.

Me, Clarey, Uncle, and Flannie are purely organic: plasmic, calcified, flesh and bones. We don't need any metal parts to live, only to function easier. Our corporeality is our immunity. An

immunity little Bonbon, the troll, and Angorla now share, considering anything metal or rusted disappeared from them with their change.

There's got to be some way I can use this power to help, maybe even to negotiate with Perish.

Clarey and I climb over and around tree roots that rise up through the earth like giant nests. This place is nothing like Juniper's boutique, but it's as alive and wondrous as her blooming displays and ivy ever were. Fruits sprout everywhere—in moss-fringed trees, on bushes, and up from the ground. It appears to be acres and acres wide—yet quickly passable. There are spots where tree roots shift underfoot and the grassy terrain rolls to propel us forward. We keep balance by holding on to each other. At moments when we can see through the canopy, the roof yawns open to a patchwork firmament—blue and sunny in places, and gray and snowy or rainy in others. Along with lacking the orb that watches our every move, this sky harbors no smoky clouds. Here, the sky looks real, like in Astoria.

However, I suspect that like the tent flaps when we first entered Mystiquiel, it's a mirage of some kind, considering vines form the real roof. But fake or not, it *feels* real. I squint in the brilliant sunlight, then flutter my lashes when snowflakes coat them. Both warmth and cold pass across my face between branches.

Along the way, we happen to see the altered troll and Bonbon. They frolic through the leaves and branches, chasing Filigree who hoots a teasing song, the trio playing like children. Bonbon sees us and waves, but continues on with its playmates. As happy as they seem, I start to wonder if they were brought here to be under the king's protection, as opposed to being kept imprisoned.

The possibility confuses and unnerves me, because Perish is not the nurturing type.

Finally, we arrive at summer, where apricots, watermelons, peaches, plums, and gooseberries grow. Through holes in the canopy, the castle's four shiny black spires appear. Clarey and I crouch behind a tangle of thick gooseberry bushes. Spring awaits somewhere in the distance; I can smell a hint of mangoes, pineapples, strawberries, and honeydew melons on the air.

I coax a few branches apart, careful to avoid the thorns, to get a better view. The spires are the only angular aspects to the palace's architecture. They rise at measured intervals along a circular, towering wall carved of tungsten—resulting in craggy edges of silvery-black metallic stone that no one could possibly scale.

Tesla coils ignite in bright white at the spire tips, their alternating electrical currents sizzling to connect to one another and form a dome of lightning over the spheric, skyscraping castle within. The castle's surface of mirrored black glass catches flashes from the spires' lights, throwing off reflections while hiding the occupants and chambers inside.

In the middle of the tungsten wall, a drawbridge forms the only entrance. The circular blockade, a flat spiral that winds in on itself to form a circle, reminds me of a giant coiled burner from an electric stove. It even glows red and emits a heat I can feel from our hiding place.

I turn to Clarey, trying to figure out a way in, when a loud humming whine clips the air as the drawbridge lowers and the red glow softens to black. Five rust-eaten royal knights trot out on the same whirring and corroded unicorn mounts that chased us earlier.

Their leader, Scourge, wears a metal helmet atop frizzed

white hair that glows like fiber-optic strands. His ghastly face—a massive bent nose, barb-edged ears, and slobbery lips—is the sallow hue of sun-bleached bones. He snarls, revealing jagged metal teeth. Veins bulge in his neck and cheeks as he whirls his mount around to face the others and holds up a thin, aluminum arm attached to a hand missing two fingers. Red flakes fill the gaping holes and sift toward the ground as he forms a fist.

Clarey and I lean forward furtively, careful not to make a sound as the king's brother shouts commands to the small regiment.

"Spread out, comb the orchards." His voice box rattles, less impressive than the king's motorized roar; more like an electric mixer turned full blast as its beaters slap an empty bowl. There are murmurs throughout the regiment. Routes are assigned and weapons rationed. Axes, swords, and daggers pass among them.

"If you find any quarry, bring it in," Scourge continues his instructions. "Dead or alive, it matters little. But keep the skins intact for him to hang on his wall in the game room. You know he loves his trophies."

Clarey's eyes pop wide, and I stifle a sharp breath at the gruesome threat. Are *we* quarry? All along, I've thought the king was indulging in a game of wits . . . that he didn't want to harm us so much as play with us. What if I misjudged everything? If he's ready to kill me and Clarey and peel off our flesh, what has he already done to Flannie and Uncle?

Heat singes my ears, followed by a rush of queasiness. No, I have to believe they're okay, or I'll spiral. And it doesn't escape me that getting flayed and put on display is too close to what Clarey went through in Chicago. I won't put him in danger again by exposing us both.

If I step out alone, I can touch each of these knights and give

them the gift of reality—of wellness. It worked for Angorla, won me her loyalty. Once I alter them, they'll be willing to act as our guards. They can help us storm the castle and find out what's really going on.

I stiffen my muscles, about to stand.

Clarey snags my wrist. "What are you planning?" He keeps his voice lower than the pop and buzz of the Tesla coils.

Nibbling on my lip ring, I stare back at him. "Just wait here."

My full intentions must show on my face, because he shakes his head so hard, I'd swear I hear pumpkin seeds rattling inside.

"No way," he murmurs. There's a sharpened edge to his voice; he's trying to be strong in spite of the heightened threat—to us, to Uncle and Flannie. "You're not going out there alone. It's suicide."

"Enough prattling about!" Scourge's command to his regiment cuts through our hushed conversation. "We haven't long before the veil closes. Get to it!"

The veil . . . they *must* be searching for us.

Clarey locks an elbow with mine, holding me crouched beside him.

The unicorn mounts ride into the trees, gears whirring along the paths on either side of our hiding place. Their movement through the grass seems to stir a strange swishing sound from the tree closest to our gooseberry bush. Clarey picks up on it first, then I turn just in time to see the bark move and take a tottery step forward.

Angorla.

Fully appearing, the hobblegob flashes a rancid grin, then grabs Clarey and me by the scuffs of our necks and forces us to our tiptoes as she grows taller before our eyes.

My feet lift off the ground, and I wriggle in her bony-hoofed

grasp, trying to break free. "You said you were on our side," I accuse in a whisper. "And faerie-kind can't lie."

"To my word be true." Her breath smells of fresh berries and warm balm—an odd foil to the rottenness of her character. "Tall as a tree, quiet as a wall. Told you our plots were aligned, and be that they do. I vowed to ne'er stand between you and any door. That counts for drawbridges, too."

With that, she shoves us out of our hiding place and into the path of Scourge. His unicorn startles and wheels around, nearly throwing him from the saddle. Sprawled at the hooves of his mount, Clarey drags me against him. We huddle as close to the ground as possible, arms folded over our heads to shield us from the shredding sting of the blades whirring on the unicorn's hind fetters.

My nerves twitch with exhaustion; the stress they've been under for hours is finally catching up. I peer between my arms as Scourge settles his mount, relieved he hasn't noticed us yet. His full attention remains on Angorla.

"We have orders to slice you up on sight, petty thief," he snarls as he unsheathes a sword, pressing its tip to her throat in one motion so it puckers the pink flesh under her fur. "It'll be a lot easier now that you're flesh and blood. I told you never to show your face here again."

My heart hammers, battering a dirt clod wedged between my chest and the ground. Clarey nudges me. We uncover our heads and belly crawl toward the orchard's border, inching like caterpillars in reverse.

Angorla hisses in our direction, incapacitated by the sword at her throat. "Where you think you be going?"

Scourge glares over his shoulder. His angry lips reshape to a

leering smile and he withdraws the blade. He spins his mount around. "What's this, Gardener? A peace offering?"

Gardener. The truth slams into me: Claws that change to harvesting tools. Her knowledge of the vine that guards the door. Her likenesses to Juniper—horns, laugh, doe eyes. Angorla is the orchard's keeper, fashioned after Clarey's aunt: the real Astoria's boutique owner. I never made the connection while drawing her all this time. Seems my subconscious truly does have a will of its own.

"Aye. An offering." Angorla catches my shoulder. I twirl around, managing to break loose, but she butts me in the stomach with her horns and knocks me into the dirt. My breath shunts out, hollowing my lungs until they ache.

"Hey!" Clarey shouts, distracting the hobblegob.

Shaking off the pain, I sweep a leg under Angorla's mismatched feet, and she topples. I pin her with my good knee, fists ready to pound her face, but freeze instantly when Scourge points the sword toward Clarey's cheek.

"Our king finds your mortal All Hallows' Eve traditions quaint and charming. He's always wanted to carve a pumpkin. I'd ask you don't force me to beat him to the punch."

The air shunts out of me again, both in terror and contemplation. Didn't Jaspar say *exactly* that? That the holiday was quaint and charming?

Snickering, Angorla scrambles up and twists me around—breaking my train of thought. She wraps my hands at my back in vines, rendering my fists *and* my touch useless. "Tell His Majesty I did his bidding, led the girl out of the open skies. I claim pardon for my crimes . . . as reward for catching the prize."

Scourge clips his head in agreement. "Begone, then. But stop flapping your tongue about, or I'll cut it out myself." There's

something strained between them that I can't put my finger on. She grumbles, then toddles away into the trees. The other knights, drawn by the clamor, have returned.

I struggle to loosen my hands. "Don't you idiots know who I am? What I can do for you? I created all of you . . . all of this!"

Scourge scoffs. "If that's so, then you should be well acquainted with the mercurial nature of all *this*. World and idiots alike."

The rusty regiment laughs, as though sharing some private joke. Without another word, Scourge shuffles Clarey forward. I follow behind, wary for signs of panic, but he seems to be numb, quietly processing everything as we step toward the gaping maw of the black castle.

We start across the bridge and I fix my gaze on the spherical glass ahead, for once longing to see Lark's reflection . . . a final glimpse of my sister before it's all over, even if she's screaming at me for my failures. But the image that stares back is distorted and disproportioned under the curved mirror's effect. It's like seeing Lark again that terrible night, but this time it's me: zippers, piercings, black triangles painted around my eyes, and red-lined mouth warping to cavernous lengths—Clarey's SFX masterpiece about to be sealed as my forever face.

Never would I have predicted the goblins that once saved me would be handing me and Uncle over on Halloween, literally bringing my family curse to fruition. Worse, never would I have guessed I'd drag Clarey and Flannie right alongside us.

Trudging onward, I try not to trip over my tired feet while anticipating the horrors that wait at the other side of the drawbridge: death, and my loved ones' skins, strung like trophies across the Goblin King's wall.

24

goblin king

I jerk awake, suspended upside down from the ceiling by my ankles in a damp dungeon. At least, that's what my senses tell me: utter darkness; slick and frigid walls that skim my hands and face as I swing from one end to another; a soured scent like mildewed wood and putrefied fruit.

My body aches, and my hands hang free below my head as a dripping sound resonates all around. I'm reminded of Scourge's callous order to bring us in dead or alive, and the king's penchant for peeled-skin trophies in his game room. My first thought is exsanguination; I'm being drained in prep for my flaying. Yet there are no points of exit, no seeping wounds. My blood still circulates through my veins. It gathers inside my fingertips and bloats my head—making them heavy and warm. Inside the skin of my palms, my heartbeat pulses, as if the organ is about to slip from reach and drop into the emptiness.

Once my mind starts to clear, the drip, drip, drip distills to a tick, tick, tick—a rhythm that drags me back and forth till I'm

nauseated. Working against the stiffness in my elbows, I ease up each palm, one at a time, to pat my clothes, instinctually searching out my dad's watch. Then I realize this tick is louder. Too loud, and it pummels inside the back of my head.

I struggle to recall how I got here, but there's nothing beyond the moment Clarey and I walked across the drawbridge and stepped into the castle. I caught one glimpse of interlocking metal stairways that moved upside down and sideways, leading to black-glass doors that shifted shapes—circular, then octagonal, then square and rectangular, opening to different rooms each time—before some sort of enchantment draped over us.

It floated down, a scented pink cloud wrapping us in warm, sweet fibers. It was as if I took a plunge into a cotton-candy car wash laced with lavender and vanilla bean; my clothes and skin retained the scent, and I felt scrubbed and clean. That's the last thing I remember before waking up alone . . . *or am I?*

"Clarey," I murmur. The lack of a response ignites a fresh spark of dread. I wriggle, bending at the waist to dig my fingers into my ankle binds. Then I stop and return to upside-down position; it's so dark around me, I'm not sure how far my descent would be, were I to break loose.

Remembering the seeds in my pocket, I fish a few out and let them drop. They hit with a pinging tap by the count of two. With my confidence restored, I resume tugging on the ankle binds. The plan is to break loose, roll into the fall, and protect my head. I need to have my feet planted on solid ground so I can search for Clarey, Uncle, and Flannie.

I grunt with the effort, struggling long enough to make my fingers ache before accepting that the fastenings on the leather straps have locks and I don't have the key. Dropping my hands

and straightening my spine, I return to dangling upside down once more. Frigid and resigned, I undulate back and forth like an abandoned scaffold at a construction site.

I've no idea how long I was unconscious, and dread thinking of how many things could've transpired in that time.

What if Perish has killed my loved ones? What if I've lost everything? Everyone? That would mean that because of me, not only did Halloween win . . . so did the Goblin King.

Maybe the two were "in cahoots" all along, as Carl would say.

Carl and Dahlia and their new baby, another reminder of a life only half-lived; the bakery, school, friends, everything in the real world that I took for granted.

The pressure of blood gathering in my head is nothing to the burden of weight behind my eyes, where tears build but can't release.

How could I have been so wasteful? Instead of disparaging that I had a future, enshrouded by guilt for living when Lark died, I should've cherished the gift—like Uncle tried to tell me. Instead of obsessing over an imaginary world, I should've lived life to the fullest with all the wonderful people who were beside me in reality, supporting me, loving me. I should've given that love back without reservation or regret.

Now, it's too late.

Every ounce of hope drains from my chest to my pulsing fingertips, then out into the dark depths around me—a spiritual exsanguination even more agonizing than the physical version might have been.

My wallowing shatters with a loud gong that shakes my surroundings, shuddering through my bones. I slam my hands over

my ears and scream, but can't even hear my own wails over the cacophony.

BONG-BONG-BONG.

Four times, five . . . again and again until it reaches ten.

Even with the sensory overload, I realize where I must be and what's happening: I'm imprisoned inside a gargantuan clock, tied upside down to a pendulum, and there's only two hours left until the veil closes.

Not that it matters. I can't go back without my loved ones. *I won't.* I have to use my remaining time to make sure this can never happen again. That no one else can fall into this wilderness crafted by my mind. That the entrance is closed forever.

It's up to me to finish what the rust and ruin started.

The moment my ears stop ringing and my head stops pounding, the swish of curtains screeching on metal hooks erupts from somewhere in front of me—and then a flood of soft light spills across the space, leaving me aligned with a clear glass door.

Giant gears and pulleys make up the floor only inches from where the hair behind my bangs flaps at the end of my scalp. The inner workings twist and churn, cranking through bits of fruit and cracking the seeds. The metal teeth gum up with pulp and rinds, yet somehow still move. The goop appears to serve as machine oil, lubricating the gears. Craning my neck upward reveals black roman numerals the size of hubcaps decorating a clock's brassy face as big as a hot air balloon stationed above me. The fruit itself falls off withered vines that sprout where the frame's rotten wood splits apart, like tufts of grass finding their way through cracked cement.

I relax my neck, setting my attention forward again as I continue to swing. The perpetual inverted movement makes concentration tricky, but through the glass front, on the other side, a black iron Victorian streetlamp comes into focus, anchored into the stone floor.

The bulb pops and wavers, casting buttery light on a pair of legs swathed in slim-fitted paisley pants tucked into grommeted knee boots. A coppery cape sweeps the floor, swaying to reveal the prismatic dagger belted at the pants' waist. The emerald and rose-gold color scheme, smeared and bright like drops of paint in turpentine, gives him away before I can even make out the goggles and smokestack-puffing hat.

When he withdraws the unicorn dagger and pierces the tip of his thumb so a bead of inky liquid wells up, fading to white upon its introduction to the air, it doesn't even faze me. His shifting blood is the clue to a secret I already know.

I figured out his true identity right before the pink enchantment pulled me under. The character who represents our deliveryman's true form . . . the one whose face I could never quite make out enough to finish a sketch.

Jaspar is Perish. Perish is Jaspar. The Goblin King is my mystery doppleganglia.

That's why I haven't seen them at the same time, not once. It's why Filigree, the king's prized pet, sat upon Jaspar's shoulder at the bakery and followed his command. It's why Scourge's remark about his brother's interest in the holiday rang a bell in my mind after Jaspar had proclaimed the same passion in the fun house.

Most significantly, it's why our deliveryman never showcased any metallic parts in the real world; why he remains warm and multihued here in Mystiquiel while everything around him

fades, cold and grayscale. He can change his inner circuitry, fashion a hologram to cloak himself in whatever form he wishes, displaying brilliant colors and beautiful features like a peacock turning his tail feathers back to front, from drab to kaleidoscopic, to captivate and entice at will.

Considering I'm the one who gave the Goblin King a predilection for illusions and mind games, I should've guessed it from the beginning. I grit my teeth, holding back a snarl of frustration.

This means the Goblin King has been with me the entire journey since I stepped into the fun house—an image stitched to my reflection in the maze, a dark figure astride a carousel pony chasing me like a runaway fox, a shadow sneaking up behind me at the bakery: prodding me with clues, taunting me with riddles, tormenting me with memories he shouldn't know.

Yet he does know, because he was born of my own mind. He's been in my life since I started dreaming of this world . . . drawing it into existence. And then somehow—for some reason my uncle has chosen to withhold—he came into Astoria when we opened Enchanted Delights.

That's the part I can't make sense of. What dropped a piece of my imagination onto our bakery's doorstep? And why did Uncle sign up to do his bidding?

Also, Perish's constant presence as Jaspar bids another question: What's the true nature of the portal . . . the veil? Is it open perpetually, or does he hold some sort of key?

A knuckle knocks on the glass in front of me. "Have a nice nap, did you?"

The voice belongs to Jaspar, but I'm no longer playing his game.

"*Perish.*" The revelation deserves a lot more volume and

emphasis than the raspy whisper I manage. Too bad I've been hanging upside down with my neck muscles overextending to hold my heavy cranium.

"Ha!" From the other side of the glass, Jaspar's swishing leaf voice morphs into Perish's powerful laugh, an engine revving for a race. "*Now* you are worthy to see the king's true face." His holographic facade flickers bright then dark, before fully surrendering to the character I could sketch in my sleep: black, silver, and white metal intertwined with lustrous flesh in shimmery shades of white, silver-blue, and palest pink; his boots, suit, and smoldering top hat replaced by an opened shirt tucked into flowing trousers with humanoid feet—bare, graceful, and long—peering from the hems. His burgundy hair shifts to ombre strands styled in four braids—two on either side above his temples threaded with iron beads—dangling over the remainder of thick waves draped long and loose across the mechanism strapped to his back. Smoke plumes into the air, seeping from the rubbery coiled tubes that span the contraption. All this topped by a pair of fuzzy black antlers that anchor a crown pulsing with electricity.

"Where are they?" I mumble, hoping he can hear the muffled question through the glass.

He crouches down so his gaze is even with my pendulating head—voltaic-burgundy eyes flaunting double pupils as white as lightning. The rest of his features emerge through the smoky haze like something from a nightmare: aquiline nose, sweeping cheekbones, brutish jaw, and delicate bowed lips housing savage fangs. Hard edges battling tender curves—a demon's face so brutal I ache to avert my gaze, yet so beguiling in its ethereal elegance, I can't look away.

He trails his tongue along a tooth as pointed and shiny as polished silver, as if considering his response to my question. "They're on ice."

I bite my own tongue hard enough to make it bleed. Faeriekind can't lie, but they can use figures of speech. I'm hoping with all my heart that's what he's doing now. That my loved ones aren't literally packed in ice, or already dead and decorating his halls. I know better than to ask. He won't give me a straight answer anyway.

He stands, and I try again to home in on his blurred image as I rock upside down, right to left, right to left. "Why haven't you killed me already?"

"And whyever would I do that?"

"Scourge said you wanted us dead or alive." My throat hurts, both from the effort of talking and from holding back a sob for Uncle, Clarey, and Flannie.

"A misunderstanding, then. Our kingdom needs you, Phoenix of the Somatic Realm. We can't survive without you."

"Because I'm your creator."

He taps a screw-shaped, steely fingernail against the glass. "Because you're the Architect."

That word again. "Artist," I correct weakly. The clock plays a spine-splintering chime to announce fifteen minutes past the hour, then continues to pendulate. It's getting difficult to hold a conversation with bile filling my mouth. "The . . . swinging . . . needs to stop."

"Oh, is that so? I've always found this a relaxing place to gather my thoughts. It's my favorite point of leisure here in the game room. At half past, it will chime two times. At quarter till, three more. And then a series of gongs count down the

official changing of the hour. Are you sure you wish to miss all that fun?"

I snarl.

He responds with a wicked laugh. "All right then, let's get you down. I'll show you my collection."

Game room . . . *collection*? I shut my eyes as my brain bombards me with gruesome imagery. I can't handle this; it will be the end of me to see Clarey or Uncle . . . or even Flannie's sweet plush hide hung in effigy—all in hateful tribute to the ugliness of a world and characters I once stupidly relied upon for safety and comfort. And I can't fall apart yet.

Even though my creation is no longer under my mastery, I have to stop it. Judging by what Perish just admitted, there's only one way to do that.

In my mind, I fixate on where I saw him return the unicorn-horn dagger, sheathed at his waist. I know how sharp that blade is. Even before seeing him prick his finger, I watched him carve the edges of his own face.

Bile rises higher in my throat on that memory . . . because it's probably the very knife he uses to prepare his morbid wall art. If he hurt the people I love, it's the last thing he'll do. I won't give him the satisfaction of controlling me. I'll end this world myself before I let that happen.

I shut my eyes and go limp on the line, a rabbit captured in a snare, waiting for the wolf to let down his guard.

My other senses resolve to brighter focus in compensation for my temporary blindness: the squeak of the hinged glass door opening; the smothering hush as the pendulum halts and the clock hands cease; the crunch of coiled metal fingernails turning the tumblers and unlocking my ankle ties, then the snick of said

nails retracting into Perish's fingertips—like an echo of a switchblade folding closed. He scoops me into his arms before I can fall into the gears, though he's careful not to touch me, skin to skin.

My cheek falls to rest against his shirt, a toned chest formed of both iron and flesh sliding underneath. Let him think I'm too weak and grief stricken to move. Let him underestimate me.

I slit one eye open carefully, noting that the chamber is small, barely a closet. All the walls are bare, and with the clock stopped, it's as claustrophobic and silent as a tomb, save for the sporadic pop of the streetlamp. Hardly what I'd call a game room.

Squeezing my eye shut again, I allow my body to slump against his unyielding torso of rippled muscle, alert to the vibrations behind a cage of steel and bone that houses motorized gears powering innards and a black, cold heart. Underpinning the scent of rust and machine oil that clings to his shirt is another perfume, warm and musky . . . a combination of animal and man.

I let my inner arm slip between us, a surreptitious move that levels my fingers with the dagger at his waist. He carries me for several footsteps, oblivious. His breath mixes with the steam and smoke sifting from the cords behind his neck, commingling to that same waxy scent of the bakery's candles. One by one, I curl each finger around the dagger's hilt and in a swift motion, donkey-kick my outer leg and pivot from his arms while lifting the dagger free.

The instant my feet hit the floor, I scramble backward against the streetlamp's pole for support, and wedge the cold blade at my jugular so the tip puckers my skin. "Game over."

Perish tilts his head. The four braids dip across his powerful shoulders, burgundy-dark twists whitening at the ends like vines

coated in ice. He narrows his electrified gaze. A sick, unwelcome pride teases its way to the surface of my thoughts. He's magnificent. At least six foot five—thick muscle tone on a sleek graceful frame, like a body builder spliced with a swimmer. Exactly how I imagined and drew him, yet so much better. The goblin and frost-elf strains in his blood have blended flawlessly to a grim, angelic sort of beauty that repels inasmuch as it captivates.

His pointed ears, the same lustrous pearlescence as every exposed inch of his skin, appear to twitch, almost as if he's trying to hear my thoughts. He seems as fascinated by my next move as I am by his.

A sudden burst of warmth radiates through the dagger's unicorn handle and distracts me with glints of rainbow light. The shock of it next to my jaw breaks our stare, and awareness rattles my core.

I'm being entranced by my own workmanship.

The revelation snaps me out of the momentary lapse and reminds me what I have to do *because* of my hand in this world. I'm the artist. I'm in charge. And now that I have my power back, I'm the one who writes the ending.

Once more, I grind the dagger's tip into my skin.

His expression teeters between curiosity and amusement. He thinks I won't go through with it, which only makes me more determined to prove him wrong.

My vision tunnels, and everything becomes surreal—this moment in time nothing but a botched panel from my novels that I'll blot out forever with water and blood. Before fear or self-preservation can intervene, I shove the blade where my pulse beats strongest, and slice my throat from ear to ear.

25

blood and skins

I stand there, knife at my neck, waiting for the spike of agony and the gush of warm blood.

Instead, I feel a ticklish chafe. I growl and push the blade harder. The metal bends—a soothing fringe along my artery. I jerk the dagger back to find I'm holding a feather with lustrous downy barbs and a pearlescent quill.

My heart races as rationale comes rushing in, the finality of what I almost did a chilling backwash in my veins. If I'd been successful, I'd be dead. No do-overs. Did I alter the dagger with my touch, instinctively protecting myself?

Perish's thunderous laugh grates along my nerves.

"I never tire of the quickening upon a human face. The proof of singularity. Each reaction a unique feast of notions and volitions dancing across your features. Such piquant confusion. Such savory fear." He licks his fingertips, as though relishing a favorite meal. "The fear is well founded and much appreciated. But let me allay your confusion." He folds open one side of his

shirt far enough for me to see a long, wide indention along his left pectoral—organic tissue piled upon itself in thick, fibrous strips. The scar is deep pink and shiny, and in places, streaks of silver shimmer through where metal pushes to the surface. "I crafted the dagger of iron peeled from my own body, then enchanted the blade so it's only deadly when in my hand. I'm the sole being who can wield a fatal stroke. As such, my own weapon will never be used against me, nor in any way of which I don't approve. Cunning, yes?"

I drop the feather, struck by the macabre genius behind it. The plume oscillates gracefully in midair for an instant before resuming its iron form and plummeting to the stone floor with a loud clang.

Perish smirks, his fang tips pressed into a full lower lip that shimmers like a carnation's petal. He gathers up the blade and houses it in the sheath. "That was a brazen move. You would truly have killed yourself rather than see me win. Color me impressed." His arms splay wide, sleeves rolled to the elbows, displaying one forearm made entirely of silver metal devoid of rust, the other of pearlescent flesh corded with thick tendons. "Color me anything, really. Just give me some color. Was that not your specialty, *Paint Slinger*? Before you lost your gift?"

The well-aimed insult, framed so callously around Clarey's affectionate nickname, slams into my chest. It's further proof Perish was somehow listening to us on our walk along Eleventh Street in the real Astoria last night. And proof he knows my biggest failing in the human world. The loss of my talent.

Perish pulls a lever on the wall, and a stone partition beside him opens with a grinding groan to reveal a giant room. "Your tour, as promised," he says. His rumbling voice is joined by

metallic pings and snarling whispers, cutting through the silence that has bound us together since the stopping of the giant clock.

All the devastation, the confusion, the dread, everything I've been suppressing kicks into overdrive as I step out behind him. The octagonal chamber is three times the size of Enchanted Delights, and is more of a cross between a war room and a torture chamber than any game room I've ever seen.

Strewn along the floor and walls and hanging from the rafters are militant and barbaric toys found in any medieval castle: weapons, torture devices, a map table with tiny carved figurines for strategizing. A convex fireplace roars at the corner to my left, formed of brick with a copper hood. Shiny strips of scrap metal in different shapes and sizes clutter the mounted shelves on either side of the forge, while several large barrels line the floor just behind a long workbench.

Standing and seated around the worktable, gopher-size creatures move in and out of the firelight, utilizing tools to shape and hammer bits of metal that reflect the flames in shimmers.

They're tinker-gnomes, the king's royal blacksmiths. Thick scaly shells fold around their backs to their fronts, a white, reptilian pattern that spreads to their heads like helmets, paints a slab between their fuzzy rounded ears, and then stops at the tip of their rodent muzzles. It's an inborn armor, as much a part of their bodies as their fur-lined arms and metal-tipped clawed feet. It's what armadillos might look like, were they to walk upright and have opposing thumbs. Even from this distance, the flames burn high enough to lap heat across my eyes and skin, and sweat beads along my hairline. Yet the tinkers continually move without stopping, because their insulated shells keep them cool as they work.

I designed them that way.

Several of the gnomes turn gray aluminum gazes our way; some have eyes dulled by rusty tears, others have empty sockets caked with red powder that flakes off with each blink—the one trait I regret giving them. They're the only creatures with the bad luck of having metal eyes. Which means because of this strange plague, they're going blind. Yet still, they attempt to build things. Or, more likely, knowing Perish as I do, they've been given the ultimatum to continue their work or die.

The sympathy in the pit of my stomach forces my attention elsewhere, skipping to the one end of the chamber I've yet to explore. Perish already waits there, facing the wall and observing the heights with interest under the tentacled nest of an Edison-style chandelier hung overhead. Through shirrs of waxy smoke—pumped from the tubes at his back—splashes of white, red, blue, yellow, and other uncountable pigments freckle the gray stone both high and low. One splash in particular, orange and globular, prickles my skin with recognition: a pumpkin head held up by spikes.

My body goes numb. The clinks and tings of hammers on metal fade behind me as I stumble forward in a queasy haze—horrified, raging—yet somehow my feet keep moving. I'm below the mask in a matter of seconds, holding my breath so I won't scream.

Once I'm up close and clear of the smoke, my sick doubts sharpen to pure relief: it isn't Clarey. I release the breath bottled up in my lungs. Not only is it not Clarey, but it's not an actual head. It's a mask, and one that's inferior to Clarey's handiwork.

Burlap forms the basis, with a jack-o'-lantern painted crudely in place around blunt-cut holes unraveling in dingy threads.

Twine dangles at either edge as a final touch to the homespun face cover. Each flicker from the chandelier's bulbs spotlights the amateur design, bright orange strokes with a black jagged-toothed smile and geometric eyes.

The discovery gives me the courage to step back and take in the entire wall—covered end to end in masks. They're not at all what I'm used to seeing at Halloween. Nothing one would find at any costume shop or retail store. No vinyl or plastic, no latex or rubber, no famous cultural icons or cartoon characters, monsters or aliens from movies, nothing popular over the past few decades or so. Instead, these coverings are obsolete and antiquated, as if centuries old. Styles I would expect to see in a documentary about the holiday's origins: half masks shaped of feathers and animal furs; actual animal heads—hollowed and dried out with ribbons sewn at the edges for adjustable fittings; early clown and jester costumes. There are even papier mâché masks, white with abnormally elongated features, evoking the memory of Lark's distorted image that always lurks along the fringes of my mind. One thing they all have in common is they're empty, lifeless, and handmade. Haunting and disturbing in their own right, but a lot less morbid than human flesh that's been exsiccated and preserved for some barbaric display.

This is what Scourge referred to.

"You collect Halloween masks," I mumble, both awed and repelled to come face-to-face—literally—with the very essence of what I've been running from for years.

"They're called skins in our world," Perish answers.

"So you're obsessed with the holiday . . . because I am."

He huffs and gives his antlers a shake—a proud buck swishing off a fly. "Such arrogance. To assume my thoughts can't spin

outside of yours. That kind of thinking can be dangerous. Or haven't you recognized that by now?"

"I only meant that since you're my brainchild—"

"I can't have a brain of my own?" He lifts one burgundy eyebrow, daring me to confirm the claim.

My mouth opens to respond, but I reconsider. What *am* I trying to say? There's no discounting that everything in Mystiquiel moves, breathes, and reacts to its environment, separate from my input. Isn't that what sentience is? The awareness to function and adapt, to protect oneself at any cost?

"These face coverings are vintage." I guide us into safer territory. "You've only been in existence since I started drawing you. Where did you find something so old?" He doesn't acknowledge the question, so I give him my full attention, mulling over Scourge's comment about quarry being brought in dead or alive. "Please tell me you didn't rob a museum."

He laughs, the electrical crackles of his crown flashing white light across his lustrous face and teeth. "Stealing masks off wax statues and busts of stone. Where would the sport be in that? I like a good chase, as you well know."

His answer provokes a fresh wave of apprehension. The rubbery coils behind his neck expand and deflate like a bellows. Circles of smoke puff out, and he inhales deeply. A release of glowing embers follows on the exhale.

After seeing how the faeries fed in the bakery, understanding the rejuvenating qualities of this substance, I wonder why he's saturated in it, constantly.

Could that reliance be used against him? I recall his breath at the bakery, how I perceived vulnerability behind the scent of decay. What would happen were I to rip those tubes from the

backpack apparatus buckled around his shoulders and fling them into the forge? Would he wind down and be weakened? Would it give me the upper hand?

As if sensing the threat, his shoulder and back muscles ripple with tension, reminding me of the sheer potency of his size and the steely bones that form his foundation. He skates a palm along his dagger's prismatic handle in assurance that I'd never get close enough to dismantle anything. He may not want to kill me, but he could easily maim me, overpower me, and put me in binds again.

"Also, for the sake of factual accuracy," he says, disrupting my musings, "I am not obsessed with the holiday." His tone is scolding—more than a little offended, and a lot haughty. Which only further substantiates the sentience theory. "This wall is sacred." He takes down a mask—a papier mâché ghoul with a beaked nose and gaping eyes. "These artifacts are priceless and revered. A tribute to our history."

History. That's what Angorla said about my mom's picture book. I study him, intent on those familiar features, a mix of man, beast, and machine, and I wonder: Does the *Goblin Market* poem somehow play a role in all of this? I've learned since being here that the enchanted fruits we've been serving our customers drain humans, that without the king's blood as an additive, our cupcakes and macarons would be fatally addictive like in the story. But that poem, those words, were crafted back in the 1800s, just like these masks that deck the wall.

Am I to believe my constant rereading of a picture book throughout my childhood informed my art—and in turn, this world—to such a degree? Come to think of it, I do remember seeing historical costumes when googling Halloween for research; it could be they stuck in my subconscious and ended up here.

Were Clarey standing beside me, he would tell me exactly that, because the reasoning behind it makes sense. But there's something missing . . . some connection I've yet to make. If only I could get one straight answer. If only Uncle Thatch had told me something, *anything*, I would have a better handle on all of this.

Clarey and Uncle. My heart skips a hopeful beat, because the mask collection—though it brushes against my own phobias until every hair on my body bristles—has confirmed one thing at least: that my loved ones weren't skinned alive. So they must be intact and still breathing somewhere.

"My uncle, my friends. They're okay?" I stare at the highest line of masks in an attempt to hide the vulnerability I know lies bare across my face. The tinker-gnomes' metalwork pings drift behind me, adopting an oddly festive tune that feeds my anticipation.

"Of course they are," Perish answers. "What value are bargaining chips if they're broken?"

The lifted weight from my chest is so palpable, my shoulders and spine rise as though I have wings. "I want to see—"

"One moment," he interrupts, placing the eerie mask back upon the wall and lovingly stroking the edges with a long fingertip. "All of you," he calls, addressing his blacksmiths across the room. "Leave us now." The blind gnomes put aside their tools and projects and single-file out, each placing paws on another's shoulders in front of them. They form a chain to keep from tripping on the way to the glass door that suddenly appears on the wall to our left with a scraping sound.

"Slag," Perish commands.

The line stalls so the gnome at the end can turn in our direction. He waits, blinking rust from his lashes.

"Have my brother bring the captives."

The gnome nods, and the line of tinkers makes its way through the door. Once Slag steps over the threshold, the glass folds in on itself with a chiming clink, again and again, forming different shapes until it shrinks to the size of a quarter, then vanishes from view.

I hold my face expressionless. Clarey, Uncle, and Flannie are coming. At last, we'll be together again. But I can't let the Goblin King see my relief. Not yet. Not until I know what he wants in return for their release.

His focus lights on me, those shock-bright pupils piercing. "You are relieved."

Annoyed with his perceptiveness, I remain silent, nudging my lip ring with my tongue.

He studies my mouth, then licks his own lips, as though tasting every emotion I'm trying to suppress. "So when you pulled my dagger, attempted to end this all . . . you truly didn't know of your companions' survival, one way or the other?"

"You said they were on ice. That can mean different things in our world."

Perish blinks, analyzing me. His four pupils grow wide enough to swallow the deep red currents of his irises—milk spreading through blood. "You were willing to be a martyr. To void your existence alongside ours. Not surprising, as a good captain always goes down with his ship. Yet these frail human barnacles that have affixed themselves to your heart, affected every move you've made since you've been here . . . you would have been willing to destroy them by ending the world they might possibly still occupy. Are you indeed that ruthless, fair Phoenix?"

I gulp an egg-size knot from my throat, overwhelmed with

the magnitude of my oversight, reluctant to admit I didn't think through the repercussions. I'd like to say I assumed they'd simply return to the real world. But in fact, I hadn't been thinking at all—not beyond defeating Perish.

"Aha." He clasps his hands, his compact, metallic fingernails catching glints of light. "You didn't consider the end result, not beyond me and Mystiquiel. That's where your true nature comes into play. You were governed by artistic pride, desperate to regain control of what you perceive should be yours. Determined to rewrite the narrative of *your* choice upon *your* paper in *your* pencraft. You wanted to win, at any cost."

I wince. His on-point accusation dredges up things I'd rather forget, unresolved feelings for Lark and the underlying competition that left our relationship in shreds.

"These qualities, they frighten you. They shame you. Yet they shouldn't. Not here. And not ever with me." Perish slants his head again, his beaded braids clacking with the motion. "Wanting power, craving greatness, I understand that desire. In fact, I respect it. Deeply. And I should like to aid you in said coup, and see you and your companions where you belong, in your proper states, before it's too late."

Finally. "Proper states? You mean our mutations, right?" I tap my zippers, igniting a twinge of pain beneath them. "Clarey's hands, his face. They'll be normal again once we leave?"

Perish lifts his thumb and buffs the nail on his shirt lapel, an unexpectedly human gesture. Then he returns his palm to the hilt of his dagger. "My enchantment upon him will release only *if* he crosses over. Otherwise, it continues until he not only looks like one of us but thinks like one of us. The devolution has been quite amusing to watch already, I must say."

A hot flash rushes through my cheeks, and I have to fight the urge to attack him. "This was all you? I thought—*we* thought it was our doing. Our imagination coming to life."

"There's no denying you both have power here. But did you suppose you were the only ones who could work magic? And besides, your man-child himself invited me to turn him into a goblin."

I swallow back a moan. Again, validation he heard us joking around last night. Where was he hiding? Or maybe it was one of his spies, too tiny to be seen by the human eye. Whichever way, I won't stroke his ego by indulging him with the subject a second longer. "So was it also you who set my father's pocket watch so we could leave before the portal closes?"

"I did. Otherwise, you must wait until it opens again, if your uncle and friends can survive that long. If any of us can, actually. It will not reopen for you once it's closed until a year has passed; it is the natural law in this place. Even magic has its limits."

I grind my boot soles into the floor, an attempt to stand against the shock of his claim. Twelve months in this place? I can't—won't—let that happen. "What about your magic? It doesn't share those limits. You have access to the real world all year round. You've been there to deliver our fruit . . . to keep watch over us . . . for two and a half years. You're always showing up. All Hallows' Eve or not. Is it because you're the king? You're immune to the boundaries somehow? Or maybe you have a key."

"*The* key. And technically, yes. But exclusively, no."

I roll my eyes. "I hate when you do that."

He smirks. "Yet isn't that exactly how I'm written, in every scene, in every panel? Wasn't it your pen that shadowed my actions with ambiguity, shaded my dialogues with nuance?

What was it you called me earlier? Your *brainchild*. Doesn't that mean, in turn, that I am a part of you, that I *belong* to you? In which case, you are responsible not only for my portrayal but for my well-being and the livelihood of this very world. You are in fact, our life*blood*—just as we are yours. You care for us, you need us, because we fill the gaping hole that craves control . . . dominance."

"No," I whisper.

"There's no denying it. I saw the depth of your devotion for Mystiquiel with my own eyes. In your discomfort as you encountered the sick and dying sea creature on the beach, in your regret as you walked the crepitating streets of our land, in your sadness as you observed the dire state of our denizens after your friend conjured rain from the sky. I know you feel it, otherwise you wouldn't have been determined to die along with us as opposed to simply *ending* us. You can't live with the thought of your creation being destroyed at anyone's hand. Not even your own."

Uncomfortable with the words, how they force me to acknowledge the ownership I feel for this place, the affection I can't seem to shake off, I turn my back on him and his hallowed wall of masks.

My skin itches; I'm antsy for Uncle, Clarey, and Flannie's arrival, worried we're running out of time. "Could we just get to finishing the game, please? The clock's ticking."

"Ah." Perish strolls toward the partitioned alcove and the giant pendulum sitting latent inside. "Thank you for the reminder." He steps within and restarts the clock. As he closes the glass door over the face, the pendulum swings too fast, and the ticking speeds, the hands spinning wildly to recalibrate and arrive at the proper time. At half past ten, normal ticking resumes, and two

loud chimes shake the room and rattle the masks, tools, and torture devices along the walls and rafters.

My entire body shudders along with them. Only an hour and a half left before we're stuck here with Clarey's humanity twisting like a candlewick beneath a blistering flame, until he's a monster—through and through.

"Tell me what I have to do," I say, sounding more desperate than I want.

"After everything I've allowed you to experience, every scene I set into play, you still don't know?"

"You want me to stop this curse obliterating your world."

"Precisely. I've seen your power, Architect." Perish's exquisitely fierce countenance gentles to something raw and unguarded as he studies my every feature. "Heal Mystiquiel, and you'll receive everything you ever wanted in return."

26

brutal bargains

Overwhelmed by Perish's faith in me, I shake my head. "How can I heal an entire world? Like you said, you saw how it worked with the troll, the pack rat faerie. Even Angorla. I'd never have enough time to touch every creature, every character, before midnight."

"Very true. It's why you must heal Mystiquiel at its very heart."

I kick myself again for anchoring this world on a weak foundation. Thinking back on my canon, my lore, I remember the strength of the kingdom lies within the power of the king. "You. If I start with you, it will reach all of them." I put out my hand.

He jerks back, just like he avoided any skin-to-skin contact when he dragged me from the pendulum. "No. I rule the kingdom, the classes, the castes. But I am not the heart."

"Okay," I say, suspicious now. "But I could still heal you. Make you stronger. You don't want that?"

"Until my kingdom is purified, I must suffer alongside it."

The selfless choice surprises me again, just like when I spotted Bonbon and the troll earlier. I tamp down the respect stirring in me, convinced there must be a catch. An angle I can't see.

"A captain and his ship?" I bait.

"Nothing quite so dignified as that. Walk with me," he urges.

Hearing the giant clock tick away the seconds, I glance at the walls in hopes of seeing an impromptu glass door and the arrival of my loved ones. When none appears, I catch up to the Goblin King's long stride as he passes the map table and torture devices, then stops at the corner where the fire laps within the forge. The extreme temperature licks my face, heats the zippers and piercings to a scalding discomfort. I ease back two steps, nearly bumping into the workbench behind me. The blacksmith tools atop it rattle and clang. I recognize most of them: anvils, vises, hammers, clamps, and tongs.

Then I notice the barrels I assumed were filled with wine or ale. Instead, they contain arms, legs, fingers, toes, even noses, antlers, hooves, and teeth. Made of pristine, unblemished metal. All of them are different sizes, but shaped to perfection and polished to a sheen.

I'm reminded of Lark's doll bits, how she used to group them in piles, clean them up and ready them for use, although this display is more significant than her plastic versions. These are replicates of the pieces that are falling off Mystiquiel's denizens, waiting to be doled out. The busted and broken faeries at the bakery, receiving replacement pieces. This is where they were forged.

Upon the bench, trapped in a vise, waits an ear canal, half-formed so it resembles a silver snail. Perish steps up, spins the handle to release the object, then carries it to the forge with a

long-armed pair of tongs. Once the metal burnishes to a reddish hue, Perish brings it back and, after pounding it with a hammer, welds another piece onto it. His savage features soften in the flame of the tool, his pale flesh reflecting the bluish light, highlighting the ethereal-elfin side of his lineage. Making him appear thoughtful and calm—heavenly, even.

But I don't dare trust that impression.

"Where did you get the material for all of these?" I ask.

Without a word, he sets aside his tools and reopens his shirt—this time divulging the right side. Along his oblique muscle stretches a gnarled scar similar to the other one. Except here, the bright flecks of silver overtake the tissue, reforming the metal panel that was once stripped away.

"All of that . . . is from you?" I glance at the shelves on the wall and back at the barrels. The revelation not only shocks me but leaves me winded.

He shrugs those broad shoulders. "Were you to alter me too soon, change the biomechanics of my anatomy, I could no longer provide what my subjects need to live. I'm the only being here who can self-regenerate. Every band of iron, every strip of steel, every ring of copper grows back."

I stand in place, gawping.

"This surprises you? Did you not have a hand in my ability . . . my burden?"

Technically, I guess I did. By making him capable of glamours and physical modifications, I enabled him to adapt in ways other characters couldn't. It also explains why he's more lustrous and luminous than his brother, and especially why he isn't rusting. His metal is torn away when it's brand new, before it has a chance to corrode.

I frown. "Maybe this is *how* I wrote you, but it isn't *who* I wrote you to be. You're not supposed to be noble. You're a cruel, barbaric king. One without mercy. One who takes pleasure in malevolence and pain." I glance at the torture devices hanging from the ceiling and aligned around the room, citing them as an example.

"Oh, I still have my amusements. We recycle our tainted metal into these injurious gadgets." He points his pair of tongs toward what looks like a rusty coffin inlaid with metal spikes, similar to the iron maidens I've seen online, yet at the ends of the prongs, balls of sparks crackle and buzz. "I had that one primed and ready for our Gardener, till she brought you to me and earned herself a reprieve. But I recently discovered another thief in my midst. He'll be here shortly to take her place."

I refrain from shivering, hoping to be far away with Clarey, Flannie, and Uncle before then.

Placing the welded ear back into the vise, Perish uses an angle grinder to shave the joined seams smooth, softening the curves and sharpening the tip with the practiced patience of an artisan. Sparks spray upward in a peaceful display of light, like shooting stars. Silver shavings curl and build beneath the vise and coat the bench's wooden top. It's like the oceanside Clarey and I walked upon on our arrival. I tap my boot along a pile of similar fibers that litter the floor. Is that where all the shavings go? To the beach? I'm struck by how much Perish does to maintain the upkeep of this world. How much of himself goes into it.

With his head turned down, the braids at his temple curtain one side of his face. He notices my silence and shoves the rope-like tresses behind his pointed ear. His gaze finds mine, urging me to speak with just a look.

"You won't let me change you, so you can continue to peel away layers of yourself . . . in what must be an excruciating process. All for the materials to cobble your subjects back together and keep them alive."

"Is that not what a king does for his vassals and dominion? He protects them, at all costs."

I blink my eyes to break the hold of his gaze. "You're—just not who I expected you to be. Like everything here; things look like how I drew them, yet act completely different." Biting my inner cheek, I take a risk and touch the shavings on the bench. Just like the ones earlier, they disintegrate into glowing golden grains of sand.

Perish graces me with a beatific smile. Even with his fangs fully bared in what could double as a feral snarl, there's no denying the expression is one of pleasure. "Do you see how your own artistic abilities have returned . . . even evolved since you've been here? They've grown, in fact, since you first began to draw this world. Is it so unthinkable, then, that we ourselves, figments of every dream you've dreamt . . . spawned of every experience you've faced, would also change and perfect? Become individuals in our own right. This kingdom may be spun from a girl's imagination, yes. But its denizens have grown to exceed what we started off to be. Your emotions, and those from whom you let read our stories, feed us."

That's when I realize the full impact I've had by giving up on my talent. "You were undernourished because I kept the stories secret . . . I limited who saw them. And then when I stopped drawing altogether—"

"We were starving, yes. Wasting away." He aims a pointed gaze at the refurbished rusted metal on the iron maiden device.

Remorse shudders through me. "The candles. You burn the wax in your factories and homes; in your shops and eateries. You were hoping it would cure you."

"It wasn't my idea. But I thought it might work, since emotions help us regenerate." He tosses a glance behind him where the tubed apparatus spews out smoke. "Which is crucial for me."

"If it wasn't your idea, whose was it?" I ask the question, although I already suspect the answer.

"When things first began to crumble to rot, I sought assistance. I entered your home one night, a few weeks before your uncle bought his bakery. Before it was even a concept in his mind. I needed help with Mystiquiel, to rebuild this place, to return us to our former glory."

Architect. He doesn't say the word this time, but I infer it. Architects build things, and in the fun house, Jaspar—*Perish*—said I'm a builder of worlds.

"You were asleep, and your uncle caught me standing over you. When he realized who I was . . . *what* I was . . . he intervened, pleaded with me, made a bargain based on a plan to supply us a surplus of emotions, so long as I stayed out of your real life and kept the other eldritch creatures away. To protect you and your fragile reality, from us."

"He lied to me to protect me?"

"He didn't exactly have a choice."

That caveat bids something to the surface: Uncle's face in the memory the piskie returned to my mind a little while ago in front of the faux bakery. How his eyes bulged last night in the storeroom, how he struggled to speak as if his tongue was swollen. How he said he wanted to tell me everything. Yet he couldn't.

Angorla's unsettling rhyme: *We shut them silent. Take the tongue and swell it tight. Seal the lips and stitch 'em right.*

"You enchanted him not to tell me," I murmur. "Forced him to remain silent with magic, because it was more binding than any human contract could ever be. But why did you care if I knew or not? You had nothing to lose if I found out."

"That's between myself and your uncle."

I glare at him. Again with his cagey half answers. "If you want my help, you're going to have to tell me everything. And stop twisting things around."

"Am I? Or will you do anything I ask to save those who followed you here? Or who chose to come before?"

"*Chose?* You forced my uncle here to lure me in!"

"Not entirely so. He forsook our bargain by providing enchanted fruits at the carnival, outside of the bakery, without pairing his wares with the necessary candles. This depleted Mystiquiel of an emotional harvest, so he came willingly as punishment in hopes of delivering you from my resulting wrath. But, yes . . . it did serve to get your attention."

I shake my head, not sure if I'm more furious with Perish or myself. "I'm to blame for what's happening here. He shouldn't be involved at all."

Perish holds the finished metal ear up for inspection, then tosses it into a barrel with a clang. "Always so dramatic. I would ask if all human girls share this trait, but I understand yours is tied to the untimely loss of your sister. I'm familiar with the complexities of sibling relationships. Believe me. But it seems the bond between twins is . . . incomparable. A metaphysical rarity even beyond magic. The premature removal of your other

half has left a parasitic wound, bound to eat you alive lest you allow it to scar."

My eyes burn at the mention of Lark's death. It's not the first time he's referred to it. I hate that he's been inside my head long enough to know my deepest and most private losses and regrets—how I've been entangled by them all this time. I roll my shoulder, expecting my sister's namesake tattoo to flutter its wings beneath my shirt. But it doesn't budge. Come to think of it, I haven't felt any movement there since I entered the orchard.

"I reiterate"—Perish shatters my introspections—"you are not to blame for our world's failing. Not entirely. It's as I told you in the fun house. You're not all-powerful, nor are you powerless."

I tuck my hands in my pockets, roll my fingers along the remaining seeds I collected off the bakery sidewalk. I contemplate their original form—metallic and tinny—before I altered them. "I drew you myself, gave you life. But I abandoned you. Even though I'm still dreaming of Mystiquiel, I stopped writing your stories because I lost . . . my vision. So if it's not *entirely* me and my negligence causing this decay, what else could it be?"

"At last. The crux of it."

Before Perish can expand on his answer, there's a tingling scrape as a triangle of glass appears on the wall to my right.

I rush to stand a few feet from it, waiting with bated breath for the door to grow and open wide. I'm almost scared to see them: Clarey, how far has his mutation developed in the time we've been apart? And Uncle—Perish said he was here for punishment . . . that could mean he himself endured some form of torture. And sweet Flannie, has she been caged somewhere—scared, hungry, confused?

When Scourge steps in alone and the door vanishes behind him, I physically deflate, an internal collapse that spreads from my shoulders all the way to my heart.

"Where . . . are . . . they?" I have to force the words out.

Scourge sneers at me, shakes his frizzed hair, and wrinkles his crooked nose as if I'm not worth acknowledgment. Then he turns all his attention to Perish. "You sent for the captives, Majesty Mine?"

Perish strolls by me, trailing a lingering cloud of waxy smoke. Without a word, he offers an upturned palm to his brother. Being a full head shorter than Perish, Scourge cranes his neck to meet his king's gaze. His clothes, similar to Perish's, hang on him, baggy and ill-fitted. Though their coloring is almost identical—minus the iridescence that makes Perish so disturbingly lovely—Scourge is physically inferior to the king. His skin sags, wrinkled and pruned, as if he's a reflection of Perish in a rippled pond.

Scourge drags three golf-ball-size marbles from his pocket and places them on the Goblin King's hand. The spheres remind me of the gazing globes I've seen on pedestals in gardens—multicolored with a lustrous, reflective depth. As I study them, the prisms swirl and turn, taking shape. Uncle's unspectacled bulging gaze, searching his surroundings blindly; Clarey's face—the orange now giving way to his natural coloring—retains the masked shape, now warped in an agonized expression as he grips his left ear in pain; Flannie's yipping muzzle and scared, wide eyes. They appear to be trapped within the balls.

I gasp and lunge toward them.

Perish closes his fingers around the globes before I'm within range. He pushes me away, barely a nudge to my shoulder, but it makes me stagger backward and catch myself against a chair

with a seat studded in rusty nails and wrist clamps. Propped against the wooden arm, I ache to shout for answers, but tension crackles between the two brothers so I take two cautious steps back and stand behind the chair, reluctant to get pulled into their current.

"Have you found the thief . . . Angorla's accomplice?" Perish asks.

"Nay, Majesty. But I will." Scourge's shoulders quiver, almost indiscernibly, but I catch it. So does Perish.

"No need." Perish drops the marbles into his pocket, then cups his brother's shoulder on the metallic arm's side—the king's large hand swallowing the entire scapula and collarbone from front to back. Then he leans down, fangs bared and snapping. "I know it was you." Though whispered, the accusation carries the weight and force of a lion's roar. "I know what she promised. And fool that you are, you believed. Should she win, your greed and envy will damn us all."

His hand squeezes tight, crushing Scourge's shoulder. The metal arm bends to the pressure with a ruinous dissonance so similar to the crunching wail of cars in the compressor behind Ebon's garage it makes my stomach turn.

Scourge shrieks and crumples to the floor, falling prostrate before his king, his arm crimped in an unnatural pose.

Without a glance my way, Perish catches his brother's shirt collar and drags him to the iron maiden contraption. He props him up inside and presses a palm over Scourge's chest to pin him in place.

"You broke my heart, Brother. I never thought it would be you—" The king's voice catches. "Should we survive this night, I'll see you on the other side of All Hallows' Eve."

A muscle in Perish's jaw spasms when his brother begs forgiveness as drool oozes from his lips. The last things I see are his barb-edged ears lying flat against his head in terror, and the veins bulging in his neck with each plea.

Perish slams the coffin-style lid, shutting out Scourge's cries. Flashing light seeps out from the seams, and that buzzing hum grows to a bedlam of pops and hisses. The odor of singed hair and broiled metal forms an acrid and repulsive stink.

Covering my nose and mouth, I tremble, tense and ready to run. But where would I go?

Perish turns to me, gaze aflicker with sparks that rival the torture device's light show. "Do not fret for him. He is not dying. He's being remade. Recast, if you will. Into a better prince. One worthy of this kingdom. One who would never betray his king."

I'm gutted, unable to speak for the brutality of the act against his own brother. It revives all my self-doubts . . . all the things I envied about my sister. Could I have saved her that night? If so, *would* I have? Or am I so selfish I'd choose my own pride and let her die?

I'll never get those answers now, and the unknowing levels me, shakes my very soul.

I want to condemn Perish's actions. But I share his devotion to this world, whether I want to admit it or not. I don't know what Scourge stole, although it's obvious the betrayal endangered Perish's kingdom. He's doing what a true king would do—as he's been doing all along. In spite of his vicious tactics, at the very least, I admire his commitment.

But my admiration fades the moment he fishes the gazing globes from his pocket and rolls them along his palm to clack

them together. "As you see, your uncle and friends are trapped. They will remain so until you accomplish our goal."

My throat tightens against a groan when their images reappear. He holds my loved ones' fates in his hands. Literally. "You're a monster."

He sighs out a cloud of waxy smoke that swirls through the tips of his antlers, then he makes a fist around the marbles. "Yes, I'm a Goblin King with elfin strains. Did you expect I would play fair? The price of losing this game is too costly. I had to hedge my bets. Because as I said earlier, there's been another player in this all along."

"My uncle?"

"He's merely a diversion. There's a weed growing in our garden, Architect. An enemy; my most worthy adversary. An entity you know, intimately."

Entity. The answer suddenly flicks on in my brain. *The Goblin King's nemesis. The only one who can match him play for play; who sits at the heart of the world.* "The Motherboard," I say, queasy at the thought. "I wrote her into Mystiquiel's story. And you brought me here to destroy her."

"Ideally. As you're the only one who can."

"Because she's my creation."

He shrugs, causing his braids to rattle. "Or has the creation become the creator? She's the one responsible for the failings of this world, not your negligence. However, you did make us more vulnerable to her goal: to destroy my lawful reign so she can have her way with this world—twist our kingdom to her will. Some might say she wants your rightful place as Architect. That you're in fact *her* one worthy adversary."

That's what he meant by offering to help me win my coup.

"But isn't she everywhere? Listening to us even now? She's omniscient."

"Precisely why I led you here, to the orchard. To the palace. This is the one place her eye can't see. And if she can't see, she can't hear."

My jaw drops with stunned recognition. It wasn't the Goblin King watching us on our journey all this time. "The sun . . . the moon. The orb in the sky."

"Is her crystal ball, so to speak. Yes."

I glance over my shoulder at the clock. In ten minutes, it will gong eleven times, and I'll have only an hour left. "Tell me how to find her," I say through gritted teeth. "How to defeat her."

That scrape of glass slides into place on the wall closest to me, but instead of forming a door, it opens to a screen . . . similar to a vintage television. The black-and-white picture flutters as it pans past the orchard to a monolithic structure in the distance, shrouded in smoke; flashes of light break through the gray billows, as if the structure beneath pulses with electricity. I recognize this image, because I drew it. It's the Motherboard's lair, rising high and disappearing into the clouds.

"It's so far," I murmur, mostly to myself. "I'll never make it in time."

"There's a shortcut. Her components and interfaces wind beneath Mystiquiel's terra firma. The underground maze will lead you through her central processor. I'll escort you as far as the opening. You'll be armed with a map, and the means to eradicate her. Just beware; once her collective consciousness senses your presence, she won't play fair. She'll distract you with illusions . . . try to lead you off course. But should you stay to the path I lay

out, you'll be protected by my magic, and the journey will take less than an hour."

I tamp down the insecurity knotting up my gut, loath to do this alone but seeing no alternative. "And when I succeed?"

"Once she's been removed, I give you my word that your uncle, the dog, and the boy will be set free and returned to the Somatic Realm. No masks, no injuries, no further obligations."

I pause, alerted to the trickery behind his phrasing. "No. You'll send us *all* home to Astoria. Including me. That's the deal."

A half smile plays at his lips, not malicious exactly—closer to begrudging respect. "Of course. I'll return you to Astoria as well." He drops the globes into his pocket again. "So long as you're the one standing victorious when the smoke settles and the rust clears."

motherboard

She's here. We feel her clunky footsteps and hot breaths, infringing, meddling. An itch we need to scratch. Gumming up our innards—a parasitic breach. We've worked too hard, too long, to let her be the crimp in our wiring, the taint in our strain. She's here on a task arranged by a Goblin King's silver tongue. We have no mouth, no voice apart, but she has wandered into our playground and her mind lies bare as a gimcrack. A masquerade, a mirror, and a memory. Beguilements are key. She still doesn't know, still doesn't see. Through riddles unsolved and doubts unbearable, she'll learn the power of sweetmeats and sorrow, of children in masks stomping bright jeweled leaves. Then lead her to her proper place before the clock hands meet, before the throne falls and the spoils rise alongside rust-grizzled wires and circuits alight with flame. She mustn't weed out our ruinous roots, or topple our victory in this harsh-fraught game.

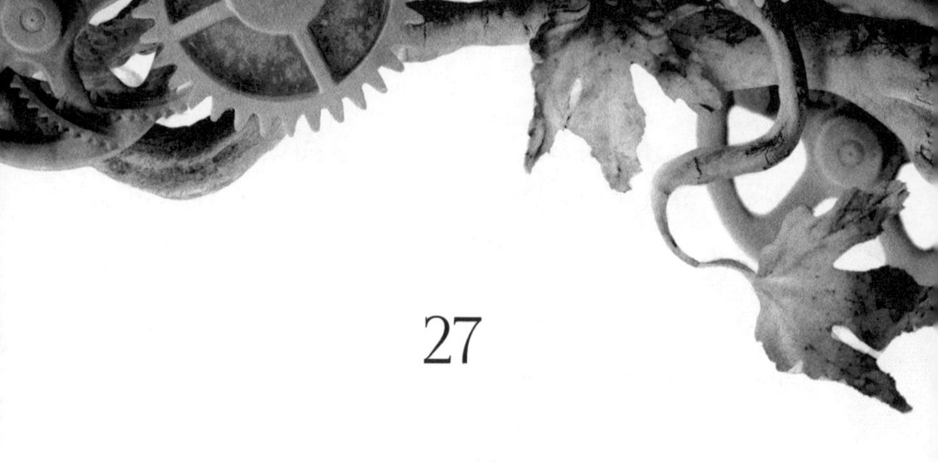

27

masque

With wool-covered fingers, I clutch the Goblin King's animated map. The paper, a deep blue, blends in with the tunnel's dim surroundings. The ink glows neon green, displaying a tangle of lines and dots. I've seen similar layouts in my computer classes, when we studied circuit board blueprints. The lines diverge in all directions, forming a maze that looks like tree roots. In the middle, where the lines converge into a square before sprouting more chaotic offshoots, rests the core of everything: Mystiquiel's central processor—the CPU—the Motherboard's hive mind, and my destination.

The enchanted ink spreads a luminous white trail to reveal the path that Perish wants me to take, and a purple X will project off the map upon arrival at each of the three connectors, so I know what to cut along the way to render her incapacitated.

This is our strategy, leaving her nothing left to fight with in the end, so when I arrive at her lair—that monolithic structure cloaked in clouds and electrical lightning—I can rip her from

the world's mainframe and destroy her. Perish will join me there, and send me through the veil along with Uncle, Clarey, and Flannie, uniting us on the other side. That's assuming I manage to beat the clock.

The gong was striking eleven when Perish escorted me to a trapdoor in the depths of his castle. He didn't let me bring my duffel, insisting it would get in the way. Instead, he gave me the four things I'd need: the map; a pair of wire cutters with blades as long as gardening shears, strapped to my thigh over my jeans; my dad's pocket watch, audibly enchanted to transmit the quarterly chimes from the giant clock in Perish's game room as it counts down the portal's termination; and a necklace with my vial of Perish's blood in case the Motherboard decides to force-feed me any tainted fruits.

"It will also work on her tricks," he said. "One drop, and her illusions will shatter around you, revealing reality. But don't drink unless you can't break her spell by any other means. Swallowing more than two drops, undiluted, in a twenty-four-hour period could bind you to this dying world, to the magic here. And you already drank a drop to enter the orchard."

Another mystery solved: why Uncle wouldn't sell more than one of his baked goods to customers per day, never by the dozen; and another reason, aside from the candle wax, that he wouldn't send them home in boxes. So he could control how much customers ate at each visit.

I fondle the vial as I walk, wondering how I'll know when to drink it. If I should at all, or if Perish is yanking at my strings just as much as the Motherboard will . . .

At this point, who can I trust other than myself?

My combat boots tromp along the ridged terrain, a substrate of laminated composite with layers of copper circuitry peering out like weeds through fissured stone. Similar to everything other than the orchard, it's one part synthetic and the other organic. Dirt clods roll under my heels and crunch, while grass and flowers splinter through the laminate. The walls around me, wrapped with leafy vines, are made of neon-filled glass tubes and other computerized components stacked together. A solid black panel forms the roof where embedded prismatic LED lights twinkle softly, reminiscent of the Lite Brite toy Lark and I shared as kids. At each turn there's something new: computer chips, flickering light bulbs, transistor switches, and buzzing motors—all giant in comparison to me.

Passing a microchip the size of a window air-conditioning unit, I can't help but compare myself to a mouse in a black-light maze. The air tastes sharp, like solder dripping and hot, with the chlorine stench of ozone underlying it all. Copper and aluminum wires act as rails along the path, as thick as pencils and humming with electrical currents. They're the veins and arteries of her system, and my own heart pounds in a frantic race to circulate my blood along an analogous rhythm—as if trying to sync up to her.

I halt at the sixth pivot outlined by the map, and the orange circle that mimics my movements on the paper, highlighting my journey along the white trail, pauses with me. I'm only a corner-turn away from the first connector I need to cut. This should be the easiest map in any world to follow, if I weren't worried about what might wait around every bend. The Motherboard won't surrender easily, so I have to keep my guard up.

Until now, she's been silent, and I can't shake the sense that she's been waiting for me to reach her first vulnerable point; that she's coiled and ready to strike. What will she throw at me? Monsters? Nightmares? Or something worse . . . something I can't even imagine?

My palms sweat and itch in the woolen gloves I left in the cave at the beginning of this journey. When I questioned how Perish came to have them, he assured me his pack rat faeries leave no stone unturned when clearing his world of foreign debris. He was insistent I not touch anything down here, for fear I might actually give the Motherboard power and life, when instead I need to be draining her of it.

Just as I'm gathering courage to step around the bend, I hear the music. So far, the only sounds have been the clicks and hums of microcircuitry and integrated currents. The melody stands out from the white noise, slow, melancholic, and familiar. A blues song—one of Breonna's favorites that she listened to back before she and Clarey moved away. Yet there's a discernible and eerie difference: instead of a harmonica or guitar accompaniment, it's the tinkling off-key swell of the music box from the carousel. No vocals, only the melody.

Underlying the music, there's a bark of laughter, then twittering and snorts. Whispers and chatters coinciding with bestial snarls and growls. Playful, yet somehow malicious.

I take a cautious step forward, stalling when a trail of iridescent, shimmery bubbles drifts from around the turn and hovers above me. There appear to be hundreds of them, gyrating and bumping into one another. As their filmy outlines connect, they integrate, each one losing itself as another swallows it. Their

numbers become smaller as the remaining bubbles grow in size, until all that's left is one giant gleaming sphere—equal to my height and as wide as the entire tunnel—wedged between me and the path I need to take.

My nerves stand at attention and all the hairs on my body follow suit as I face the Motherboard's first move. Why did she choose something so fragile? All I have to do is prick the bubble with my finger. Frowning, I tuck the map into my jacket pocket and start to lift my hand toward the filmy globule, but hesitate. To burst it, I'd need to take off my glove. Is that what she's trying to get me to do? I debate using the wire cutters instead, but would the bubble capture them and carry my one weapon away?

I drop my hand to my side, contemplating.

The music box continues in the background. Before I can figure out the song title or artist's name, it shifts to another tune, a sultry ballad I've never heard before. The plinking notes resonate lower to form a haunting but sensuous mood that makes my hips sway. I cup my hands over my ears, but the music continues to swish in my head and swim in my veins.

As I struggle to break loose of the song's spell, the bubble casts back a reflection trapped within its center: a girl covering her ears with black satin gloves—me, but different. I'm wearing a long-sleeved, high-necked gown. The bright red vinyl fabric—glossy like cherry skins—hugs every curve from my chest to my waist, then falls in a gathered, flowing skirt that drapes the toes of my combat boots. Tiny mirrors line the bodice, cut in the shape of diamonds to resemble a corset which ends where a black lace-up belt cinches tight. On my head sits a black bunny mask. The ears stand tall, obsidian mesh stretched around wire frames.

My eyes, the zippers, and my piercings glimmer under the lacy fabric where the mask stretches down and slopes beneath my nose, leaving my shiny lips bared.

Lark had mastered the skill of playing dress-up, but I never felt comfortable primping and preening. Pastel ribbons and gauzy frills were something I wouldn't be caught dead in; yet I can't deny this dress is extreme in a way that's entirely *me* . . . the brutal sensuality is empowering—intoxicating even.

I press my lips together, wondering what flavor the slick red lipstick might be, were I the girl in the reflection. Would it taste of ripe cherries, like the color of her dress? Or would it be something more layered, such as the raspberry cordial Uncle uses in his Berry-Truffle Roonies?

I lift my arm again, wanting to touch the reflection, wanting to taste it . . . to make it real. My gloves bend the bubble's wall, then my hand disappears inside, the wool becoming black satin. Next, my wrist and my arm plunge through, as my leather jacket gives way to the cherry vinyl sleeve. Then finally, all of me slips inside until I *am* the reflection: Nix in the red dress and bunny mask.

I watch through the translucent casing as my bubble shrinks, resizing me along with it. Then I'm floating, floating, floating, around the bend and into a ballroom filled with gorgeous gowns and debonair suits—velvets and satins of every color and trimmed in lacy frills that glimmer with fiber optics. Everyone's dancing and laughing, kissing and embracing. The bubble stretches toward a checkered floor blinking in a succession of silver and gold squares. I expand along with the membranous walls, and once my soles hit ground, the casing bursts with a loud pop that leaves me full size and surrounded by a cloud of rainbow glitter.

I rake off several sparkles stuck to the mask and lick my lip gloss, savoring the sweetness of icy watermelon on a summer day. The bunny ears sway atop my head when I glance at the ceiling, admiring a line of crystal chandeliers twinkling with warm rose-gold lights.

The crowd around me dances to the music box's alluring, tinkly song. I stand there in the midst, surrounded by a whirl of feathered and furry half masks, hollowed-out animal heads, the stiff and frightful smiles of handmade clowns and jesters, and most unnerving of all, white and red papier mâché masks locked in silent, expansive screams with gaping eyes and elongated noses. It's an exhibition of the face coverings I saw on Perish's hallowed wall. If the dancers' heights and body types weren't so humanlike, I'd guess they were the creatures and characters born of my imagination. As it is, I have no idea who or *what* they are.

My pulse resumes a frantic beat, no longer entranced by the music but awakened. Determined to spark reality, I feel around my neck for the chain, for the vial. But I'm reluctant to uncork it and put the rim to my lips. There has to be another way to break this illusion so I can reveal where I really am . . . find the connector I'm supposed to cut.

I search for the map in my pocket, but now that my jacket has transformed to a dress, it's no longer accessible. Neither are my jeans and the wire cutters. A wave of panic begins to rise but then instantly ebbs once I spot *him* across the room—the only guest not wearing a mask.

I know that face, the square clefted chin, the high cheekbones, the same beautiful boy who's been by my side since our childhood. His true flesh shines, without any unnatural streaks of orange, and his dual-toned eyes twinkle; everything is back to

normal. He's himself once more, and relief swells inside me. He meets my gaze and smiles, showcasing the divots in his cheeks. *I've missed those dimples.* My heart speeds up again, this time for an entirely different reason.

He opens his mouth to shout something over the music, then vanishes as the crowd shifts. I push through the surge of bodies, following the flashes of his white forelock through sporadic openings in the sea of swishing fabrics while he seeks a way to me.

Playing louder, feeding on our need to find each other, that tinkling, hypnotic cadence captures me once more, igniting fires inside my blood. Finally, Clarey reaches me. His slim jacket and tight slacks match my gown, sharing both the color and high-gloss fabric, though his is stamped with a design resembling crocodile skin. He's wearing the same loafers he arrived in, the only part of his ensemble that hails from home.

I'm at a loss for words. Thrilled to see him, yet unsure if he's real. Then all doubt fades once he catches my hand and pulls me to him, enveloping me in the scent of flowers and chemicals.

"Nix," he whispers. "I found you."

The dancers spread out, as if to give us room. The glimmer of chandeliers zeros in on his wonderfully bared face, a blush-pink spotlight that causes everything else around us to bleed into darkness. It feels like we're back in the orchard, only the two of us, as he draws me against him, one hand at my lower back and the other running a finger along the edge of my mouth until he reaches my lip ring.

"You're a sight for sore eyes," he says in his outdated lingo.

Giddy, I trace every inch of his face with a satiny fingertip. A cluster of white curls dips down over the pale skin of his forehead, hiding his scar. He catches my hand before I can move the

strands aside and presses his mouth to my wrist. Satisfied to find his lips as soft and perfect as his touch, I lean into him. Folding my arms around his neck, I rest my forehead against his and sink my gloves into the dark ringlets at his nape. I let him lead, lost in the feel of our bodies swaying to the ballad. The sleek fabric of our clothes squeaks with our movements, a sound at odds with the dreamy atmosphere.

I hug him tighter, triggering more rubbery creaks between us. "I'm so glad you're okay."

"I am, now that I know you will be." He hovers his lips inches from mine. My knees feel weak as our breaths mingle. He drops his mouth closer, making me ache for contact.

Yet instead of the kiss I'm anticipating, he whispers against my piercing, "It's all a lie."

Startled by the words, I trip over the long hem of my gown and push against him, though he doesn't release me.

He holds my gaze. "Look around us. *Really look*."

I do as he says, scanning the attendees that are now watching us with strange lights in their eyes. They drop their masks, one by one, revealing human faces underneath from every corner of the world, in every gender. Though all of them are teenagers, like Clarey and me. They look artificial, their expressions frozen in place. Sad, haunted, lost.

I turn my eyes back to Clarey, grateful his features are animated and genuine. He grabs my hand, wearing a somber expression. "We escaped the Goblin King, and the Motherboard led us to the portal. She only wants us gone, so she can finish what she started. So that no one will ever be lost and victimized here again." He casts a sidelong glance at our audience. "Your uncle, Flannie and me . . . we already stepped through. I came back so

you could see, so you'd believe. You need to come with me now, before time runs out."

The crowd rustles, and the vacant faces bow low, opening a path for us. Clarey leads me through the space toward a silvery light at the end of the room . . . an archway cloaked in thick cobwebs. A briny-scented wind gusts in, ripping through the gossamer strands so they gape to reveal the sea cave that brought us here. The closer we get, the clearer the view. Just outside is the beach, but not Mystiquiel's glowing golden sands. It's Cannon Beach, lit up by moonlight. It's home. The real world, wide and waiting.

Along the shore, Uncle Thatch paces in circles and Flannie follows at his ankles, as though anxious for Clarey's return and my arrival. Clarey's harmonica, mask, and gloves are piled on the ground close to them, where he shed the instrument and costume before coming back for me.

In the depths of the ballroom behind us, I hear the attendees grumbling and hissing, sounds that are strangely similar to the hums and pops of circuitry. The tinkly music grows quieter.

Something niggles at me, warning me. The cobwebs over the cave's opening. How long does it take a spider to weave something so seamless, so thick? Hours . . . days. Maybe even weeks. Long enough to make me question how Clarey got back in without breaking them. He would've had to be here all along. Unless of course, they're magic.

I glance again at the sea cave's portal to the beach. Clarey's shoe prints speckle the rocky edge where he stepped out, then returned, their shapes formed in wet mud.

Mud . . . Muddy. I remember now, the blues song I heard playing at the beginning of all this, before the bubble carried me

into the passage. The title, “Still a Fool,” rings disturbingly apropos in this moment. As for the artist . . . I grapple for the singer’s name. This is more than a game now. It’s life or death: Clarey’s, Uncle’s, Flannie’s, and mine. I have to be sure. Then it comes to me . . .

I meet Clarey’s gaze again, wanting to believe him. Hoping this is really over. But I need proof. “You remember that song ‘Still a Fool’? Your mother loved it.”

“Yeah.” He looks annoyed and drags me closer to the portal. “Nix, we need to go. We’re losing time.”

I stiffen and dig my heels into the floor. “First, tell me the artist’s name. The singer, it was Muddy *something*. Right?”

He frowns and tries to tug me out of the cave and onto the beach. He herds me close enough that the spiderwebs reach out and stick to my gown, to my mask.

I jerk free and back up two steps, pulling off the sticky threads. “Tell me, Clarey. Was it Muddy . . . *Rivers*?” I offer the wrong name on purpose, then watch his face, counting on that typical flash of exasperation that both flusters and charms me. I wait for him to correct me, to tease me. That’s all I need, and I’ll know this is true. That this thing is finally over and we can be together, back in the real world, with Uncle and Flannie and all this weirdness behind us.

His expression remains unreadable. The longer I study him, the more unreadable and blurred his features grow. Rattled, I glance down at the mud smudging the metal toes of his calfskin loafers.

“Shoes,” he says, as if reading my line of sight for clues. “Muddy Shoes.”

My stomach drops. “Muddy *Waters*. And Clarey . . . you’re

the lie." My throat catches as I reach up to move the curls hanging over his eyebrow and find the scar isn't there.

I swallow a whimper, watching his skin petrify to porcelain.

The crowd behind us converges, approaching in agonizingly slow increments. With each minuscule movement, parts of their faces crack and slide off—breaking into enameled chunks. Noses, ears, lips, and teeth. By the time they're a step away, the guests have shed yet another disguise and returned to their true selves—in shape and size. The creatures I created: trolls, elves, sprigs, piskies, gnomes, sprites, and hobblegobs, dressed in ensorcelled ballroom attire that obscured their savagery under a veneer of false sophistication.

Their discarded human faces lie in broken pieces on the marble floor. They hiss and snarl in accompaniment to the fading song, gyrating and pirouetting in ungraceful and off-tempo movements. Crunching and crackling the false features beneath their corrosive metallic feet, they leave behind bloody streaks of rust.

Heartsick, I turn to Clarey's expressionless face and drag his mask away. I half expect to see the pumpkin prosthetic looking back at me. Instead, shadowy emptiness waits underneath. The shadow grows, swallowing up all the other guests, my dress, my mask, every part of the illusion except the mirrors on my bodice. Those clatter to the floor and gather at my feet, a sparkling array of multiple reflections: a girl in ripped jeans, a T-shirt, and leather jacket. I'm left standing in the passage in solitude, chilled and trembling at the Motherboard's decisive assault.

She's wily, and she hit me where it hurt. But I beat her. *This time.*

Shaking off a wave of nausea and grief, I kick the mirror bits

aside and reach into my jacket to pull out the map. The purple X projects itself onto a black cord next to a large microchip at my left. I drag the wire cutters from their sheath and crouch, placing the long, open blades on either side of the pulsing rubber duct. I pause momentarily, resting one glove upon the microchip's surface to hold my balance as the substrate beneath my boots shudders like an earthquake. A niggle of sympathy threatens to stop me, that same part of me that hates erasing my sketches.

Then, I hear a lone chime transmitted through the pocket watch clipped to my jacket's zipper, marking eleven fifteen . . . forty-five minutes left before we're stuck here forever. That's all the incentive I need. I force the blades closed, slicing through the tubing to release a gush of oil and blood.

28

mirror

The tunnel rumbles, and I scramble to escape, slipping and sliding in the muck rushing from the severed cord. I sheathe the wire cutters and try not to wonder where the flow of blood and oil could be coming from, or what sort of pain I've caused this entity I created; just as I try not to question why there's blood at all, when the other beings here bleed machine oil and rust. I shove any warped sense of empathy from my thoughts, knowing I can't let artistic affection override what's most important.

I check my dad's pocket watch to confirm the chime I heard was real. It was; I have three-quarters of an hour to find the other two connectors and win our freedom. Following the direction of the white trail on my map, I push onward. Beneath me, the diamond-cut bits that once made up my mirrored corset drift along the same course, carried by the goop still spewing from the damage behind. The surge is shallow—barely high enough to lap at the soles of my boots. I try not to step on the glass while managing the slickness.

After several turns, I arrive. The X casts its mark onto another cord that runs along the ground beside some frayed copper wiring. Upon pocketing the map, I attempt to cross the passage to get to my target when the bits of mirror in the sludge begin to melt. They come together and overtake the dark greasy mix, like water mixed in oil. I step onto the hardening glass surface to keep my feet from being swallowed by it.

Soon, a seamless mirror spans the entire passage, beneath me, over me, around me . . . covering up the X and boxing me in. I'm surrounded by silhouettes I fear will become Lark's angry image looking back at me. Yet I don't have time to slam my eyes shut against the onslaught before reflections begin shuffling inside the glass panels, from floor to wall to ceiling to floor, over and over in a spinning motion, as if I'm locked inside a slot machine and someone has pulled the lever, sending me into rotations. The effect leaves me disoriented and dizzy. I kneel clumsily and wince at the pain in my scraped knee as it wedges against the cold glass.

The spinning slows to a stop. I rise to gather my bearings, the haziness in my brain clearing. I don't even have to fight for my eyes to stay open against that old habitual fear, because I'm not the object looking back at all. Much like in the fun house, it's a presentation playing out. Yet this time, I'm not part of it. I'm only a spectator.

Trees form in the scene all around me, lit by moonlight and stars. The branches, laden with autumn leaves, rattle in a cool wind. A sweet scent carries along the gusts—spiced with fresh peaches and cranberries, apricots and pears—so inviting and tempting, I long to step within and follow. But when I press my hand to the mirror, it meets a solid plane of glass. I'm on the wrong side, invisible and irrelevant. So I stay in place, my feet

lodged on the slick surface, searching for any crack in the veneer, any means to break the glass and find the cord I'm to cut.

Meanwhile, inside the diorama, movements begin to shift through the tree trunks. I inch closer and peer around branches and brush as a parade of creatures wends through the woods toward a glimmering hole in the ground. Violet mist and yellow light billow upward, revealing an enchanted doorway that opens into the depths of the earth.

The creatures are varied in size and shape, part humanoid and part beast: one tall and lean with a cat's face and whiskers, one short and plump with a bushy squirrel's tail flicking behind; one a stump-legged, horned wombat man covered in fur; and one that tromps forward on rat's feet. They're dressed in vintage hats, from felt derbies to aviator helmets, paired with knee britches and suspenders. Yet they wear no shirts or shoes. Others filter by, harder to see in the shadows, small and grotesque and singing gruesome lyrics ending with the chorus *Bid goodbye to our orchard fruits; goodbye, goodbye.* It's similar enough to the "Come buy our orchard fruits" verses from the *Goblin Market* poem that it leaves me with a sick churn in my belly. Many of them carry fruits in baskets or plates; others pull carts that one might see at a farmers' market.

Though somewhat different, this scene parallels illustrations I've seen of goblins tracking to and fro, in hopes of selling their seductive harvests. The logical part of me reasons it out . . . surely this snippet is taken and twisted directly from all the times I read the poem. It makes sense the Motherboard would choose to guilt me over my careless treatment of the book my mother presented as a gift.

I wait for Lizzie and Laura to make an appearance as confirmation.

There's a rustle from inside the misty, otherworldly doorway as two new creatures push their way out, coming onto the forest trail and headed toward the retreating parade. One, a huge, slug-shaped wretch without legs, squirms forward on its belly at a snail's pace. A flat-headed, pointy-nosed fellow follows, his black hide split by a white stripe from forelock to back—reminding me of a badger. The snail-paced one wears a harness and reins, and lugs a golden sleigh so heavy with produce the runners score troughs in the trail.

The creatures pushing carts and toting baskets pass their goblin companions without a word and disappear down into the murky, glowing doorway, taking their wares with them. The snail creature and its badger companion stall in front of my vantage point, as though, like me, they're waiting. My stomach does a flip when a coarse buzzing sound emits from under the fruits in the sleigh. I realize it's a snore in the same instant it stops.

A human arm plunges out from beneath some pears and grapes, hanging over the side. Next, two bared feet push free at the opposite end, followed by ankles and legs encased in lace-trimmed bloomers. When a girl's head appears, shoving out from beneath an avalanche of apples, I slap my glove across my mouth to keep from gasping.

She sits up all the way, brushing twigs and stems off a dusty blue floret gown and ruffled petticoats that belong on a mannequin in a Victorian era museum. A mask made of a hollowed-out fox's head covers her face. A golden frizz of hair bursts from the

ties around her nape, the tattered ends of a braid left short and uneven—as though cut off with a pair of dull shears.

The badger waggles a clawed finger at the girl. "Naughty Laurencia. You weren't to awaken yet." His vocal cords seem to be rioting, like shrill notes clashing, as if someone plucked a violin with a wire-toothed brush. "Not until your sister arrives and the trade be made." He opens his palm and blows pink sparkles into her face. She sneezes, then flops backward into the fruits once more, rolling them beneath her as her snore resumes.

Laurencia. A name so similar to Laura that the latter could be a moniker.

Out of nowhere, two girls shuffle into place in front of me, dressed in the same antique clothes as the one in the sleigh, both hidden from the waiting goblins and oblivious to my presence. They're around the age of fifteen or so—one with golden hair that matches the goblins' captive, and the other with chestnut locks. The blonde shushes her darker-haired friend, who mumbles the blond girl's name: *Elizabeth*.

Having heard "Lizzie" as a nickname for "Elizabeth," I have all the confirmation I need. The girl in the sleigh is Laura, Lizzie's sister who sold her hair and became addicted to the fruits. I'm seeing the part of the tale where Lizzie comes to bargain with the goblin men, to save Laura, yet it's not the way it was written at all. In the poem, Laura was never kept in a fairyland deep beneath the ground; she was at home, wasting away.

"Stay to the shadows, Christina," Lizzie whispers. "They mustn't find you with me, or they will bind you to tell lies for them."

I gulp down the surprise knotted in my throat. Christina . . . as in *Rossetti*? The author of the poem? What kind of a twisted

fantasy is this, where the author plays a part in her own fictionalized tale?

I stifle a snort when the irony hits. After all, where have I been this whole night, if not Mystiquiel? And now the Motherboard hopes to use my knowledge of an old picture book against me. I won't let her get the upper hand.

My attention perks as golden-haired Lizzie whispers again to Christina. "Since Jeannette never made it back, you're the only one left who knows the truth."

Jeannette. Another name similar to the poem . . . Jeanie, the sisters' friend who disappeared.

"You must be our historian," Lizzie continues. "Tell my family everything, so I won't be believed dead, or the curse forgotten. Tell them why I did what I did. Warn them of the true meaning of All Hallows' Eve. How goblins were the 'spirits' our ancestors hid from beneath their face coverings. How the costumes instead drew the attention of the goblins like flies to honey, attracted them to our imaginations. How the creatures captured young people in their masks, and tempted them with their fruits into years of servitude underground, draining them of life and emotion. Remind Laura, so she never forgets. Have her pass it down to our future generations . . . in case the fey forsake their side of my bargain and try to entrap humans one day again."

Lizzie's account of human sacrifices forced into a fairyland makes me edgy; it too easily explains the wall of old-world masks I saw in Perish's castle. But then I remember how just minutes ago I was trapped in a delusion that tried to convince me there was a roomful of human victims. Yet when I broke through the false reality, their masks fell away and revealed them as faerie tricksters.

I remind myself the Motherboard knows everything I know and is simply exploiting my doubts to hold me at bay so she can beat the king and win the destruction of his reign. All so she can replace the world I've drawn with one of her own making, to rule as she wishes.

I glance at the pocket watch. Seven minutes have already passed. It's 11:22, and I need to find the loophole out of this deception. If I could just get to the map, it would project the X.

I reach for my jacket pocket, but my gloved hand slams to the floor beside me, held in place by some unseen force. I'm able to peel free so long as I don't search out the map. Each time I try to get to it, my hand is pinned again. I grit my teeth in frustration and place my palm against my chest where the vial of Perish's blood waits. I still can't bring myself to use it.

My attention returns to the two girls as they continue to mumble.

"Once the doorway closes," Lizzie says, "wake up Laura and take her home."

Christina nods. Kissing her friend on the cheek, Lizzie clambers bravely out onto the path, leaving Christina safely behind the brush.

Lizzie scrambles into the path of the badger and snail goblins.

The furry one looks her up and down. "Did you bring what you be bidden?" he asks in his tumultuous timbre.

Lizzie pulls a dress from the pocket bag strapped at her waist. Streaks of blood mar the floral print.

The badger sneers a feral grin. "Very nice. The king be pleased you follow his instructions to the line. Who did you kill?"

Lizzie scowls. "He never specified a *who*. So I chose a *what*.

Our mother had to prepare a chicken for my sister's wake. There was blood to spare."

"Resourceful." The badger turns to his sluggish companion and laughs. "No wonder he like her, aye?"

The other arches his long snail neck in an almost graceful nod, obviously unable to speak for the bridle's bit in his mouth.

The badger focuses again on Lizzie. "Twisting words into riddles with the lot of us. You be fit in perfectly. And take heart. The chicken won't go to wasting. It sustain those attending your wake now."

Christina kneels lower behind the brush, and I know she must be thinking of Lizzie's final request, to ensure her family knows she didn't die.

Opening his sharp teeth to a grotesque snarl, the badger bites and slashes at the bloody dress Lizzie gave him, then tosses the fabric bits to the ground so the breeze picks them up, carrying them away to snag upon underbrush.

"There." The badger claps loose threads from his claws. "Your poor mum. Get one daughter back the same eve the other be tore apart by wolves."

Tears stream down Lizzie's face as she leans in to kiss her sister's blond head. "Don't forget me, Laurencia. But don't regret me, either."

My heart goes out to them. I ache to tell her that her sister will never forget, but that the regret is inevitable. I know only too well the agony poor Laura will face when she wakes up to the absence of her other half and wonders what she might've done to make her stay.

"Give me her skin," the badger barks. "Be part of the bargain. The final seal upon your contract."

Lizzie nods and unties the fox head, then hands it over. The baring of Laura's face reveals strange marks upon her neck, jaw, and temples, and over her eyes. It's almost as though her skin has been tattooed, but instead of ink, they're embossed—indentions in her skin in the shape of leaves, vines, and flowers. The imprints retain a pinkness to them, as if stamped so recently the skin hasn't healed.

I watch closely as she's lifted out of the sleigh by the badger and Lizzie. The same kinds of marks embroider her wrists, ankles, and shins where the hems and cuffs of her clothes pucker and shift while the two strain to place her under a tree trunk, her limp body propped to a sitting position.

Lizzie wipes tears from her face and corrals her features to a stern scowl. "The Goblin King . . . he swore she'd be safe here."

"She be under a spell of protection till she be found," the badger confirms.

Casting a surreptitious glance Christina's way, Lizzie climbs aboard the sleigh and settles into the indentation in the fruit left by her sister's body. The trio turns about. They're met at the fairyland entrance by a silhouette I recognize: ram's horns, hobbled misshapen limbs, goat's head.

Angorla.

"You're here to place a seal over the veil?" Lizzie asks.

The Gardener nods. "As per the contract, so none can stumble in or be taken. Plant these enchantments at the border," she directs Lizzie, dropping some seeds into her hands. Lizzie leans over the edge of the sleigh to do as she's told. "His Highness will come to bathe them in his royal blood, so they blooms. Nothin' else will flourish in their shade, no grass, no weeds. No winds will blow, no snow will snow. Nor even rain in the barren spot where

only daisies grow. And there be no more trades nor loss, where only the Goblin King and his blood-chosen may cross."

I think of my jeans' front pocket and the remaining seeds I have tucked away inside, wondering what kind of plant they might've become had they been sown and nurtured by the king's blood.

Within moments, the duo has accomplished their task and the small band vanishes into the mists of the fairyland doorway.

Christina stirs in front of me. Caught up in the scene, I forget it's an illusion and will her to wait . . . let the doorway close, make sure she's alone. But overly anxious, she tramples through the brush toward Laura a moment too soon.

She doesn't see what I see: a shadow creeping up behind her. The instant the outline swallows her small, frail form, she spins around, coming face-to-face with the king. Or rather, face-to-abdomen. He's huge. Tall, muscular. Antlers protrude from his head, though sharper and more pronged than Perish's. Strands of silver-lilac magic wind through his crown. He looks like my Goblin King in his complexion and build, but he's organic like the other goblins from earlier, not a touch of metal anywhere. His hair is gray, with a grizzled beard, and his features grow long, older and more weathered than Perish's.

"Ah, the poet I've heard so much about," he croons, bending low. "Laurencia couldn't say enough of her talented friend." His voice is deceivingly lovely—rich and sonorous. Too much like a human man's to reside in that monstrous, fanged mouth. He must be casting some sort of audible glamour.

Christina gapes and stumbles backward, falling to the ground next to Laura's drowsing form.

"Fear not, child. I am here merely to wake our dear Laurencia before my realm closes, as I'm the only one who can." He places a pearly hand next to Christina's cheek and strokes it with a thumbnail as long and menacing as an eagle's talon. "I am Blaze, king of Mystiquiel."

Blaze . . . I've never written any character with that name.

Blaze's thumbnail heats to a bright red and presses deeply into Christina's scalp where her dark hairline begins, as if to hide the scar he plans to leave behind. "By the time you trudge home to your pen and paper, you'll remember only the lure of goblin men, the brilliant beauty and wickedness of their fruits. Their pristine rinds, and the blemishes they leave upon tender human flesh. Outside of that, you'll be unable to speak of the bargain or the veil, or Elizabeth's whereabouts to her family. You'll not even be able to spell out her or her sister's true names. Unable to fashion words or symbols of any sort, in print or otherwise, that would allude to their secret or our unique history. It will be only a fantastic twilight tale, cautionary but questionable. Dancing on the fringe of the ephemeral. Make it a tribute to sisterhood, if you wish. For even I, a monstrous fiend, can admire Elizabeth's sacrifice. But nothing more. And should you ever see words anywhere that remind you of this experience, that threaten to awaken a forgotten memory, you will blot them out with ink or paper, and hide them eternally from your sight."

Angorla's cryptic taunt in front of the bakery comes back to me once more, how she said the history was forbidden, and why the creatures in the book looked nothing like the real denizens of Mystiquiel; that writers were the enemy. Now I see; they put a silencing enchantment over Christina, which also explains her

nervous breakdown as a teen, and even why she pasted strips of paper over passages in other books.

Yet . . . no. I shake my head to clear the cobwebs. This can't be real. I drew Mystiquiel; so it couldn't possibly have existed during Christina's lifetime in the 1800s. I shift uncomfortably behind the trees, needing to burst this vision, to get out of here. This is wrong . . . it's all wrong. Yet it's also confusing because it somehow plugs the holes in all the theories I've heard, which makes it feel completely right.

Again, I attempt to reach the map and fail. It doesn't matter, because I can't look away once the king's hooked claw begins drilling deep into Christina's skull with a grinding sound like metal scoring wood. Her eyes roll up into her head as a stream of blood dribbles down from the perforation. When he releases her, she shuts her eyes and the skin closes along her hairline. She slumps sideways, her chin resting on Laura's shoulder.

Blaze swipes away the red streaked along Christina's temple, then presses a palm to each of the girls' foreheads. "You will both awaken once the veil seals shut, and not a moment before. You'll remember nothing more than I've allowed you to retain."

He retreats, his large footsteps thundering along the trail. Upon arrival at the entrance, he uses his thumbnail to slice his own palm, then drizzles bluish oily blood across the freshly planted seeds. The liquid turns white before it hits the ground. Immediately upon contact, a harvest of deep pink gerbera daisies sprouts up from the earth—petals, leaves, and stems fully formed. I'm struck another emotional blow upon seeing them, as they were Lark's favorite flower. She used to make daisy chains for our necks and petal tiaras for our heads.

The sentimentality lasts only a moment, because once Blaze

steps into the hole and disappears from view, a torrential wind siphons through the forest, tugging at branches, ripping up grass, stripping bushes, trees, and vines of their leaves. The ephemera forms a whirlwind that funnels into the portal as it slowly cinches closed. I catch my breath, captured in the fray. The momentum drags me backward toward the opening, and with nothing but glass beneath me, I have no traction. Feet first, I'm flung toward the mirror, slipping inside to become part of the illusion, being hauled toward the doorway where mist intertwines with detritus in a vortex of suction—ready to swallow me whole before it closes forever.

My hair flings around my temples. Vines pelt my face and snag the zippers along my chin, cheek, and forehead. I thrust my left hand forward as I'm dragged across the enchanted daisies, clenching my fingers around a tendril growing out from a tree. I come to a halt, wrenching my shoulder with a painful jerk, but strain to hold on, keeping myself aloft in midair against the sucking pull.

The hems of my jacket flutter out around me like broken wings, and a corner of the map shifts from my pocket, just enough to imprint the X on a small patch of the magical daisies beneath me. Catching a breath at my luck, I force my right hand toward the wire cutters and unsheathe them. I'm not strong enough to squeeze the handles closed with a singular grip, so I work my fingers over the tool to cup the opened blades in front of their hinges. I pinch them shut around the cluster of petals and stems. In the same instant the blossoms snap in half, the wind ceases and the mirror box vanishes from around me. With a thud, I fall to the floor, finding myself in the open passage again.

Fresh streams of blood and oil gush from the daisies that have transformed back to the now-severed cord. Hundreds of fuchsia petals remain behind, floating atop the liquid. I scramble to stand. Gathering up my map and wire cutters, I race into the next tunnel to escape the gory petal-strewn current, the shuddering ground, and the grief and confusion burbling up within my chest.

29

memory

The double chimes transmitting through Dad's pocket watch tell me I've only a half hour left. I move on, following the map's white trail while I shiver from head to toe—more from my dark mood than the quaking ground and walls around me. My clothes, soggy with oil and blood, cling to my body, prompting goose bumps all along my skin.

A sense of loss weighs so heavy inside my chest, my heart strains beneath it, as if it's being smashed flat, too thin to function. I have difficulty breathing but convince myself it's a reaction to the claustrophobic narrowing of the tunnels—the Motherboard's desperate attempt to keep me from reaching the last leg of my journey. It can't be that sense of ownership growing more cumbersome with each step I take, leaving my emotions as muddled as the murky liquid beneath my feet. I feel as though a part of me has shattered alongside the two cords I've severed. How am I ever going to manage a third?

The oily reddish rivulets, speckled with bright pink daisy

petals, have risen to the point they swish around my ankles, just inches away from reaching the tops of my boots.

I press forward, my footsteps sloshing along. Although the sludge is thick, I'm able to round the next-to-last bend in a matter of minutes, leaving one long tunnel between me and the final corner I'll turn. Despite the ache in my muscles and behind my sternum, I embrace a sense of hope. It's almost over; if the Motherboard hurts as much as me, maybe I've incapacitated her enough that she has nothing left to throw my way.

My feet stumble to a stop as I'm proven wrong: two gazes, one set amber and one set green, appear out of nowhere just ahead, then morph into a solid feline form—bigger than Flannie.

Slinx and Binx.

I lean against the rumbling wall, fearing the grimalkin's jagged teeth if I risk passage. With the sludge slowing my steps, there's no making a run for the corner.

But I can't turn around and give up. I won't . . .

The grimalkin's eyes shimmer brightly atop its two heads. Its long, coiled, serpentine necks cojoin in a V at a furry black torso merged by a zipper from the chest to its belly. Its four legs disappear under the muck as it sits on its rump, whipping a wiry tail left to right along the surface, stirring currents on either side.

I wrote the character so the zipper is its vulnerability. If my canon holds true, I could unzip it, and the innards—gears and wires—would spill out and leave it paralyzed. It seems the logical answer to bypassing this barrier. But how to get close enough?

The whir of a motor hums on the air between us, a precursor to the grimalkin's taunting voices, and I know in that moment why the Motherboard conjured this particular creature. Not to mangle me, but to level me.

"There be no friend like a sister, Slinx," Green-eyes hisses—a wet, greasy sound like a leaking tire skidding through a puddle.

"None that I can see, Binx," Yellow-eyes answers with a purring mewl.

A sob breaks from my throat, loosened by the haunting final verse of the poem. I clutch my ears in an agonized bid for silence.

"Yet only Father Truth can clear the dreary gray . . . ," Slinx says, its voice slipping directly into my head. "To fetch a mind that's gone astray."

Binx winks one eye coyly. "Aye. Then is up to us to lead the way."

The change in the wording knocks me off balance. What are they planning? The two sets of luminous eyes narrow as the black slitted pupils elongate, long necks entwining in a snaky dance.

"Shall we end her pain, Slinx?"

"Elsewise, we be nothing more than monsters, Binx."

The grimalkin's two heads bob as it stands up to full height, dark liquid streaming from its fur. It struts forward, slinky-slow, on all fours, scoring rivulets through the deepening mire. It lowers its necks, a graceful move that reminds me more of black scaly swans than snakes, and opens both sharp-toothed jaws.

I stiffen, prepared to shove off the wall and duck out of the way, then realize I'm not a target. The grimalkin moves its gaping muzzles from side to side, swallowing up the pink petals and letting driblets drain from both mouths in oily streaks.

Within moments, Slinx and Binx have trekked all around me, leaving no petals behind. Gulping down the last of the flowers, the feline faerie plops onto its haunches, its lower torso submerged again. Two forked tongues flick out to lick its muzzles

clean, then each side of the creature lifts a forepaw to finish grooming.

Before I can make a move, the dreaded voices sound off again.

"Time to sow the final seed, Binx."

"Aye. A cruel reaping that can't be avoided, Slinx."

The grimalkin makes the long splashy walk to the end of the tunnel, then, tail flicking, turns the corner, leaving me with a map burning a hole in my pocket, and my deepest dread branding a crater in my heart.

I force myself to follow. The resulting pull of the current—sooty and dismal without the bright fleck of Lark's favorite petals—slows my stride.

As I trudge along, stopping often to catch my breath and nurse the deep ache of exhaustion in my bones and muscles, an epiphany takes form: the blood and oil forming this tragic tributary surrounding me, they're the embodiment of all the regret I've lived with over the past few years; every pang of doubt and culpability I've wrestled for the sake of Lark and her untimely death.

The Motherboard knows my regrets, my weaknesses. And she's capitalizing on them. She saved her cruelest trick for last; the gerbera daisies should've clued me in the moment they sprouted.

I muse over the scene of the sisters in the prior illusion. How much that event mirrored Lark and me. When Lizzie had to leave and told Laura not to forget her, but not to regret her. I'm stunned to open-mouthed shock as Perish's earlier observation rides upon the tails of that thought: *The premature removal of your other half has left a parasitic wound, bound to eat you alive lest you allow it to scar.*

That's exactly what has happened since Lark's been gone. I've been bleeding out, withering away, a shadow of who I was meant to be. Letting my own gifts, my own dreams, decay and rot, then stepping instead into Lark's. So that her essence would survive by proxy, through my symbolic death—the ultimate penance I could pay.

I plod forward again, sloshy step by sloshy step, and recite the verse aloud—this time all the way to the final sentence I could never bring myself to say.

For there is no friend like a sister
In calm or stormy weather;
To cheer one on the tedious way,
To fetch one if one goes astray,
To lift one if one totters down,
To strengthen whilst *one stands.*

That's what I kept overlooking. I could never make it to the end before the grief broke me. *Standing* is the same as surviving. A tree stands against harsh winds. A sea wall stands against inclement tides. That last line refers to spiritual support, on the chance just one sister is left behind.

The competition between us could never change how much I loved her. Could never break the bond that connected us with a power deeper than magic. Both remain even now, after her death.

That has to be why I kept seeing her face in my reflection: the anger, the frustration—it wasn't to guilt me; it was the essence of her telling me to let go and stand strong.

I deserve to heal, to stop hurting. I deserve to be me. Lark would've wanted that. Subconsciously, I think I knew this all

along. I was just afraid to clamp the exposed artery, for fear I'd stop feeling *her* once the bleeding stanched.

A new courage wells up within, alongside a certainty I've struggled until now to find: This is my trial by fire. The one chance to cauterize the wound, to close it and let it scar, just like Perish said.

I *must* beat the Motherboard . . . not just for my loved ones and our freedom, but for me. The only real way to honor Lark is to stand up and embrace my future.

I glance at the pocket watch. I've twenty-five minutes left. I propel myself forward until I'm at the turn, prepared for my final slash with the wire cutters.

I inhale a sip of solder-scented air as I slosh into the next tunnel, with twenty-four minutes left to spare. I'm forced to a stop at the entrance, shaken to find it dry as a bone. The sludge is now somehow dammed up behind me with an invisible barrier. Is it because I've unburdened myself from the pull of all that guilt?

The map in my hand springs to life, marking an X upon a cord attached to the wall only feet away. Yet one thing still stands between me and victory. The grimalkin's motionless form slumps in my path, its eyes shut. Both heads and necks lie slack on the ground, mouths gaping and tongues lagging, a gruesome reminder of the dead kelpine on the beach. I fight a gagging sensation at the slimy brownish-red substance oozing from the corners of its muzzles. Its torso has been unzipped, though the belly is flush to the floor, keeping the innards from view.

I want to believe this is my doing, that I've incapacitated the Motherboard's last illusion by freeing myself of my regrets. But why am I still seeing the grimalkin at all?

Refocusing on the X and the cord I need to cut, I inch ahead with my hand clasped over the wire cutters sheathed at my thigh. I nudge the grimalkin to get around it, then jump backward when it rolls over, listless as a corpse but emitting a rustling sound from its gut.

Instead of gears and wires spilling from the belly gape, thousands of flower petals begin to pour out, the momentum growing until they cascade upward as if from a busted water main. The passage begins to fill with them—the whooshing force of a tidal wave. I'll be enveloped in minutes and suffocate if I can't break this illusion.

Having no other option, I grab for the necklace and the king's blood. Yet before I can pull out the stopper, the petal torrent swells up to my collarbone, confining my hands at my chest. My tattoo flutters its inky wings, the first movement it's attempted since I landed in the orchard.

The green-herbaceous scent of daisies surrounds me, a nauseating parody of cow manure and grass. Gasping for air, I stretch my neck and tilt my chin above the petals' surge. At the moment they reach my jawline, they stop and sweep away. Only one long strand of pink and green remains; whole daisies, their blooms, stems, and leaves, are linked and wound around me, acting as shackles upon my arms, legs, and ankles and holding me immobile.

The rest of the petals slap against the walls and stick in place. There they reshape and change colors like a puzzle, shifting until the pieces join in a clear and vibrant image that animates in front of me.

There's no sound . . . only visual and tactile cues. In the back of my mind, I agonize over time ticking away, but I'm a captive

audience—imprisoned by daisy chains—unable to break loose or maneuver the wire cutters from their sheath.

The background resolves to an apartment building. In the distance behind, late afternoon sunlight paints red-dirt plateaus with streaks of pink, orange, and purple. Outcroppings of pine, spruce, and fir dot the horizon. It reminds me of photos I've seen from Arizona that Uncle took during an internship there, a couple of years before he became our guardian.

A third-floor apartment door comes into view, guarded at the threshold by a crudely carved jack-o'-lantern alongside a paper skeleton, tied with yarn to the stairwell's post and skittering on a dry, arid wind. A hooded figure ascends the cement steps and casts shade upon the pumpkin, then knocks with its left hand. The visitor's bone structure is graceful and feminine, and a band—made of the tiniest dried forget-me-nots and baby's breath—encircles her ring finger. Along the wrist are the same raw marks, imprints of ivy and flowers pressed into the skin, that I saw on Laura's limbs in the Motherboard's *Goblin Market* delusion, when the goblins brought her back from their underground fairyland.

A taller hooded form moves into place at the woman's side—his broad shoulders bent with the weight of an infant car seat gripped within the clasp of each hand. He also wears a wedding ring made of corded threads, but has no puncture marks on his wrists. Pink blankets swaddle both babies in their carriers, hiding their faces and hair. But even without seeing them, the sick feeling of familiarity in my gut is enough.

The door opens. A spray of buttery golden light reveals the lanky silhouette of the occupant, holding a bowl of candy. It's Uncle Thatch, but younger. The lenses of his glasses aren't so

thick. The smile and frown lines around his mouth and eyes aren't yet defined. The moment he sees his visitors, he drops the bowl of treats, casting candies along the landing and stairs in a prismatic rain of cellophane and silver foil.

A bone-deep unease unwinds inside me. I wriggle against the daisy chains, struggling to break loose so I can slash the cord and be free of the Motherboard's twisted taunts. But unable to budge, I slump in place, resigned to watch the nightmare play out.

The puzzle pieces shift . . . spanning into another scene. This one showcases the inside of the apartment, thick curtains pulled to shut out any daylight. Soft candles flicker along the walls of a bedroom I've never seen, spotlighting a calendar turned to October thirty-first. I recognize the duffel bag tossed by our mother onto the messy bedspread, and two of the items that tumble out of its half-opened zipper: a picture book and a pocket watch. Other things scatter across the covers that aren't so familiar: onesies and newborn gowns and dresses, diapers, a rattle shaped like a white ghost, and baby bottles with pink lids, all with price tags made of masking tape and permanent marker . . . as if recently purchased at a garage sale.

The image zeroes in on my uncle again. His mouth mimes the words "my sister" over and over as he stands toe-to-toe with Imogen, whose hair, coloring, and features match his so perfectly, yet softer and daintier: smaller nose, eyes wide but almond shaped, jawline more curved than angular. Mom mimes back the words "my twin." Why didn't he ever mention he and Mom shared that trait with me and Lark? He holds out her wrists, fussing over the wounds there, and does the same to her neck and

temples. Then he drags her close, hugging her as their bodies quake with weeping.

I bite my lip, caught up in their emotional backlash. She looks so much like Lark and me, I could be staring in a mirror—if not for the dark, thick eyebrows accenting each of her green eyes. Then the man comes into view, our father, and the source of our own white eyebrows, pale freckles, and gray irises becomes clear.

The albinism of his coloring is much more pronounced than in us. His white-blond hair, cropped short, fades into skin so snowy and wan he could be a ghost. But he's beautiful, and he's my father. The man I've only known through a few stray photographs, an obituary, a broken watch, and an old army duffel.

Dad holds out his hand, and I see the name "Owen" form on his lips. After shaking hands, Uncle crouches on the floor beside the infant carriers, peeling away the blankets to showcase my and Lark's bulbous little heads—pinkish scalps under newly sprouting tufts of fine black hair. We're tiny . . . can't be much older than a week or so. Maybe even less. Is this the first time Uncle met us? Our first visit with him? Did my parents live in Arizona during our three years as a family, before they died? If so, when did we visit a beach?

How my ears ache to hear their voices as the three of them speak. To know what they're saying. Uncle stands suddenly, then slides a suitcase from under his bed as Mom and Dad open his drawers and closet, helping him toss clothes inside, not taking time to fold or remove hangers. They're flustered, hurried, scared. It shows in every trembling move. Then my logic catches up to my sense of wonder, and I realize something's very wrong with

this enactment. Lark and I were born in August. So why do we look like newborns on this Halloween day?

I growl in fury as the puzzle pieces shift once more. That scene had to be fake, considering the discrepancy of our birth date. Regardless, I wasn't ready to let the moment go. To finally have seen my parents' faces, even if it wasn't real, was something I've always longed for—which is no doubt why the Motherboard played that card.

The new scene opens up, and night has fallen. Imogen and Owen are in a car. Heavy darkness fades in blinks as headlights pass on the other side of a highway. The back seat holds no child carriers, and if it wasn't for the ghostly rattle gripped in Mom's hands as Dad drives, I'd think it was a different night altogether. But Mom still has the same fresh markings on her skin, and she and Dad wear the same clothes under their dark hooded cloaks. I have an uneasy intuition that Imogen kept the rattle as a keepsake, which rekindles that sense of dread and wrongness inside me. They raised us until we were three. Maybe they had to go somewhere and came back a day or two later. Or maybe Uncle is following behind them, although I don't see any car lights in the rearview mirror.

Outside the windshield, Owen's headlights illuminate a large yellow sign with the words Welcome to New Mexico, The Land of Enchantment in pink and black letters. Along the shadowy landscape appear more sandy plateaus. Sparse gatherings of yucca and desert willows stand leafless and spindly, like skeletal sentries in the distance. Then, as they drive past the sign, a giant stag appears in the road a few feet ahead, as if by magic. Its eyes catch the light and glimmer a brilliant white as it freezes and stares them down.

Dad's jaw clenches, and he jerks the steering wheel. Mom loses the rattle to the floorboard and clutches the console as the car swerves out of control toward a clump of barren trees that wasn't there moments ago.

Although I know what this is . . . the night they died, I can't stop watching as their car hits the trees with a crumpling crash that I can't hear, yet it shudders through my spine.

In a horrific moment of clarity, I see the white stag trotting over to the crushed car. The animal changes, morphing into a Goblin King. Not Blaze, not Perish, but one who somehow resembles both, from his antlers to his luminous coloring. He pulls my mother's listless form from the car's wreckage, leaving my father to bleed to death. The ground opens up in the middle of the clump of trees, revealing a softly glowing doorway, just like the one in the *Goblin Market* vision. Mom rouses and reaches over the goblin's shoulder for the car, screaming soundlessly. Then, as if spotting me, she waves her hand, bidding me to follow her into the misty hole.

I'm jerked to the ground as the daisy chains tighten around me, dragging me toward Mom's beckoning fingers and the fairy-land doorway. I slam my eyes shut, wanting to unsee everything. Maybe it's not worth fighting anymore. Maybe I should just let the Motherboard take me. The tattoo on my skin begins to flap fiercely. It shakes me from my despondency and reminds me what's real. What I'm fighting for.

I'm stronger than this illusion.

My body continues shuttling toward the light. With my arms and legs bound, I can't catch onto anything to hold me in place this time. So instead, I turn my attention to what I can control . . . maybe. I drew the lark tattoo, like everything else here, and

although I can't command the characters in Mystiquiel due to their evolution, the tattoo has never left my flesh. It's part of me; but it seems to want independence, to be able to fly away. Maybe I can use that to my advantage.

I concentrate on the wings of ink flapping against my skin and grant the tattoo permission to fight for escape . . . to claw and rip through my clothes. Within moments, the lark's black beak punches through my leather jacket, revealing a threadbare hole in my T-shirt beneath. The razor-sharp bill gnaws along the daisy chain, snapping it apart at my shoulder. Then the tattoo takes flight into the air and escapes the tunnel. My skin feels cold, bruised, and bare without that stamp tying me to my sister, but it was a necessary sacrifice. I've no more regrets.

I cast off the broken link of flowers and crawl free from the enchanted doorway's pull. Suddenly, triple chimes, marking fifteen till midnight, set fire to my determination. Scrambling to my feet, I leap over the grimalkin and drag out the wire cutters, slicing the cord without pause, desperate to burst the vision before I see anything more.

Just as the tableau starts to collapse into petals, a scintillant flash of light blinds me as the car explodes and flames eat up all that remains inside, including my dad. An agonized moan escapes my throat.

Blood and oil flood the passage and swell around my feet as the petal puzzle crumbles. I did it. I cut the final cord, but despite the momentary purge of relief, I drop to my knees as everything I've witnessed and the feeling of loss hit me anew.

The Motherboard has managed to plant doubt in my mind, and I can't help but speculate: Those pictures in Uncle's attic are

only likenesses—other families, other parents with their babies, similar in coloring and form so they could resemble our mom and dad to stanch our curiosity—but nothing that showed a clear enough depiction to enable a search online for matches; our birth certificates—counterfeits with falsified birth dates; Imogen and Owen's obituary spotlighting their death along Highway 101 in Astoria, another fraudulent document. All to cover up the most inconceivable truth of all: that Uncle raised us from the beginning, because the Goblin King stole our parents away.

What purpose could there possibly be to weave such an intricate tale for a set of insignificant twin girls?

My veins shudder in agonized pulses, the plasma inside them a loud swish in my ears. My lungs squeeze painfully, needing air. Sweat beads along my hairline and nape, yet I quiver from the chill. I can't catch a breath . . . is this what Clarey feels like? Am I having a panic attack?

Wheezing, I watch through bleary eyes as the grimalkin dissolves into puddles along with the daisy petals, melting away one by one, until the tunnel and the final severed cord are all that remain. The current tugs at my waist, my legs. A soul-shattering tremor shakes the walls and ceiling around me. Multi-lit panels and mechanical components slide loose and plummet into the liquid, splashing my face. I lick my lips, tasting blood. Is it the Motherboard's . . . or mine?

My heart beats queerly, a dual-flopping sensation, as if the wire cutters reached into my chest and cleaved the organ in half, leaving two grisly sides unfit to function. I go limp, allowing the sludgy river to lift me. In a daze, I ride its current out of the passage, escaping only moments before the walls collapse.

30

the motherboard

The gushing water wends through a huge cement pipe, then plunges out to deposit me with a thud onto a muddy bank, black with sludge. Soaked to the skin and aching all over, I cough to clear my lungs of the vile liquid I swallowed. Yet even that doesn't ease the irregular rhythm of my heartbeat.

Overhead, the orb that watches over Mystiquiel—the Motherboard's eye—comes into view. It's now bloodred and cloaks everything in rusty shadows. Blotting muck from around my zippers and piercings with the back of my wet glove, I squint at Dad's watch; I've only thirteen minutes left, but I'm almost there.

I've landed in a shallow drainage trench, a few feet away from my destination. I crane my neck to make out the top of the structure. The electrical flashes lighting up the billows of smoke are dissipating, and what I see breaking through the haze floors me.

The steel structure is shaped like a giant head, with embossed features that are painfully fresh in my mind after the final illusion I just endured. It's Imogen, my mother. In tribute or in

effigy, I can't be sure. I've come to the conclusion that since I'm the creator of Mystiquiel, this false history must've been supplied by thoughts in my own subconscious—ones the Motherboard distorted to fit her purpose. This is her final ploy to scare me away, to finish what she started . . . cut me off at the knees and leave me in shreds.

I refuse to quit, but the wave of nausea that churns in my stomach forces me to stop long enough to retch. Frothy bile sours on my tongue. I spit, then swipe my lips with my shirt's wet hem. I push up to standing, and nearly double over when my pulse drops, leaving me light-headed. I haven't eaten anything since I entered the orchard earlier, so no surprise my blood sugar's low. Panting, I lean against the cement pipe's edge and contemplate the climb ahead of me.

A tall copper scaffolding supports the metallic likeness of Imogen, and the long, winding aluminum stairway that leads into the structure seems to go on for a mile. Since Perish isn't down here to greet me, he must be inside. I'll be making the climb alone.

Every muscle in my body protests, and a bone-deep bleakness zaps my strength. Still, I force myself to limp to the first step and start the ascent. When the stairway jostles to a hum beneath my aching feet, accompanied by a *chink-chink-chink* like the chain pulling a roller coaster to its highest point, I'm not even fazed. Why wouldn't it be an escalator? After all, I drew such contraptions into my novels.

I laugh then, drunk on fatigue and hysteria. This entire journey, nothing's acted quite like I sketched it; yet this last leg . . . this one instance . . . followed my rules, and in a moment when I needed it most. An overwhelming sense of gratitude anesthetizes me. I prop myself against the mobile handrails and ride the climb.

Within a matter of seconds, I'm nearing the top. I glance down, the heights both dizzying and inspiring until I see the result of my destruction to the Motherboard's mainframe. True to Perish's word, the world is no longer rusting. The brownish veins in the cement and soil have faded away. Yet everything else also fades—as if being erased.

Beneath the orb's tinted shadows, Mystiquiel slowly disappears into a colorless void. The buildings, the homes and landscapes, all of it being swallowed by a snowy wave, as if someone spilled a bottle of Wite-Out across the panel, leaving a blank page.

The biomechanical characters and creatures—be they winged or footed—all gather into shivering, panicked masses along the evaporating streets and terrain, watching helplessly as the vortex of emptiness surrounds them. Bonbon, the troll, and Angorla float into view. Soon they're all adrift in space—pencil-line sketches without any background to anchor them. The same event has already removed the beach, ocean, and carnival tents, as demonstrated by the sea creatures and corpses afloat alongside the others. The wave slows within a few yards of the orchard and the Motherboard's lair, as if held back by the two most powerful beings' magic.

An agonized moan escapes me. I thought I was saving everything . . . that I was stopping the Motherboard from blotting out my creation. But it appears I did the opposite. Is this what Perish wanted to accomplish all along? Did he deceive me? Or did I fail somehow?

An audacious idea enters my mind . . . a frantic last bid to save my creation. Once we get safely home, I can draw everything from scratch. Now that I've worked through my depression, my guilt, my ability to see colors has returned. I can revive

Mystiquiel on the page, breathe life into my works. But should I even try? I don't want to endanger anyone ever again, yet now that I've finally embraced my gift and understand it, I want to pursue it. And most of all, I don't want to leave my characters and creatures orphaned here, adrift forever, lonely and helpless, with no world in which to exist. I can rebuild this place with a strong foundation, a good heart.

As if in response to my musing, my heartbeat takes another odd tumble behind my sternum. Breathless, I slide down to sit on the automated stairs—unable to look at Mystiquiel's cleansing one second longer.

A slot above me opens, ferrying the escalator into the steel head, then closes upon our passage, thankfully shutting the sad plight of my world and its denizens from my view. The stairs flatten to a conveyer belt, and I'm funneled through a dim coolness—lit by sporadic penlights and red beeping alarms. The scent of machine oil and burnt cables singes my nostrils. Tangled electrical cords hang from the ceiling, many of them frayed, with orange and white popping sparks that fall like fiery rain to the floor. It's both dreadful and beautiful, holding my attention in the way only chaos and destruction can captivate.

The belt slows, chugging toward a figure waiting in the shadows, blurred by split-second intervals of light. It's not hulking enough to be Perish, and the face's profile is too long and lumpy for Uncle. Once I see the furry dog dancing beside the silhouette, and hear the tapping of her mechanical foot against the floor, I gather what little stamina I have left and leap off my transport toward Clarey and Flannie.

"Nix!" Clarey catches me in an embrace before my knees give out.

Flannie yips in greeting and sniffs at my feet, wagging her tail as I wrap my arms around Clarey's neck and hold on for dear life.

"It's okay . . . we're all okay," he says, his shoulders stiffening with pent-up emotion. The fronds of his mutating hands snag at my lower back where my T-shirt is tucked into the waist of my jeans. Nuzzling my nose at the place where the BAHA has enmeshed with his mask, I breathe him in. He feels real . . . he smells real. But is he?

"Midnight Pumpkin," I whisper against the molded ridge of his ear. It could be a term of endearment for him in this absurd moment, but what it really is is a test.

He leans back with a confused expression, and I fear I've fallen into another trap.

"I can't hear from that ear anymore," Clarey says, tracing the zipper that runs along my chin. "When the latex melded to my hearing aid, it started bugging out. I'm telling myself it will be good as new once the spell wears off and I can lose the mask. What did you say?"

"Midnight Pumpkin?" I present it as a question this time.

"Oh! Toni Price," he answers back with a sad, crooked smile, correctly naming the singer of the album that once haunted me with its Halloween design. A holiday that no longer holds any power over me after this crazy night.

I yelp with relief, pulling him in for another hug. Then remembering the portal's deadline, I force us apart again to check the pocket watch. There's ten minutes left. I don't want to admit that a part of me dreads this last step. Killing the Motherboard is suddenly feeling way too real and final, taking into account the devastation caused by just incapacitating her.

Rubbing Flannie's ears, I look her and her master over as quickly as possible in the blinking lights and sparks. Dust, grease, and mud cake along Flannie's damp fur, but other than that she seems as rambunctious and playful as ever.

Clarey's wearing the same clothes he's been in since we went to the carnival on Cannon Beach—the *real* Cannon Beach—though they're spotted with grime and torn in several places. Strangely, they're also almost as wet as mine. His natural complexion breaks through the orange latex while his flesh still retains the shape of his prosthetic; so that detail was true. He's becoming permanently fused with his costume.

The question is, why are he and Flannie already here, broken out of the Goblin King's marble spell? "I thought you were at the castle, trapped in Perish's pocket. Is he here?"

Clarey frowns. "I was never trapped. I must've only been at the palace for a few minutes. Scourge snuck me and Flannie out, and I woke up here sometime around ten thirty or so. The king's brother made some kind of deal with . . ." Clarey stops himself, his altered features folding to worry.

"The Motherboard," I finish for him, realizing what Perish meant when he accused Scourge of stealing and conspiring. Which also means the Goblin King was bluffing with the gazing globes; it was merely illusions trapped inside. Hedging his bets, indeed. "Uncle?"

Clarey nods. "Angorla helped him escape early on. He's been waiting here the whole night."

My thoughts shift to the first illusion I endured. Was the Motherboard using her imagery to try to tell me she had Clarey and Flannie; that she had my uncle, too? "Why would the Motherboard want to help you . . . us?"

A deep sadness lurks behind Clarey's bright eyes. "Because she's—"

"Clarey." Uncle Thatch's voice drifts down from the second-story platform shrouded in shadows. An odd crackling sound sputters from the upper level, but I can't make anything out other than a couple of burlap tarps draped across indefinable shapes. "Let me be the one to tell her, okay?" Uncle descends the steps and wipes some grime from his hands with a rag that he then tucks into Dad's duffel on his shoulder. Uncle's busted glasses sit crookedly on his face, the cracked lens lit up by flickering sparks. When he reaches us, he's as wet and dirty as Clarey.

I throw myself into his open arms, so happy to see him I can't find it in me to be angry at the secrets he's kept, or to even ask what he means by stopping Clarey midsentence. I breathe him in, the scent of baked goods and lemony dish soap still lingering underneath the muck on his Enchanted Delights T-shirt and khaki jeans. His familiarity—and the unconditional acceptance and love he's always given so freely—fills those lonely spaces inside me, all the gaping holes that reopened when I thought I'd lost the last remnants of my family.

Uncle hugs me close and mumbles against my dripping hair, "Aw, Nixie-girl. I'm sorry I didn't realize who Jaspar was. I thought he was a henchman, not the king himself. I really wish you'd stepped back through the veil. She was trying to lead you out."

"*The veil?*" I'm slammed with the one consistency in each illusion: doorways. One that opened to Cannon Beach through a cave, and two others in the ground, filled with light. All three were the way out of Mystiquiel. Two of them even tried to

physically suck me in. "What about you guys? Did she open a door for you, too? Why didn't you go?"

"We can only pass the threshold alongside you. You're holding the key." Uncle taps the vial on the chain around my neck, reminding me of the contents I once naively believed to be squid ink.

Another moment in the tunnels comes full circle. Angorla's rhyme: *No more trades nor loss, where only the Goblin King and his blood-chosen may cross.* So that's what she meant.

"The opening responds to royal blood," I conjecture aloud.

Uncle shrugs. "Exactly. The veil can appear anywhere in the world, but for anyone to step through at any time, be they fey or human, they either have to be accompanied by the king or have a sample of his blood in hand—willingly given by him—to cross over."

Willingly given: in our case, provided for our bakery.

"We tried to get to you by taking the drainage tunnel, but the flood kept us out," Clarey answers. "It was too slick for us to climb in."

This explains their wet, grimy clothes. I wonder if they know I was responsible for that particular flood. "Wait . . . so the Motherboard was going to send me alone, without you three? Didn't you tell her it would kill me to leave you behind?" My entire body quivers, an all-encompassing chill that is one part rage and one part exhaustion.

Uncle tries to get me to sit on the lower step, but I refuse. "You were her only concern," he insists.

I clench my jaw tight. Right. Because, like Perish said, I'm her one worthy adversary, and she wanted to shove me out of the way so she could finish what she started. I grind my teeth. "Where is she . . . this . . . *thing*? I want to talk to her."

Uncle and Clarey exchange heavy, meaningful glances.

"Talk to her, or finish her?" Uncle asks, wearing an expression that teeters awfully close to accusation—confirming they do know what I've been up to.

"She's my creation, and I have to deal with her," I snap, all the confusion and frustration bubbling up inside. "You haven't seen all the stuff she threw at me in those tunnels. All the horrors, all the lies. I have to finish what I started. Perish is the only one who can get us out—together."

Clarey and Uncle stand there, looking indecisive.

"Seriously?" I ask. "What's with you two? This entire world is being erased. There's going to be nothing left. I'm not sure we can survive that. Even if we did, we'd be like all the characters, floating around in empty space." I glare at Clarey. "And you—you'll be locked in goblin form, forever." I hold up the pocket watch. "Come on, guys! We've only eight minutes left before—"

"Perish padded the truth, Nix." Clarey's rippled jaw twitches as he interrupts me. "Yeah, every year the veil magically opens at dawn on Halloween and closes at midnight. But there's no limit on it for the Goblin King. Perish can reopen it for us whenever and wherever he chooses—day or night, any month of any year. He just wanted you to feel pressed for time, to weaken the Motherboard before she defeated him and broke the contract for good."

"Contract?" I look at Uncle. "The one you made for the goblin fruit?"

He places a hand on my arm. "No. The one our ancestor made centuries ago, to save her sister and preserve the human world."

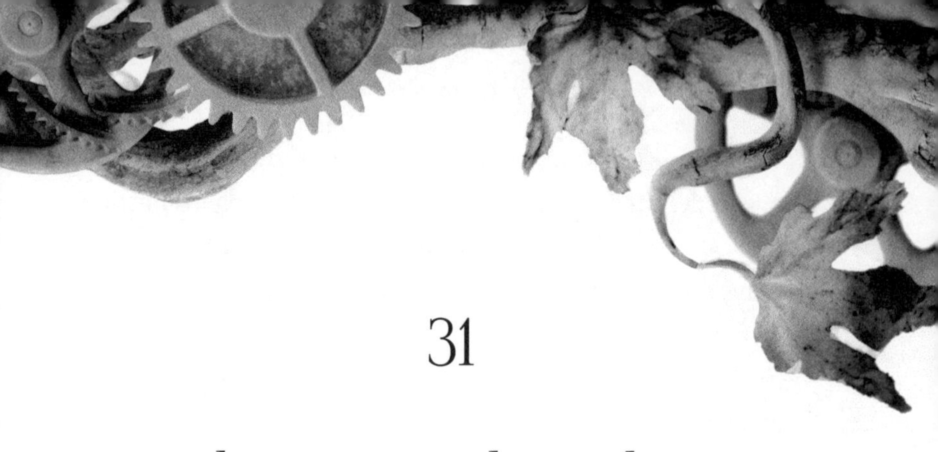

31

revelations and predations

I shake my head, the room spinning in a swirl of lights and sparks.

Numbly, I shove the watch into my pocket; I'm no longer its bond servant. This time, I sit on the step when Uncle guides me over. Flannie comes to my side and lays her muzzle atop my lap. I curl woolen fingers into her neck scruff, seeking comfort . . . stability.

"Those things the Motherboard threw at you in the tunnel," Uncle continues, sitting on the other side of me. "They weren't lies. They were the truth . . . at least to the extent she could tell you. She can't speak, so she had to help you visualize things, and hope that you could somehow believe it."

"But if she can't speak, then how do you know what she showed me?"

Uncle points behind him. Clarey, having climbed to the second-story platform, drags a burlap sheet off a huge screen—one that is eerily similar to Perish's vintage television. The image

flips back and forth between the two final scenes I saw in the petal puzzle: Mom being carried away, and the explosion that swallowed up my dad's unconscious form. A snow of static curdles the clarity, but there's no denying it's exactly what I witnessed in the tunnels.

So Clarey and Uncle Thatch were watching alongside me—from here.

I feel the urge to be sick again, but my stomach has nothing more to give. "The *Goblin Market* poem, it's *real*? And it's about my . . . *our* . . . ancestors?"

"That book your mother left for you was as close as she, or I, could ever come to telling you the truth. It's why I didn't change the date of your parents' 'accident' on the death certificate, and why I dedicated the bakery's theme to Christina Rossetti's masterpiece. All of it was in honor of my sister and our family's sacrifices. Because although it was vague, there was still a trace of the truth in that poem . . . of how the eldritch world tore the limbs off our family tree."

Clarey descends the stairs, glancing behind at that shadowy corner of the platform where the sputters and crackles originate from under another burlap tarp. He wears an expression I can only describe as devastation.

He trembles when he sits on the opposite side of Flannie, and I wonder how he can be buying any of this. Maybe, after all we've seen here, it's no huge leap.

So why, then, is it so hard for me to accept?

I hear the words Uncle says, his curse of silence finally broken now that we've all crossed the borders to this world; I soon feel as if I'm drowning in details I only *thought* I wanted to know.

He tells me Perish gave me a partial truth: that human

emotions rejuvenate his kind—much like food can restore and rebuild a mortal body. However, eldritch beings also rely on human artistry and vision, as these provide the building blocks of their terrain, homes, and architecture. Only humans have the ability to "glamour" the infrastructure and keep the foundation of the fey world thriving; thereby its appearance changes according to who "builds" it with their imagination.

This is why both Clarey and I had the ability to affect things slightly upon our arrival. But an actual *Architect* must be connected to the world's "heart" in order to make global changes. Since the beginning of time, the fey have been luring young girls and boys into their kingdom with their addictive fruits when the veil between worlds thinned, forcing them into servitude so Mystiquiel could flourish.

"But that was the biggest problem," Uncle points out. "Since each Architect grew up in a human world, they felt no loyalty or love for this one. They often ached for home, and it drained them of the will to create. Which meant the Goblin Market had to return every year at All Hallows' Eve to attract fresh batches of Architects—enough to last them until the next season."

I gasp as the true significance of Halloween falls squarely into its logical slot, giving Perish's hallowed wall of masks a new grisly meaning: they were the costumes worn by each victim who became an Architect to be used up and thrown away.

I pivot a glance to Clarey, who stares down at his twiggy hands folded across his lap. The leaves sprouting from his fingertips are as green as I feel.

Uncle continues his telling, that when Lizzie's sister was taken, Lizzie made a deal with Blaze, Perish's ancestor. She vowed her family would serve the goblin hierarchy if they would

stop abducting innocent human souls. She proposed her future offspring be born in Mystiquiel, and their descendants after. The children would be raised among the eldritch creatures, thus cementing their loyalty to the faerie-kind, the one characteristic other humans lacked. And in so doing, they would be able to service the Goblin Court their full lifetimes.

Blaze bound his bloodline to the veil as part of the contract, ensuring no human could stumble in, nor could anyone from his kingdom cross the borders ever again to steal away mortals, putting a stop to the annual Goblin Market event.

The new ritual began with Lizzie. Once she came of child-bearing age, she was escorted out of the faerie world on All Hallows' Eve—blending in with all the other costumed humans milling about so her loved ones wouldn't recognize her. She had one night to find a suitable mate to bring back into Mystiquiel, who would help her produce the succeeding creative anchor; when she didn't find him, she was taken out the following year and the next until she finally met her match. Once she conceived, the father of her child lost all memory of the event, his brain scrubbed with piskie dust before he was deposited outside the veil and left to awaken alone and confused.

Lizzie's baby—a girl—was then born and raised inside the faerie realm. This continued for almost two centuries. Over time, only girl offspring were kept—encouraging a maternal attachment toward the fey—and only one daughter from each generation. That was the rule. Girls who were extras, along with every boy born, were left on the doorsteps of assorted orphanages and churches in the human realm, everywhere around the world.

Uncle was one such baby. He never knew he had a twin sister until he found her on his doorstep one late Halloween afternoon,

begging him to hide her two babies as her life was in danger. She told him all she could of their family history, and that's all he needed to hear. Uncle stepped up and took responsibility for two tiny infants he'd had no inkling existed, driving them in one direction while Imogen and Owen drove the other in hopes of leading their hunter—Perish's father—off track. Uncle Thatch also fixed both babies' birth certificates to make them appear to be born in August, so if any of the fey searched for babies born at Halloween they would overlook them.

And it worked . . . for a while.

"When Imogen's life began waning," Uncle says, "Perish was being groomed to take the throne. Every firstborn goblin prince remains young, little more than an adolescent, until his coronation. That's when he inherits his power, and the magic ages him, transforms him to adulthood. To earn his crown and become a 'man,' Perish's assignment was to find Imogen's replacement. Here he was, barely a teen himself, seeking a missing girl bound to his realm—born into a bargain that was unbreakable so long as his lineage reigned."

"That's why the Motherboard was trying to dethrone him," I whisper, seeking sense in the senseless. "She's the Architect, and she wanted to stop his reign to end the bargain."

Uncle nods.

A torturous epiphany threatens to choke me: Imogen must be the Motherboard. It explains the metallic head's features, and the intimate details in that final illusion. I brace myself against the unthinkable realization that I was tearing my own mother apart—snip by snip.

Oblivious to my torturous introspections, Uncle continues. "Yes, the Architect had concocted a plan to destroy Perish's

monarchy. Using her knack for biomechanics, she introduced metal into the infrastructure of Mystiquiel . . . into the very genetic makeup of its denizens, full knowing it had a poisoning effect on the fey. Iron, tin, copper, brass—all of it acts like an infectious plague. Her goal was to taint Perish's dynasty so he'd either step off the throne to save his subjects or die with them, ending his reign that way. Either result would've freed our family of the contract. Instead, Perish chose to fight back, hoping to find something more valuable to his nemesis than her taste for vengeance, and placing it in her path to derail her."

The conjectures in my head turn too fast, spitting out thousands of questions and thousands of possibilities. How did Mom manage to give birth outside the faerie world? How did my father still remember her? But one takes precedence over them all: Uncle mentioned the Architect's knowledge of biomechanics. Did Mom share Lark's interest?

And then the logic comes rushing in: Uncle said Perish wouldn't receive his crown and become full grown until he had Imogen's replacement. There's no denying he's king, and that he's no longer an adolescent.

I moan, my mind snagging on that one detail, as the night we lost Lark revisits. This time, I don't fight it; this time, I dissect it, moment by moment, to strip it down to its horrifying truth.

I let the darkness fold over and spit me into my moonlit bedroom. I jerk out of sleep, but instead of popping out of my top bunk to check on Lark, I peer from under my sheets, my muscles too heavy to move. It's as if I'm paralyzed. I'm silent, trying to decipher the sounds that startled me awake—raspy unfamiliar voices and fluttering wings; I look past the colored pencil sketches on the

wall and see the dark silhouette, hunched down, blinking two sets of eyes that spark bright with electricity.

But now, I see them clearly: it's only one set of eyes, a glow behind the burgundy depth, with dual pupils of white. Not electric, merely luminous.

A younger Perish—devoid of metal parts, smaller, lither, and still lean, barely at the cusp of manhood—sits on the floor next to Lark's bed, riffling through the pages of the Goblin Market *book. A creature that's half squirrel and half frog and the size of a sparrow with wings to match clambers along my sister's sleeping form. Lark's forehead glows with a pink hue. As I watch, I realize a matching pink fuzziness floats around me, that same pink vanilla-and-lavender-scented cloud that coaxed me to sleep in the castle, although mine has begun to evaporate.*

"This one is the artist. She must be." Perish lifts Lark's right hand, holding it up to the moonlight to showcase the sparkling hints of glitter glue dried upon her palm and between her fingers. "See, there's her pictures strung up. My Royal Father says you always know an artist by their medium. They wear it like a second skin."

My Frankenstein and mummy monster sketches flap on the wall, curling in the wind, each spotted with sparkles that match Lark's hands. What these otherworldly intruders can't see, what they miss, is Lark's glittery-legged mechanical doll, tucked underneath her bed. And I can't correct them or even scream for help, because my tongue won't move.

"Take her away, Frets," Perish commands.

The froggish faerie shakes a furry tail in agreement. He hiccups, and his bulbous chin grows until a bubble escapes his jaws. It's

iridescent—beautiful and mesmerizing as flashes of moonlight reflect off its surface and vibrate along the walls like a strobe light. It stretches across Lark's prone form, swallows her, then shrinks down, adjusting her size to fit it. The frog faerie uses his suction-cup fingers to capture and hold the small bubble, fluttering his wings toward the window where the screen has already been cut and waits for their escape.

The moment they leave, Perish changes—eyes hollowing, mouth gaping, skin withering and shrinking along with his limbs—as his form converts to a glamour that mirrors my sister. I whimper under the sheets, outing myself.

Perish, looking like Lark now, climbs the mattress and waves a hand, enveloping me in a fresh cloud of gauzy pink mist. "You woke a mite too soon, dear sister," he whispers in a voice exactly like hers.

I snap myself out of the memory . . . the harrowing revelation creeping up under my skin. Uncle's words last night to Jaspar in the alley: "This is the consequence of *his* choice, so you'll all just have to suck it up."

The goblin monarchy got one chance, one daughter per generation. And Perish chose wrong. He meant to get the artist, not the mechanic.

The goblins came for me that night. To carry me to the land of Faerie.

This land.

All the time I blamed myself, now I know why. It was too horrible to believe, too ghastly to be real. So I blocked it out, weaving together only a few threadbare details when I woke up from my enchanted sleep, making it something tolerable enough to accept.

Lark never had a seizure, never took a last breath. Just like it

was never me inventing Mystiquiel. The name, the motifs, they originated from Lark . . . drawn from her memories of Astoria—while seeing it anew in my life each day through our twin lens. This became her source to create the alter-world while adding her own unique, destructive touches. In turn, I saw everything she created in dreams that I then sketched out—some of which she pooled into her own creative well and recycled for the world's foundation.

An endless loop of shared ideas and imagery. That must mean that as Mystiquiel's stage was being set by her conceptualizations, her likeness imprinted itself on the Motherboard's head, easy for me to mistake as Imogen, because my twin and I look so much like our mom.

Didn't Perish's own words at the castle warn me? He said the Motherboard had stolen my rightful place, which made us worthy adversaries.

I sob, realizing what's on the upper platform, crackling and hacking beneath that tarp. I know now why my heart has been breaking with each cord I snapped, the attachment I felt being severed with each cut. *I've been killing my sister—my other half.*

I lunge for the stairs, but Uncle clasps my elbow and Clarey blocks me from the step above.

"Sweetie, wait. It's better you don't see—"

Before Uncle can finish speaking, a gush of prismatic bubbles floats into the chamber. I use the distraction to my advantage, jerking free of Uncle and pushing Clarey aside. The enchanted spheres surround them while opening a path for me. I can't make out the passengers inside the bubbles, but I know at least one of them is Perish . . . that this entire night has been an elaborate

and calculated hoax to bring me here to this very moment—to fix his mistake from three years ago.

I plunge up the stairs with more brute force than I thought I had left in me. Flannie nips at the bubbles in an effort to herd them as Uncle and Clarey swat at the onslaught. Before they can make a dent, the bubbles expand, each one spitting out beefy-boned boggles in chain mail and metal helmets. The royal guard forms a barrier between the upper and lower levels, enabling me to arrive at the tarp alone. I rip the blanket away, and my soul shatters as Lark's glassy, empty gaze meets mine. All this time, I thought my world was being drained of color, when in reality it was my sister being drained of life.

32

no fairy-tale ending

My beautiful, broken twin sits upon a throne carved of tungsten, the same rigid and unforgiving stone used to bolster the Goblin King's palace walls. Behind the dilated pupils of her empty gray gaze, orange lights flash where electrified coils—those connecting her temples, wrists, and ankles to openings in the floor—short-circuit.

In an ironic and heartbreaking tribute, the lark tattoo that escaped from my flesh has found its way under the tarp and is perched on its namesake. As if spooked by the unveiling, the inky bird flutters into the shadows, only visible by the sparks running through its outline—having absorbed some of my sister's erratic electrical currents.

Lark wears a gown of black vinyl, as shimmery as a puddle reflecting a starless sky. A crown of tangled copper wires—alive with snapping sparks—sits upon her head: a mangled queen presiding over a gruesome world of metal, rust, and scrambled circuitry. Her pitch-dark skirt sweeps all the way to the floor,

curling beyond the throne's frame and enveloping every inch of her, all but the tips of her bared toes and glimpses of her ankles.

Her pale face, though tinged with a gray pallor, mirrors my own, and her black hair is slicked back from her temples and forehead with the crown to showcase white eyebrows and freckles along with the lack of a widow's peak.

Her mouth, hanging slightly open, displays the gap between her central incisors. It's the only confirmation I need that my twin never died . . . if anyone could call this living.

Her head slumps against the throne's back and she stares up at me with a hollow expression. What I wouldn't give to see that angry, accusatory expression that has taunted me in mirrors since I lost her. All that time, she must've been trying to reach out to me, to keep me from coming here.

Her hair, grown far beyond her waist now, has been swept into a side braid that hangs thick and shiny over the left edge of her jagged seat, and her long neck and collarbones skim a graceful V-shaped trail to her brimming décolleté, held up by a bustier and spaghetti straps. She's aged and filled out over the past few years, just as I have, even while trapped here. Which means she's been given the nutrition she needs somehow.

The same sparks that race behind her eyes also skitter through her veins—rolling balls of light moving to and fro beneath her skin like luminous superhighways—spilling in and out across the circuitry that disappears into the floor and connects her to the soil beneath the surface of the world. These links must be how she feeds the terrain and everything living upon it, and how it sustains her in return, while siphoning away any waste her body emits. It's demented, parasitic, and cruel.

An agonized yowl pierces my eardrums and grates along my throat. It echoes through the chamber, underpinning the manufactured whirs and bleeps of the surroundings, a visceral reaction to a twisted and grim situation.

Seeing Perish's shadow loom behind me, I glare up at him. "How could you just *trap* her here? Paralyzed? How could you do that to anyone?" Fury boils my blood, but I resist the urge to attack him; I don't dare leave my sister's side even for a second.

"This is not the organic exchange our progenitors agreed upon," Perish answers in his deep rumbling timbre. Having discarded the bulky smoke-emitting apparatus strapped to his back, he appears more svelte and graceful, despite his musculature. "Fey are respectful of the elements. Obeisant, even. Because we were born of the old ways . . . put here as guardians to the natural world, and guides to humanity's relationship with it. The orchard you drew, that is what the land of Faerie should look like."

That's why he put his palace there, where it was safe from my sister. Because that particular element wasn't poisoned since it came from me.

"There was never a Motherboard among us until now," he continues. "This hive-mind lair"—he waves all around us—"is not natural. Every other Architect has had the ability to walk and live in our midst, a reciprocity that aids in the bonding process. They're connected to Mystiquiel's framework by nature—vines, flowers, leaves, roots act as living links that adhere to them yet are as flexible as a change of clothing, allowing them to refill our emotional wells as they get depleted, while still giving the Architects their freedom."

I remember the vinelike and floral scars I saw upon Laura in

the tunnels . . . the ones upon my mother—images fed to me at Lark's own hand. They substantiate Perish's claim.

"I don't understand." I rub my gloved palms against my thighs, restraining myself from reaching out to tug at the coils protruding from Lark's temples. Those lethal beads of electricity rolling through her body hold me back. She would have to be unplugged first, and I'm not sure what that entails. If it's even possible. "What went wrong?"

"She *chose* to set herself up as judge and executioner. To entrench herself within the very core so her imaginings could warp Mystiquiel and usher in an artificial age, in opposition to our sworn symbiosis with nature—so she could dominate everything, to poison not only the terrain but us as well. To graft us with metal, wires, cords, and electronics . . . in hopes of assimilating us. Make us mindless, synthetic robots that she could corrupt, then switch off at will with her hive mind."

I remember how aimless the creatures all seemed upon my arrival to Mystiquiel's streets. How they appeared so lost. I assumed it was because I'd stopped drawing them, yet it went so much deeper.

"Ironically," Perish continues, "in so doing, your sister became entangled in her own twisted attempts. Now, she's a biomechanical being in her own right and can't be removed from the circuit board she created, lest she die. She did that to *herself*." His white-bright pupils mimic the electrical storm zigzagging through the prongs of his crown. The currents seem to reroute through me, a shared regret that pulses between us.

I can't blame him for his anger, but I do hold him responsible for his manipulations . . . for using me to destroy her. I fall to my knees at her feet, just inches away from the cords running from

her ankles into the floor. Oil and blood ooze out everywhere the cords connect to her skin. My fingers itch inside my gloves, aching to help.

I study the swarms of magic and electricity spreading out from her as if she's a living CPU. Removing her would kill her. Yet she's going to die if she stays connected. I've healed others on this journey, broken them from their synthetic bonds. Why would I be given such power, if not to use it on my sister? I have to at least try. What do any of us have to lose at this point?

Absolutely nothing.

I remove my gloves. Perish holds my gaze as I do it.

"It was supposed to be me," I mumble. The explanation is for Uncle and Clarey, so they'll understand my responsibility.

"Yes," the Goblin King says, that thundering motor-revving voice now quiet and humming like an engine idling in neutral. If I didn't know better, I'd call it gentle. "I couldn't undo it once it was done. One daughter chosen per generation. We tried to coexist with her, move forward. But her rage . . . her vengeance. It was untenable. She withheld every positive emotion from us; pumping our populace with only vitriol and misery, throwing off the balance of the world, making such a mess of things, we couldn't heal or recover."

"So you brought me here," I murmur, "forced me to rip her apart, so I'd have to volunteer to save her."

"Oh, I haven't forced you to do anything."

I grit my teeth, wanting to pound that smug smirk off his face. His sharp metal fangs hold me at bay.

"All along," he continues, "you've made your own choices. Each one driven by your artistic pride, by your jealous love of this world."

I ignore the taunt, because the truth is so much bigger than that, and he knows it.

A rustle of clothes and muffled grumbles drift from the lower level. I don't have to look to know that Uncle and Clarey aren't having any luck in their efforts to get past the knights.

My attention returns to my sister. "Lark, can you hear me?" I push the question past the dread clogging my throat, but she doesn't answer. Other than my heart feeling as if it's torn in half, I no longer sense the connection between us. I must've severed it with every cord I cut. "We have to unplug her."

Perish's opalescent fingers curl over my jacket at the elbow. The silvery sheen of his metallic forearm peers from the cuff of his shirt and reflects the sparks around us. "I can shut off the power holding her in its thrall for a few moments. Perhaps just enough time for you to restructure her. But Mystiquiel won't truly release your sister, so long as she's living, unless it has an acceptable replacement. You've all the tools you need to convince our world that you belong here."

I don't ask what he means, don't even bother to shake him off. He's referring to the seeds that Angorla encouraged me to pocket, and the vial of blood at my neck that I thought it was my own idea to collect. Now I know the truth. Perish said the blood would bind me to him, his magic. And Angorla said that to swallow the seeds and blood simultaneously would call the roots of the world to me—the roots that follow the Architect. This must be how one becomes inundated, connected to the world.

It was all part of the setup. Angorla was following a script laid out by Perish to get back into his good graces.

"Once she's free," I tell Perish, "and *only* if she survives, I'll do whatever you want."

He shakes his head, his ombre hair loose and long now, so the waves rustle across his back with the gesture. "You must do it first, so the world will release her. And remember, it's not simply what I want, Architect. It's what we both need. Let's be clear on that point."

"No, Nix!" It's Clarey's voice. "Don't do this!" He's finally broken free and rushes toward the first stair step, but no sooner does he lift a foot than he's captured again.

"You can't make this sacrifice!" Uncle takes up Clarey's plea during the distraction, before a boggle intervenes by gripping his shoulder. He stiffens under the knight's touch. "There are only two acceptable options here. The Goblin King can either send all of us back, including your sister, or we'll die together alongside him and his world, to stop this deplorable practice."

"You're only partly right," Perish answers, seemingly unfazed. "This world won't release Lark without a replacement. And as for all of you staying, well, it won't have quite the ending you're hoping for. Yes, as mortals, you won't survive once the emptiness breaches these walls. But your four lives will be martyred in vain, because I'll still live, as will my subjects. We've already been purged of the plague put upon us, with Phoenix's help. Soon enough, our metal deformities will fade without the Motherboard's vicious mental grasp. My kingdom will survive in limbo until next All Hallows' Eve. We've managed before. And since you'll all be gone, leaving me with no tie to your ancestors, I'll no longer be held to the confines of the contract. The Goblin Market will be reinstated; we'll go back to the old ways, which means more human souls will be collected at each turn of every year. More families losing their precious children, more broken hearts and suffering." He shrugs his massive shoulders. "We had

a good run, until Imogen decided to cross us, merely because she couldn't bear for her precious daughters to grow up without each other. Such a selfish act."

"You know there was more to it than that," Uncle snarls. "You know what your father was planning for them . . . what he'd already attempted before they were even born!"

"Enough." Perish nods to the knight restraining Uncle, and the boggle slaps a stony gray hand over his mouth to silence him. "Another word out of either of you, and I'll cast you back into the Somatic Realm without the dog."

Clarey, standing between two boggles, holds on to Flannie and opts for silence, but the expression wrinkling his latex features lays bare the fear and frustration he's battling.

The knights tighten their circle around my loved ones, once more making it difficult to see them. It's better this way, because I'd have misgivings about my decision at the reminders of what I'm going to be leaving behind, of the dear people I'll never be with again.

Perish crouches beside me, his powerful form blotting out the blinking lights in the chamber, so the only flashes radiate from his crown and eyes. "Your sister never had the love for us that you do," he says, low and hypnotic. "Of course, one could argue that developed from your time drawing us, learning about our world. It evolved to an ownership she lacked. Perhaps then, I didn't make a mistake after all. Imogen made the mistake, by taking you both away so you felt like aliens here. As a result, my error of judgment became the solution. For it gave you time to grow into the mother of Mystiquiel. The true Architect."

The true Architect . . . Angorla's phrase at last comes full circle.

"I'm not your mother," I seethe.

Pressing a fist against the floor, he leans over me so I'm curtained by his long hair, unable to escape his scent: man, beast, and machine. "Oh no, I'd never think of you as such." His antlers curl so close to my temples they could be protruding from my own head. He fills my line of vision with every graceful contour and hardened angle of his terrifying beauty. "I was referring to them." With his strong chin, he gestures to the screen on the wall that has shifted at some point to my—*the*—eldritch creatures afloat in an empty void outside. "As for what you are to me, we have your lifetime to figure that out." He taps the zippers on my face, one by one, and they fall away, each hitting the floor with a ping.

I ease back from his touch, all my hairs standing on end at the shocking current that runs between us. Rubbing my thumb along my skin, I find it's smooth and normal again.

But for how long? What am I to become once this is done and over? I shake off the question. It doesn't matter. What matters is that my sister lives. I once thought I let her die. I've just been given a second chance to save her. This time I'll be strong enough.

"You're sure we can free her?" I ask Perish.

"Together, we can," he answers. He lifts the vial at my neck and unstops the cork so the liquid turns a pearly white.

I glance at Clarey and Uncle. They both duck then stretch to toe tips behind the wall of boggles, as if seeking a glimpse through the branches in a dense forest, the kind of forest where this warped nightmare originally began. I allow myself one final memory of Uncle's kindnesses all my life, of his paternal care; then, of Clarey's kiss, and how amazing it felt in that moment, to

truly believe we had a chance to grow into something rare and new, after all our years together as friends.

My chest gives an agonized twist, because several of those years were stolen from him and Lark. It's only right I give them back, although imagining him getting over me and moving on feels like I'm ripping my own guts out.

"You'll see them safely across the veil—all of them together," I press Perish for one last assurance.

"I will," he answers.

Scooping the seeds from my pocket, I toss them into my throat and tip the vial up, letting the royal blood wash everything down. Somewhere in the distance, I hear the striking of midnight, tied magically to my father's watch. I struggle not to look directly at the Goblin King, for fear he'll pull me into that intense gaze just to sample every torturous emotion hacking away at my insides.

Against the odd sensations beginning to stir in my innards, like foreign objects taking root and altering my very DNA, I stand up, bolstering my muscles despite their tremors. Then I lift my hands to catch Lark when she falls from her throne, so my touch—and our pinkies tightly linked—will be the first thing she feels, so I can heal her and set things right.

"Do it now," I command the king. "Unplug her."

❋

The clock strikes twelve, and we know we failed. We lost. All our work, discarded for dross. Our eye in the sky grows dim. Our ears deafen. Our tendons, once stretched into the deep—snap free and fray at the edges, sparks fizz and sibilate. We wither, we waste. Our heart groans and careens, a ship caught on the waves. It collides and

fractures, smashed upon a reef. We weep without eyes, shed rust for tears, shout without voices. We hurt. We fear. We feel.

We feel. We . . . feel?

We . . . me . . .

I.

I hurt. Muscles reawakening, a twitch and a needling tracery of flame across nerves too long dormant. Lungs stretching, brimming. A vacuous void filled to capacity. I cough.

My eyes blink open, and warm moisture seeps from the edges. *My* eyes . . . and only mine.

I recognize her, this face looking back—a mirror that slices me through. She's my other half. My sister. The one I love above all others. The one who envied everything I once was.

Her hands hold me tight, fingers linked with mine and pulling me against her, cheek to cheek. I block out her apologetic thoughts and drain her instead, my skin drinking from hers, starving for what she has, for what I've so long been deprived of.

Individuality . . . separation . . . nonconformity.

The barbed hooks circuited through my heart, the wires that skewered my will to this parasitic realm, release with shivery snaps like ropes being cut, fortifying my bones and enriching my marrow. The immense multitude of heartbeats, too many pulsations to count, grows singular, rhapsodic. One beat . . . one beautiful strumming tumble to carry my breath and feed my needs. My cells reassemble, my veins swollen with red, iron-rich plasma. My skin pinkens and warms, drizzles of red blood leaking from open puncture marks where my connections have severed.

As I take and take, my sister weakens. Yet she gives, and

gives, until I'm me again. Whole, at last. Then Nix turns me loose.

My legs and arms feel heavy, unwieldy and awkward. They've forgotten how to move. I fall backward into another set of hands, those that once held mine as I learned to toddle, first steps building to skipping hopscotch and springing runs. He holds me up now again, my muscles too weak to work alone, and helps me walk toward an opening . . .

He's everything good: family, warmth, security. Kindness and gentleness. Hero.

Uncle.

I glance behind one last time. Uncle pauses, guiding me over the threshold, and my ears hear their first sound: his gasping sob at the burst of light spindling from my twin's flesh like rays of sun . . . too searing for my unseasoned sight. I wince as electrical cords become green, leafy vines, as they wind through her hair, sink into her scalp, massaging . . . caressing. More sympathetic in their gentle suction than my drilling, puncturing connectors. Buds, moss, and petals bloom, wrapping her like a soothing ground cover. My cold, jagged throne, my circuit board, my lair, they all fold up and disappear. She's now the heart, and from her flesh bursts a vision of flowers, roots, and vines, in every color and texture. They spread out, plunging into the ground like my copper coils once did, shifting the world from a cold and grayscale industrial nightmare to a verdant paradise, radiant and prismatic—worthy of a fairy tale.

My optics blur, weaving in and out of focus, as two birds swoop by—one the tiny, flat, black tattoo set free from its anchor of my sister's skin. It now houses the scant remains of my broken

circuitry, and lands upon Nix's upheld palm, its dark form shifting in lightning-strike flashes.

The other, an owl of purest white feathers tipped in rusty red, with no electric eyes or circuitry anywhere, inside or out. Nothing synthetic, purely real. Filigree lands on the Goblin King's shoulder just as Perish discards his own metal parts and transforms to his radiantly brutal flesh-and-blood form. The way he first looked when I saw him being crowned.

"Goodbye, Lark of the Somatic Realm," he says, white fangs glistening in a smirk. "Game well played."

A competitive flame kindles inside me at the smugness of his words, at the innuendo only I intuit, but I stifle the blaze until it's an ember. It was just a gut reaction; I'll learn to forget. I'll learn to tamp the regret. But I will never forgive my sister for forcing me to play. For letting him take me to begin with. She was awake when he stole me away; I saw her peering under the sheets.

At the horrible memory, I shut my eyes and fall through the veil with my uncle holding me tight. Something cushioned softens our fall. I dig my fingers and toes into the damp, gritty depth.

Sand.

I'm aware of what it is without even looking; in fact, I choose not to see, but instead let my other senses flood over me—as I've been without them for so long. My ears fill with the cries of seabirds and splashing wavelets. The scent of salt and fish pulls a stitch in my stomach and triggers a hollow growl. At last, I'm hungry for something other than destruction. I'm hungry to *live*.

Another scent then: petrichor. Earth, saturated and nurtured by rain. And my hunger grows. I listen as the voices surrounding

me no longer blend to animalistic snarls and vicious, bestial complaints. These are familiar, kind, beloved sounds.

"Lark. Come on, little songbird. Open those eyes. Let me know you're in there."

I squeeze my uncle's proffered hand and blink my lashes open, caught between bliss and disbelief at the vision around us. The sands glitter as a brilliant, winking light on the horizon gilds the ocean's froth and the white clouds with a pinkish haze. The palest carnation blush blending to silvery blues. Pink used to be my favorite shade in the world. Until Perish and his iridescent complexion overtook my every thought.

Yet I can't deny that I've missed dawn, just like I've missed breathing. *Living.* So I embrace the moment and the clarity of color. I'm back . . . on Cannon Beach. It's really over.

A yipping bark makes me jolt, worried it's an eldritch creature come to force me across the veil again. The vinyl of my gown squeaks and stiffens as I move, an intolerable grating against my ears and skin. I ache to be free of it, of all memory of that world.

Then I see a common dog, a bundle of fur and energy, and release a relieved breath. Her back leg clicks into view and I recognize the resemblance to my robotic designs, too strong to be a coincidence. My invention, stolen and altered to another's specifications. I'm not sure how I feel about pieces of my life being parceled out, as if I was never coming back to claim them.

"It's okay, it's just Flannie." A boy leans over me, peeling orange pumpkin skin away from his features, revealing a brown complexion and bright, two-toned eyes. White curls flop down over his forehead, covering a scar that shouldn't be there. "Lark . . . I—I can't believe it. All this time . . . three whole years thinking you were—"

He stops himself as my uncle pats his shoulder and hands him Dad's duffel for the mask. I swallow a knot from my throat and glance at the parts of my body I can see: my ankles, my arms, my wrists . . . the puncture marks there, still raw and open, waiting to heal.

Three years. Was I truly attached to Mystiquiel for so long?

I focus on the boy again, now that the face covering is gone. I know him. That's why he seemed familiar in Mystiquiel. With my free hand, I reach up to touch his tear-wet cheek, another needling activation of muscles and nerves that remained comatose until now. He presses his fingers over mine and says my name again. His voice is deeper than I remember, yet comfortable and nostalgic, as if from another lifetime. A lifetime that to me was only yesterday.

Clarey.

His name melts the ice around my heart, replacing it with a gentle, happy glow. I can't bring myself to speak aloud yet, so I rest in silence, observing them both, touching them both, loving them both. So grateful just to be with them again.

"We can't leave Nix there." Clarey disrupts my blissful peace by prying his cheek from my grasp and glancing toward Haystack Rock. There are fresh tears on his face. "We have to get her back. *I* have to—"

Watching him, sensing the misery behind his plea, I'm slammed with the memory of how he and Nix looked at each other just before being dropped into the orchard. I saw what was there. A spark being born; something unexpected and rare.

Something that once belonged to me.

My uncle shakes his head and looks in the opposite direction, off in the distance where red and orange carnival tents are being

taken down. “There’s no way Perish will open the veil for us now that he has her. But by the law of nature, it thins on its own every Halloween. That gives us twelve months to make a plan. And we already have our key to walk through.”

“Back at the bakery,” Clarey says. “Shipments of squid ink.”

Their talk of a bakery feels out of reach, just as this place and time feel foreign to me now. *They* feel foreign to me. I feel foreign to myself.

Because of her. Because the goblins took me instead, and she made everything hers while I was gone.

How do I make it mine again? How do I reclaim that time?

Then, I know. I’ll start from the beginning—pretend to be the same girl I was when I left. The one who loved pink; the one who lived to tinker; the one who wasn’t afraid of anything. Doesn’t matter that it’s all a lie. That no one could participate in such a game and be unchanged.

I weave my fingers through my uncle’s and struggle to sit up. He helps steady me as Clarey puts an arm behind my back.

Looking into their concerned faces, I rasp the first words I’ve spoken aloud since the night I woke up a captive in the land of Mystiquiel: “Unca-thunk, take me home, please.”

acknowledgments

Writing a book is always a solitary endeavor, but this one was especially challenging. I penned over half of *Shades of Rust and Ruin* in 2020, when the entire world was quarantined during the Covid pandemic, so it was more difficult to spark creative motivation than ever before. There were days I was so heart-weary and worried over missed loved ones, unattended graduations, funerals, and weddings, and feeling so out of touch with the people and activities that keep me centered as a human being and inspired as an artist, it took every ounce of willpower to sit in front of my computer and craft a story. But finally, word by word, day by day, I started to gather momentum and my gritty, dark world of Mystiquiel became a solace. My characters' trials served as a catharsis for my own, and the monsters they faced—both internal and external, horned, fanged, or humanoid—personified the fears and insecurities of our very scary real world, giving me the chance to fight them on my own turf. This book was a journey in and of itself, and I love the resulting story all the more for

it. However, because of the isolation we all experienced, there's a smaller cast than usual in my acknowledgments.

As always, the lion's portion of gratitude goes out to my husband and children: Vince, Nicole, and Ryan. It takes an abundance of patience to live with an author on deadline, and you were stuck with me under the same roof 24-7 during the thick of my writing neurosis. Yet you never complained when I hijacked the bandwidth for research and interrupted your streams or Zooms, nor did you threaten to unplug my speakers when I pumped up the mood music during difficult scenes. Instead, you pitched in with the housework and cheered me across the finish line. Thank you!

Although my local crit group disbanded during the pandemic, I'd like to thank them for their input on the earliest chapters: Jennifer Archer, Linda Castillo, April Redmon, Marcy McKay. But my most heartfelt appreciation goes to my out-of-town critters, Jessica Nelson and Bethany Crandell, who have been by my side for over a decade and continue to this day to hold my hand and read chapters, seeing me through every manuscript's freefall moments. I admire and adore you both as dear friends and colleagues, and wouldn't want to ride this rollercoaster without you!

Thank you to my fantastic agent, Jenny Bent, who's always there to go to bat for my stories. Also, to Cindy Loh, for seeing the potential in my book proposal and bringing me into the Bloomsbury fold. I'll never forget how you advocated for Mystiquiel, and hold hope that one day we'll find some other project on which to work together.

I'm so blessed to have two discerning editors, Mary Kate

Castellani and Camille Kellogg, who help me preen my grammar, pacing, and characterization so that my stories can take wing without crash-landing. And much appreciation to Phoebe Dyer and the Bloomsbury marketing team as well as to copyeditors, sensitivity readers, proofreaders, and all the unsung heroes behind the successful flight of every book in the industry. Thank you also to Marcela Bolívar for crafting such an atmospheric and moody cover that captures the steampunk/Halloween elements so beautifully, and to our in-house designers for carrying this concept across to the interior with skillful and creative formatting.

A nod of recognition and respect to the poem and the movie that inspired this dark tale: Christina Rossetti's *Goblin Market* and Jim Henson's *Labyrinth* each lent surreal coming-of-age moments alongside a healthy dose of sibling loyalty and dark, mystical imagery that would one day spark the beginnings of Mystiquiel in my mind.

Ceaseless gratitude to the many vloggers, bookstagrammers, and booktubers—for all you do to help authors promote their books—and in fact to every person who reads for the pure pleasure, thank you for giving my stories a chance to take you somewhere new.

And most of all, a humble thank-you to my Lord and Savior for giving me the ability to weave words into these worlds, characters, and adventures that in turn connect me to agents, publishers, reviewers, booksellers, librarians, teachers, students, readers of every age—a most unique and wonderful society of people who champion literacy every day on every level, and who are also kindred spirits.